P9-CFH-080

IT ALL
COMES DOWN
TO THIS

Also by Therese Anne Fowler

A Good Neighborhood

A Well-Behaved Woman

Z: A Novel of Zelda Fitzgerald

IT ALL
COMES DOWN
TO THIS

———————

THERESE ANNE
FOWLER

ST. MARTIN'S PRESS
NEW YORK

THIS ONE IS FOR ALL OF YOU WHO, AS I DID,

NEEDED SOME BRIGHTNESS DURING A DARK TIME.

———————

First published in the United States by St. Martin's Press,
an imprint of St. Martin's Publishing Group

Title page painting by Henry Isaacs

Designed by Michelle McMillian

www.stmartins.com

Library of Congress Cataloging-in-Publication Data

Names: Fowler, Therese Anne, author.
Title: It all comes down to this / Therese Anne Fowler.
Description: First edition. | New York : St. Martin's Press, 2022.
Identifiers: LCCN 2022002310 | ISBN 9781250278074 (hardcover) |
ISBN 9781250278067 (ebook)
Subjects: LCGFT: Novels.
Classification: LCC PS3606.O857 I86 2022 | DDC 813/.6—dc23/eng/20220120
LC record available at https://lccn.loc.gov/2022002310

Our books may be purchased in bulk for promotional, educational, or business use.
Please contact your local bookseller or the Macmillan Corporate and Premium Sales Department at
1-800-221-7945, extension 5442, or by email at MacmillanSpecialMarkets@macmillan.com.

First Edition: 2022

10 9 8 7 6 5 4 3 2 1

When we are not in love too much,

we are not in love enough.

—ROGER DE RABUTIN, Comte de Bussy
Histoire amoureuse des Gaules: maxims d'amour

1

Certain Expectations

How differently the Geller sisters' lives would have turned out had C. J. Reynolds not been released from prison that February. Or suppose he'd been released but had not decided to restart his life on Mount Desert Island, Maine, where Marti Geller's old waterfront house might or might not be coming up for sale. Suppose that instead of getting a flight from Columbia, South Carolina, to Bangor, C.J. had instead returned to his hometown of Aiken to try to make amends.

But he did take that flight, and in doing so, he altered his future and theirs—the three Geller sisters, Manhattan born and raised, not at all the sorts of women C.J. had been used to back before he was locked up with some thousand men whose coarse behavior made him feel like he was in the ninth grade. Misfit. Scared. Wishing yet again that he'd been born into a different family, a different life.

You'd be amazed at the volume of prison conversation that had centered on women's breasts. On body parts generally. On sex in every possible form—incarceration made some men *really* creative. C.J. had chosen not to take part in those conversations. He'd chosen not to take part in most everything optional in the pen, a place he was *not* meant to be. And yet there he had been, and this made him wonder about *meant to be* and about fate in general.

He'd also wondered whether Jesus, who he believed had been a real person who'd done at least some of what was credited to him, would approve of all the ways he (Jesus) was being put forth as the personal savior of a lot of hardened criminals who really only hoped the connection might help get them paroled. C.J. had not relied upon Jesus to aid in his defense; for that, he'd spent a good deal of money on an attorney whose relationship with Jesus (if any) was unknown to C.J., but whose relationship with law, evidence, and specific judges was certain and solid. This had not, however, been enough to keep him out of prison. It had perhaps made it so that he wasn't in prison longer, and this was worth far more to him than the money he'd spent.

C.J. was extremely fortunate to have had that money in the first place, especially as he hadn't earned most of it himself; he'd inherited a pile—no, a mound—of money from his paternal grandmother, who had never judged him for wanting to take a different path. But he didn't have more millions coming to him the way some of his kind did, because he had not returned to Aiken to make amends and was determined not to do so. Ever. He was also out of a job. And a wife. A daughter, too, damn it all, though he hoped to rectify that, if not the rest.

Would any of this matter to the Geller sisters? Beck: a journalist, pragmatic but also sensitive and stalwart; Claire: a doctor, caring but skeptical, too, and sometimes quick to judge; Sophie: an assistant gallerist, forgiving yet cagey, self-protective. If any of these women discovered his past (and maybe they would not), they wouldn't be the pushovers one might wish to have as a jury. But how much would that matter to C.J., who wasn't looking for new entanglements? An inspiring, peaceful setting in which to live and paint was his central aim.

The Geller sisters, too, had particular aims. They had certain expectations, desires, long-held beliefs. They had no idea that everything safe and familiar would be undone at the intersection of a man and a house and a secret—not C.J.'s, but another's. Of course, each of them had their own secrets, too, hidden and protected by long and careful habit. Revelation is risky; suppose it leads to a fall?

Ah, but suppose it leads to flight?

2

Tough Situations

Knowing for certain now that there was no chance she would outlive what money she had, Marti Geller left the clinic and hailed a cab to take her to her apartment on 19th Street in Gramercy Park. She gave the cabby the address and told him, "I should have taken more cabs in my life. I was too cautious about everything."

The cabby said, "This I think is very wise. Please you spread the word."

Marti was one of those unlucky nonsmokers who'd developed lung cancer mysteriously, then spent four years playing tumor whack-a-mole with diminishing success before today's appointment, where her oncologist told her there was nothing more to be done. The high probability of her dying from the cancer had been known and (more or less) accepted by Marti and her three daughters. That she would die *soon*, though, likely within the next couple of weeks, was news Marti intended to keep from them until it became a fait accompli.

Just the same, once she got home from the clinic where she'd been given her final prognosis, she would ring up her middle daughter, Claire, to tell her that the doctors had run through all possible treatment options and it would be palliative care from here on out. If Claire asked for a timeline and particulars, Marti would be vague. She chose Claire for this and not her oldest daughter, Beck, because Claire was a doctor herself, though not here in New York, and because Claire was not Beck.

The day was cold but clear. Marti leaned back and watched the cityscape as the cab wended its way over to Gramercy Park, where, almost five decades earlier, she and her late husband, Leo, both of them eager to play house like grown-ups, had lucked into the spacious south-facing two-bedroom on the top floor of a five-story that had been a walk-up at the time but was now outfitted with an elevator just large enough to hold two people, a bag of groceries, and a small dog. She and Leo had been relieved when all of their children turned out to be girls and they didn't need to find an equivalent three-bedroom here in Manhattan (impossible on their income) or leave the city for the suburbs, a lifestyle that Leo had rejected long before.

Three children, two bedrooms, one bathroom, five flights of stairs. Take-out that you ordered by calling someone on the telephone. Physical books that you purchased from a store *in person* or took out from the library. Bulky television sets that got only three or four stations and gave you the news just twice a day. Young people in the city today could not appreciate the everyday efforts and limits Marti's generation had taken as basic matters of fact. No, now they had every need answered by their smartphones. They lived their lives with their faces angled toward glowing screens and never even saw what was around them. Ninety percent of the people Marti observed in her neighborhood had a coffee in one hand and a phone in the other, and very often a leash looped around one wrist, tethered to a trailing dog that was seeing all the sights its person was missing.

The cabby pulled up close to a gap between parked cars, making space for Marti to get out safely. "Here you go."

"Let me ask you a question," she said while swiping her credit card to pay. "Are you from here?"

"No, I come to New York from Bulgaria."

"When you're not driving, I hope you don't walk around with your phone in your face. This is a wonderful city. It's terrible, too, it some ways, but it's an exceptional place and I hope you aren't sorry you came from Bulgaria to work and live here. I hope you notice all the wonderful things."

He said, "I love Shake Shack. Best cheeseburger in my life."

"Well, I don't disagree with you there."

After living five decades in the same location, Marti still liked her neighborhood, and she liked her controlled rent even more, since she was now getting by on Social Security and Leo's pension from the city, where he'd worked for the comptroller's office. She knew many of her neighbors, knew their dogs and their children, felt valued for her talent in remembering small details about myriad things, like which days and which markets had the freshest produce, and whether to take a bus or the subway (or a cab) to any given destination in the city depending on the day and time of travel, and how or whether to scare off a stray cat. The talent for details had served her well over the years in her various apartment concierge jobs—which, not incidentally, had made for excellent part-time work especially around the holidays, when the big earners liked to show their largesse by slipping her "just a little something," usually in an envelope, usually in cash. She should have spent more of it on cabs.

Until exhaustion and pain had made it impossible to continue, in retirement Marti had been volunteering at Mount Sinai Beth Israel three mornings a week, responding to patient call buttons when the nurses were busy, and keeping lonely people company while they recovered from illnesses and surgeries. Her days had been as full as she wanted them to be, and who could ask for more? No one got to live forever. Her sweet, adored Leo had made it only to sixty-six.

Once Marti was back in her apartment, she sat down in front of the window to sunbathe for a few minutes and regather her energy. Then she called Claire. She delivered the news about ending treatments, then said, "I've got hospice coming on Wednesday for an orientation. I've heard they're terrific people."

"You sound almost happy about it," Claire said. "Are you stoned?"

"What? No, I'm saving that for if I really need it."

"Ma, don't ration it. You can get more."

"Okay, well, no, I am not high, I'm just relieved to be done with treatment. All those days of feeling terrible." She coughed, and coughed some more, then, after catching her breath, said, "I'm so tired of that. And food doesn't taste like anything. And I've got all these damned pills. Surgeries. Infusions. *So* many trips to the clinic. It takes up your whole life! It's too much, and I'm glad to be done with it. Is that crazy?"

"You were really tough," Claire said. Her voice sounded thick. "I'm sorry all of that failed you. I'm sorry I failed you."

"You? Don't be ridiculous. You do hearts, not cancer. Even the oncologists couldn't fix me, so how could you have done any better? Anyway, tell your sisters, all right? I don't have it in me. Sophie's . . . somewhere. L.A., I think. Tell Beck first."

"She'll call you the minute I hang up with her."

"I know. That's fine."

Marti had another coughing spell, then said, "About that marijuana Beck got for me—"

"On *my* recommendation," Claire said.

"Yes, honey, on your recommendation. Can my lungs handle it?"

"You only need a couple of puffs. It'll make you feel nice, and it'll help with the pain. I thought I explained all of that to you."

"You must have. But chemo brain, you know. Okay. I'm going to find the pipe and try it. I hope if the neighbors smell the smoke, they won't give me any trouble about it."

"I doubt they'll smell it, or mention it even if they do. But if there's any trouble, call me."

"Okay, I will," she said, though she wouldn't. For that kind of thing, she'd call Beck.

Who, as predicted, rang her up about ten minutes later:

"Oh, Mom, Claire just told me. Why didn't you call? They can't just cast you off like that. I wish you'd told me you had an appointment today. Do you want me to talk to Dr. Cooper?"

"No, don't call her . . ." Marti let the sentence trail off, then reminded herself to keep speaking. "This is just the way it is. Sometimes people don't beat it. Some people are just unlucky. I'm not *that* unlucky. I've had some good luck, too, not all bad. But sometimes the bad is not really the person's fault, not completely, and what could they do? If they think about it too much, though . . ."

"Mom?" said Beck.

"Hmm?"

"You kind of went off on a tangent, there."

"Oh. Well. I just tried some of that marijuana you brought me. Do you have any for yourself? Are you a secret smoker? If you aren't, you should be! It will make you feel *m-u-u-c-h* better."

"I—no, thanks. I just . . . Oh, Mom."

Beck was on the verge of tears, and that wouldn't do. Marti wasn't gone yet. She said, "I know, honey. I know. Okay, so, I'll call you tomorrow. You relax now. Don't worry about me."

Marti hung up before Beck could fret further. Then she cooked a pot of egg noodles and set about finalizing her funeral plans.

Consistent with Jewish tradition, there would be no viewing of her body, nor would she direct the girls to have her cremated, though the practice seemed eminently more sensible than burial. She believed in ecology and economic efficiencies, but she was certain that Beck would feel conflicted by a cremation directive, as it risked marking Marti as a bad Jew—which she was not, or at least not anymore; leave the past in the past. But with Beck's feelings in mind, she'd decided to be interred at Woodlawn next to Leo. Leo had chosen Woodlawn because Irving Berlin was buried there. On her own, Marti might have liked to be laid to rest in Maine.

"Good enough," she said, and closed the file that held her notes and directives.

This being early March, if she was as efficient as Dr. Cooper predicted she would be, she might, for a little longer, continue to have the pleasure she derived every year from reading about the Mets' spring training, and even better, she wouldn't need to worry about filing her taxes.

Marti weeded out her clothing and books, because some of her choices were questionable even by her own standards, and she didn't like to imagine Beck pulling out that old paperback copy of *Fear of Flying*, for example. Ditto the fringe-trimmed skirt she'd bought at Saks two years ago, knowing that not only was she too old for it by about forty years (though her legs were still good), but in buying it she had been satisfying the latent hippie in her. She wore the skirt only once, on a summer day when she was feeling pretty good and had let herself pretend she'd lived that other life, the one where she left Maine before ever meeting Leo. The one where she'd come to the Village to write poetry and hang out at the Gaslight. To escape her alcoholic, depressive father and her addicted, depressive mother, and the hardscrabble potato farm they'd lost to foreclosure. That hippie life might have turned out badly; who could say? But unlike the life she'd led, it would not have been predicated on a secret and lies. This is what sat at the center of Marti's regrets.

As for that original secret and the lies that followed, she knew that she was weak for not revealing any of it while she was still living. But regrets or not, she refused to do the deathbed-confessions thing. Her girls would find out later.

Would they judge her harshly? Claire might. Beck probably would. Sophie, though, would try to temper their reactions. This was Marti's prediction. If there was a heaven, and if Marti was let in, maybe she'd be able to look down and see their reactions for herself. She visualized this as standing knee-deep in a fluffy cloud and peering over the side of it to see the girls gathered around a firepit to discuss what they'd learned. *But, look,* Sophie would be saying as she stood facing her sisters, *you have to see it from Mom's point of view: if Dad had known any of it back when they first met, he would never have asked her out. And then we wouldn't even exist.*

Oh, my girls, Marti thought.

Having already put aside the few belongings the girls reluctantly said they wanted for themselves, Marti was giving the rest of her household goods to charity. As for money, there wasn't a lot of it. Some savings, a 401(k), a life insurance policy that would cover all of her final expenses with a bit left over for each of the girls. Smaller bits for the grandchildren and the new great-granddaughter. Her largest asset was the house she and Leo bought on Mount Desert Island with money he inherited after his parents died in the blizzard of '78, stranded in their car somewhere in Ohio while on their way to Leo's great-aunt's funeral. How terrible but also idiotic of them to die in a blizzard! It was the twentieth century, for god's sake. It's not as if they didn't know the storm was coming. They weren't traveling in a wagon train. Marti hadn't said anything like this to Leo, but it was clear that his father, good man though he had been, lacked the sense God gave a hamster. Her mother-in-law, too timid to resist his insistence on traveling just then, also froze to death. It was tragic.

Leo, though, being a good, sunny soul through and through, had been determined to transform his sorrow into happiness:

"Let's use the money for a summer place in Maine," he'd said, a few months after they died. "On Mount Desert Island. It'd be so fitting, don't you think?"

He and Marti were in bed, postcoital, when he made this declaration. It was a night in late spring. Things were blooming and greening. She understood he was attempting a grand romantic gesture. They'd met and fallen in love amid the island's summer lushness, its flower gardens and sighing pines.

He said, "The kids will love it," referring to preschooler Beck and infant Claire. "I know it's a long drive from here, but it'll be worth it."

"It's a really nice idea," Marti said, though she wasn't sure she thought so. "But we could just rent a cabin there from time to time and save the money for more essential things."

He said, "No, no, don't you see? It's the *having* it that matters. The owning. It's us making a permanent claim." He raised his hands as if framing a sign: "Leo and Marti Met Here and Went On to Have a Wonderful Life."

"I adore you so much," Marti said. "I think you're crazy, but I adore you."

Leo said, "Death reminds us that we need to make the most of things. I'm thinking Mets season tickets and a little place on MDI."

"You don't care that the island is crawling with rich WASPs?"

"Beth and Bruce aren't WASPs," he said. This was the couple whose Bar Harbor wedding had brought Leo to Maine from New York, the summer they met. "Anyway, diversity is good. That's why we'll send the girls to public school."

"They'll go to public school because we'll have spent your inheritance on a summer house."

Leo got on top of her. "Do you love me?" he said.

"I do."

"Is Mount Desert Island as special a place to you as it is to me?"

"Of course it is," she said, though the truth was a bit more complicated than that.

"Then it's settled."

For all her silent reservations, Marti had never regretted having the house there. In fact, to her surprise she'd found that being on the lake every summer was a balm.

There had been parts of her history she might have revealed to Leo, parts that in and of themselves were innocuous—but you couldn't pull just one thread on something like this. The entire thing might unravel, and then where would you be? Even the girls could not be counted on absolutely to love her once they learned she'd lied about her past, and so she had decided never to risk it.

Marti still called them that—*girls*; her girls, the girls, our girls, though all of them were adults and had been for some time. (Sophie was youngest, and she was thirty-six.) Even so, Marti wanted to make her passing easy on them. Death was difficult for the bereaved under even the best circumstances; there was no getting around it. She remembered the pain she'd felt at her own mother's death—and the surprise of that pain, given their decades-long estrangement. Some things never leave you, even if you've left them.

Being a daughter hadn't gone so well for Marti, but being a mother had been much better than she'd expected. The girls had sometimes fought with one another but not often with Leo or her, and none of the girls had gotten a venereal disease (that she knew of), or become pregnant by accident (that she knew of), or overdosed, or shacked up with the wrong sort of boy. The most serious difficulty Marti could recall in their teenage years involved Beck—Beck, of all people!—being arrested and locked in jail for taking part in what had devolved into a disorderly protest against the Gulf War. Apparently nudity was part of the effort, and something about motor oil and an effigy of President Bush. Leo had been upset (about the nudity, mainly), but Marti was proud of Beck for being bold and, if not quite fearless, willing to face what consequences might come.

Regarding the financial matters attendant to her demise, Marti told Delia, the Puerto Rican woman who was one of the hospice nurses who'd be caring for her, that she wanted the girls to have "three-part harmony." She said, "Everything will be equal, so that they don't have lasting bitterness toward each other. They aren't that close as it is, and I don't want to make that worse."

Marti also wanted to see her girls individually happy. Lately she'd gotten the sense that there were sharks in the waters of all three girls' lives, dark shapes lurking below the surface and threatening the equilibrium each seemed to have. Maybe this feeling was simply a side effect of her meds, but Marti didn't think so. The girls were troubled, and she was not going to be around to help.

Not that they'd sought her out much for aid and advice; she and Leo had raised them to be independent, capable women—so much so that she sometimes wished she had more influence. She wished they had more influence on one another. That being the case, she had devised a situation that might— might—bring them closer together, so that they'd want to rely on one another in the years to come. Would it work? And would she, in the beyond, be able to see whether it did? She supposed she would find out before too long.

Marti made Delia swear that none of the nurses would alert the girls when she reached a point of no longer having the interest or energy to communicate further. "I absolutely do not want a death watch," she said.

Nor did she want to die surrounded by the girls and their families—well, Beck and Claire had families; unfortunately, Sophie was a late launcher in that facet of *adulting*, as the young people put it. And Claire's family was no longer a family in practice, as Claire and Chad were recently divorced after one of them had done something heinous to the other, but no one would or could tell Marti what specifically had gone on—not even Sophie, who Marti could usually count on to reveal far more than she wanted to know about most everything.

For example, Sophie, who worked for a tony gallery in the West Village, once described to Marti—over dinner at Veselka, where Marti always went for veal goulash when her appetite was good—an exhibit she'd seen that celebrated a wide assortment of less traditional sex practices, including fisting, which she then googled for Marti on the spot, even playing her a how-to video that had been made, it seemed, for the purpose of instructing prospective fisters on best practices. Marti (who knew what fisting was but hadn't wanted Sophie to know she knew) had not asked Sophie if her knowledge went beyond artwork and instructional videos. She had not asked Sophie to tell her more about the exhibit. She'd changed the subject to politics, which in those days was a far safer subject than sex.

Why not have the girls and their families at her bedside when her time finally came? Well, Marti knew from seeing a few patients die that death wasn't especially flattering or tidy, and in her several hospital stays during these whack-a-mole years, she had suffered more than enough indignities, thank you very much. For her, death was a private matter, not a spectacle. Let them remember her as she had been.

She worried about all of her girls in the routine ways a mother does when her children no longer need her materially, but she had a special corner in her heart for anxiety about Beck. Claire and Sophie would weather her death like grizzled sailors getting through a monsoon. Beck, though? Marti imagined Beck as a rain-lashed stowaway cat climbing under a lifeboat's tarp for safety, paralyzed by uncertainty and reluctant to even try to move.

She told nurse Delia, "Beck is stuck. I don't know if *she* knows it, but she is."

That was not the life she wanted for her daughter. Marti knew that Beck needed a push, and didn't want her death to become an excuse for Beck to stay stuck as she was. *This is what wills are for,* she decided. To pull the strings you weren't able to, or willing to, in life.

3

Special Circumstances

Arriving at the Callaghan estate on Mount Desert Island, C. J. Reynolds viewed the setting with his out-of-practice painter's eye: the sky on canvas would be ultramarine, the flocculent clouds titanium white and opaline gray—same for the snowy areas, of which there still were many. The tree branches required an array of grays and browns speckled with Indian red buds that promised spring *would* come; be patient a little bit longer, folks, we're all in this together. The temperature was only forty-three degrees Fahrenheit, but C.J. didn't mind the chill. South Carolina's highs were already pushing seventy. He preferred this climate to that. Even better was the prospect of a summer he could spend outdoors in comfort—part of Maine's appeal. The greatest draw, though, was that his daughter was in Portland, just three hours away. At some point he'd have his own place here on MDI, and at some point she'd agree to see him. He hoped.

C.J. had stayed here in the Callaghans' grand four-story Victorian for part of one summer during college and felt like he belonged on this island that many artists and writers called home. Unlike the Callaghans, with their houses and horses and yachts, and unlike his own family, who also lived extra-large, those were his kinds of people—though he had not identified himself this way while in the pen. Better to let the other inmates believe he was hardened like they were, that he was capable of murdering his own father—or capable of meaning to, since he had not in fact done so. In prison it had been enough to *appear* capable of it, to *enact* that capability and keep his mouth shut about pretty much everything else.

At the front door, he pressed the entry code his friend Joseph had given him, waited for the lock to accede, then let himself inside the spacious wood-floored foyer. A few lights were already on and the heat was running. According to Joseph, the whole house had been rewired a year or so ago to allow for remote control of everything—lights, thermostat, music, security—which C.J. figured must have enabled this warm welcome.

Currently Joseph was in Greece for his third honeymoon, this time with a woman much closer to his own age. C.J. was confident that Joseph, who'd been a happy-go-lucky fuckup in the way only certain kinds of rich boys get to be, had finally figured things out. He was *not* confident that, in his installations of remote controls and automations, Joseph had not also installed hidden cameras here, for security purposes or otherwise. So C.J.'s plan was to be out as much as possible, seeing properties, hiking, running, eating, and doing little more than sleeping here. This was not paranoia. Or if it was, it was paranoia he had come by honestly: in prison there was not a private corner anywhere. That is to say, someone or something had its eyes on him for every moment of his three-year lockup at Broad River. For C.J., this lack of privacy had been worse than being shut in and cut off. Whatever house he ended up buying on MDI, privacy was foremost.

C.J. had just dropped his bag in one of several guest bedrooms furnished in solid old furniture, Persian rugs, and handmade quilts when he heard noises coming from downstairs. Footfalls, then voices. He went to the landing and called down the stairs, "Hello? Who's there?"

A silver-haired woman in a red wool coat came to the foot of the stairway.

She held her phone in one hand and was poised to press its screen with the other. Though surely in her eighties, she looked ready to command cops or troops as a given situation might warrant.

She said, "Who are you, and what are you doing here? Talk fast."

He raised his hands in front of him. "C. J. Reynolds—Joseph's friend? You must know Joseph. Maybe he's your . . . nephew?"

She made no reply.

"I guess he didn't mention I was going to be here."

"How did you get in?"

"He gave me a code. I can show you the text message."

"You'd better do that," the woman said.

"Yes, ma'am." He took his phone from his pocket and came down the stairs. As he did, he saw a child's face in the doorway to the drawing room, peeking out at the encounter. Caught, the face disappeared.

"Here you go," C.J. said to the woman, holding out his phone with the text message displayed.

She took the phone and squinted at its screen, then squinted at him and said, "Why are you here?"

"I'm aiming to buy a house, ma'am. Joseph offered to let me stay here while I see some places. Do you know Carol Barksdale? She's the real estate agent I'm working with."

"I don't know her. Which agency?"

"I can't remember the name of it just now. But if you like, I'll call her and you can ask her about me yourself."

"Yes." The woman handed his phone back.

"Really?"

"What, you think I'm taking your word for it? I don't know you."

"Right. No, of course."

"Where are you from, anyway?"

He hesitated. His intention, in coming to live here, was to create the cleanest slate possible so that no one would associate him with his past. He wasn't going to lie outright about anything important, but he did mean to make the trail tougher to follow, which meant prevaricating on a few details, including his hometown as well as his name. Not the Reynolds part, which was common enough as to be untraceable, but *C.J.*, the name he'd used in college and for his artwork. At home, he was known only as Coleman or Cole or Junior, and all the many, many news stories that had been written about his arrest, trial, and conviction, referred to him as Coleman.

He had better not try to mislead this woman too much, though; Joseph knew the facts. C.J. said, "I'm from South Carolina."

"I see. I honestly don't know why people from the Deep South all have to sound like they're missing IQ points."

He didn't think he'd given that impression. He hadn't used *ain't* or *cain't* or brought up his mama, Jesus, fried okra, or guns. "Something about the drawl does that," he said. "But I am a college graduate, I promise you. Joseph was my freshman-year roommate. I actually think you and I might've met when I visited here back then." When she failed to look impressed in any manner, he said, "Let me get you Carol on the phone."

He felt completely asinine as he told the Realtor, "Hey, Carol, it's C. J. Reynolds. I just got into town, and I've got a woman here—that is, a lady— I'm sorry, ma'am, I didn't get your name . . ."

"Deirdre Callaghan."

"Mrs. Deirdre Callaghan," he continued.

"*Ms.*"

"*Ms.* Deirdre Callaghan is here wanting to make sure I'm where I'm supposed to be, so would you talk with her for a minute?"

Again he handed off his phone. Deirdre Callaghan took it, asked a few questions of Carol, thanked her, and ended the call.

"All good?" C.J. asked.

"Good enough." Deirdre sighed, returning his phone. As she removed her coat and hung it in a closet beneath the stairs, she called out, "All right, Arlo," and the child C.J. had seen revealed himself.

"My grandson," she said.

The boy, who looked to be about eight years old, was slight, with floppy dark hair and big blue eyes—that eerie, almost surreal shade that makes you wonder if the person had been engineered in a vat. Arlo, though an attractive child, had a homely look about him, a woebegone quality. He came to Deirdre Callaghan's side.

"Hey there," C.J. said.

The boy said, "Hello."

"This is Mr. Reynolds," Deirdre said. "Now that we're all acquainted, I'm going to get supper started. You'll eat with us?"

C.J. had intended to find himself a lobster dinner somewhere in Bar Harbor. He also had intended to be staying here alone, but that, too, did not seem to be going according to plan. So, curious though he was about what would be on the menu—not to mention why Deirdre Callaghan was here and how long she and the boy were staying—he was a little bit intimidated by this woman. He said only, "Yes, ma'am, thank you, I appreciate the invitation. What time?"

"Six sharp."

"I'll be there. And now if y'all will excuse me, I was about to get changed and go for a run."

"I suppose that's a thing people do," she said.

Alone in his room, C.J. texted Joseph, not expecting an immediate response, given *Greece*, and given *honeymoon*. He just wanted to say a sort of polite *what the hell?* and get some information.

When C.J. got outside, he stopped for a moment to recalibrate, to breathe deeply. Deirdre Callaghan aside, what a blessing it was to be here now, to be free! To have unlimited fresh air, to look forward to home-cooked meals, to finally have the ability to paint again. That's how he intended to spend the coming summer: just a man and his canvases in a studio filled with gentle light, and unstructured days to revel in it all.

As a boy, he'd reveled in beach time at his family's Hilton Head Island home, shirtless in the summer sunshine, mindless of the UV damage being done to his skin—one of the great pleasures of being young and invincible. In his youth, he'd also been mindless of the effects of the Everclear cocktail his sister, Maya, liked to make and share with their friends. Though *cocktail* was a more refined term than the drink warranted; usually its base was Kool-Aid. She made batches on mornings when their father golfed and their mother race-walked with her girlfriends, all the women in flouncy tennis skirts and visors and gigantic sunglasses (to hide the signs of hangovers, surely; those women had elevated their own cocktailing to high art).

C.J.'s fondness for that Everclear punch and for Denise, one of the girls who shared it, had led to consequences any of them could have foreseen but had chosen not to, and now one such consequence—his daughter, Avery— wasn't speaking to him for reasons that had zero to do with sunshine, punch, or ugly sunglasses, and everything to do with him having gone to prison.

In front of the house, Arlo, still wearing the blue fleece jacket and black wellies he'd had on at arrival, squatted beside one of the barren planter beds. He had a hand trowel and a bucket and peered closely at the dirt.

"Whatcha up to?" C.J. asked, positioning himself for a hamstring stretch.

"I'm digging for precious gems."

"That so? What are you hoping for? Diamonds? Emeralds?"

"Sure, or opals. They're miniature galaxies."

"Wow."

"I mean, not *real* ones," the boy said, looking at C.J. over his shoulder. "You shouldn't get your hopes up."

"Oh. Sure." C.J. continued his stretching regimen. "Find anything yet?"

"I found this." He brought the bucket over to C.J. Inside was a dime-sized piece of a bird's pale eggshell.

"Cool. Any idea what sort of bird?"

Arlo shook his head. "Not a chicken, though, I'm sure of that."

C.J. was less sure, this being too early in the year for songbirds to have hatched their young. Also, eggshells were an ordinary component of kitchen compost. He wasn't about to ruin the boy's fun, though.

He asked, "Do you think it could be from a dinosaur?"

Arlo tilted his head. "Pr-o-o-o-bably not," he said. "But I'm not going to rule it out."

"No, right? Good science means considering all possibilities."

"Even though dinosaurs are supposedly extinct."

"You have a favorite?"

"Velociraptor—they're dangerous, but they're really smart. What's yours?"

C.J. said, "Hmm. It'd have to be Parasaurolophus. Just because I like saying the name."

Arlo smiled slightly. "That's a bad reason."

C.J. had been accused of bad reasoning before—most recently during his trial, by the prosecutor who wasn't buying his account of what had gone on the day of the shooting. *Do you really expect the intelligent people on this jury to believe that when you fired that weapon, which was aimed at Mr. Reynolds, you had no intention for that bullet to strike its target?*

He said to Arlo, "Bad as that reason may be, it's all I've got."

He was about to set off on his run when Arlo asked him another question: "Are you a friend of my mom's?"

"Nope. I've never even met her."

"Oh. Okay. I just thought maybe you were her friend. She had a lot of friends."

Whatever murky situation might be behind this subject and Arlo's raising of it, C.J. had no desire to pursue it. He started down the long driveway, calling, "Good luck with the digging! See you later."

"See you later," Arlo echoed, and squatted down to dig some more.

C.J. went for a short run, six miles out and back, sticking to the main road in order to avoid the need for any sort of navigation. At 108 square miles, MDI was a big territory, and he'd need some time to learn his way around. The Acadia trails were really calling his name, though, and if he was up early enough tomorrow morning, he aimed to catch sunrise on Cadillac Mountain, one of the first spots in the country to see the sun each day. Cheesy as it might sound, sunrises were among his favorite rediscovered pleasures, along with spicy Asian food, birdsong, singing aloud to the Talking Heads, privacy in the bathroom, sleeping in full darkness, and going barefoot any damned time he pleased. There was a high probability that when he got the right opportunity to add sex to the list, it, too, would make the cut.

He wasn't rushing that, though. After three womanless years, what was a little more delay? Now more than ever he wanted simplicity. He wanted peace. *No drama*. No exceptions.

The Callaghan house, which might once have been owned by a Rockefeller or Vanderbilt, sat on a knoll where the winter-browned lawn sloped to a stony beach and waves ran up against rocks again and again, etc., spraying salt water into the air. The ocean smelled different here, possibly because the water was colder or possibly because this northern Atlantic coast was unsullied by C.J.'s summertime recollections. How many times had he and Denise made out in the dunes after nightfall while the adults sat on the patio beside the pool and downed drinks with names like Stinger and Negroni, Tom Collins and Mai Tai? He remembered hearing their voices—his father's fey sort of cackling laughter, his mother's hooting whenever something tickled her, his uncle Lindsey's booming baritone—as the backdrop to his own drunken frolic, *frolic* being a polite substitution for the other F-word, which is what was going on there in the dunes as frequently as he and Denise could make happen. C.J. being twenty years old, booze-brave and stupid in love, meant it happened often. Like, three times in one night once.

Had Avery been conceived that night? She might have been. At any rate, Denise, who lived most of the year in Atlanta, didn't get word to him about her pregnancy until five months later, after she'd made the decision to keep the baby.

Denise: how differently all of this might have gone if she'd been on the pill, or if she'd insisted on condoms every time, or if *he'd* insisted on condoms every time, or if she'd had an abortion or given the baby up, or if she'd agreed to marry him first, instead of her father's new young surgical partner, a Duke grad who was thirteen years older than they were—that is, thirty-two at the time, and already a whiz at resecting livers. C.J. had been a whiz at little more than charcoal sketches and pretty watercolors—which Denise had loved, along with his smile and his eagerness to please her. These affections, though, were not enough to build her future on; he'd understood that. And he understood that his resistance to living off the Reynolds family teat was not as attractive to a young woman with a newborn as it had been to a young woman with an Everclear buzz. Actually, Denise had never cared that much about his determination to be his own man; she'd mainly just enjoyed having sex on a beach towel under the stars. And in the boathouse. And in a golf cart once. If her choices were either to marry a sweet but brooding college boy working on a fine arts degree or to stay secure in her elevated, southern-girl world, she couldn't be faulted for that.

Nor could he fault her for their on-again, off-again, on-again romance, which had followed her short marriage to the surgeon. Or the bumpy marriage to C.J. that followed *that*. Or the divorce that came on the heels of his conviction. He just wished it had all been different.

Inside, neither Deirdre nor the boy was in view, but the foyer and drawing room and kitchen were fragrant with sautéed onions and garlic. There was hardly a better scent where food was concerned, and it reminded C.J. just how much he'd missed the everyday textures of domestic life. He'd been out of prison for close to a month, but living in a hotel room with only a kitchenette meant he ate a lot of microwaved meals or ate out, alone. There was just something dispiriting about cooking for himself in that too-slick, corporate-style garret. And so it was with genuine pleasure that he joined Deirdre and Arlo in the dining room at six o'clock for a meal of ricotta-stuffed shells and a red-sauce gravy that was, he thought, the best he'd had in his life, ever. "Ms. Callaghan," he said, "I sure wish I had grown up in your house," which he'd thought would be taken as the supreme compliment it was, but instead caused both her and the boy to purse their lips and make no comment at all.

By the next morning, C.J. had learned the reason his compliment failed to land: Arlo's parents had three months earlier crashed their King Air on approach to the Saba airstrip, killing themselves and a third passenger (who might have been an underage boy toy, Joseph said, though no one talked about that). Arlo had been at home in Boston with his nanny. Preflight, the trio had gotten elevated on a chemical high, there in the Caribbean's playground for the rich, giving no thought to the risk of island-hopping in that condition. The result: Deirdre, old as she was, stepped in to raise Arlo, whose other relatives were either unwilling to be bothered or were already gone. Joseph had texted, It's a hell of a thing. But my life is just too complicated for raising a kid. Right, thought C.J. Jet-setting and horse racing and big-game hunting were complicated matters.

Does your aunt know about me? C.J. asked Joseph.

Not from me. So what if she does, though? You didn't kill anyone.

Arlo's family situation was an example of the kinds of reasons why C.J. had turned to F. Scott Fitzgerald's *Gatsby* while in prison. Fitzgerald, even as he'd aspired to wealth and its attendant privileges, understood that there could be consequences.

They were careless people . . . they smashed up things and creatures and then retreated back into their money or their vast carelessness or whatever it was that kept them together, and let other people clean up the mess they had made.

C.J. had reread *Gatsby* to remind himself of his own mistakes—and concluded that although his method of breaking off with his father (that mean-spirited SOB) might have been less than wise, the shooting had done the job he wished he'd been capable of thirty years earlier.

After eating breakfast with Arlo (Grape-Nuts, which the boy declared to be his favorite), C.J. met up with Carol Barksdale, the real estate agent, at her office in Bar Harbor. Carol was at least a decade older than she appeared in her website photo, and had that generic style he associated with women of a certain age and class. The black dress pants, black loafers, polyester top with a vaguely floral pattern in shades of blue against a white background—it was a kind of uniform, a Lands' End wardrobe made especially for women who valued practicality over fashion, or who understood that paying $590 for a plain white T-shirt (for example) was not only impossible for their budgets, it was stupid, or who just liked to be comfortable in their clothing and didn't want to have to worry about disguising their softer parts with shapewear. C.J. could not speak for every man, but in his view softer parts were just fine! Softer parts were natural! If God had meant for women to look like praying mantises, he'd have made their ability to bite men's heads off literal.

Carol's highlighted brown hair was neither long nor short and had no particular style. The tops of her cheeks were pink, as if she'd spent the previous day out in the sunshine. Clearing out the dead leaves from her flower garden, maybe. Or fishing. That seemed like something women up here might do on a clear March day. Whereas C.J.'s mother now spent many March days sunning on her southeast-facing Miami condo's balcony, then ostensibly undoing the sun damage at her favorite spa, with the occasional visit to her favorite cosmetic surgeon as needed.

Carol greeted C.J. brightly. "Well, hello! It's a pleasure to meet you in person. I guess you had a little bit of a rough start there, with Deirdre Callaghan. She can be a pill."

"It wasn't so bad. Can't blame her for being cautious."

"They're an interesting family, that's for sure. The money comes from cleaning sprays, of all things. But I suppose you know that."

C.J. nodded. His own family's history was similarly unsexy: the money had come from fasteners—snaps, buttons, zippers, hooks, clasps, buckles. Try to get through a day without using even one of these and you'll see how dominating the market early in America's history might lead to great prosperity.

Carol said, "Did you get a chance to look over the listings?"

"I did. Seems like there might be a good prospect or two here."

"Usually there's more to offer. It's a little early for the market. Things will heat up when the weather does, but it's smart of you to try to get the jump on that. The early bird."

C.J. waited for her to finish the phrase. When it was clear that she would not, he said, "Sure. So, yeah, I thought I might get ahead of that hot market and be in residence by the time the warmer weather brings the tourists."

"Really smart of you. So many people come for vacation and want to buy a house while they're here! And I don't turn them away, of course, but I do always think to myself."

Again C.J. waited for her to complete her thought, and again she seemed to have already done so. "Sure," he said again.

"We have some celebrities, too. They turn up in town from time to time. I'll bet you've heard of Susan Sarandon. *Such* a shame about her and Tim. And we've got Martha Stewart, at Skylands. That used to be Edsel Ford's estate. I sat beside her on a flight once. Martha Stewart, I mean. Edsel Ford was a man. What a funny name, Edsel. Old-fashioned. Though so is Martha, come to think of it."

C.J. didn't say what he was thinking: that he and ex-con Martha had more in common than just a desire to live on MDI.

Carol said, "I know none of these homes satisfy your entire wish list— but then, here's the truth: nothing is truly perfect, but there's always something that's perfect for *you*."

"Always?"

"Eventually. Meantime, the hunt is half the fun!"

For her, maybe. C.J. didn't want the hunt. He wanted the kill, quick and decisive, so that he could get on with his life. He'd spent so much time in purgatory as it was.

When they were in Carol's car, she said, "Here's something I've always wondered about people from the South: do you really use the expression *all y'all*? I've seen it on Facebook, but you know, not everything on Facebook is accurate, so . . ."

"We really do."

"Huh. Well, I guess every place has its ways."

"I guess so."

"Sometime back I had a client tell me that *cunnin'* doesn't mean *adorable* anywhere else but here in Maine."

"When we say it in the South, it means *diabolical*."

"Language is so interesting."

"It surely is."

Carol was an easy companion, and just the sort of real estate agent C.J. wanted: she didn't pry with personal questions; she didn't talk incessantly; when they got to each of the properties she wanted to show him, she reiterated the features that corresponded with his wish list, then let him tour the houses and grounds without interruption.

The first four properties were easy to reject. One of them lacked the density of trees he was aiming for, two were on summer-busy roads, and one was in such serious disrepair that he'd need to spend twice its cost to make it habitable year-round. Not until they were on house number five did C.J. see anything that got him excited in that necessary way you need to be if you were going to commit to spending several hundred thousand dollars. However, the source of his excitement wasn't house five (which was just okay), it was the next property along the road.

That house was set on a large property dense with pines and firs—which was exactly its appeal—and beyond the house, water. "That's the setting I'm looking for," he said from the driveway of house five. "End of the line, lots of trees, waterfront—idyllic."

"It is, I know, and if I'd had one like that to show you, we'd have seen it. *This* one"—Carol gestured toward the house they'd just toured—"is the closest thing on the market right now in your price range."

"Sure, I understand," C.J. said. "If I were to buy this one, I wonder if the folks who own that one would mind my cutting through to the water sometimes."

"The owner is a seasonal resident from New York, though the house has sat empty for the past several years, I think. Leo died maybe ten years ago? I heard that Marti's been sick for a while. It would *probably* be okay for you to go to the water, unless one of the kids was there or they plan to rent it. That could vary from year to year. I can certainly check on it for you."

"Do you think he might consider selling? Being sick, and all."

"She. It's Marti with an *i*. And I don't know, but I'm guessing the family would want to hang on to it regardless."

C.J. nodded. "I would, if it was me."

"Also, it would be priced higher than what you're looking at."

"Sure," he said. "Waterfront. Probably ups the value by a couple hundred thousand."

"Exactly. Even for a relatively modest camp like this."

"Camp?"

"It's what we Mainers call our seasonal houses in the woods or at the lake. You'd probably say *cottage*, but up here, a cottage is what we've always called houses like the one you're staying in, the Callaghans' big place. Language! There it is again," said Carol. "Do you want me to make a call and see if Marti's willing to share her frontage?"

"Hold off for now," he said. "I'm not sure I'm sold on this one regardless, and I don't want to bother her for no reason."

He turned back toward the house they'd just toured. The *camp*. It had some things going for it. The location was quiet and somewhat private, and there was enough space. It was in fair condition. He didn't love it, though. It was boxlike, with few windows and low ceilings. Still, some selective remodeling might be all it needed.

He told Carol, "How about I walk through once more?"

"Absolutely! 'Tour twice, offer once,' I always say."

"Let's not get ahead of ourselves."

As they went back inside, Carol said, "If this isn't 'the one,' don't worry. Inventory will increase soon. And now you've got me wondering whether Marti *would* be open to selling. I'll have to make a few calls."

That evening over a dinner of crab cakes and asparagus with hollandaise, Deirdre asked C.J. for a report. "What did you see? Anything worth buying?"

"Well, there's one fairly good prospect," he said, "but to tell you the truth, I'm not in love."

Arlo, who'd been silent while scraping the sauce off his asparagus, spoke up. "My mom said love takes time."

"Sure," said C.J. "That's why it's good to not rush into it. I guess you've got some hard experience there?"

"When I was little, my dog jumped on me a lot and bit my clothes and I pretty much hated him. But Mom said I had to give him a chance, because he was just a puppy. She said that when I was a baby, I was annoying, too."

"I bet I know how this turns out," C.J. said. "After a while, he was your best pal."

"How did you know?"

C.J. wondered where the dog was now. Another casualty of Arlo's reckless parents? He also wondered what was being done as regards the boy's schooling.

He said to Arlo, "Lucky guess. Too bad a house can't improve itself through growing up. It's a lot of work and money to change or fix things. Best to be picky."

Arlo said, "Yeah, Gram says, 'Make your choices with your eyes on to-morrow, not just today. Then you're not sorry as much.'"

"I do say that," said Deirdre.

C.J. nodded in agreement. "Those are wise words."

Arlo was quiet as he fit his butter knife's blade between his fork's tines. Then he said, "My dad should've waited for the weather to get better. I know planes can fly in rain and everything—even inside hurricanes. But that's special circumstances." Arlo spoke the last two words as if reciting a self-soothing excuse for why his father had failed so spectacularly: the man was just an ordinary pilot; he hadn't been equipped for *special circumstances*—with, say, a weatherproof aircraft and fighter pilot training.

C.J. said, "Yeah, it's a tough situation, losing your folks. I'm real sorry that happened to you."

Arlo lifted his chin. "I cried for like three weeks in a row. I'm doing better now."

Deirdre brought an apple pie to the table. "You're planning to leave Monday morning?"

C.J. said, "Yes, ma'am. Which will be a hardship after eating so well here."

"I suppose you have to get back to your work. What *is* your work, by the way?"

"These days, I'm a painter. Artist, not house. So my time is pretty much my own. It'll be easy enough for me to come back when there are more places on the market."

Deirdre said, "A painter. Is that right? Family money, then."

The woman was direct. If most folks here were like this, he'd need to be especially cautious not to give openings to the curious.

He said, "Yep, there was some family money. My grandmother was generous. But," he added, misleading her with a truth from twenty-five years earlier, "I've made a little headway in the art world."

"Noted," she said. "Is there a lady friend awaiting you at home?"

"There is not. Where are you going with this?"

Deirdre handed him a plate on which she'd put a generous slice of pie. "Do you know anything about setting landscape timbers and field stone? Or are those hands too precious?"

"I have done some landscaping."

"Power tools?"

"All the basics. Why?"

"It seems to me that it'd be foolish for you to go home only to have to fly back every week until you find true love here. Arlo and I came out to build ourselves a big summer garden—"

"We drew our plans like engineers do," Arlo said. "Gram taught me how to use a compass. Not the navigation kind, the drawing kind."

She said, "Some of the beds will be circular, some will be square or rectangular; it's an ambitious project."

"It's going to be big," Arlo said with great seriousness. "A *lot* of vegetables. Gram's letting me choose ones I like best, which are carrots and corn and watermelon—that's a fruit, but I'm not cheating. Fruit is allowed, too."

"Nothing green?" said C.J.

"Gram chose the green stuff. And flowers."

Deidre said, "I intend to hire laborers, unless you'd like to stay on for a few weeks. I'll keep feeding you, and you put in a few hours a day laying out the plan, installing the timbers, stacking stone, and so on—you see what I mean."

"I do," said C.J.

"I'm sure Arlo would like to have the company of someone with a bit more vigor than I've got. You two seem to be getting on nicely."

Before answering, C.J. weighed the complications against the advantages. To extend his visit would mean keeping the rental car a while longer, suspending his return flight, buying new clothes—a hassle, for sure. On the other hand, it *would* save him the back-and-forth and give him the ability to see houses as soon as they got listed for sale. And he wouldn't have to sit alone in his uninspiring hotel room night after night.

He said, "Just so I'm clear: would Arlo be bossing me, or would I get to boss him?"

Arlo's whole demeanor brightened. "I would let you boss me," he said, "if you'll take me hiking sometimes. Gram isn't good at hiking."

"Well then, yeah, man, count me in," C.J. said. "A hiking partner is exactly what I need."

While he and Arlo were cleaning up the kitchen after dinner, he texted Carol Barksdale:

> Not going to bid on house #5 but I'll be hanging around MDI for a
> little while, so hit me with any new prospects as they happen. Also
> please do inquire re: status of neighbor's place on water.

A few hours later, Carol replied:

> Marti Geller says she's not ready to sell just yet but we should check
> back in a couple of weeks.

Geller, thought C.J. The name had a familiar ring, but he couldn't place it. A client, probably, or someone who worked for his father's company, Reynolds Fasteners. The company that would've eventually been his, if he'd been willing to stick to the Faustian bargain he'd made. A whole other future, gone now, no looking back.

4

The Effort and the Effect

The last time Marti spoke to any of the girls—in fact, the last time she spoke at all—it was to Beck, by telephone, and she said, "Honey, it's okay; I've got it all arranged. Please just take care of each other." There were more thoughts in her mind, but because of her pain meds and because of her disease, she was too tired to push them all the way out of her mouth and through the phone, which Delia was holding up to her ear. "We'll talk soon" was the last thing she said.

By the time Beck called again two days later, Marti was effectively gone. Delia said, "She's sleeping now, but I'll let her know you called," which was what Marti had directed her to say until she could replace *sleeping* with *dead*, at which time the nurse would be the one making the phone call to Beck, as well as to the funeral home. Call them first, Marti had said, the idea being to ensure that her body would be removed from the apartment before Beck was able to get there from Irvington.

Marti Geller's soul departed her body a little after one o'clock on Thursday afternoon, just eleven days after her doctor's pronouncement—something she would have been happy about because it was proof that her doctor had been correct. Hardly anything pleased Marti more than having her faith in someone or something rewarded, as with the Mets in '69, '86, and very nearly in 2015 as well.

As deaths went, Marti would have said hers was a good one. She was unconscious and free of pain. The girls, though, were rather taken aback by the news.

"Obviously we knew she was probably going to die from the cancer," Sophie said to Beck and Claire on the three-way phone call Beck initiated after the hospice nurse called her. Sophie (youngest, blondest, prettiest) was currently in Dubai, while Beck (oldest, tallest) was at home in Irvington, and Claire—you could ID her by the massive curly hair, when she wore it down—was at work in Duluth. Sophie said, "But I didn't know she was going to do it *today*."

Claire felt betrayed personally: she knew the basic end-stage-cancer timeline and suspected that Marti had duped her about her progress along that line. She said, "I was led to believe she had months yet. That was really unfair of her. Really wrong."

"It's not *wrong*," Beck said. Being a writer, she was particular about word usage and could be a bit schoolmarmish—though less so in recent years, as her kids were grown now, and she was no longer reviewing schoolwork or correcting their speech. She was, however, still married to an editor. She said, "*Wrong* implies a moral failing. The real issue is that you just don't like it."

Claire said, "Oh, and I suppose you're fine with it. Well, you would be. You're the one she talked to last."

"Pure happenstance," said Beck, though she secretly (gratefully) felt it was not. She said, "Anyway, I'm just waiting for Paul to get home so that he can watch Leah, and then I'm leaving for Mom's. The funeral home is already on their way to the apartment. I'll head down there as soon as I can and start sorting things out. God, I can't believe she's gone."

Claire said, "Why does this feel so different from when we lost Dad?"

"Maybe because Mom was the glue. You know? Dad was . . . he made us like dandelion seeds, scattering us all over the city so that we could see and do everything. But then Mom held us all together, and now we're adrift because neither of them are here. I don't know if that makes sense—and it's sure not poetic, I know, but you take my meaning."

"No, you're right," Sophie said. "I feel like . . . like I could hang up with you guys and FaceTime her and she'd answer. Except I also feel like there's this huge blank wall standing between me and wherever Mom is. If she's anywhere. But never mind me, I'm really wiped right now—no sleep. Beck, did you say you have Leah there? Send me a picture."

"Yeah, Zack and Binta are doing a retreat to explore whether they're ready to cohabitate," said Beck, referring to her son and his . . . girlfriend? Partner? Future wife? "I'd better wind this up so I can call them, and Cammie. I don't know if Mom told you, but Cam's in Nicaragua right now, backpacking with friends. Oh—and I need to call Paul, too. God, I can't believe I was forgetting Paul."

Claire said nothing.

Sophie said, "Zack and Binta had to go away to figure out if they should live together?"

"Look who's talking," said Claire. "You went to Paris when you were trying to decide on a *hair color*."

"Because the colorist everyone said was best was in Paris."

"I'm just saying."

"I wanted to have an in-person consult. And the trip was free, or almost free, so."

Beck ignored the bickering and answered Sophie's question. "They need some couples time, and I don't have any problem with taking care of my granddaughter. It's win-win."

"I am a great-aunt," Sophie said wondrously, in reference to the baby. "*You* are a grandmother. A *grandmother*. God. It still blows my mind."

Claire redirected them. "I'll see how soon I can get a flight. Tonight, possibly, or tomorrow for sure. David can stay at Chad's and then go out there just for the funeral, and I can reschedule my patients."

"No need for you to come early," said Beck. "I can handle things. Wait until I know when the service will be. My guess is Sunday or Monday."

Sophie said, "I'll be back late tomorrow. I can help with whatever."

"Then I should be there, too," Claire said.

Beck sighed. "Fine, but we've converted the kids' rooms to home offices, so you'll need to stay in Mom's place or bunk with Soph—at her housesit, I guess. Sophie, you sublet your place, right?"

"Right, yeah, I did," said Sophie.

Claire said, "Can I, Soph?"

"Ugh. I will be *so* jet-lagged."

"And?"

"Well, I mean, no one will be at Mom's, so . . ."

"The apartment is going to smell like a death chamber," Claire said. "Because that's what it is."

"Why come early at all?" said Beck. "Just come for the service, stay with Soph or at a hotel, then head back the next day."

Claire said, "I just want to, okay? Let me decide for myself."

"A hotel makes *way* more sense," Sophie said. "I don't know if my guest bathroom's clean."

"Aren't there four bathrooms?" said Claire.

"How would you even know?"

"I looked it up when Mom said you were housesitting there. I knew it was going to be something great. There are pictures from when it was on the market."

"Okay, yes," Sophie said. "There are three and a half bathrooms, actually. But if you *must* have the truth, I already have a guest in residence, and we like our privacy."

Claire said, "Why didn't you just say so? Anyone I'd know?"

"Not unless you follow the international urban art scene."

"Is it Banksy?" said Beck.

"Ha-ha," Sophie replied. "And even if it was, I wouldn't tell you."

Claire said, "Chad had a light fixture made from a bicycle wheel. Does that count as urban art?"

Beck heard the baby and said, "Listen, guys, Leah's awake; I have to go. I'll call you both later—or, Sophie, will you even be up?"

"Text me," she said. "If I don't reply right away, I'll catch up with you tomorrow."

Claire said, "I'll bet she parties all night at these things." She sounded simultaneously envious and annoyed, which was par for the course where Claire's views on Sophie's life were concerned.

"Goodbye," Beck said, and ended the call before Claire could derail the conversation further.

If Marti was watching over the girls as they had this conversation, she might be unhappy to see that even with her death to unite them, they were still failing to treat one another with the version of sisterly affection she'd naïvely imagined possible when Sophie was a newborn being adored (briefly) by four-year-old Claire and eight-year-old Beck. They needed one another, whether they thought so or not.

She might be unhappier still with the soon-to-come addition of an ex-con to the mix. But maybe Leo would be beside her with his arm over her shoulders, assuring her—as ever—that there were larger forces at work here, and she should give it all a chance to play out. Years of following Major League Baseball taught you that if your team was in a slump, you could still hold out for a rally—whether that was in an individual game or for the entire season. And of course there was also the wisdom derived from knowing that the World Series championship sometimes came down to a single game, or even a single inning. In fact, a single pitch could be the clincher. He would say, *Try not to worry.* Marti, though, would remind him that one team was going to lose no matter what.

I don't like to look at it like that, Leo would say.

I know, she would tell him. *That's why I love you.*

5

This Is Mine

What people tended to notice first about Beck Geller was her height. She stood five nine and a half in her bare size 10 feet. Her neck was long, her cheeks and chin and shoulders angular. Had she been striking when she was young, she might have found work as a model. Maybe on the runway, although most of those young women were even taller: sleek greyhounds in human form. Beck sometimes encountered such women strolling along in pairs on Fifth Avenue or in SoHo. Away from the runway and out of couture, they seemed alien. That was not Beck.

One benefit of Beck's height was that it made it her more visible, and thus it was slightly easier for her to get a cab streetside, which is what she did today when she left Grand Central after taking the train in. Admittedly the cab was an indulgence, but it was raining/sleeting outside, and she'd forgotten to bring the umbrella she'd need for the walk from the station at 14th to her mother's place five blocks away. Also, in one of their last conversations, Marti had encouraged her to take more cabs.

When Beck got out on 19th Street, there was no hearse at the curb, and this was not a surprise, exactly; nearly four hours had passed since Delia's call. Still, Beck had expected something to look different here upon her arrival, something to indicate that what she'd known as her life—that is, her mother, Marti Geller, residing in this building, in that apartment on the top floor where a small lamp shone from a table that had been positioned beside the living room window for as long as Beck had been alive—was forever altered. There was no Marti Geller up there now, and never would be again. Before very long, that table and that lamp and the photographs and books and tchotchkes, and every other material good that had defined the Gellers as their distinct selves on this island that housed millions of others, would be carted away. The apartment would be scrubbed and painted—fully updated, probably, in whatever ways would bring it up to the standard of its current market rent, whatever that might be. Certainly more than Beck, whom some might call a dilettante freelancer, and Paul, an executive editor for a big publishing house's smallest fiction imprint, would think to spend on housing.

So no runway work for young Beck—but what about print? For a time, this had seemed not impossible. She might do fashion ads like the ones in *Harper's Bazaar* or *Vogue*, her wavy dark bob tamed and slicked back, her pale skin made paler with powder, her eyelids made vibrant and enormous in purples and reds or greens and blues. Copper. Silver. Violet. She'd loved paging through the magazines with their heavy, glossy pages and their sophisticated take on what New York City life could be for a young woman if she was styled correctly and wore the right lipstick. Beck, at sixteen, had very much wanted to be and do those things, to have that version of life here, which might, just *might*, be accessible to her if she got work as a model.

She had the right kind of skinny legs for the trade, but her facial features were, alas, too ordinary. And anyway, around this time she got turned on to Joan Didion and New Journalism, and became as keen to get into the pages of *Rolling Stone* or *Vanity Fair*, *The New Yorker* or the *Times* as she'd been to be one of the glossy girls. Keener, in fact, because doing so would be a result of her talents, foremost, not her looks. She'd read Candace Bushnell, too— that enlightening columnist in *The New York Observer*—and concluded that she, Beck, would choose love over money if she should ever be faced with the choice. She'd been young enough to not be cynical.

That Beck had managed to write professionally still felt surprising; she had no college degree, no formal training, just some natural talent and a strong desire to get good at saying things with it. And while her long-form journalism might never win her a Pulitzer, she could hold her head up in New York's literary circles. That Beck had not emulated Didion (or for that matter, Bushnell) well enough to crack the literary scene with her *novel* was a disappointment. Of course, your novel couldn't get noticed if you were still failing to write it.

But focus on the successes, Beck: A high point in recent years was being the subject of a small photo spread in *Marie Claire* that accompanied a piece she'd written herself. This was a best-of-both-dreams situation, though she'd been wearing her own clothes, and the pedestrian makeup did not lend her any kind of exotic appeal, and her mother had kept forgetting to buy the issue so Beck had brought her a copy, and upon seeing it, Marti had said, "That's really nice, honey. I'm not sure about your hair, though. Did you see Sophie got a mention on Page Six?" which had confused Beck for a moment. Page six of this *Marie Claire* issue? Then she understood that Marti meant the *New York Post*, where, it turned out, Sophie appeared in a photo with Tania Uccello and Taylor Swift. Marti had the newspaper at hand.

Beck's habit, now that she was over forty, was to take the stairs whenever the climb was ten floors or less, as part of her effort to get healthier and to avoid losing muscle mass as she aged. She'd started Pilates and kickboxing as well. Menopause might still be a decade off (some days she hoped so; other days—with the cramps and the clots and the bloating—she wanted it *now*), but if she established these fitness practices early, she'd be ahead of the aging game later. Or at least this was what she told herself as she trudged up the five flights to her childhood residence. Deliberate exercise was really not her thing—had never needed to be—but when you had a mother who was fighting stage 4 cancer, as Marti had been when Beck initiated the fitness plan, you started to think differently about biological causes and effects, about chance and prevention, about living long enough to become the person you were still working at being.

She let herself into the apartment and had to push through a heavy wave of nostalgia and loss. Very little had changed here over the years. On a dreary afternoon like this one, she ought to see her mother in the armchair by the window, a mug of tea steaming at her elbow as she read the latest Louise Penny mystery or did the *Times* crossword. Seeing the empty chair made her choke up. God *damn* cancer.

She cleared her throat, then called out, "Hello? It's Beck."

Delia emerged from the kitchen drying her hands on a dish towel. The woman had strong cheekbones and a husky voice that were at odds with the sprinkle-donuts-and-flamingos print scrub top she wore today. When Beck had met her the previous week, Delia was wearing a zany tree-frog print.

Delia set aside the towel and said, "Oh, sweetie. I'm real sorry for your loss."

Beck burst into tears, surprising them both. Delia pulled her into a hug. "All right now."

"I'm so sorry," Beck said. "I don't know what came over me." She wiped her nose on her coat sleeve. "I guess . . . I just wasn't ready for this. I wasn't *ready*."

"No, but she was."

"Why didn't she say? I just don't understand. She told me *everything*." Beck paused. "That is, I thought she did."

Delia released her. "I've finished tidying up her room—"

"You didn't have to do that."

"I know. But some people get upset by the death scene, so why not make things a little easier?"

Beck said, "Mom loved you, and I can see why. You are a truly caring person."

Delia shrugged. "I just think about what I'd want for my own family. So, okay then, I'm gonna go ahead and be on my way. You're all right?"

Beck nodded.

"Good," Delia said. "You have the funeral home info. They were real careful with her. Real respectful. They said if you want to see her—"

"I don't!" Beck shook her head. It would be too much. Neither had she seen her father after his death, which had occurred in surgical post-op after his heart bypass. Jews didn't do open-casket visitation. A mercy, in Beck's opinion.

She said, "I mean, maybe I should want to. Probably I should. But . . ."

"That's all right. Understandable. There's no rules, sweetie. Oh—she said to tell you she left everything set for you, there on the table."

"Thank you." Beck went and put her arms around Delia as if embracing one of her own beloveds. Speaking into Delia's hair, Beck said, "Thank you for being here with her. I mean, I know it wasn't a favor or anything, I know you're paid—probably not nearly well enough; I wrote a piece once about hospice workers—but you chose this work and hardly anyone does that. You have to be an angel to do it. Thank you."

Beck continued to hold her until Delia said, "All right," and gently extricated herself. "Is anyone coming to help you out?"

Beck nodded. "My sisters are getting their travel arranged."

"But no one tonight?"

"No," Beck said. "Paul's babysitting our granddaughter. But it's okay. I'm okay. I'm just . . ." Beck still couldn't understand why Marti hadn't warned her or wanted her there. "I'm okay, really."

Delia put on her coat, a bright fuchsia North Face like one Beck had admired in a shop last fall. The color was what had attracted her and was also what had kept her from buying it. So vivid! A fully confident person wore that coat. A person who was comfortable in her own skin. A person who didn't shy away from interpersonal interactions that she hadn't initiated herself. Beck's own coat was a tentative navy. It was long and puffy and suggested a person who feared cold, whereas Delia's suggested someone who faced it—which did seem appropriate for a woman who tended the terminally ill, who oversaw passages to the afterlife while covered in donuts and flamingos. Beck imagined that Delia, who appeared to be in her late thirties, was also willing to bike in the city and walk alone through Central Park at dusk and eat dishes whose ingredients she couldn't easily identify at a glance.

Beck, ever the journalist, said, "Before you go: if you don't mind, I have a question. What does success look like for you?"

"What do you mean?"

"Well, everyone you work for dies. Usually we think of death as a failure. My sister Claire is a pediatric cardiologist. If one of her patients dies, she takes it personally. In my work, success is me placing an essay or article I've written, or writing something that's commissioned and seeing it in print. If I wrote things that were *always* rejected . . ." She paused, thinking about it. "That seems like your job: a negative result every time."

Delia said, "Yeah, okay, I see what you mean. Well, all of my patients are dying, no matter what—and that's not because of anything I did or didn't do. So I succeed whenever someone dies the way Marti did, the way they decide to."

"And you aren't afraid of . . . ? I mean, seeing dead people . . . Obviously you aren't. I don't think I could do that."

"You've never seen someone who has passed?"

Beck shook her head. "Not so far. Not in real life. In photos, yes."

"If the death isn't violent, the bodies look peaceful. Beautiful, actually. I see God in their faces."

"Really?"

"It's nothing to be afraid of."

"That's a nice thought," said Beck, though she felt that death was the ultimate thing to be afraid of.

When Delia was gone, Beck draped covers over all the mirrors, then stood at the living room window for a few minutes watching the rain on the glass, the people walking along the street with their dark and bright umbrellas, the headlights and taillights of cars. She was trying to imagine her mother's face as Delia described it. What did that look like—seeing God in the faces of the dead? She might have asked for more information, but she'd felt in that moment that Delia wouldn't be able to describe it satisfactorily, that it was something that wasn't seen so much as perceived, an ineffable thing no words or even a photograph could relay.

Gone.

Her mother was gone.

Beck sighed. The pain and illness were over, at least. That was a kind of blessing. Her worst anxiety, as regards her mother, had been that Marti would have an excruciatingly slow and painful decline. That she would struggle and beg for release and Beck would be unable to help her. The Beck who had dutifully mastered her Torah trope murmured, "God is good." The heartsick skeptic in her added, "Except when He's not."

Her phone rang. It was Paul. "How are you holding up?" he said. "I thought I'd check to see if everything is okay—relatively speaking."

"I had a few moments where I was a little bit of a mess, but Delia was very patient with me."

"It's okay to be a little bit of a mess."

"I'm an orphan now," said Beck. "I hadn't really thought about that before."

Paul said, "It puts you in esteemed company, if that's any consolation."

Beck couldn't think of any esteemed orphans. "Who do you mean?"

"In literature. Dickens could hardly write a story without an orphan in it."

"Oh, right. True."

"And, you know, things worked out well for Harry Potter."

Beck smiled. "Jane Eyre—depending on your point of view."

"Tom Sawyer. Mowgli." Paul laughed. "Remember how badly Cammie wanted to go live in the jungle after she saw that movie?"

"Oh my god, *Jungle Book*. She insisted on watching it every day for weeks, and probably once or twice a month after that until she was, I don't know, five? The songs are burned into my brain. Anyway," Beck said, sighing again, "I need to go through the stuff Mom left for me, so I better get to it."

"Yes, you should do that and then call me back."

"Oh?"

"Yes—damn, Leah just spit up on me. Hold on a sec. Actually, just call back afterward. You'll see what I mean." He hung up.

Beck seated herself at the kitchen table, where a file box waited. Inside, atop a collection of other things, was an envelope labeled READ THIS, which she set aside for the moment. Also in the box were a few other file folders holding a bunch of old cards and letters and drawings she and her sisters had made; a spiral notebook; three baby books; a photo album; several of Beck's early articles and a "book" she'd written on notebook paper, bound with red yarn (this made Beck teary); Claire's college graduation program; birth announcements for all the grandkids and Leah; and the recipe binder that had been in use for as long as Beck could recall. At the bottom of the box: Marti's keys, kept (improbably) on a ring with a red enameled heart that read *I ♥ NY*. Beck hooked it onto her own key ring, loving that her mother, a girl who'd come to Manhattan from Kentucky via Maine, had embraced this city and never let go.

She opened the READ THIS envelope, humming "The Bare Necessities" without really realizing it. It held a folder whose contents were: one envelope on which Marti had written *The Girls*; lots of papers relating to Marti's hospital bills and insurance; a printed list of information about her bank accounts, her IRA, her life insurance; contact information for her friend and attorney Audra Berg, for the volunteers coordinator at Mount Sinai Beth Israel, for her friend Elise from the mah-jongg group, her friend Michelle from book club, and so on; a stapled copy of her will, on which COPY was stamped across the top of the front page; a handwritten note listing passwords to various accounts (*delete my Facebook!*); and a sheet of instructions that specified the details of her funeral preparations, as well as directions for sending out some already-addressed thank-you cards that were bound with a rubber band.

After making this quick survey, Beck opened the envelope addressed to *The Girls*.

Dear girls,

I don't have a lot to say here, I just want you to know I love you all very much. You have been the best daughters a mother could have. Beck: you did good with Paul. He's like a son to me. Forgive me for choosing him and not you.

If you three have any disputes about the will, I trust you to work it out amongst yourselves.

My greatest hope is that you will each find happiness. It's not simple, I know.

I'm sorry if I upset you by dying by myself. If there really is an afterlife, I will be there watching the Mets beat the Phillies every time they play them, and eating a hot dog with Dad.

Love,

Mom

"Choosing him for what?" Beck said. She picked up the phone and called Paul. When he answered, she said, "What did Mom choose you for?"

"What do you mean?"

"Her note." Beck quoted that part to him.

"Ah," he said. "Then you haven't read the will yet?"

"*You've* read it?"

"I saw a draft. She swore me to secrecy."

"Are you kidding me?" said Beck. "The nurses, and now you? Who else knows Marti Geller better than I do? The *real* Marti Geller?"

"I was afraid of this."

"Just tell me what it is she chose you for."

"It's nothing major. She just wants—wanted—me to be the executor, that's all."

"That can't be right; she told me *I* was going to be the one handling everything. She *told* me. I feel like I'm going to lose my mind."

"It was deliberate subterfuge, so that you wouldn't argue with her about it. The idea was that she didn't want you three to be at odds over anything. If no one is the boss, no one can get mad at anyone else."

"Except that you're my husband, so I'm sure to be accused of having undue influence over you if everything isn't to everyone's liking. But what is there for us to even get worked up about? Isn't it all straightforward? Everything basically in thirds? Or did she change that, too?"

"No, it is . . ." Paul said.

"But?"

"The whole estate's value will be divvied up equally between the three of you. What may surprise you—all of you—is that she wants the house in Maine sold off."

"No, she doesn't. She wouldn't."

"See for yourself."

Beck scanned the will, looking for the relevant information. There it was: their camp was to be brought up to salable condition using funds Marti had set aside for the purpose, then sold and the proceeds divided equally between the three of them.

"I can't believe this," she said. "How could you let her do it? I never would have allowed this."

Paul said, "I didn't 'let' her. It's hers to do with as she wishes. She said maybe the money would be more important to each of you, since no one was using the place."

"Not lately. But eventually we would. I mean, that's what I thought would happen, once things settled down again."

Her intention was that when her mother was either cured or her mother was (God forbid, she'd thought) gone, she'd use the camp regularly—not only as the summertime family retreat it had been for most of her life, but as a writing retreat, too. A place to go off for a while to work on the novel she'd been dabbling with for years, a coming-of-age story about a young woman in a Pennsylvania coal town in the 1980s. She was basing it on a girl she'd read about in the *Pittsburgh Post-Gazette*, whose story had then been picked up by the *Today* show. At the time, she'd thought, *This could make an important novel.* Like something Joan Didion might write if she cared about girls from coal towns. Which, maybe she did—but probably not; the subject wasn't culturally sexy the way hers tended to be, and she seemed to have stopped writing fiction, and that was good because it meant she wouldn't beat Beck to it. *If* Beck actually wrote it, that is.

Eight years of dabbling, to be precise.

This failure to execute was not Beck's usual modus operandi; she was long accustomed to deadlines and to setting goals and slaying them. This was how she'd managed to make everyone—family, teachers, editors, friends—believe that she was as bright and capable and important and interesting as her sisters.

A novel, however, was an intimidating goal. She had no idea whether she could pull it off. Paul often talked of how many bad submissions he read, about how most writers needed a decade or more to study craft and write two or three shitty attempts before they could produce a novel worth reading. So she kept her dabbling to herself, revealing the ambition only to her mother, who'd said, "Then don't wait."

Good advice. But for Beck there were two main dangers in making a serious effort: she'd be so bad at it that not only would the work never see publication, but she might also lose faith in her ability to write anything, ever again, *or* she'd be good enough at it to sell the book and have it published, but before it even had a chance to be found and read by the public, it would be mauled and shredded by one or more critics at one or more junctures. She'd seen that happen to a few of Paul's authors, as well as to authors published by some of his peers. Beck had ached for each of them, knowing they had put their hearts into their work. She also feared that if that happened to her, her skin might not be thick enough to withstand the pain. She would want to stick her head in the oven and crank up the gas.

On the other hand, she might—*might*, it *was* possible—write a whole readable book *and* get good reviews. She might get to be the author du soir at her local bookshop, maybe even in other stores in other towns, too. Instead of sitting in the audience feeling the weird mixture of envy and awe and determination and terror she experienced every time she went to a novelist's event, *she'd* be the one speaking with pride and affection about the characters she'd invented, the story she'd told, the journey of ten years that it had taken for her to gestate the baby they all had come to hear about. She'd be the grateful author hugging angel booksellers, God bless every one of them.

But for this dream to become reality, she needed the camp. It was the one place in the world where she was confident she could feel focused and comfortable and safe enough to finally write the book.

She'd told her mother exactly that. They were in yet another medical facility waiting room, where yet another doctor was running behind schedule. "I think I just need to get away from Paul's influence," Beck said. "I feel him judging what I write even though he doesn't know I'm writing it. At camp, it would just be me and the story."

"Then go," Marti said. "You don't need to come to every appointment with me. I appreciate you being here, but I could manage without you sometimes."

"Well, okay, but I have other obligations, too. Committees, and babysitting Leah when Zack needs me, and, you know, my paid writing assignments. I just need to find the right time."

Marti said, "If you want to, you will."

Yet here her mother was, Beck thought, basically telling her, *Never mind, forget it.*

Beck said to Paul, "I just don't understand. Everyone loves the camp. It's like a member of the family. We can't *sell* it."

"But we haven't been up there since Zack was sixteen, I think."

The kids hadn't wanted to be ripped away from friends and jobs for a stay at Grandma's musty old place on the lake, where they'd have to share a bedroom and a bathroom. One bathroom for the entire family! This fact alone had constituted a horror sufficient to dissuade their teen selves. Every summer when the kids had been small, though, Beck and Paul had taken them up to MDI for at least a long weekend, usually for a week. Sometimes Claire (and later Chad and David) would be there, too. Sophie might pop in. Marti and Leo would welcome and accommodate all of them, in any combination. They would eat (a lot), often at Geddy's in Bar Harbor, and swim and kayak and hike and take boat rides to see whales or catch lobsters. And before all of that, teenage Beck had lost her heart there, to a boy of summer. That memory had stayed with her all these years, a tender spot she still probed every now and then for the bittersweet pleasure of it, the knowledge that she had once been young and passionate. And foolish. And heartbroken.

She'd learned so much in those early years—not only about love, but about life outside of New York. About nature. The sea. The tides. Native peoples. How to read a sundial. How to tell a female lobster from a male. What the ocean sounds like when it rushes into and out of a cave. The peculiar pleasure of picking sand out of her hair hours after lying on a beach being kissed by a college boy who smelled like warm coconut.

But, time being a river, etc., all of that was past now, no way to recapture it.

Which, however, did *not* mean they should sell their camp!

Paul said, "Marti set aside some money to get the place shaped up for sale—do you see where it says so?"

Beck found the passage. "I see it. And wait, what's this? She wants it on the market within a *month*? This is ridiculous. I'm not doing this."

"She stipulates one last hurrah there for you three together, before it goes up for sale," Paul said. "You have to admire her thoroughness. Anyway, if you want to be in charge of doing those improvements, consider yourself so directed."

This rubbed Beck wrong. Had he not heard anything she'd said? "Oh, gee, thank you, sir, that's my heart's desire."

"Come on. Don't be an ass."

"Don't *you* be an ass," Beck said, and ended the call.

Paul and Beck were twenty-five years into their marriage at this point, yet Beck could not recall a single time either of them had deliberately hung up on the other. She was mortified by her behavior. If the two of them were anything to each other all these years in, they were kind. Polite. Unfailingly polite. *Ludicrously* polite, Sophie had once remarked, as if it was a failing. Beck did not see it that way. Their actual failing was deeper than the two of them treating each other like favored partners at a global summit: they were living a lie.

It stemmed from a matter they never spoke of: sex. From lack of sex. From the complete dearth of sex in their marriage nowadays, which was only a little less sex than they'd been having in the years before "nowadays" had begun, which had followed a decade of occasional sex, which had been just a bit less than the amount of sex they'd had in the early days.

Beck never talked about all this with Paul (or anyone). Really, it had not seemed to be that much of a problem. A lot of busy parents had little to no sex; Beck had written about it for *Cosmo*. And none of the sex they'd had, ever, was especially impressive in its vigor. Paul was not that kind of guy, and Beck had known this and married him anyway. Their relationship had been based on other things—*truer* things, she'd told herself. Whenever Beck wanted more than what she had, she'd pick up a steamy romance to read in secret, indulge the vicarious thrill.

She'd told herself that whatever explained Paul's diminishing interest, it didn't seem to be about her. After all, she was more or less the same person she'd always been. Some people might even say she had grown more attractive with age and experience. Also, she and Paul got along great, co-parenting and cohabiting with far more ease than many couples they knew. They were genuine friends, through and through.

So yeah, fiery, frequent sex was probably great, but it wasn't what marriage was supposed to be about. She'd believed this twenty-five years ago, and she still believed it. Now, however, she also believed she knew what lay behind their situation: Paul was gay. Women just didn't quite do it for him, though he'd tried in good faith to be heterosexual, maybe unsure, in his younger years, which way he was meant to go. Paul was gay, and closeted out of shame, she supposed, or embarrassment, or an admirable desire not to upset the kids and her.

Beck had not undertaken her theory lightly. She'd resisted it for a long while, in fact. He might just have a low sex drive, low testosterone; not every male was compelled to daily spread his seed like a desperate farmer flinging it over a tilled field before the rain came. But then a year or so ago she read an article that linked to a surprisingly thorough *Is he gay?* questionnaire, and her result was *Strong Probability*.

She'd tested her theory on Sophie, pretending that the man in question was the husband of a longtime friend of hers on staff at a major magazine. Beck outlined the diminishing sex in years past, how it had pretty much ceased altogether a couple of years ago, how it had never been vigorous. Sophie asked some questions that Beck had to pretend she didn't have the answers to (like, how many women had the guy been with in the past? Before Beck, Paul had been with only three). But even going just with the basics— close friendship with his wife, caring, intelligent, warm, interested in things like literature and interior decorating, frequent nights out for "work"— Sophie had said, "He does sound like he *could* be a closeted gay man who's stepping out for sex. Someone should open the door for him. This is twenty-first-century New York, after all; what's there to be afraid of?"

Beck knew there was a lot to be afraid of if you were the things Sophie was not—i.e., already long-married, parent of two adult kids, child of traditional-minded parents.

The more she thought about it, the more convinced she became.

Beck had sympathy for his plight and was waiting for him to talk to her about it—which surely he would, and probably soon, since Cammie was moved out now and had become openly fluid in her own sexuality. Given that science had shown a biological component to homosexuality, this was even more evidence for Beck's theory.

Beck and Paul were reasonable people, best friends, genuine allies (his secret about Marti's will notwithstanding). She knew they'd be able to find a path forward for their relationship that also allowed him to be open about who he was. The question that niggled at her was whether he was right now involved with someone, and whether that someone was his editorial assistant, Geoff. She wasn't crazy about Geoff. He seemed a little too slick and ambitious; Beck worried that he might be using Paul as a rung on his climb up the publishing ladder. She'd raised that issue already, and Paul was mildly defensive. She hadn't pushed.

Now, feeling that she'd been unnecessarily petty toward him (though, she maintained, not quite an ass), she called him back and apologized. "Forgive me? It's just . . . it's been a really hard day."

"No, of course. I'm sorry, too."

"I hate thinking of Mom alone in some . . . in some *cooler* or some *drawer* or whatever, at the funeral home."

"Try not to think about it."

Beck's eyes flooded. "She was my *mom*, you know? And now she's just . . . gone."

"I know. But I'm here for you." Beck heard a cooing sound, and Paul said, "Leah is here for you, too."

Beck wiped her eyes with the back of her hand. She found a tissue and blew her nose. Then she said, "So, okay, sure, I'll get the camp ready to sell. It makes sense, since I'm the one who's closest and has time."

"And you're good at it. Tell you what: I'll call your sisters and tell them about the executor duties and selling the camp, all right?"

"Thanks." It'd be one fewer thing for Beck to fret about getting wrong. "Although you might not reach Soph; she's in Dubai. Text her and say to call you back when she gets the text."

After they hung up, Beck went to lie on her mother's bed, which Delia had stripped after Marti's removal. Rain pattered against the window. Night was falling in New York, the city lighting up to its fullest wattage as the restaurants and Broadway theaters and music venues and movie houses and dance clubs and sports arenas all came to life. Millions of people. Thousands of places. The combinations of what a person could have and be and do in this city were just about incalculable. And yet the one thing Beck wanted most was impossible. No, it wasn't to keep their camp, though that, too, wasn't possible. What she wanted most was to have Marti alive and well—which, admittedly, would offer the side benefit of the family keeping the camp.

"You are a selfish wretch," she said to the ceiling.

But the ceiling knew the truth: Beck had loved Marti and had done well by her all these years—and especially in the recent ones, during Marti's illness.

The question was how dutiful Beck was going to be from here on out. Right now she was merely going to break the law: Marti's remaining stash of marijuana was in a Rubbermaid bin in the top dresser drawer, next to the pipe Beck had bought for her in the East Village. Though Beck was not a regular user, Cammie had been (and presumably still was), and so when Claire suggested Marti try it for her pain, Claire had also suggested that Beck procure actual weed, if possible, not the medical grade products that were the only legal forms in the state.

"It's simple and effective, it works faster than edibles—which, with her appetite, may not appeal. And she won't get those nasty oils they put in the vape fluids," Claire had said. "But if you're too nervous about getting caught—"

"No, I'm not," Beck said.

"You aren't?"

"*No.*"

"I was expecting resistance."

"Well, you don't know everything about me. I'll get some for her."

And thanks to Cammie, she had. And now she would smoke some herself, which she hadn't done in probably fifteen years or more—not since the kids had gotten old enough to know what was going on if they caught her.

After filling and lighting the pipe, Beck took two deep hits. Then she cleaned out the pipe, put on her long, puffy navy blue coat, tucked the bin and pipe into her pocket, pulled on her gloves, gathered Marti's file box and umbrella, and went down to the foyer, where she collected Marti's mail before heading out into the cold, sleety evening with a lighter step than when she'd arrived.

Beck headed to Fifth, then went south toward the subway, all the while enjoying the soft patter of sleet against the umbrella. Such a soothing noise. *Tap-tap. Tap-tap-tap-ta-tap.* It made her almost happy. It made her sort of hungry. Dope-hungry? Actually hungry. So she passed the subway stairs and continued down Broadway toward Ribalta, to get a bite to eat before the long ride home (their meatballs were *won*derful!). And, oh, The Strand was a good idea, too. A new book or three. Support an author. Support a bookshop. Support one's mind and heart. Books. She loved books. She really should write a book, starting (again) tomorrow. She didn't *have* to go to Maine for that, right? Carpe the damn diem!

As she passed the Regal movie theater where Claire used to work, she sang to herself, "Raindrops on 'brellas and books in the bookshop, meatballs or pizza would be really yummy . . ." Then, seeing the bright Zumiez storefront, she veered inside to see these bright things, these vivid things on this dim, gray, sad night.

Her first thought, once she was in the shop, was, *Oh, I'm* way *too old for this stuff.* But, wait—that orange coat! Beck set down the box and umbrella and took her coat off, letting it drop onto the floor, then took the orange coat from its hanger and put it on.

"Hey, cool choice," said the salesclerk, a cute Asian boy who reminded Beck of a boyfriend she'd had back in high school, before this kid had even been born. "Plus, it's on clearance. You going to hit the slopes somewhere?"

"Slopes?" Beck said, admiring herself in the mirror. She looked tall. She looked strong. Kickboxing was a miracle.

"Skiing, snowboarding?"

"Me?"

"Why not?"

She turned to face him. "If I told you the year I was born . . ."

"Hey, age is a state of mind," he said.

State of mind prompted Beck to remember that she was stoned. Stoned was good! Stoned was so much better than not stoned, at least right now, when a minute ago she'd been navy. She petted the sleek orange fabric. "This is mine," she said. "Ring me up."

6

Some Excellent Perks

About a week earlier, on a day when Sophie Geller's mother had been preparing for the end, Sophie was hustling to get to LAX in time for a flight to Dubai. Leaving L.A. was not what she wanted to do; her place there (which was not hers, but anyway) was possibly her favorite spot in all the universe. However, her Amex bill had exactly zero sympathy for favorite spots and was one hundred percent about work that paid in actual money.

Sophie spent half of her life in airports and on airplanes and in rideshares and cabs. What this meant was that she was nimble in every way, intellectually and physically. Her mother believed she worked in a gallery, and she absolutely did, but that was only one element in the performance that was Sophie's life. In short, she was a professional doer. Sort of like being a fixer, except without having to beat anyone up or break any laws (usually). She was capable. Quick. Smart. Fearless, some would say, and sometimes she felt exactly that. Other times, she wrapped herself in whatever was the coziest thing at hand—a blanket, a spa robe, a towel when that was the best she could do—and made herself as small as possible. She would find the snuggest space in which to tuck her smallest self, then sit there, thumb pressed to lips—because she was too old to suck her thumb, and either way she didn't want to ruin her corrected overbite.

Her smallish size belied the physical strength she'd worked hard to gain and to keep. For that, she credited the do-it-anywhere body-weight fitness regimen she'd learned from Zoë, trainer to the stars—well, actually, trainer to the wannabe stars, some of whom were getting *a lot* of work nowadays, what with all the streaming channels producing a dizzying amount of content. *Real* stars, that is, actors whose names you knew, whose faces sold magazines and opened movies, had higher-profile trainers who were nearly equal in their celebrity. But that was okay; trainer Zoë was working her plan and being intentional and manifesting success daily. The young actors could relate.

Sophie, too, could relate—who was better at intentionality than she was? And acting? She was a top talent, for sure. When you hustled for rich people, you had to be whoever they wanted you to be or the tap would dry up as quickly as Kevin Spacey's career had after the accusations. She had the occasional yen to see if she could get an actual acting gig, but her life was already fraught in ways she struggled to control; why add yet another layer of shit?

From the back seat of her rideshare, Sophie took a photo of her hand making a peace sign, with the L.A. freeway in the background. On the visible fingers of that hand were three artisan gemstone rings: two in silver, one in gold. She queued an Instagram post for her SimplySophie! account and wrote, *Stay hot, Los Angeles, back soon!* plus the sparkling heart emoji, then tagged the jeweler who'd made the rings and added six carefully chosen hashtags—only six, because she'd determined that she got the highest number of interactions with a less-is-more approach. Within ten seconds she had more than forty likes.

"Hey, I'm low on fuel," her driver told her, tapping his gauge. "I'm gonna get off at the next exit."

Sophie sat forward to see for herself. The needle was close to E, but not so close as to be dire. They'd get to LAX, easy. "Um, no, not an option," she said. "I have an international flight."

"You'll make it, don't worry."

"*You'll* make it. Don't worry. Get fuel after you drop me."

He smiled at her in the rearview mirror. "Ha, so you're one of those chicks. Sense of humor. I like it. But yeah, no, gotta refuel in case there's a slowdown. L.A. traffic, right? You'll get the quoted rate, if that's your concern."

"Yes, but also I'm pressed for time. I'm meeting colleagues at check-in."

She was not meeting colleagues at check-in. But being the veteran traveler she was, Sophie had learned to assess these kinds of situations quickly. More to the point, she'd learned to assess these kinds of men quickly. This one, for all that he was smiley and casual, was also muscular and tattooed and had a look and a tone that raised a mild alarm in her. Not enough to cause her to signal for help on the app—not yet, at least—but enough to make her wary of pushing him. A woman alone in a car being driven by a man she doesn't know is a woman who could easily end up dead and defiled in a drainage canal. This had actually happened to a woman she'd followed on Instagram, except it wasn't a drainage canal, it was a bridge overpass, and it wasn't L.A., it was someplace in rural North Dakota. Sophie couldn't imagine having any reason to go to rural North Dakota to begin with, and she sure as hell wouldn't go there now.

Her driver was not deterred by her meeting-colleagues declaration. He said, "There's an exit coming up. A station I like—prices are better than anyplace around. California's gas taxes . . . Jesus Christ. I came here from Birmingham, and I'm telling you, this kind of taxation is un-American. You do know it's the Mexicans that are behind it."

"How's that?" Sophie asked, keeping her tone casual even though she was angry. If by taking this exit to get fuel (or whatever) he made her late and she missed the flight and did not arrive in Dubai in approximately twenty hours, she could lose her job at the gallery, for which she was being sent to the annual Dubai art show, flying business class, in order to close an exclusive deal with Jordan Morgan, who was in demand and knew it. Therefore, it was imperative that she not be delayed, and therefore, imperative that she not aggravate this racist asshole. She did not give a shit about his opinions on gas prices or anything. She just needed to appear relaxed and friendly, funny, smart, a good conversationalist—in sum: the kind of woman you wanted to impress, not murder.

She arranged her minimal luggage on the seat beside her while saying, "The Mexicans are responsible for the gas prices?"

"Believe it. Our bleeding-heart governor needs all these Mexicans to come into the state to vote for him, and getting them here and keeping them here costs money. So, voy-la."

Voy-la, Sophie thought. Well. There you have it.

She said, "Okay, well, that's a theory, I suppose. Really interesting, actually." She wanted him to think she was mildly, platonically impressed. Meantime, she had already pulled up a map on her phone and was familiarizing herself with their location, seeing what was nearby, where she might go for help if she needed it. This was one of many strategies she'd learned in her years of globe-trotting, and she had never yet needed to bail for safety, but as with coke, as with unwanted sex, as with stepping in for the sick nanny to keep a client's kids for a week in a Tokyo hotel, there was a first for everything.

They took the exit and continued on, the driver taking them farther away from the freeway while telling her, "I study these things. I'm making a documentary about it—got my own production company and we're taking meetings right now to see who wants on board."

"A documentary, huh? That's cool," she said as they stopped at an intersection and she contemplated bailing now, while they were stationary. "Good luck with it."

"Thanks! I'm confident. I used to work with a guy who's now at Hulu. We were hibachi chefs together back in the day."

He turned the corner and drove on, taking them farther still from the freeway. Sophie checked the time. Even if this was a completely legitimate side trip (they *were* low on fuel, and the best prices *were* away from the exits), she had already been cutting it close on getting checked in on time for the flight, and was now cutting it even closer. As they pulled up to a red light, she used another rideshare app to see if there were drivers nearby. Seeing several, she put an arm through her pack's strap, reached for her carry-on, opened the door, and climbed out of the car onto the sidewalk adjacent to an automobile dealership where glossy McLarens, Bentleys, Ferraris, and more beckoned the moneyed class. "Sorry, thanks!" she called, shutting the door and striding away, across the street to the opposite corner, where her new driver would meet her in less than two minutes. Enough time to get a strategic selfie with those cars behind her, if she framed it right. And she always framed it right.

Nimble.

Not long before Marti breathed her last, Sophie was heading out to ladies' night in Dubai, which had once been just a single night in each week wherein the ladies who lived in or were visiting the fantastical futuristic city with its backward politics could go to a club and bare some skin and get specially priced cocktails that they rarely ended up paying for themselves, thanks to the extreme imbalance in the number of men to available women.

That's more or less how it had been during Sophie's first visit, eight years earlier. She'd been such a tourist then, new to the Middle East and its robed men and its sexist attitudes. Though she'd been told it was unwise to wear anything sleeveless or short in public, she'd walked through the airport in the sleeveless minidress she'd worn for the flight (an unwise choice in itself) as if to show that she was an independent, actualized female who could and should dress however she pleased. Also, she'd been twenty-eight years old and her body was a-*mazing* and she was in the habit of making that clear to everyone who looked at her, wherever she went.

Well, that day in DXB, everyone looked at her. And suffice it to say the gazes were not merely disapproving. Some, in fact, had been (she felt) murderous.

As she'd neared the exit doors, a dark, attractive man in an expensive suit took her arm to stop her. "Please excuse me. You speak English?" he asked.

"I do," she said, hoping for a question about directions, maybe, or a recommendation for a hotel, neither of which she'd know the answer to, but he couldn't know that.

"Excellent." He withdrew a business card from his jacket pocket and offered it to her, saying, very politely, "I know several men who will pay good money to fuck you."

"Fuck *you*," she said, and turned around to go to the nearest restroom and change her clothes. Even back then she'd been nimble, if a good deal less wise.

Now there were ladies' nights *every* night somewhere in the city, and more women baring more skin inside the safe-ish spaces like the club Sophie went to on the third night of this trip, having overcome her jet lag and made her initial date with Jordan Morgan and requisite first appearances at the fair. Now she knew to don a thin silk jacket and long wrap skirt when moving from her hotel to the clubs, then to remove them on arrival and stow them in her bag. Which she did tonight, popping into the ladies' room to perfect her look while the lights strobed and the music thumped, the bass so deep it made her bones vibrate.

There had been a time in her life when this combination of free time and upscale club environment filled her with excitement and anticipation. Tonight was not such a time. This year was not such a time. She might—*might*—be getting too old for this. That she could even entertain this thought without cringing in horror was itself a sign, wasn't it?

Still, the bathroom lighting and decor were photo-perfect (not an accident, surely; Dubai clubs knew their clientele). After ensuring that her blond updo was the precisely right amount of messy, she angled her head and her phone to the mirror just so and snapped a photo, then cropped it just so, then wrote a pithy, perfect caption tagging the appropriate sponsors, chose her six perfect hashtags, and posted. In twenty seconds, ninety likes. "Coming in *hot*," she murmured, then left the bathroom for the bar.

"Hey, girl," a friend greeted Sophie when she came to the bar.

"Hey! *So* good to see you." Sophie kissed her cheek.

The two women looked each other over in that way women do upon meeting, silently assessing and comparing, deciding whether their own choice of dress, makeup, hairstyle, shoes, accessories had been correct, was better, was lacking, was likely to be sufficient for the purpose, which was to be admired and desired by others—for friendship, for sex, for opportunity.

Sophie pointed at her friend's breastbone and said (really, yelled), "I *love* that necklace. Oh my god."

"Damien," the friend said (yelled). Her name was Eloise, and she was a Brit. Milk-white skin, black hair, leonine face. She fingered the diamond pendant. "It's a full carat."

"Well done, Damien! Is this a reward? A precursor? Tell me."

"Both," Eloise said. "We've been kind of sort of feeling our way toward a bigger diamond for *this*." She extended her left hand, where the ring finger was still bare. "And in the meantime, as I had been holding out on letting him do anal . . ."

"*Mm*, yes, you said." Sophie signaled the bartender.

"Yes, well, I felt the time was right to reward his patience, show him there really could be fringe benefits to being locked down, so to speak. Try it before he buys it, you know?"

"Hendrick's martini," Sophie told the bartender. To Eloise, she said, "Yes, but do we think he thinks the pendant was itself a sufficient trade for the treat?"

Eloise shrugged. "He may, but if there's no engagement ring soon, he'll discover a return of my reluctance. I can be quite stubborn."

"No doubt."

"And you? What progress with the new boy?"

"What, Marco?"

"He's the band boy from Colombia, yes?"

"No, that was Sergio. Marco's an artist, and I like him just fine."

"And?"

"And nothing. He's very smart and very talented. Last fall he had a show that was written up in *Vanity Fair*, so that was pretty great."

"Then why do you sound less than excited about him?"

"Are you excited about Damien?"

"I'm excited about Damien's stock portfolio and Damien's yacht. Damien himself is not terribly exciting, but that's all right with me. I have different expectations of my relationships."

While Eloise spoke, Sophie finally smiled at a man who she knew had been waiting to catch her eye. She raised her drink as if to toast him while saying, "I wouldn't be disappointed to have an empty but grossly rich boyfriend."

"Temporarily, perhaps."

"A girl has to be practical, after all."

"*I* always say so. But how long have we known each other? Five years? I happen to know you have that thing some people refer to as *values*. You want your rich man to believe the right things, vote the right way, and so forth."

"Which explains why I'm a never-married thirty-six-year-old."

"Surely such men exist. Look at Bill Gates."

"The exception that proves the rule, I'm afraid."

Besides, a wealthy, liberal man with high intelligence and a sense of ethics like Sophie wanted was probably not going to look at her and see spouse material. Leaving aside her fine-tuned physical appearance, what did she have to offer? Being nimble, being wily, being conniving when that's what was necessary to do the task at hand—this was not a compelling attribute list for a future Mrs. Liberal Billionaire. Sophie had no college degree—she'd dropped out her junior year. She had no creds connected to anything highminded, save for being employed by Benji Ochoa as his front-line scout, his chief assistant. Benji, with his blue-chip gallery, had the creds. He was the one who banged the social justice drum. He was the one who volunteered and marched and donated and spoke out. He set the example, and if Sophie were not always teetering on the edge of the abyss with regard to her finances and living arrangements, she might have time to follow that example. Working for

Benji did have some amazing perks (annual trips to Dubai among them), but the salary was anemic. To be able to afford her desired lifestyle in Manhattan on her own (and if she could not afford her desired lifestyle, what would even be the point of living there?), she needed at least three times what he paid her. Not for the first time, Sophie thought of how she'd put herself in an impossible position for just about everything related to those values Eloise mentioned. Why did she do this to herself? Why?

Eloise and Sophie were presently joined by two more girlfriends, and for the first couple of hours, they all danced and talked and drank and flirted with the men who paid for their drinks. There was a kind of system to this scene, and Sophie was expert at working that system such that she never had to pay for more than her first drink, if that, and nearly always got a fantastic meal out of it, too, if she wanted one, and sometimes she even got gifts, all without needing to remove any of her clothing.

Admittedly that standard permitted (in theory) activities that could be enacted using either her mouth or her hands, but in practice she had not had to barter this way more than a few times over the years. And when she had, she'd shored herself up with the "Julia Roberts in *Pretty Woman*" philosophy of "I decide! *I* say who, I say when."

Tonight, fortunately, her agenda was merely to have some stimulation, some way to pass the time rather than sit alone in her hotel room or mill about the hotel lobby and grounds, solo, which she was fine with during daytime hours but in the evening it smacked of desperation, even when she wasn't desperate at all, just desirous of a stroll or whatever. Most evenings when she traveled were scheduled to the hilt, but she'd learned to build in at least one free night if it was possible to do so, some me time when she didn't have to schmooze for or with anyone, didn't have to enact the business she was there for, could be the *real* Simply Sophie, her off-duty self—in contrast to her IG SimplySophie!, whose life was a madcap swirl of luxe travel and celeb encounters and high-end product endorsements that helped her alter ego make the minimum payments on her overloaded credit cards. *That* Simply Sophie really ought to be star of a TV series where in every episode the heroine blows off whatever her day job is and goes on titillating adventures. Of course, TV Sophie would probably have to be late twenties, tops, and taller than her namesake. Not thinner, though, so there was that, at least.

A song ended, and Sophie, who'd been dancing with a cute but forgettable man whose name she couldn't remember, said so long and headed for the bar to get a glass of ice water. Such was thirty-six: ice water after eleven-thirty, to ensure she'd be sharp for her eight A.M. breakfast meeting.

"That looks refreshing," said a man she hadn't noticed coming up behind her. His mouth was close to her ear.

She turned, and he stepped away slightly, to give her more space. She liked that. "Water is life," she said.

He nodded. "Especially here."

Sophie liked the look of him. He was very dark, with good features, nice clothes, straight teeth. She said, "Let me buy you one."

"Big of you."

"It's the shoes." She pointed to her platform heels.

He laughed. Very good, she thought, appreciating that he appreciated her joke.

She thought it again approximately two hours later, when the two of them were naked and spent in his villa at the Jumeirah Dar Al Masyaf, the luxury hotel many Art Dubai goers stayed in. The villas reportedly went for more than $3,000 per night, and therefore, Sophie would never be booked into one. Generous with the travel perks as Benji might be, there was a (far lower) limit.

"That was *great* fun," Sophie said, rolling off the bed and gathering her clothes. "Thank you."

"Thank *you*," said the man, whose name was Hanif. "Won't you stay?"

Sophie was tempted. There was Hanif himself, with his gym-toned body and his lilted British English, and there was his villa, which had a balcony that overlooked a picturesque canal. Likely there would be additional energetic sex and excellent champagne and a spread of delicacies worthy of its own IG account. But for all of that, she'd have to stay, and stay up, and she was really tired just now and there was work in the morning. So.

"Love to, can't," she said, pulling her dress over her head. "I might call you tomorrow, though." *Might.* After she'd googled him, after she'd checked out his claims, after she'd gotten a feel for his possible net worth. This was entirely a practical matter: her credit card debt was now in the tens of thousands of dollars and growing by the day.

It wasn't until she was on the water taxi returning to the city that she thought about Marco, who was staying at her place (that was not hers) in New York. Marco, who had evidently not been thinking about her, either, as she had no calls or texts from him. She couldn't decide whether this made her feel good or bad. *But, no matter,* she thought. What was done was done and que será, será. Her mind moved on to the next item on her agenda, the breakfast meeting in which Jordan Morgan would be made to succumb to her charms every bit as effectively (albeit with a different emphasis and outcome) as Hanif had done. She would succeed; the conclusion was almost foregone, because Benji Ochoa's star was rising fast and Jordan Morgan, whose trajectory was (so far) like a jet's compared to a rocket's, wanted to hitch a ride. Nothing wrong with that. This parasitic system underlaid Sophie's whole existence, and she was as much a tick as anyone.

Her phone pinged, reminding her to pay her Amex bill. A minute later it pinged again with a text that would lead to the news that would change everything: Beck, saying, *CALL ME.*

7

Those Illogical Bastards

Earlier on the day that her sister Beck called with the news of their mother's death, Dr. Claire Geller (who still sometimes got mail as Mrs. Chad Handelman, despite having kept her name and lost the husband) was being doctored herself. Her annual physical. Except that it had been almost three years since her last, so, not quite annual. She was busy! She had a preteen son, a geriatric dog, a now-ex-husband whose career, like hers, was demanding. Her mother-in-law (the actual Mrs. Handelman) was, like Claire's own mother, ailing, but doing so here in Duluth, where Claire had often been tasked with tending to her needs. Claire had patients who had emergencies, and some emergency cases who became patients. She was a hockey mom, a soccer mom, a chess mom. Now she was also a single mom. The only reason she'd finally made time for this appointment was that her IUD had expired and needed to be replaced (such a hopeful act!). So, in for a penny, in for a pound.

"Let's get you on the scale," said the nurse, who'd led Claire back from the lobby.

(Not that kind of pound.)

"Let's not," Claire said, though she lay her coat and purse on a chair and dutifully followed the direction. The scale told its sad story: Claire ate meals out far too often and was perhaps too fond of the innocuous-looking vodka tonic, its colorless appearance hiding its calories so persuasively. Though, too, she was wearing long underwear, wool socks, and boots, which added a few pounds.

In the exam room, the nurse fitted Claire's arm with the blood pressure cuff and let the machine take over while she busied herself laying out pap smear supplies. Claire watched the monitor's numbers climb. And climb. And climb.

The nurse turned back to view the result. "Hmm, 160 over 101? Let's try that again."

"Yes, let's!" said Claire.

This time they both watched the monitor. This time, it delivered the numbers 163/105.

"Well," said Claire. "You might need to get that recalibrated."

"This is unusual for you, I assume."

"Very," Claire told her, though she didn't actually know that was true because she hadn't checked in forever. "What's it say in my record?"

The nurse looked. "Last time Dr. Martinez saw you, it was 140 over 89."

"It was that high?" Claire said. She didn't recall being told about it, though that didn't mean she hadn't been. Her life was so constantly full of stats and stresses that this might've gotten lost in the mix. Dismissed for the moment, with an intent to think about it later when she had more bandwidth for her own health matters.

The nurse said, "Says so right here. When did you last have it checked?"

There was a knock on the door, and the doctor entered. "Claire, hello, good to see you again."

Claire said, "Hey, Josie. You're looking fit!" This was a safer way to say *You've lost a lot of weight since I last saw you,* since (a) you didn't want to convey that you thought the person was overweight previously, and (b) weight loss wasn't always a sign of good health.

"Marathons," said Josie, whom Claire had known since residency but hadn't seen much of since their kids got older and were in different schools. Josie continued. "I started running last year—it was May, I think?—and now I'm one of those obnoxious converts who thinks everyone should do it."

The nurse, who'd been waiting for an opening, said, "Dr. Geller's BP reading is elevated." She pointed to where she'd noted it on Claire's chart. "We took it twice. This is the lower figure."

Claire said, "It's probably the machine."

"Okay, well, let's try it the old-fashioned way."

As Claire sat still for the manual cuff and stethoscope reading, her mind raced ahead to what awaited her later in the day. Get David from school for an orthodontist appointment, then return him to school; see patients until she picked David up from after-school care and delivered him to Chad's; Women in Medicine board meeting at seven-thirty . . . Somewhere in there, she'd need to grab dinner. Chinese food, maybe. Hot and sour soup? No, egg drop—

"The machine is telling the truth," Josie said, removing the stethoscope from her ears.

"Really? What'd you get?"

"I read 166 over 104. Given your history, I think we need to consider medication. I'm going to step out and let you undress. Then we'll talk about it some more."

Left alone, Claire sat unmoving for a moment to take in what she'd just heard. While being hypertensive was neither unusual nor an immediate crisis, she was surprised the condition applied to her. A stupid response, she knew. Being a heart doctor wasn't protective against heart disease. Also, her father had atherosclerosis. Plus, she was forty years old and stressed out by most every aspect of her life, and to top it all off, she was more or less sedentary when she wasn't popping in and out of exam and hospital rooms. It fit. Just the same, she didn't *like* this news. She didn't *want* it. It might fit her facts, but it didn't fit her self-image of a woman who had everything under control.

By the time Josie and the nurse returned, Claire was ready with a plan. She said, "I'm going to restrict my caffeine and sodium and step up my cardio regimen. That should bring me back in line."

"O-kay," said Josie. "Far be it from me to tell a cardiologist how to manage hypertension. But I do want to see you back here in sixty days for a follow-up. Lie back, and we'll get you set with a new IUD."

Claire lay back and put her feet in the stirrups. "It's the same advice I'd give any otherwise healthy adult."

"Yeah? With numbers like yours?"

"Maybe I'll take up running marathons," Claire said, bracing herself for the speculum. "I don't know if I'll like it, but it'll be way more fun than this."

After her appointment, she stopped into the pharmacy to use the blood pressure testing booth there. *Trust, but verify,* she told herself, as if this wasn't at all about denial or about control. The machine displayed its glowing red result. Claire revised her Chinese-food dinner plan to a plain baked potato and an undressed salad, then donned her coat and scarf yet again for the walk to her car.

At David's school, Claire pulled up to the pickup line curb, where David, a slight, loosely bundled ten-year-old boy with curly dark hair, waited for her. Behind him stood a snowbank higher than he was tall. So. Much. Snow. Snow piled so high that the building's windows were partly obscured. So high that it might never melt completely because this part of Minnesota would continue to have snowfalls well into April, and because spring wouldn't really arrive until June, and because summer lasted approximately four days. Claire loved summer here in the Northland, *loved* it with a passion, but that passion was born of ten months of heat denial, of her desperate longing for sun-generated heat, a longing that began in September and lasted well into June.

When she'd moved here after finishing her residency, nervous about the sinking polar vortices that pushed deadly cold down from Canada to the Arrowhead Region, the locals all told her, *You'll acclimate before long, don't worry a bit!* Eleven years later, she was still waiting for her body to cooperate with this rule that seemed universal for everyone but her. It was maddening.

A failure. And though she had not mentioned her cold feet/hands/nose/body to anyone for years now, every day that the temperature stayed below sixty-five (approximately 270 days per annum), she yearned for what she didn't have. A familiar emotional state for Claire, as it happened.

David, however, stood at the curb bare-handed, bareheaded, with his coat unzipped.

"I don't want to go to Dad's tonight," he said when he got in the car.

"Where's your hat?" Claire asked. "It's twelve degrees." Even with the heat blasting in her Volvo wagon, even with the seat heater on high, even with her boots and hat and gloves on, she was chilled.

David said, "I was only outside for a minute. Why do I have to go?"

"It's Dad's night with you," Claire said, turning onto a roadway that, like every other in town, was bordered by towering snowbanks. There had been so much snow this season that the excess had to be trucked out of town and dumped at a site near the airport—a not-especially-rare occurrence here. "And I have a meeting," she said, "so you'd be with him anyway."

"He's a Nazi."

"Sorry, what?" Claire glanced at him in the rearview mirror. David was slumped in his seat, scowling. "Did you say *Nazi*? We need to have a talk about history."

"It's just a saying, Mom."

"Words mean things."

"Whatever. I can't leave *anything* sitting around, not even in my own room. 'Put your socks away. Put your iPad away. Hang up your shirt.' Plus, he makes me wash the dishes."

"Oh god, that's awful! We'd better call social services."

"Why is he like this now? He didn't used to be, before you got divorced."

Claire said, "He likes to keep things tidier than I do. He just had to compromise a little when we lived in the same house. In his own place, he can be as neat as he likes. He's not exactly abusing you, you know."

"He lectures me *all the time*."

"Maybe behave better and he won't feel the need."

"Mom, you aren't listening. He doesn't even *like* me. He won't care if I don't stay there."

"Oh, honey. He loves you very much. He's just not used to having you all to himself."

David slumped farther down in his seat. "I wish you didn't get divorced. This is all stupid. Why can't you guys work it out, like you always tell me to do with my friends?"

"It's too complicated for a ten-year-old to understand."

"I'm smart for my age," he said, not bragging, just repeating what he'd been hearing his parents say regularly since not long after his birth.

Claire said, "You are—but this isn't the kind of thing even an above-average kid can understand."

"Can I go with you to your meeting?"

"You'll be fine with Dad. Give him a chance. It'll improve with time."

"It's been so long already!"

"It's been three months, David, and you're only there three nights a week."

"Plus sometimes on the weekend. You guys ruined my life."

What could Claire say to this? His life was not in any way ruined; he was still a child with tremendous privilege in comparison to ninety-five percent of other children in the world. His father was the city's chief prosecutor. His mother was a pediatric cardiologist. He had his own bedroom in two different homes (and in their cabin on Island Lake), three meals plus snacks and dessert daily, a dog, a snake, and a computer, and Chad was pushing Claire to move David from a flip phone to a smartphone so that it would be easier for David to text.

It was no use to debate someone's feelings, though, and no use in succumbing to the guilt she worked hard to keep at bay. In med school, the emphasis was always on acknowledging error and moving forward, taking whatever you'd learned with you. The dead could not be resurrected; try for fewer deaths.

Claire parked at the orthodontist's office. As they walked to the building, she told her son, "Maybe life isn't picture-perfect for you, but you have it so good compared to other kids in the world, even in our country—do you recognize that?"

David said, "Whatever."

But no wonder he didn't recognize it, not as well as he ought to; he was an upper-middle-class boy living in one of the whitest places in America. Being a Jew in Duluth made him a minority, but not in any way that mattered. None of this was his fault. It factored, though, in how he saw things. His situation was so different from her own childhood, where she'd mixed with kids from just about every named country on the planet. Now she couldn't recall the last time she'd seen a person of color in real life.

While David had his wires adjusted, Claire watched the tropical fish swim about in the huge tank of presumably tropical-temp water and let her mind rest, let it meander and drift with the fish. She didn't need pharmaceutical intervention for her hypertension, she needed an aquarium. No—she needed a hut on a Bahamian beach and good snorkel gear.

David returned to the lobby and Claire returned to reality, brought into even sharper relief a short time later when David, as she dropped him back at school, responded to her "I'll see you later" with "I hate you and Dad. You both suck."

Not two minutes later, her phone rang. It was Beck, who told her, "I don't even know how to say this. Mom's gone."

Expected though Marti's death may have been, Claire, now in her Duluth hillside four-color Italianate with its distant view of icy Lake Superior, felt hollowed out by the loss.

"It's as if I have a hole in my chest that goes straight through me," she told Paul, who'd called to tell her about Marti's wishes and the will. "Like, you could see through it. Like a part of me is literally missing."

She'd tried to explain this feeling to Chad earlier, when she dropped David off, but she hadn't been able to express herself as well as she wanted to. The feeling had been too fresh, maybe. Or Chad had been too cold. He was not finished punishing her, and who could blame him?

Now she spoke to Paul via her earbuds with their built-in mic (brilliant invention) while pulling her suitcase from the spare bedroom's closet, while taking clothes from her drawers, while stocking her travel kit, while letting the dog out to pee. She was saying, "I don't mean to be overdramatic, but that's the best way I can describe the feeling. I didn't talk to her that often—every few weeks, maybe. But in some ways, it seems like I measured everything against what I thought she'd think. Is that lame?"

"Not a bit. I can only imagine how badly it hurts," Paul said in that warm way he had. The man could hug you with his voice. She thought it was his being the only child of Soviet émigrés, growing up with one foot in each culture, that made him so empathetic. And though he was American by birth, the language of his home life had been his parents' soft, almost apologetic Russian, and Claire believed she still heard echoes of that in his cadences.

She said, "I'm surprised by my reaction, to tell you the truth. I knew she wasn't going to beat it—I mean, of course I hoped I'd be proven wrong, but that didn't seem likely. When Dad died, I felt shocked, since his surgery was pretty routine, but when the shock wore off, I had run-of-the-mill sadness, you know? I didn't feel any less . . . complete, I guess you'd say, the way I do now."

She felt newly anxious as well. Wounded and oddly vulnerable, and sort of angry, too. Why hadn't Marti told them, or at least told *her*, how soon the end would come?

Claire valued stability, predictability, order. She needed to always know where she stood, she hated loose ends, and she had no tolerance whatsoever for her own personal failures. If she undertook a project or signed up for an activity or enrolled in a class or accepted a challenge, she followed through for as far as the ride would take her. For example: in middle school she decided she wanted to be a doctor, and to be a doctor meant she had to be excellent in biology and chemistry. So for high school she'd applied to Bronx Science, was admitted to Bronx Science, and then every school day for four long years, she'd gotten herself out of bed at four A.M. in order to be dressed and fed and ready to take the 4 train up to Fordham—basically riding the length of Manhattan almost to the end of the line.

Knowing how expensive college was going to be, after school she schlepped back down to 14th in time to run home, eat, change clothes, and go to work at the Regal, where she'd sold gigantic servings of popcorn and candy and sugary drinks (enabling the very sorts of illnesses some of her adolescent patients now suffered from. *Kids* with *acquired* hypertension and high cholesterol, not to mention diabetes. On the other side of the coin: kids—mostly girls—who were starving themselves trying to get Instagram-celebrated thigh gaps).

When her shift at the Regal ended, she'd gone home and done her homework, often staying up past when the rest of the family was asleep. Those years had been a grind, and she'd sometimes felt out of her league in a school that had among its alumni winners of the Pulitzer, the Nobel, and a panoply of other awards. Her classmates were so incredibly smart! Whereas Claire felt she was just a hard worker who'd gotten lucky, or maybe made her own luck by working rock with a pickaxe, chiseling away obstacles one strike at a time. So as to ensure she didn't waste that luck, she'd worked even harder and graduated in the top five percent of her class.

Where had that gotten her? Into Rochester on scholarship, then into med school at Northwestern, where she'd met Chad, who was there at Pritzker for law. Confident, persistent Chad, with his smart-boy horn-rims and his motor scooter and his stovepipe jeans. He'd prefigured the Brooklyn hipster bros, guys like Sophie dated when she was in high school. Of course Sophie attracted them; Sophie was hip. Sophie was also stupidly pretty, like some little shiksa goddess, born golden blond with fire in her eyes. Everything came easily to Sophie. Sophie hadn't needed a pickaxe; all she needed was a smile.

Claire, though? Even then, Claire had to watch her weight. She'd had to use acne medicine and needed four different products to control the frizz in her hair. Then there was the hair on her upper lip and legs (and let's not mention that bikini line). Chad thought she was pretty, but she knew that, hair excepted, when compared with her sisters she was ordinary, vanilla in appearance.

And all the while, at every point when Claire could have just said, *Screw it, this is all too much, it's too hard, I don't belong, I shouldn't have dated Chad, why did I accept his proposal,* she had instead pushed on, stuck to her plan, honored every commitment, even the minor ones. You did the thing you said you were going to do. But Marti had not done the thing she was supposed to do, the thing Claire had been determined that Marti must do—that being to survive her disease. And when Marti knew absolutely that she wouldn't survive, she hadn't gathered her girls at her side for the end. She hadn't allowed Claire a proper goodbye. And because Marti had not, Claire felt like a failure. What unreasonable, illogical bastards feelings were.

She told Paul none of that, instead pushing her focus outward, forward. She said, "I'm actually glad Mom chose you and not Beck, which is what I expected to happen. I mean, I love Beck, of course, but it's better this way."

"You aren't upset about having to sell the place in Maine?"

"Me? No; I haven't been there in forever. David was a toddler last time we went. Nothing against Mom, it's just been so much easier to have the cabin at Island Lake." Which she had not been willing to part with in the divorce, and why should she? She paid for it. Her finances were tight now, though, without Chad's income to round things out. She told Paul, "My share of the proceeds will be really useful, if you want to know the truth. I'm still paying off my med school loans."

"Hey, so is it all right with you if Beck spearheads the repairs?"

"God, yes. I'd be grateful. I have more than enough to deal with."

"Do you think Sophie will mind?"

"Please. I can't imagine she'd have the slightest interest in being part of that. Can you?"

"Not really. All right, good. I will, of course, still ask her when I get the chance. Oh, and maybe this is unnecessary, but I was wondering whether you've already spoken to Chad about your mom. If not, I'm happy to make the call."

Claire stopped folding the sweater she'd been about to pack. "You are so incredibly thoughtful. Thanks for the offer. But I did already talk to him."

"I thought maybe you had, but, well, Beck says the two of you aren't really on speaking terms, except about David."

"He'll be at the funeral, by the way—Chad will. He'll bring David out. But yeah, it's true, we generally aren't speaking."

Because Claire had done Chad wrong. She had done him wrong and she'd failed David and she'd failed herself in a way that continued to embarrass and haunt her. She had not completed the undertaking of marriage according to the vows she'd recited thirteen years earlier, when she and Chad stood under the chuppah and swore they'd be parted only by death. Ha! Death of their mutual trust is what that turned out to be. Death of honor (hers). Death of pride (also hers). "Go with God," Chad had told her sadly before he left to start his new, genuine life in a rented waterfront house out on Park Point. Go with God, he'd said. He wasn't even religious!

And she wasn't either, mostly. But Claire sometimes asked God why He, in all his supposed wisdom, had made her incapable of loving the right man. The man she'd been married to, for example. It made no sense! But then so many things made no sense, she knew that. You couldn't be a pediatric cardiologist and not know this all the way into your own bone marrow. Her personal suffering was minor, it was inconsequential, it was, she sometimes believed, a small but real penance for her failures as a physician, for the kids whose hearts could not be made to function correctly, or not for long enough.

You want to know suffering? Suffering, she sometimes told herself, is a kid who has just come out of a surgery where their sternum was sawed in two. Suffering is a parent who sits day and night with a child whose pain isn't responding well to drugs. Suffering is hearing from a doctor such as Claire, "I'm so sorry, there was nothing more we could do."

Unrequited love for a man you can never have is difficult, yes, but she had lived with that torment for a long time and could continue to do so without it ruining the new life she was building for herself in the wake of Chad's departure. A life that now had to confront the pain of this new, sharp loss.

Claire said, "Mom really thought the world of you, you know? You were her kind of guy."

"It's because I'm a Mets fan," Paul said.

"No, it was more than that. Obviously. She didn't make Chad the executor."

"Well, no, since you two split. But I always thought she was partial to him, his being a big-time prosecutor and all that. He's an impressive guy—sorry if that sounds disloyal."

"No, it's okay," said Claire. "He is impressive, kind of. Definitely not like most guys. Mom was partial to his suits." Chad insisted on getting bespoke menswear for work rather than buying his suits at Brooks Brothers or wherever. He went to a Filipino tailor in Minneapolis once a year. She said, "Being Duluth's chief prosecutor is not *that* big a deal, though, I promise you. Mom knew that."

"All right, but I'm not exactly Max Perkins, either."

"Don't sell yourself short. He wasn't a legend in his own time, right? Look at your roster—especially Jessalyn Chukwu. She's brilliant. Her book is brilliant. She's your Hemingway."

"You read *Yankari Springs*?"

"Of course. I bought it the day it went on sale. Totally deserving of the National Book Award; she got robbed."

"Thank you. But *all* of the finalists deserved to win, if you ask me; we're not alone in our loss."

"That's very fair of you, but you can't blame me for being Team Paul."

"I appreciate the sibling loyalty. *In-law*-sibling loyalty," he amended.

Claire's response was an *mmm* sound of acknowledgment. *Sibling*, she thought. Naturally that was how he regarded her. The only way he regarded her. The only way he *ought* to regard her, given that she was his wife's sister.

Claire knew it was very wrong of her to entertain even for a fleeting moment the fantasy of Paul regarding her in any other manner.

The kind of wrong that could end an otherwise reasonably good, high-functioning marriage of two respected professionals.

Had ended one, in fact: hers.

Because the Paul fantasy wasn't merely a moment's whimsy; it was decades-long. Paul, her older sister's husband, was the longtime unrequited love of her life.

(No wonder her blood pressure was so high.)

If only she had kept her mouth shut about it last fall! (Really, she ought never to drink.) Then Chad would not have left her. She would not now be embarrassed and untethered and alone. Thank God there was only one person besides Chad and herself who knew her sad secret, since Chad was too proud to reveal details to anyone. Unfortunately, that person was Sophie. Who had sworn she'd never tell. But still.

"So anyway," Paul was saying, "I'm in the process of getting the will in probate. The things that pay out irrespective of probate all need death certificates, which we won't have for a couple of weeks, minimum. I'll keep everyone posted on all of that."

"Thanks—for everything. It's really good of you to take on the responsibilities when you're already so busy."

"The Geller family is my family, too," he said.

Much as Claire wanted to keep Paul on the line, she knew she had better cut herself off. But oh, the piquant pleasure of having even this kind of connection to him, of hearing his voice so intimately in her ear. *Bad. Wrong. Stop it.*

She said, "Well, I should let you go. Thanks so much for calling."

"No, sure. It's lucky I was able to get Leah down without any trouble, so we could talk uninterrupted. Babies—you forget how much work they are."

Listen to this man, thought Claire. So polite, so thoughtful, so good. She didn't deserve him, which was why she didn't have him. She was a rotten person, deceitful, heartless—that's what Chad said, at least, and how could she deny it?

She said, "They really are so much work, it's true." Stop talking, she thought. Let the man get on with his night. "But you know, I miss my little David. Of course he's a great kid *now*, too. Mostly. When he isn't sulking."

"Been there," Paul said. "But at least you don't have to feed and change and rock them at that age, and feed them again, and change them again." He laughed. "I'm glad to get to do it, though. And it's easier when you know Mommy and Daddy will be back soon to collect the little darling."

"Well, I can't wait to meet her. So, I guess I'd better get back to packing," Claire said, again trying to force herself to do right. "And I need to drop Goliath at the kennel. My flight's at five-thirty A.M."

Paul said, "I miss having a dog. We've been thinking about getting another, but Beck's reluctant—we've been talking about traveling more, now that Cammie's out of the house, and . . ." He stopped mid-sentence. "Sorry, I'm just blathering on, here. Travel safe. We'll see you sometime tomorrow."

"I'm looking forward to it. I mean, the reason is terrible—"

"It is," said Paul. "But it's going to be good to have the family together again."

"Yes. Okay. 'Bye." Claire pressed *end* and tossed the phone and earbuds onto a chair. "Define *good*," she said.

For this trip to New York, Claire decided to splurge on the NoMad Hotel, where she'd stayed once before. She loved the Beaux Arts building and the hotel's enveloping warmth (good for the wounded soul), its deep, luxurious bathtubs, and the neighborhood, which wasn't too far from Gramercy but far enough for her to feel like she wasn't stepping right back into her youth. Just a three-minute walk to Madison Square Park, onetime home of Madison Square Garden before it got poorly reimagined and relocated to 34th and Seventh. Claire was not a fan of that part of Manhattan, which was ever-packed with tourists and grime and noise. Losing the original Penn Station—which had been as magnificent as Grand Central in its way—in order to gain an ugly sports and concert arena was among the bigger architectural travesties of this city. (On the other hand, the resulting Madison Square Park was an oasis.) Had Claire not been so determined to be something impressive enough to offset not being the eldest child and not being the boy her parents had hoped for and not being the pretty, charming child, she might have become an architectural historian or preservationist. Instead, she tried to fix sick kids—and wasn't sorry for that. It had its rewards. It did also take a toll, though, when fate or God or luck or she, Dr. Geller, failed them.

Claire left her suitcase with the desk clerk and set out for the park. Raw as the morning was, already the sky showed more blue space than clouds. The Chrysler Building (her favorite) glinted in the occasional sunlight. What a change from the place where she'd started her day, the place she'd made her home after her residency in the Twin Cities.

Duluth had felt to her like a town on the Hudson but without all the attendant New York baggage those exurbs have. Minnesotans were hardy, good-natured folk who embraced winter like the Scandinavians so many of them were, setting a good example for transplants like Claire. What's more, living in Minnesota meant she was never in competition with her sisters—except when she got on the phone with Marti; then the old rivalries were activated in her. Had she seen Beck's exposé (of some suddenly crucial-to-her-mother subject) in *Vanity Fair*? Did she know that Sophie attended the Met Gala as Reese Witherspoon's plus-one? Beck had marched in D.C. wearing a knitted pink pussy cap. Sophie vacationed with crown prince Someone of Middle Eastern Somewhere. Her sisters were busy with important or impressive visible things, the kinds of things that were easy to point at when her mother's friends asked how the girls were.

Claire, though? What had Claire ever done that Marti (and Leo, when he'd been alive) could point at? Her work didn't appear in the New York newspapers. Still, Claire had proven herself worthy of her M.D. and worthy of her position at St. Mary's and worthy (almost always) of the kids who were her patients. She tried every day to be worthy of David, too. She had felt mostly worthy of Chad, and the friendship and respect of his colleagues and her own—until last Thanksgiving on the drive home from her in-laws' house in Menomonie. If only David had been in the car with them instead of staying to hang out with his cousins, or if Claire hadn't been drinking boilermakers with Chad's sister before they left, or if Chad hadn't been so high on praising Beck . . .

New Yorkers were hardy, too, in their way. Look at all the people out this morning in their scarves and hats and gloves, moving about the city with purpose and energy. The pace rarely slowed here. That took a catastrophe like the towers falling or the subways flooding, something that scared people or stranded them. Claire admired this, but also she was forty now and saw the city through the perspective of a woman who'd come to appreciate a six P.M. cessation of business, or the stillness and absolute hush that followed a foot-deep snowfall. Manhattan could get quieter, but it was never quiet. It could get stiller, but it was never still. That said, she always liked to visit, which usually she'd done solo because Chad hated Manhattan; he said it was too much everything. Claire suspected the problem was rather that there wasn't enough Chad. Very small fish, *huge* pond.

Claire got a coffee, then found a park bench where she could see the clock tower and the Flatiron Building and keep an eye out for Beck, who would be meeting her here any time now. Beck, who'd first met Paul at Eileen Greenburg's bat mitzvah, same as Claire had, but Beck had been eighteen to Claire's fourteen and Paul had never looked at Claire twice. When Beck and Paul got engaged, Claire remembered complaining to her mother, "Beck gets everything," and Marti said, "Your turn will come." But Claire had wanted a turn with *Paul*; did her mother not understand that?

She spotted Beck and stood up. "There you are. Hi!"

Beck looked tired as she came toward Claire, but healthful. Vivid, even, inasmuch as one could apply the term to Beck. They hugged, and Claire said, "I *love* that coat."

"Yeah?" Beck looked pleased. "Impulse buy last night, when I left Mom's."

"I approve."

"I almost returned it this morning."

"No, it's great. Really."

"You look great, too," Beck said.

Claire wore her usual winter uniform of a long gray wool coat with a col-

orful Fair Isle knit scarf and a toque, as such knit caps were referred to in the
northern Midwest. Her calfskin gloves had rabbit fur lining, which did not
offend her as much as it delighted her (sorry, rabbits). When she'd bought
the gloves, she'd reasoned that if she could engage in a profession that relied
heavily on science that involved animal testing, choosing not to buy fur-
lined gloves (also, hello, *calfskin*) would be a certain kind of hypocrisy.

Beck said, "Last time you were here you had pinkeye."

"Oh god, I'd forgotten about that. Yeah, David got it at school, so of
course we got it, too." Meaning she and Chad, who had not been with her on
that trip to see Marti shortly after Marti's third lung resection. Pinkeye had
given him a great excuse to stay home, and that was fine, as it meant Claire
could sleep alone in her old bedroom the way she'd so often wished were
possible when she was growing up.

Beck said, "So how are you today? I'm . . ." She paused, her eyes filling with tears, which she blinked away. "It feels all wrong, doesn't it? Even
though we pretty much knew it would happen."

"During my layover I took my phone out to call her, then caught myself.
What *is* that? It's not like I don't know she's gone."

"I was crying when I woke up. It was so weird."

Claire nodded as if in empathy; she hadn't cried, though. Not so far, anyway. She'd woken after only three hours' sleep feeling strung out. She would
bet that when Beck woke up crying, Paul had wrapped her up in his warm
arms and stroked her hair and kissed away her tears.

Quit it, Claire told herself. *You're just making everything worse.*

Beck was saying, "I'm impressed that you got your travel arranged so
quickly."

"I almost didn't. I had to try four airlines before I found one that had a
seat. I was wedged in between two manspreaders. You can imagine what a
fun couple of hours that was. Like the old days, riding the subway—if less
fragrant."

"I meant everything—work, David, your dog."

Claire shrugged. "My life is not all that complicated," she said, mentally adding *logistically*. Emotionally it was complex and, at this moment, somewhat fraught, as this was the first time she'd seen Beck since the confession and subsequent divorce. That Beck didn't know she'd played a key part in Claire's drama mattered not at all; Claire's guilt about her behavior and her longing to be what she wasn't (honest, open) operated on their own wavelengths, independent from reason. What's more, every moment that she was in Beck's company, she was fearful that either Beck would somehow be able to read her mind or that she, Claire, would buckle under her own nervous anxiety and just tell Beck the truth. When she *wasn't* in Beck's company, she worried that Sophie would be the one to buckle. And if Beck ever learned how badly Claire had betrayed her—just in her imagination, but still!—that would be it for them. Beck would hate her. Ridicule her. Punish her. Despise her. And she'd deserve it.

Beck was saying, "I'm glad you got things sorted out. But—and I don't say this to be pushy—you still haven't told me what happened. I'm not going to judge you, you know."

"I appreciate that," Claire said.

"And?"

"And . . . I will, okay? I just . . ."

"It's all right," said Beck. She took Claire's hand and gave it a brief squeeze. "I know historically we haven't confided in each other, but maybe that was a mistake. When you're ready, I'm here for you."

"Thanks."

Beck drew a breath, then said, "Okay, so, I talked to the funeral home. They can see us at two-fifteen. Are you hungry? Do you want to get something to nosh on first, or go straight to the apartment? There's some food there, but not much. Mom seriously cleaned house."

"Such a *Mom* thing to do. Let's go home first, then get lunch before the appointment."

They set off through the park. "It's funny to hear you call it 'home,'" Beck said.

"What, don't you still think of it that way?"

"It's been twenty-five years since I lived there."

"Twenty-two for me," said Claire, "if I count when I was home summers from Rochester. So?"

"So I've lived elsewhere a lot longer than I lived there. I think of it as Mom's now. Before Dad died, it was Mom and Dad's."

"You're so pragmatic."

"And you're so sentimental," Beck said.

"Me? I am *not* sentimental."

"About this place, you are. I think it's because you *left*-left. Like, away to other states. And you stayed gone. Maybe I should've done that."

"Please," said Claire. "You love Manhattan. That's why you didn't ever leave."

"I live an hour away. It's nothing like here."

"How often do you come in?"

"I guess maybe once a week—but that's only been in the past few years, because of Mom being sick."

Claire said, "She didn't need you around that often, not the whole four years. You love it here, that's why you come so often. Just admit it."

"No, I mean, sure, I guess I do. So?"

"So who's the sentimental one?" Then Claire said, "Why don't you and Paul move back?" and the feel of Paul's name in her mouth was like pressing a bruise.

"He likes living in Irvington. When they started letting the editors do Fridays and most of summertime at home, he practically threw a party."

"But you come in to go to shows and all that, right?"

"Have you seen the prices? Even the minor shows are too expensive. Getting good seats for *Hamilton* would require taking out a second mortgage."

Claire said, "Maybe you should consider getting a regular job."

"By which I assume you mean a full-time job outside the home." Beck sounded defensive, and Claire took a little pleasure in that.

Claire said, "A full-time income to go with the full-time job, yes. Your kids are out of the house, your dog died, *Mom* died. Maybe now's the time for that."

This was a practical suggestion, but maybe this was also Claire's envy speaking. The part of her that was cranky over Beck's having been able not only to spend every night in a bed beside Paul but also two decades choosing when she wanted to work and when she wanted to do whatever else she did with her time. It was a little galling.

Beck said, "Then I'd need a work wardrobe, and that means a big initial expense plus dry cleaning, and probably heels every day, and if I worked here in the city I'd be commuting daily and eating out all the time . . . I'd spend as much as I made."

"So what? Haven't you ever wanted the pride and satisfaction of a full-time career?"

"Who says I don't have all of those things? I don't have to be a doctor to be a valuable person in the society. I mean, good for you for having that drive, but my interests are different."

They turned off Fifth onto 19th Street, and Claire, already knowing she shouldn't say what she was about to say, said, "Didn't Paul think you should work?"

"Paul? You're suggesting that I should shape my life to accommodate what my husband might think I should do, regardless of my wishes? My god, that's backward. Besides, I *do* work, and I *have* worked, but I also wanted to be home with the kids. Day care costs a fortune, for one thing."

"You guys had the money from his grandparents," Claire said, digging into this argument even though she didn't actually believe in it. She added, "I know it wasn't a *lot* of money, but it would've paid—"

"Why are you even bringing all of this up?" Beck said, stopping on the sidewalk and turning to face her.

"Why are you getting so defensive?"

"You know what? Let's just drop it. This isn't . . . It's all academic, isn't it? My kids are grown up. I have a granddaughter, for god's sake. I'm forty-four years old. Having a Claire-approved career is not high on my list of priorities."

"Some women are having their first babies at your age. Look at you: you started early, and now you're done with that. All I'm saying is that you can still have a full-time career if you want one."

Beck stared at her for a moment, then started to laugh.

"What's so funny?" said Claire.

"*You*. You're like . . . I don't know, you're like a . . . a bulldog with a stick. You just will not let it go."

"Fine," Claire said. "It's done. Forget it."

"I will!"

"Good."

"Good."

But Beck was still laughing. "I love you, Claire. Never change."

Claire thought, *If only you knew.*

8

Terrible, Wonderful

Had a much younger Paul Balashov imagined what his life would look like when he reached that ripe "old" age of fifty, he'd have seen himself as a Norman Rockwell gent: a man of ease in slacks and a cardigan with a pipe in hand and a dog at his feet. Mister Rogers, basically. This made sense; he'd watched a lot of *Mister Rogers' Neighborhood* in his childhood, had taken comfort in the message that he, a Jewish boy whose former-Soviet parents spoke broken English, who had no siblings, who had a profound love of tree frogs and those primitive handheld video games of the 1970s and, of course, books, was genuinely fine—even lovable—just the way he was.

Paul, who'd been cute in a soft rather than a rugged way, had been bullied in junior high and high school for being too smart, for being uninterested in playing sports, for spending his free period in the biology lab or the library. If any girls had liked him, he couldn't tell. He liked girls, though, and it was this, not the bullying, that had tormented him most. All those appealing girls! Short, average, tall; skinny, average, plump; dark skin, light skin, freckled or plain. He liked them all. The bared shoulders, the short skirts, the scents of floral shampoos and teen perfumes and the hair spray that kept white girls' big hair elevated in ways nature had never intended. Surely every heterosexual teenage boy went around half crazed all their waking hours from either being near girls or thinking about what it would be like to be able to do with girls or to girls all the things nice girls weren't supposed to want to do or have done to them.

Thanks to Mister Rogers, Paul was pretty sure that it was okay to feel this way. The trouble was that, okay or not, protracted horniness was a misery, and masturbation barely took the edge off. Sixteen-year-old Paul, if he'd had the forethought, would've yearned to be fifty-year-old Paul—that is, supposedly far too old to care anymore about girls and sex.

Sixteen-year-old Paul was an idiot in that way.

Of course, there'd been more to him back then than libido, same as there was more to him now. He played chess. He was fascinated with geology. He rooted for the Mets, same as Marti and Leo had done. He'd traveled the country with his parents, their self-designated navigator, great at reading maps, and he stayed in close contact with them even now that they'd retired to Portugal. If he was still sometimes preoccupied with sex, it was because his circumstances had gotten so far out of alignment with his desires. Imagine being hungry and getting to eat a little something now and then, but rarely feeling full. What he wanted—needed, really—did not match up with what he had. He knew, however, that this was a common truth, and he was obliged to simply live with it.

Mostly, he did.

However, there had been some exceptions.

Paul's first encounter with The Resident happened on a mild fall evening about two years into Marti's whack-a-mole treatment, when it seemed she had a fair chance of beating the cancer into a lengthy remission or maybe even a cure. At that time, the family members were quite optimistic, no one was in crisis mode, there were no surgeries on the near horizon; Zack hadn't impregnated anyone yet; Cammie still lived at home, and she and Beck had just begun taking kickboxing; Claire and Chad and David were off in Hawaii;

and Sophie was—well, who knew what Sophie was doing just then? She was really tough to track.

Before the encounter, Paul had been having ramen at Ippudo with Sinclair West, one of his authors who lived nearby. They'd been talking about sex, which wasn't something Paul did much of (the talking or the having), but West's work in progress had a lot of sex in it, much of it between a white person with a vagina and a black person with a penis, and this was a sensitive matter, and West wanted to sound Paul out about the issues at hand, as well as the story. Over the course of their meal, the conversation, which had initially been specific to the book, evolved into a lively conversation about sex in general, and about the challenges of being queer in a time when most people still thought queer meant homosexual. Paul did not admit that this was also what he'd thought, having been only recently educated by Cammie.

West was in the early stages of exploring their nonbinary identity and ungendered pronouns, which Paul supported and found unproblematic during face-to-face conversations. Letting go of the gendered pronoun when speaking of West to others, however, was something he still had to work at. And so when West had gone to use the restroom and their (the plural *their*, in this case) coolly charming, attractive waitress (or was it waitperson now?) asked Paul whether West's remaining ramen should be packaged to go, Paul said, "I'm not sure whether he's—they're—finished eating."

"No problem," said the waitperson, who presented as female. *Very* female, by Paul's assessment, an assessment that had been heightened by all the talk of sex. This female—this woman, Paul thought, presuming that this person had a vagina—had a figure with pleasing roundness in all the places that the average male of the species was hardwired to take note of: ass, hips, breasts. Plump lips, too, but not too plump, not duck-face plump like some images Cammie had shown him and Beck of a few girls in her senior class. (Their parents had *paid* for that?) And because Paul had been thinking and talking about sex during dinner here, and because Paul had been having so little sex of late (that is, none in months), this fresh attention to the waitperson's features had the effect of arousing him. The arousal itself wasn't a surprise; he might be middle-aged now, but he was no less influenced by his hormonal imperatives than he'd been at sixteen, or thirty. It was the force of his arousal that was startling, this immediate hard-on that made him shift in his chair so as to give it some space.

Paul, embarrassed but determined to disguise the erection, crossed his right leg over his left and said to her, "While you're here, though—would you mind getting me the check?"

"Glad to," she said. "Separate, or together?"

"Together," Paul told her, then, conscious of the possibility that she might interpret this as them being a couple, he added, "But we're not *together*. Not that there's anything wrong with two men—" He stopped himself, unsure of how he was supposed to, in this context, describe a person with XY chromosomes who was not presenting as male right now. "Anyway, I mean, I don't know if you overheard any of our conversation—"

"Don't worry; I don't judge."

"No, of course. He—*they*—that is, my dinner companion, was just telling me about something they're writing. I'm their editor."

"Yeah? Of what? Books or a zine or . . . ?"

"Books. Fiction, mainly. Novels."

"I read," she said. "Any recommendations?"

"Where to start?"

Paul wished she would go away so that he could stop trying so hard not to look at her breasts, and at the same time he was glad that she was right here where he could sense, just below the line of his deliberate face-only view, the swell of them. Did this make him a sexist pig? Possibly it did. Or possibly it made him an ordinary product of nature. Surely it had to be okay for a person to notice someone, as long as they didn't behave badly.

Paul named a few of his recent favorite novels, then said, "I especially like immigrant stories. My parents are both immigrants. I was born here, but I guess you could say I have heightened empathy." Heightened empathy was a good trait, and he did possess it; he wasn't just saying so to score points. Possibly this trait helped offset his momentary objectification of the polite young woman?

"Thanks for the recs," she said. "I'll look for them. And I'll be right back with one check."

Smiling warmly, she left him sitting there alone with his embarrassment. Paul felt the heat in his face. He felt the unabated stiffness of his erection. He felt miserable.

West returned to the table, the check was presented, leftovers packaged up, credit card charged, receipt given, and Paul sat there throughout all of this still hard, damn it. It was as though the more he wished to cease his body's response to the woman, the more his dick defied him, berated him for the self-discipline he exercised in limiting how often he masturbated (once a week, tops) and how he mostly avoided porn. If he had been one of those men who one way or another got off daily, this might not be happening now. But no.

Of the many reasons Paul was grateful to be an editor, the one he was most grateful for as he and West left their table was that he always carried a messenger bag, even in this day of electronic everything. He'd used to tote around manuscripts—and once in a while he still did, but now the bag usually held a notebook, his iPad, and galleys of books his colleagues were publishing, most of which he shared with Beck. This current bag was a canvas-and-leather design in gray and black. Paul held it in front of his crotch in a manner that surely looked a little unnatural once he'd navigated the tight space between the seated diners and was out in the open. So be it. Better that than a visible trouser tent.

"Thanks so much," West told the waitress as they passed her.

Paul, trailing behind West, said, "Yes, thanks."

"Hope to see you again," she told them.

Paul was nearly out the door when he felt someone tap his shoulder. "You dropped this," the waitress said. She held out a business card that had been folded in half.

"I did?" he said. This was unlikely, as he couldn't recall having any such card in his possession. Still, he did not want to prolong the encounter, so he took the card and put it in his pocket.

Outside, he and West talked for a few more minutes—not, thank God, about sex. As they did, Paul's erection finally subsided enough for him to loop his bag's strap over his head so that he could carry the bag normally. Once they'd said their goodbyes, he headed south toward the Astor Place station, but had walked only a few strides before he remembered the business card in his pocket. Embossed on the front was *The Resident* and a phone number. Handwritten was *Good rates/no complications. 7:30 tomorrow night? Call me.*

His half-conscious thought—simultaneous with surprise and the questions of whether this card had come deliberately from the waitperson herself, or the waitperson was some kind of middleman (so to speak), or the card truly had been dropped by someone and mistakenly assigned to him—was his appreciation for the correct spelling of *night*. He hated the corrupted *n-i-t-e*, much the way he hated the missing-*d* or-*ed* endings of words, and their ungrammatical results. For example: "They stocked the pantry with a variety of *can* foods." And then there was the epidemic of misplaced apostrophes and underused commas. For a certain kind of person, this was crazy-making.

At the entry stairs to the Astor Place station, Paul paused to consider the possibilities attendant with *good rates/no complications* at *7:30 tomorrow night*. Who was The Resident? The resident of what? The resident of where? Good rates for what service or services, exactly? Massage? Sex? Dope? Something harder than dope? Something harder than sex? Paul, whose whole adult life was predicated on *story*, was attracted to the mystery of this.

But just the same, he wasn't a person who acted on illicit opportunities of any kind. Or perhaps it's more accurate to say that he hadn't been such a person before this night. And, he reasoned, he would not necessarily become such a person, even should he call the number. He would merely be someone resolving a mystery.

People streamed past Paul, heading downstairs, coming up, all of them taking action. The action he was meant to take was a 4, 5, or 6 train to Grand Central, then the Metro North home to Irvington, where Beck, by the time he got there, would be curled up with a bowl of popcorn and a book, or maybe watching one of the British dramas she liked. He liked those shows, too, but most evenings he was tasked with reading for work—either novels that agents had sent him as new prospects or novels he was in the process of editing for publication. Cammie, if she was home, would be in front of her computer, headphones on, gaming. This was what awaited him. This, and a short walk with their old dog, Beanie, a black Lab mix whose given name had been the incredibly original Blackie (it was the kids' choice) but who as a puppy of maybe ten months had climbed onto the backyard picnic table during the July Fourth party prep and helped herself to an entire Pyrex dish of baked beans.

Paul loved his dog. Paul loved his wife and kids. Paul called the number on the card and made a date for the next evening.

The Resident was, yes, the waitperson, who, she told Paul at a coffee shop on 9th, worked part time to help cover the expenses of med school. This gig—that is, offering sexual services for money—was a newish endeavor and would soon replace her restaurant job completely, once she had a sufficient roster of regular clients.

As for what her actual name was, she wasn't telling. As to her handle, she said, "I chose The Resident as an aspirational title. I still have a year to go before I graduate." She planned to specialize in trauma surgery, spoke three languages other than English, and was interested in joining Doctors Without Borders.

The other information she was willing to divulge was that she was thirty years old, single, childless, and disease-free ("I'll show you my paperwork"). Doing sex work was an idea she'd first gotten when she was a kid watching *The Best Little Whorehouse in Texas* with her grandma. "Men will pay a lot for sex," she explained to Paul while he sat there not drinking the coffee he'd bought, "so why not exploit that, as long as I can do it on my terms?"

"You're not afraid of being . . . harmed, or, you know, catching something?"

"I'm more afraid of the president getting reelected."

"I can see that," Paul said.

"So, anyway, it's your call. Here are my terms: I don't kiss. I don't do anal—that is, I'll give, but I won't take. Also—"

"Give?" Paul said. Possibly he'd been mistaken and The Resident did not have a vagina after all?

"Strap-on, handheld—"

"Oh, okay. Yeah, no, that's not for me." As he said this, he realized he could no longer fool himself that this conversation was meant only to satisfy his curiosity.

"To each their own," she said. "Also, I charge by half-hour increments. Soft BDSM is fine, if that's your kink. But I have found that most of my clients are looking for the basics. So what do you say?"

Paul thought a lot of different things in this moment where a decision was expected of him. He was fascinated—by The Resident herself, somewhat, but more by her manner, the practical way she approached this endeavor, the completely unromantic vibe. Too, he was fascinated by his own response to all of it: he was physically turned on, same as he'd been earlier, yet his attraction wasn't to her as a specific individual he hoped to have a relationship with; it was merely to her as a sex partner. This had never happened to him before, possibly because he'd never before approached the matter of having sex without it being attached to the issue of having a relationship. Even as a teenager, even as a college student, even in the years after college when he'd dated Patricia, Jules, Cindy, and then Beck, he'd conflated lust and love.

This kind of attraction—lust without love—was what The Resident trafficked in. She didn't want involvement. Involvement was against the rules. No complications.

He said, "How did you come to be so . . . so bold? I mean this in the best way. I admire your boldness."

"Are you a Bowie fan?"

"Bowie? Yes, I'd put myself in that camp."

"So I once read in *Vanity Fair* that his answer to the question 'What do you regard as the lowest depth of misery?' was 'Living in fear.' That's me, too. That's my motto. I don't want to be miserable, so I refuse to live in fear."

Paul wanted to rise to the occasion (so to speak). He did not want to feel miserable. He wanted to let go of his fear.

"I think . . . I guess I could try it," he said. "I mean, I'm a little bit worried, since I'm married. I've never . . . That is, I haven't cheated, even though I've wanted to. Not cheat. I don't mean that. I misspoke—I'm nervous, sorry. What I mean is, sometimes I want, I don't know, to magically have a whole different life. To have made different decisions, maybe. You see, there's this other woman . . . But, well, never mind."

The Resident gazed at him impassively while he stumbled through all of that. Then she said, "Do you jerk off?"

"I—well, sometimes, sure. What man doesn't?"

"Are those ejaculations a betrayal of your commitment?"

"No, of course not. I see where you're going with this, but I think that's too simplistic."

"Totally your call," she said, checking her phone for the time. "But I've got an eight-thirty, so . . ."

Paul considered the masturbation analogy. Sexual release was all it was. Sexual release would be all this was. The math did sort of work.

He said, "We'd just go . . ."

"Upstairs. It's not my place; I just use it. My friend bought it as an investment. I give her a cut."

"And that offsets her carrying costs?" If that were true, The Resident would have to be servicing an awful lot of clients.

"God no," she said. "Two different situations. She bought a foreclosure. She'll sell it at some point, when she thinks the market is topping out."

"Oh. All right, I get it."

"So?"

"Okay."

"Okay? Like, we're on?"

He nodded. She led him outside, then to the door that led upstairs, then to the apartment. The one large window looked out at a photography studio across the street. Inside, a young woman posed with her small spotted dog while the photographer moved about, taking flash photos.

In this time before everyone was using Venmo, The Resident attached a square plastic thing to her phone and asked for his credit card. "Payment first, please. Don't worry; satisfaction guaranteed. But no money back; credit for a future visit only."

"I can't pay in cash?"

"Credit cards only. The charge will show up as RES-BK."

"All right," Paul said. He gave her his card and attempted to say with confidence, "Just a blow job."

"You got it."

Shortly after, he did get it, and it was a terrible, wonderful relief. He'd kept his eyes closed the entire time and thought only of the woman he loved, in a scenario of very different circumstance than the one he was in. To his everlasting shame, he thought of Claire.

9

Charmed or Cursed?

I t was morning when Sophie, just home from Dubai, let her sisters into her current apartment (that was not hers), giving each a quick hug the moment they hit the threshold—because as soon as they got a look at the view, they'd be pulled toward the windows by the same irresistible gravity that had captured Sophie (and everyone) on their first visit here, and for a short while, at least, it would be as if she didn't exist.

Brief as the hugs were, she needed them badly: her mother was dead. Her mother was dead, and she was jet-lagged from no sleep on the flight because she couldn't turn her brain off. There was some trouble with the gallery, and she was basically broke, and her boyfriend had ghosted her, and god damn it, did everything have to go wrong all at once?

Her boss, Benji, sounding serious and nervous, had told her just before she left Dubai that he was going to be audited. "The IRS has discovered some irregularities," he'd said. "Keep it to yourself for now." Irregularities? Could this virtuous man—her hero, basically, for the way he'd turned his love of high art into a profitable, even lucrative, endeavor, and then put both name and dollars behind good causes—also be a cheat?

To top it all off, during her travel home the aircraft Wi-Fi was offline for hours and she'd missed making one of her Visa payments by maybe ninety minutes. By the time she was able to log back on to pay it (the minimum, but still), she already had an email saying she was being charged a penalty and her interest rate was being jacked up. God, the vultures were so fucking efficient.

But, okay, the view.

Beck said, "Oh, wow, are you serious?"

Claire said nothing, she just followed Beck, slack-jawed, to the fifteen-foot-high walls of glass.

The apartment was a voluminous ninety-first-floor southeast corner unit in 432 Park Avenue, the city's tallest (for the moment) and newest (for the moment) residential high-rise. From up here, every other building in sight appeared quaintly truncated, with the exception of the new World Trade Center and Sophie's favorite landmark, the Empire State Building. On Valentine's Day, she and Marco had turned off the lights and danced in the rosy glow from its holiday-themed red spotlights and talked about how they'd get their own penthouse when his career took off. Nothing quite so grand as this, probably; he was an artist, not a pop star. Then again, David Choe had gotten commissioned for Facebook's HQ, which had led to his getting in on Facebook's IPO to the tune of two hundred million dollars. Everything came down to who you knew, and between the two of them, Sophie and Marco knew a lot of people who had influence over a lot of other people. Opportunities could come knocking at any time.

Just the same, Sophie understood in a way Marco seemed not to that who you knew was only one of the essential factors necessary for stratospheric success. Also in the mix were talent and personality and skill and hunger and timing. Really, if you hoped for lightning to strike you, you had to be the one most appealing key of many possible keys that might have been strung on Benjamin Franklin's kite and flown during the perfect thunderstorm.

How different might Sophie's life be today if she had been able to write and sing like her friend whose apartment this was, or paint like David Choe, or tell a story like J. K. Rowling, for example? Talent was a raw material, and for certain people it became literally as good as palladium. Someone in Sophie's position—that is, someone talent-adjacent—could get rich, too, but usually that happened as a result of cheating the talent whose business they managed. To her disappointment, it appeared that she was both too ethical and not sufficiently talented to ever get rich on her own. Which didn't mean she wasn't still trying; she had a YouTube channel and her Insta game was strong, and monetizing both was helping to keep her in a style to which she really did want to remain accustomed. God, if only the best places to live (best cities, great apartments within those cities) weren't also so fucking expensive! If only becoming a capital-I Influencer with tens of millions of followers was as easy as Kim Kardashian had made it look; Kim had gotten famous by being Paris Hilton's friend, and come on, Sophie had famous friends, too.

Was it a character thing? Was she, Sophie, just too much of something or too little of something to be able to spin these friendships into gold if not palladium? She could (and often did) conclude that it was possible that her only remaining viable path to happily ever after was to marry money. Yet even that situation, which had come so easily to some of the women she'd known over the years, continued to elude her.

Beck, still gazing out the windows, said, "You'd think we were too jaded to be impressed."

Claire turned to Sophie. "I once took Chad and David to the Top of the Rock and they both got vertigo. How high are we here?"

"I'm not sure," Sophie said. "Beck, that coat is *excellent*. Is it new?"

"It is. I needed a lift."

"Very well done."

Claire said to Sophie, "You didn't ask her how high it is?"

The *her* of Claire's query was Tania Uccello: pop star, actress, spokesperson, cover model, entrepreneur, a dynamo who made Sophie's nimbleness look like somnambulance. And, sure, coke had been part of that equation early on, but lots of people did coke and merely got separated from a few hundred dollars each snort. Tania, though, had really made it work for her; her net worth was now in the hundreds of millions. Was there a bigger return on investment in the history of coke? Sophie couldn't think of one. As for this penthouse, Tania had needed a place to put some money, and where better than the Park Avenue high-rise that let her gaze out upon not only all of Manhattan below 56th, along with both rivers and three boroughs and the Atlantic Ocean beyond, but also her hometown of Maspeth way off to the east, that place where "those fuckers at my high school didn't think I'd amount to anything."

Now Sophie told Claire, "No, I didn't ask her, because what difference? This is not one of the metrics that matters to me. I mean, it's way fucking high up, right?"

"Do you know what she paid?" Claire asked. "Does that metric matter to you?"

It did matter, or at least more than knowing the precise height of the penthouse mattered. It mattered because she'd been following Tania's stratospheric rise for almost twenty years in the way that some people had followed Tom Brady's ascension from his days playing high school football at San Mateo's Serra prep. Some people simply knew potential greatness when they saw it. In fact, this was Sophie's one true talent, the reason she'd been able to advance relatively quickly through the art world ranks (so far as she had, which was not far enough). And she continued to feel that her one true failing was being unable to parlay that talent into a money factory for herself.

"Tania paid a lot," Sophie said.

Beck was still standing at the window. "I'll bet the common charges are fifteen grand a month."

Claire said, "How would you even begin to—"

"I wrote about this building for the *Times*. The financial politics of the project's early stages looked pretty shady—Trump's cronies, Trump's lender, some Russians, Ukraine, etcetera. But then again, when in this city is some version of that not the case?"

"I'm sure Tania Uccello doesn't bother herself with those kinds of details," Claire said. "She's too busy being insanely rich."

"Don't diminish her that way," Sophie said. "She's a cognizant person. But to Beck's point, if she were to only deign to buy a place that passes a purity test, she wouldn't have *any* Manhattan penthouses to choose from."

"Evidently she's not living here anyway," said Claire. "Which just seems insane to me. Spending god knows how much money, and then just leaving the place unused—by her, I mean."

"I told you, she's touring and she wanted someone she trusts to housesit. Plant-sit, really." Sophie indicated the dense array of potted plants positioned throughout the living room. "I'm sure the concierge has people who'll do that, but think of it: would you want some hourly wage slave like we all used to be poking around here if it was your place?" They all took in the top-end modern furnishings, the artwork, the collected bits and pieces of a life lived internationally, lived in small bites. Sophie said, "Tania feels it's violating to have people she doesn't know in her space."

Claire said, "She doesn't have a relative willing to do this? I mean, lucky for you she must not."

"No, her mom tours with her. She hates her dad. Her brother stays at her Panama estate. So she asked me. I'm probably her closest—or at least most trustworthy—friend in the city."

"Oh, her *Panama* estate," said Claire. "Well, next time, swap with the brother. I want to go to Panama."

Sophie didn't mention Tania's other properties—the farm in Norway, for example, which was under professional management, or the Singapore flat, currently occupied by their friend Danica. There was a wonderful London town house as well, looked after by Tarik, Tania's current squeeze, and a Paris flat that she lent out constantly. Tania had *so* much, and not only materially. She had pride. She had love. Sophie wasn't jealous, exactly, but she was envious. Tania had *found the way*, whereas she, Sophie, had taken a left turn into a hamster-wheel life, with no off-ramp (off-wheel) in sight.

Beck said, "Her Tokyo dates sold out in two hours. That's insane."

"What," said Claire, "did you write about that, too?"

"No, but I do read."

"Some of us are too busy to read celebrity gossip," said Claire.

Beck said, "Some of us have to pay attention to celebrity life as part of their profession doing occasional celebrity interviews. Minor celebs— authors, mainly, but famous in their ways."

Claire ignored her. "Soph, remind me, did you give up your apartment, or is Tania paying your rent, or what?"

"I sublet it," Sophie said. (A lie.)

"How long have you been in that apartment?" said Beck. "Why have I never seen it?"

"I don't know. Timing?" Also a lie. Sophie knew why Beck hadn't seen that apartment: that apartment was fictional.

The story she'd told her mom and Beck was that she'd rented a fantastic Williamsburg loft with skyline views, when the truth was that she'd been in a succession of short-term housesitting gigs for people who didn't actually know anything about her but who'd been told she was trustworthy and then hired her and relayed her name to others. These people were what Sophie thought of as the careless rich: young women and men who'd never had to work for their money and so were not assiduous about protecting their things. Their concern was casual, their oversight minimal, which was why they were so easily cheated by those they hired—and why they didn't even know they were being cheated. For these people, she was Sophie Silverberg and had a web presence to match what they believed to be true about her. There was no harm in this deception; unlike the cheats, she actually was as trustworthy as she was made out to be. What difference was there between her practice and that of someone who operated the same kind of service business using a company name they'd invented for the purpose?

None, except that hers flew below the IRS radar. She needed to keep every dollar she could—*keep* being the momentary verb that occurred before *send*, as in *to her creditors*.

In between housesitting gigs, Sophie had camped out in a seedy hotel in Long Island City. This was where she'd been when Tania, who was unaware of Sophie's housesitting side job, texted her to ask this HUGE favor . . . I know I've been a bad friend, SO busy, OMG I can hardly even think straight, but please say you can watch my new place while I'm on tour. Nine months, BIG ask, I know. Call me.

Tania, of course, knew Sophie's actual identity. They'd met at a Brooklyn rave as boy-crazy, badass sixteen-year-olds and became fast friends. At eighteen, Sophie, with her bush-league drawing skills and a fascination with the art world present and past, enrolled at the School of Visual Arts for a BFA, and Tania started kicking around the Northeast, writing songs and performing them at dive bars and basement clubs. Sophie had felt mildly superior to her friend back then—more together than Tania, more probable. She'd badly underestimated what could happen when a talented young woman with chips on both shoulders and a burning desire to transcend a shitty home life launched herself at the world in a way that was at once heedless and calculated.

Sophie had called Tania later that day from work, at Benji's gallery where she was surrounded by high-priced paintings and sculptures by in-demand artists, where she was wearing Stella McCartney (marked down due to a tiny rip; an incredible deal) and this season's Louboutins (a necessary splurge, she couldn't help it), and so felt halfway worthy of the arrangement she was about to make. She said, "Hey, I got your text. My travel schedule is pretty light, so yeah, I think I can help you out."

Now Sophie told her sisters, "Let me give you the grand tour."

They were admiring full bathroom number three when Claire said, "So the new guy must be *really* tidy, because I don't see any sign of—"

"Oh, yeah, no, that's over."

"Since when?" said Claire. "You got home a few hours ago."

"Since then," Sophie said. "We basically had a difference of opinion."

Beck said, "So it was a real thing?"

Sophie frowned at her. "What? Yeah—I mean, we probably weren't headed for the altar anytime soon, but it was real . . . *ish*. What makes you even ask?"

"I don't know, I thought maybe you were his beard."

"What, Marco? Um, no, he's absolutely hetero. Also, why would I do that?"

Beck shrugged. "To be a good friend?"

"And scare off my actual prospects? I'm nice, okay, but I'm not that nice."

Claire said, "Wait, what is a beard?"

Beck explained. "It's a cover for someone who's gay but not out and needs to appear to be straight."

Claire looked at Sophie. "And that's not what you were."

Sophie said, "Correct."

"So what happened?"

Sophie considered for a moment whether to invent a story that would make her look less pathetic than the truth might. But right now, when she was grieving and hadn't slept and hadn't eaten and had, for most of the hours since arriving home, been curled up on the window seat wrapped in Tania's chunky-knit alpaca comforter, cocooned in the faint whisper of huge air handlers and staring out at the gradually lightening city, she couldn't muster the energy. She said, "Actually, he was gone when I got here. Totally ghosted me. Not a note, not a text, nothing."

Beck turned to her. "What? Oh, honey."

"I'm fine. It was . . . whatever. He's kind of a big baby anyway. I was gone for two weeks and he couldn't deal, I guess. He doesn't need a girlfriend; he needs a mother figure that he can fuck."

Claire's eyes widened. "Oh my god, listen to you."

"What? It's the truth."

Beck told her, "You forget Claire is a prude."

Claire said, "I am not. I'm just not used to women speaking so . . . well, *coarsely.* I know you both do it, but it's impolite, for one thing. Also, that imagery is off-putting."

"Oh, sorry, Dr. Geller," Sophie said. "I didn't mean to offend your refined sensibilities."

"Look, just because *I* don't use crude language—"

"Which is because you're uptight and uncreative—"

"Quit it, both of you," said Beck, which after a moment made all three of them smile.

"Bossy Beck. Just like old times," Sophie said.

Beck said, "When were we last together, all three of us in one place?"

"Dad's funeral," said Claire. "God. Ten years."

"But we're together now," said Sophie. "And we're going to do breakfast, right? I'd offer to feed you here, but the cupboards are pretty bare. We *could* eat downstairs in the private dining room, but what do you say we do our old pretend-tourists thing and get breakfast at Sarabeth's?"

Claire was pulled back to the view and stood looking out at the city. "Can't we order in?"

"From downstairs or Sarabeth's?"

"From I don't care. I'm not ready to leave here yet. I may never see anything like this again."

"Then stay here while you're in town," Sophie said, surprising herself. She hadn't intended to make any such offer, and especially not to Claire. Yet the words had left her mouth. She really was very tired. But, okay, having her sister here with her in this voluminous penthouse might make it feel less lonely. She doubled down: "Check out of the NoMad. I obviously no longer need privacy."

Beck said, "Why only her? That's not fair at all."

"You too," Sophie said, liking the idea better and better. She would not have to be alone here with all Tania's plants and a head full of angst. "It'll be just like when we were kids—except with separate bedrooms and triple the space."

"To say the least," Claire said.

Beck said, "High-speed elevator."

"Fitness center, personal trainers," Sophie said, ticking off a list. "Pool, spa, sauna, billiards, library, private restaurant, studio apartments for the help, and concierge services that include but are not limited to arranging chartered flights and shipping sports cars, should you need your Bentley or Lamborghini to join you somewhere abroad."

Beck said, "Not exactly the level of concierge Mom used to be." Marti had been more of a glorified doorman in staid Upper East Side prewars and midtown towers that attracted mid-level executives of middling companies.

"I accept," said Claire. "I'll lose a few hundred dollars, but I don't care."

"Not a loss, really," Beck said. "Think of this as a room upgrade."

Claire said, "A gift from Mom, thanks to the insurance money and all."

The money, thought Sophie. *The money!* God help her, she almost salivated at the thought. She was in every way sorry that her mother was gone, but in no way sorry that if her mother had to be gone, at least there was a small windfall coming soon.

Her eagerness to have more cash was in no way a measure of her grief, of course, and if Marti was able to know this in the afterlife (such as there might be), Sophie was sure that she did. She said, "Everybody happy, now? Remember to pack your toothbrushes and jammies and favorite snuggly; I don't want anyone getting homesick, and I'm not sharing mine. Now, can we go eat?"

After breakfast (the scrambled eggs/smoked salmon/cream cheese Goldie Lox for Sophie, as ever), Beck hailed a cab for their trek down to Marti's apartment. The sisters were mostly quiet as they rode, each of them taking in the sights with fresh attention. For Claire especially, the city seemed different than she remembered. The luxury mega high-rises (Tania's included) spiking out of the uptown streets made the area feel a bit strange, futuristic. Sophie said, "That new Central Park Tower is basically giving 432 Park the finger." Beck said, "Where will it end?" As for midtown, it looked cleaner than it used to, refreshed somehow. Throughout the city, the bustle of people going about the day's business seemed orderly and purposeful. So much life was happening here, every square foot maximizing its potential, or trying to.

The Manhattan of their youths was grittier, less like a Disney attraction and more like a dark circus being run by that clown, Rudy Giuliani. Even so, it had felt like a place people *lived* rather than a place people *went*, this parking spot for the super-rich and a spectacle for tourists. How soon before someone started stringing ziplines between skyscrapers and charging $100 per five-second thrill?

When they got out on 19th Street, they stood on the sidewalk looking up at the building that had been the cornerstone of their lives. None of them spoke right away, each lost in her own thoughts. The place was nothing special, yet for their family it had, for a long time, been everything. Leo and Marti's pad, in the early seventies. The Geller girls' home, in all their growing-up years.

Finally Beck said, "All right, let's do this. You guys take the elevator; I'll do the stairs."

"I will, too," Claire said.

Sophie said, "Meet you up there."

The dramatic contrast between Tania's place and this one, though not unexpected, felt starker than it might have if Marti had been there to enliven it. "Is it just me?" said Claire, and her sisters said no, the place really was kind of sad—or maybe it was that they were so sad to be here under these circumstances and this sadness leached into their assessment of the place each of them had learned to crawl and walk and talk in, the place where they'd fought one another over bathroom time, where they'd sat elbow to elbow at the round supper table chattering to their father about their days. Leo, who was universally regarded as the epitome of *mensch*, took time to listen to each one of them, drawing out their stories, asking questions, praising good behavior or good judgment, challenging them with insights about the world around them. Yes, he'd seemed to favor Beck a little, but maybe that was because he and Marti had four years with her before Claire's arrival, and eight before Sophie's—so much more time to bond. In any event, the apartment seemed dimmer and smaller and dingier now, the furniture more worn, the linens and dishes and books more dated than any of them remembered—even Beck and Claire, who'd been there only a day earlier.

"It's so tidy," Sophie said. "Last time I was here, it looked like—well, like Mom lived here. Now it's just a mausoleum."

Beck removed her coat and draped it over a dining chair. "She wanted to make this easier on us."

"There's not really *that* much to do, is there? I'm not trying to weasel out of anything; I just have to be at the gallery by three o'clock to touch base with Benji in person. He's insecure like that."

"Mostly we need to organize everything based on where it's going and coordinate with those agencies for pickup. I've got boxes, and I made a task list for each of us." Beck paused as if awaiting complaint. None came, so she went on, "So, okay, Mom's instructions were pretty clear about it all, but if there's something you want to keep that you didn't prearrange with her, let's talk about that. It's not like she'll know it didn't go to charity. Some personal belonging, say. For example: I'd like to keep that red chenille sweater she wore a lot."

Claire said, "Are you talking about the one I gave her for Hanukkah a few years back?"

"I don't know where it came from; I just know I associate it with her. Are you suggesting I shouldn't have it just because it might've come from you?"

"Well," said Claire, "I'm just saying that since I gave it to her—"

Sophie said, "Oh my god. It's going to be like this? There are a thousand items to fight about. *I* don't want anything except what I already picked and the stuff I've kept stored here."

Beck said, "You say that, but it's likely you'll come across something. Like that sweater. I never would've thought about it ahead of time, but for me—and I saw her so often—it's Mom. Did either of you ever even see her wear it?"

"No, fine, have it," Claire told Beck, turning away. "I'm sorry. I shouldn't be so possessive. It's not like it's mine in the first place. If it makes you happy, have it."

"Okay," Beck said. "Thanks." She looked around the apartment. "I guess we should divide and conquer. Do you have preferences? Who wants to do the kitchen?"

The three of them stood there, looking around at the evidence of existence, all of it soon to be relegated to other lives, other homes, people and places they'd never seen and would never know.

"This is going to be so hard," Claire said.

Blame the gin martinis they'd mixed in a Swedish mouth-blown martini pitcher, or if you're inclined to believe in otherworldly forces, maybe blame Marti's posthumous influence, but late that evening, when the sisters were showered and relaxing in Tania's penthouse while the city lay twinkling below, Sophie's earlier confession of having been unceremoniously dropped by Marco led her to inquire about her sisters' relationship statuses—something she would never have been inclined to do before, because the three of them were not the kind of sisters who shared those kinds of things.

Their age differences may have had something to do with that; each one of them had matured independently of the others. When Beck had her first menstrual period, Claire was eight years old, Sophie four—hardly out of training pants. When Beck received her high school diploma, Claire was *still* waiting to get her period and Sophie was obsessed with the Littlest Pet Shop. Two years later, Beck was married and the mother of a newborn, while Claire fought acne and fretted about whether any boy would ever love her the way Paul evidently loved Beck. Sophie had just discovered masturbation.

Their personality differences surely played a role, too. Beck: self-counseling and watchful. Claire: defensive and judgmental. Sophie: independent, and striving always to be something different/better/more than her big sisters, to be the best possible Sophie, whatever that meant at any given time.

Tonight, however, the best possible Sophie had been waylaid by the effects of a third martini, and seated with nighttime Manhattan laid out beyond her, she said to both sisters, not caring which answered first, "So, okay, tell me one thing about your marriage that made you think twice about what you'd done—that is, get married in the first place. Help a girl out: I'm trying to justify my ever-single status."

Beck and Claire glanced at each other as if seeing who'd brave going first. There was a pregnant pause, then Beck blurted out, "I wish I'd known that Paul was gay. That is, *probably* gay. I'm-pretty-sure gay."

Sophie's mouth dropped open, while Claire, who'd been reaching forward to set down her glass, fell off the sofa. Actually fell off. Toppled down to knees and hands. She righted herself, saying, "Please tell me you're joking."

Beck said, "I wish I were!"

Sophie started laughing. "Oh . . . my . . . fucking . . . god! Well, that does it. The whole thing is hopeless. I'm joining a convent."

Beck was laughing, too. "A Jewish nun! Now there's a thought. Let me know if they'll take you; I may want in."

Returning to the sofa, Claire stared at them both. "I don't think this is funny at all. I also don't believe it."

Sophie said to Beck, "That 'colleague' you asked me about—it was Paul, wasn't it?"

Beck nodded. "Yes, sorry. I didn't want to out him. I shouldn't have now."

Sophie said, "I can't believe I didn't see it before! It was his idea to wallpaper your bathroom, right?"

Claire said, "Don't traffic in stereotypes. Straight men can decorate. Straight men can be nice."

"Also, the sex," said Beck.

"What about the sex?" said Claire.

Sophie said, "They don't have any."

Beck said, "I think he might have something going with Geoff, his assistant. Which, good for him? Except I worry Geoff might be using him."

Claire got up and went, somewhat unsteadily, to the bar cart. The martini pitcher was empty. She dropped ice cubes into the cocktail shaker and added gin while saying, "Then it was all pointless. I mean utterly *fucking* pointless. Not that I didn't think so already."

"Hooray!" Beck said. "Claire has finally learned to curse!"

Sophie laughed again, but, too, she was watching Claire's grim expression. Poor Claire! All this time, pining for a man whom she not only couldn't have because he'd married her sister, but now really couldn't have—couldn't ever *possibly* have because women weren't his thing after all. Claire shot her a look that threatened murder if Sophie gave voice to any of what was going through her mind.

Sophie said, "Wow, all these years—you must've felt so rejected!"

"Not really," Beck said. "I think maybe a part of me knew the truth, because—TMI?—I was never all that hot for him to begin with."

"Never," Claire repeated flatly.

"Not really. Not that way."

Sophie said, "And you just *settled*, all these years?"

"It was fine," Beck said. "Sex is overrated anyway."

"Not *all* sex," said Sophie. "Some. But definitely not all."

"Anyway, what will you do?" said Claire. "You don't seem to be terribly upset about it."

"What would be the point?" Beck said. "I don't love him any less."

Her phone rang. She glanced at the screen. "Speak of the devil." She held it face out to show that it was Paul. Then she answered, "Hello there, we were just talking about you."

While Beck excused herself to go talk in the bedroom, Sophie said, "I know what you must be thinking. But look at it this way: if she's right about Paul, you dodged a bullet."

"He's not gay. I would know."

"Oh, you'd know, but his own wife wouldn't? Maybe you just don't want it to be true."

Claire swirled her drink. "Maybe."

"Listen, it might not be too late to fix things. Chad might be willing to take you back."

"Um, no."

"I'm serious."

"He'd love it if I came groveling," said Claire. "Which is why I'll never do it."

"Fair enough." Sophie, too, was not the groveling type.

She carried her drink, unsteadily, to the window seat, thinking about Marco, about Chad, about Paul. About her sisters and herself. "Would you just look at us," she said. "Is it only ever about men? What would Mom think of that?"

Claire said, "Mom had a charmed life that way, and she wanted the same for us."

"That's what makes witchcraft so interesting," Sophie said.

"What are you talking about? You're drunk."

"Oh, no question. But hear me out. You said *charmed*. For some situations, a spell is a charm, but for others, that spell is a curse. Same incantation, different effect."

Claire raised her glass. "I don't know if that's right, but I'll drink to it."

Sophie was standing on the window seat, her back pressed to the glass. "I hope she didn't think I'm a failure."

"Please. If anyone's a failure, it's me."

"You? Ha! *You're* drunk," Sophie said.

Beck returned to the living room. "Paul sends his love."

"I should've stayed in school," Sophie said.

"Why didn't you?" Claire asked.

Beck sat down, saying, "She met that DreamWorks guy, who was at SVA recruiting seniors."

"Yeah," said Sophie. "Then I followed him to L.A., for a couple of years."

"I was *so* envious," said Beck. "Joan Didion lived out there. She did her best work there."

Sophie had not done her best work there; she'd done her best coke, however. And gotten hired at the William Turner Gallery while she was there. And met Benji, who was *so* charming, so eager to emulate Turner's great operation. He lured her away, back to New York, with promises of better pay and a bigger role and real opportunity for growth. He had Hollywood connections. He had a Greenwich Village lease. This was when her money troubles began. She'd wanted to be the Carrie Bradshaw of the art scene, and that had meant looking the part.

Claire said, "Women do a lot of stupid things for love."

"Never mind love," said Sophie. "I mean, yes, it's about love, sometimes. But also, what men grant us is power. *If* we're lucky. It's a bullshit system. We should start a revolution."

Beck said, "You've been listening to *Hamilton*, haven't you?"

"That's the second time you've mentioned *Hamilton*," Claire said. "Are you obsessed?"

"Please," said Beck. "You can't live here and not be."

When Sophie started humming "The Story of Tonight," Beck said, "Okay, everybody go brush your teeth; it's bedtime."

Claire said, "I'll clean up."

"Leave it for the maid," Sophie told her.

"The maid," said Beck, shaking her head.

"What?"

"Nothing. This place!" Beck waved her arm at their surroundings. "We are swimming in opulence. We are at the top of Manhattan. It's wild. Think of those buildings Mom used to work in. I thought they were *so* posh, but they were nothing compared with this. I wish Mom could see us now."

They were all quiet for a moment, thinking of Marti.

Sophie said, "I was going to have her up here, once I got back from my trip. I mean, she kept saying, 'I'll wait for Tania to get back,' because she *loved* Tania and wanted to hang out here with her. She didn't love Marco. And I did think, what if she doesn't make it till Tania's tour is over? But I didn't do anything about it. And it was too late."

Beck said, "I was planning to take her to Maine this summer. She hadn't been up to camp since she got sick. I think Helen—you guys remember her, the neighbor?—she's been doing spot checks. They were friends for a long time."

Claire said, "I was thinking I'd bring David here for Passover. See Mom, the cousins, meet Leah . . ."

"We should talk about the camp," Beck said. "As in, I don't want it sold."

Sophie said, "We have to sell it. It's in the will."

"We don't *have* to, if we agree not to. That was in Mom's letter, remember? She said if we have any disputes, we can work them out ourselves."

"Okay, but just the same, I can't see a reason to keep it."

"Claire?" asked Beck.

Claire said, "I don't see a reason, either."

Beck looked troubled. "You guys aren't attached to it at all?"

"What I'm attached to," Sophie said, making this up on the fly, "is a really great project I didn't think I'd be able to invest in, but now, with the proceeds, I can. Anyway, didn't you say it's bedtime? I'm wiped." She couldn't wait to burrow under the covers and shut out all the stress for a little while, at least. Tomorrow they would bury their mother. A horrible thought! Impossible! And yet.

They each went to their bedrooms and settled in. Sophie piled extra blankets onto the bed and slid beneath the covers. "A little bug in a rug," Beck had used to say whenever she saw Sophie snugged in like this. Sometimes Beck would sit on the end of Sophie's bed and tell her a story—about bugs in rugs, or cats that roamed the Paris rooftops, or pixies and sprites that lived on the fire escapes all around Manhattan. Sophie, tucked now into this bed so high up in the Manhattan sky that no pixie could ever get here, wished Beck would come tell her a story. Something happy. Something silly. But of course Beck did not come.

All was quiet for a few minutes, and then Sophie heard Beck call out, "Good night, John-Boy."

Claire called out, "Good night, Jim-Bob."

And Sophie, who'd never watched *The Waltons* reruns but always loved how Beck had made this a ritual of their childhood and had learned her part, called, "Good night, Daddy. Good night, Mama. Good night, everyone."

10

Getting a Feel for His Intentions

For Marti's funeral, the sisters had done their best to follow her directions to the letter. She'd be laid to rest in a traditional wooden casket. The service would be held graveside and would be brief, inasmuch as that could be prescripted. There would be no songs of prayer, just a short speech by the rabbi from Marti's synagogue followed by remarks from anyone who wished to speak. Marti had prepaid for fifty kriah ribbons—not because she expected so many attendees, but because buying that volume meant the price was the same as for twenty.

Marti had asked for donations to her favorite causes in lieu of flowers, and they'd dutifully passed along that information, as they had passed along the containers of food that had been arriving at the apartment—unless the food arrived in a container that needed to be returned to sender, as was the case with Mr. Abraham's noodle kugel, Mrs. Leavitt's rugelach, and the chocolate sprinkle cupcakes made by the Kasey twins, five-year-old girls who lived in the apartment below Marti's. Beck and Sophie had eaten one cupcake apiece.

Then Sophie distributed them to eager college kids at Union Square before giving the twins back the emptied Aladdin's Magic Carpet tray.

Here at the cemetery, amid a crowd of nearly forty mourners (a solid turnout, this being a weekday), Paul wore the black suit he wore for every formal occasion. As with Paul himself, the suit could not be said to be stylish by New York's impossible standards, yet it had a certain something that made it stand out among the sea of other suits of similar price points worn by the men who had gathered with the family to say goodbye to Marti. Only Chad's suit outshone Paul's (and everyone's): he'd chosen a dark-toned and subtle wide plaid in deep sapphire blue and black, with a plum accent in the warp. Paul admired the suit, and he admired Chad's willingness to be at the funeral in that suit; not every ex-husband whose wife had cheated on him egregiously (or so Beck had said, though her conclusion was still based only on speculation) would take time off from work to come pay respects to that wife's mother. It was a testament to his character, Paul thought. If Chad was a bit cool toward him, well, that was to be expected, family loyalties being what they were.

Grizzled old Rabbi Schneider, who'd married Paul and Beck, who'd buried Leo, now stood at the head of Marti's grave. "Al molay rachamim, shochayn bam'romim, ham-tzay m'nucha n'chona al kanfay Hash'china, b'ma-alot k'doshim ut-horim k'zo-har haraki-a mazhirim, et nishmat Marti . . ."

Paul, though, had a head full of Claire.

Seeing her today for the first time since she'd arrived in New York, he was suddenly less certain of what he thought of her in the wake of her split from Chad. That is to say, if she had in fact cheated on Chad egregiously, she was not the woman he'd thought she was. And if she was not that woman, who was she? And what did it matter who she was? And who was he to judge her, anyway?

Though, in fairness, what he'd done a few times in that year before The Resident graduated med school and took a residency somewhere out of state (she did not divulge which hospital or even what state), and what he'd done a few times more recently with a woman she'd referred him to, was not *cheating* per se. To cheat was by definition *to behave dishonestly in order to gain an unfair advantage.* That's not what he'd been doing. There'd been no advantage gained by him or anyone. If anything, his encounters benefited Beck as much as himself. He was doing Beck a favor by relieving her of the burden of marital sex, in which she had little interest anymore.

In their early days, they weren't particularly good at sex, but he had expected they'd improve. In those days, Paul, being older and slightly more experienced, felt obliged to lead, and Beck followed that lead. His confidence was more faked than earned, so the sex was tentative, occasionally awkward, and usually not long-lasting. She never complained. In fact, she sometimes seemed relieved that it was finished as quickly as it was. And she didn't ask him to do anything extra for her—which he would have done if she'd wanted him to, which she evidently did not. Modern women asked for what they wanted, right?

Beck was a decisive, intelligent, strong woman; Paul had to figure she just wasn't enthusiastic about sex. And he hadn't conveyed his desire for more enthusiasm because he hadn't wanted her to feel judged or hurt or inferior. For that same reason, he'd felt inhibited from showing it himself and hadn't known how to even begin to broach the subject in conversation. It was terribly difficult to talk about sex when you didn't talk about sex.

She'd gotten pregnant with Cammie almost right away. Then Zack came along eighteen months after Cammie, and before Paul knew it, years had passed and their life had developed a sort of rhythm, a logic that mostly worked. To raise the subject of her lack of enthusiasm for sex, for sex with him, would have been unfair to her, wouldn't it? He was also unsure that he was prepared for the other possibility: that *he* was what underlay the tepidness of her interest, and that if he asked her, she'd have to admit that yes, this was true, and she just hadn't said so because she hadn't wanted to make him feel judged/hurt/inferior. This was entirely possible.

And then came the summer they'd taken the kids to Duluth to visit Chad and Claire and David, who was three years old at the time and as cute a child as God made, a ringer for Claire at the same age. They were all down at

Canal Park to watch the massive, nearly silent ore boats enter Superior Bay by passing beneath the Aerial Lift Bridge. On this particular day, one of the thousand-footers was coming in, and Chad and Beck had raced ahead with the kids for a closeup look from the canal wall, leaving Paul and Claire to walk together alone.

Though Paul had always found Claire appealing, he didn't know her well. She'd been a high school kid when he and Beck paired up. Then she'd gone away to college and stayed gone. Having spent more time with Claire in this one visit than in any before, he now saw, or maybe *felt* was the better word, that he and she were kindred spirits. Where Beck was firm and confident in her assertions, Claire's manner was that of a woman who spent her days tending sick, worried kids—competence wrapped in softness, he thought. As with the plan for this day's outing: Beck had said, "We should do Canal Park at ten-thirty, to beat the lunchtime crowds," as if she were the one who had experience here. Whereas Claire had said, "Why don't we see where the kids are with their interest once breakfast's done? Does that sound all right?" Also: "I'm thinking tuna-noodle casserole for dinner will go over well with everybody. What do you guys think?"

And, okay, these were banal matters, yet they pointed to something Paul hadn't realized about himself, back when he and Beck had gotten together: Paul preferred to operate by consensus, while Beck blazed the trails and expected others to follow. Or to blaze alongside her. He admired her tremendously, but it was Claire he resonated with; he'd noticed it again and again during the visit.

As they'd strolled toward the canal, Claire said something to Paul, something innocuous, he couldn't even recall what, but he'd turned toward her and she was just *luminous* to him. So intelligent. So lovely. Paul saw her anew, and that was it. If a Renaissance artist had painted the scene, it would show Claire standing with her face upturned toward Paul's, her entire being lighted by a singular beam radiating from a break in the clouds. He was struck as surely as if Cupid had fired the arrow point-blank. The right word for it was *besotted*.

How was he supposed to deal with this? Paul spent the rest of the trip struggling to navigate the opposing forces of attraction and denial—not denial of what had happened to him, denial of the fervent urge to act on it. An urge that didn't abate afterward and flared fresh each time he saw or spoke to her after that. He hated it, yet he loved it; it made him feel alive, in a tormented, terrible, wonderful way.

So, all right: he was a shit, there was no denying that—but it wasn't because he'd paid for some blow jobs; it was because years ago he had fallen in love with his sister-in-law and had not done one thing about it since. Yet what could he possibly have done?

And now look at her, standing beside Marti's grave with her son's hand in hers. The color black, which made some women look severe, suited her so well; it made her pale skin look milk-glossed, her dark eyes even darker, her long, curly hair shiny and healthful . . . Paul knew he was romanticizing her, but he didn't care. He decided that he also didn't care that she might have had a flaming extramarital affair; maybe an affair was a good thing, a sign that she could be passionate, a sign that Chad didn't do it for her anymore, if he ever had. What Paul remembered about Claire and Chad's origin story was that Chad had pursued her relentlessly and she'd been worn down by it and gave in. Gave in cheerfully, it had seemed at the time. Still, more of a capitulation than a strong desire to be wed? Possibly.

Rabbi Schneider was speaking, and Paul made himself pay attention to him, and then to the women and men who took turns telling anecdotes about Marti. They remarked on her sense of humor. Her doggedness. Her generosity. How good she'd been at soothing others. How much she'd loved goulash. What a terrible cook she was, except that she could assemble a Chicago-style hot dog as if she favored the Sox or the Cubs, when in fact she just favored loading the thing with fresh vegetables instead of sauerkraut. The grandkids spoke of how accepting she'd been of their life choices. Supportive. Interested. Sophie talked about how open Marti was to everything: "Pretty sure I taught her some valuable stuff about sex," she said. Beck— who was stoned, Paul was pretty sure—told a funny story about Marti trying to learn to ride a bicycle one summer in Maine. When Claire took her turn to speak ("Mom was the most genuine person I know . . ."), Paul looked elsewhere—out over the wide expanse of still-brown lawn, the headstones that marked the passages of those who'd gone before him, some of them surely poor fools like himself.

Later that evening, the entire family (Chad excepted—he had his limits) assembled to sit shiva at Paul and Beck's Irvington home, as Marti's apartment was now in full disarray and, regardless, would have proven a tight fit.

It seemed to Paul that Claire was avoiding eye contact with him—was mildly hostile toward him, even, and he could not think why. She had been so vulnerable with him on the phone, and he thought he'd been a good listener. Best not to think about it at all. But when she was close like this, his entire being thrummed with that knowledge. It was thrilling and humiliating. It led to encounters like:

"Oh, Claire, hi, I didn't know you'd wandered off." (This, upon discovering her in Cammie's former bedroom, now his home office.)

"I was just putting my purse in here so that it's out of the way. Sorry."

"No, *I'm* sorry. I didn't mean to intrude."

"What? No—it's your office. I'm the one who—"

"Really, it's fine." He tried to laugh to ease the awkwardness, but the sound came out more like a gulp.

Long, awkward pause.

"It was a really nice service," she said, eyeing the door. Obviously she couldn't wait to get away from him.

He stood aside. "It was."

"So I guess I better get back, to help with—"

"Yes, sure."

She moved past him at what seemed to be almost a run.

He stood there in a fog, having forgotten what it was he'd gone for in the first place. Maybe subconsciously he'd been following Claire, hoping for . . . what? He didn't even know.

On his way back to the kitchen, he passed Cammie in the hallway. He said, "Where are you going next, and will you take me with you?"

"You're funny, Dad," she said.

He watched her continue down the hallway toward the kitchen. His little girl, all grown up. She was tall, like Beck, but with his Slavic cheekbones and eyes. Strong-minded like Beck, but freer—maybe because she hadn't let herself get tied down. Not by anything or anyone. How long this would last, he couldn't predict. Nor could he guess how long they'd stay supportive of Cammie's footloose ways. It might depend on whether the lifestyle was a whim or something they'd be dealing with long term. He and Beck both were prone to saying (only to each other), "But what is she planning to *do* with her life?" Imagine if she could know how ridiculous her father was; she'd rightly wonder what it was he was doing with *his*.

In the kitchen, the conversation centered on some big gathering long past. Beck was saying, ". . . and that's when I knew that those boys were *trashed*."

Paul observed Zack (who'd also gotten Beck's genes for height) holding Leah on his shoulders. Binta, whose dark skin and lyrical accented English had once made her seem so exotic in their rather homogenous suburb, stood with her arm around Zack's waist in a picture of complete harmony. *Good for them*, thought Paul as Beck continued: "But it was summer, and we were on Sand Beach, and, you know, we were a bunch of teen girls looking for—"

"Action," said Sophie.

Beck laughed. "Adventure, I was going to say."

"Sometimes one and the same!"

David was standing in front of Claire, leaning against her. She covered his ears with her hands. "Tender minds," she said. She glanced at Paul. Glanced away.

Beck said, "Well, I ended up getting my heart broken, but I don't hold that against the island. It's such a special place, you know?"

Cammie said, "You sound like Grandpa Leo. Except *he* got the HEA."

"The what?" said Claire.

"Happily Ever After," said Paul. "It's a story trope, for romances."

"Not only those," Beck said. "Would we say Jane Austen's books are romances?"

"Some would."

"Point being," said Cammie, "Mom sounds like Grandpa, who I hope is this minute romancing Grandma again."

Come eight o'clock, they'd all shed shoes and shapewear and ties. Sophie aided Cammie, who funded her travels by doing odd jobs (like bartending) wherever she could find them, in mixing creative travel-inspired cocktails for all takers. They'd eaten an assortment of foods put into their hands by a number of funeral attendees who, though they weren't going to make the trip up to Irvington, had still wanted to contribute food to the shiva. The foil tins and plastic containers and loaves and spreads and baskets were still laid out on every surface in the kitchen when Paul, who'd again disappeared into his home office for a short while, asked the others to join him in the den.

He waited for everyone to find a spot to settle into, then said, "I've got two bits of business: a development about the camp, and a message that Marti recorded and asked me to screen for everyone tonight. She didn't say what it is, and I haven't seen it, but I'm assuming it's some kind of goodbye."

"Oh my god," said Sophie. "Camp first, please."

"Yes," Claire said.

Paul said, "Beck?"

"Sure, yes."

"All right. So, I had a very interesting phone call just now. A woman named Carol Barksdale, who's a Realtor from Bar Harbor, called on behalf of a client. She said she'd shown him some homes recently and he was somewhat interested in the Barretts' place—"

"Which one is that?" said Sophie. Her drink in hand was inspired by Australia's red monolith and was made up of Fireball Whisky, apple vodka, and grenadine.

Beck said, "It's the one right across the road from ours." To Paul she said, "And?"

"And she said he had been wondering whether, if he bought it, he might be able to come over to the shore when no one's at the camp."

Claire said, "That shouldn't be a problem, right? At least for the time being." She'd chosen Cammie's version of a Midnight Sun, a pale blue cocktail nod to Iceland.

Paul started to speak, but Beck, who'd let their daughter mix her a double-strength jalapeño margarita (Mexico), said, "I don't know; I wouldn't want us to be responsible for anything that might happen to the guy, not to mention whoever might be with him. It's a liability thing."

"What could happen?" said Claire. "He'd just be cutting through the woods. It's more than two acres, right? We couldn't be held responsible for him tripping on a rock, or whatever."

Paul said, "Hang on—"

"We might be," Beck said to Claire. "Do we want to even risk a lawsuit?"

"Hey," Paul said, waving his hands to get their attention, "I'm trying to tell you that there's more: Carol, the agent, said she'd been in touch with Marti maybe two weeks ago and Marti said to check back—which, when Carol did, she got Marti's voice mail directing her to contact me no sooner than today's date. I had six voice mails waiting, all from folks who'd tried reaching her over the past week. How's that for planning?"

Binta said, "Wow. I can barely plan ahead to lunch."

Beck patted her shoulder. "Welcome to motherhood."

"Anyway," Paul went on, "the agent says the client is actually keen to consider the place, if it were to be offered for sale—which, obviously, we know it will be."

"Did you tell her that?" Beck asked.

"I didn't want to sound overeager. I said you guys were considering the possibility and we'd let her know. But this is fantastic; you could save tens of thousands of dollars right off the top by not having to list it for sale."

Sophie said, "What, you mean by just dealing directly with this agent?"

"And a real estate lawyer we'd hire, yes."

"That *is* fantastic," Sophie said. "We should sell it now, as soon as possible.

Forget fixing it up. If he's this eager, just price the place as high as its condition warrants. We can split the money Mom set aside for improvements."

"We're getting ahead of ourselves," Beck said. "We don't know who this
client is or whether he actually has the funds or can get them. We don't know
what the house is worth in its current condition, or how much more we might
be able to get after it's fixed up. A little spit shining could be worth a lot more
than we'd get splitting the repair kitty and saving some commission. We
need to take our time with this."

Claire was nodding. "Yeah, I can see that."

Sophie said, "Okay, sure, I'm not saying you're wrong. But at the same
time, this buyer-bird may be sitting *right in our hands*, you know? Why beat
the bushes for another one? We owe it to ourselves to find out more. Could
be he's some careless rich guy who'll pay whatever price we name—I mean,
within the most generous range of reason. Maybe he wouldn't even want
it repaired; maybe he wants to tear it down and put up some gorgeous new
house."

"What? No," Beck said. "If that's his intention, he can't have it."

"It's all the same to us. We're not going to be there."

"*No*," Beck said again. "No. I won't agree to sell it to anyone who's got
that intention. Paul, we all have to sign off on any deal, right?"

Claire said, "Beck, the will doesn't say anything about the future disposition of the house, post-sale. A new owner can do whatever they want. You
can't stop it."

"Look," Paul said, palms raised, "all I need to know right now is whether
you three agree that we should let him see the place. That's all, just *see* it."

"Just get more information," Claire said. She was watching Paul intently.

Paul, uncomfortable under her gaze, said, "That's right. And if so, Beck,
you can go there this week to do a once-over, tidy things up, and give the
agent a key. She said the client is from out of town but is currently staying
with friends nearby. If you like, you can stick around, be there when she
shows him the place, maybe get a feel for his intentions. Yes, everyone?"

"Yes, please," said Sophie.

"Ditto," said Claire.

Beck, who was sitting with her arms wrapped around herself, was silently crying—leaking tears, really, the way she'd been doing off and on for days. She said, "Why did Mom want this? I just wish . . . I mean, really, this isn't what I . . . That is, I'd rather not deal with any of it." She used a tissue to wipe her eyes and nose, then said with resignation, "But okay, I will."

"Wear your new coat," Sophie said, taking Beck's hand.

Paul said, "And if for any reason this buyer's not the one, the house goes on the market the second weekend of April as per the will's timeline. Is it a plan?"

It was a plan. *Best laid*, and all that.

"And now for Marti's message." Paul cued the video to play on his computer screen and turned it so that all could watch.

Marti appeared, seated at her kitchen table with an oxygen cannula clipped to her nose. Her wavy silver hair was dull and thin, her face pale and devoid of makeup. Her natural beauty had been eclipsed by her illness and treatments, yet you could still see it in the warmth in her eyes, a reminder of the person she was behind and beyond the disease that had dominated her last few years.

The tender goodbye they were all expecting was something else entirely. This was a dying woman unburdening herself, finally, as the clock ran out. Marti spoke slowly and with difficulty, tears streaking her face toward the end.

When it was over, no one seemed able to speak. Finally Cammie broke the silence. "Whoa. I didn't have *that* on my bingo card."

11

The Courage to Continue

W hen Beck later wrote about her mother's little bombshell, she told
the story like this:

The day Marti Newman first met Leo Geller, it was high summer on
Mount Desert Island. As always in places like this, summertime meant opportunity for romance between tourist and townie. The girls who lived there
counted on it. Cute boys arrived from Boston, New York City, Philly, DC,
and from southern cities, too, their families in love with the rugged coastline,
the ponds and pines, the long, long days of June and July. In love with Bar
Harbor and the other harbors, with the villages that dotted the mountainous
land, in love with the mountains—quite modest by standards like the Rock-
ies and the Alps, but mountains nonetheless. In love with Acadia, its almost-
tamed wilderness, its stony, picturesque, well-worn trails.

The visiting adults loved to gather for regattas, for clam and lobster bakes,
the men freed of suits and hats, the women in sleeveless sundresses, naked
shoulders draped with fine cotton sweaters. Those slim cigarettes. Sandaled
feet. Alfresco dining. (They all wanted to be Italian; more specifically, Ro-

man, or at least *in Rome*; to be Audrey Hepburns with their Gregory Pecks.) Children chasing one another along rocky beaches and clipped lawns, running races, collecting stones, catching frogs, building forts in the woods. Summertime as an ideal realized, delivered to them whole cloth via generous salaries or generous relatives' trust funds and wills.

That was not Marti's life.

On this day, two weeks or so after her eighteenth birthday, she was no longer thinking about cute young men living la bella vita when she encountered a group on the steep trail that would take her down from the Beehive summit to Sand Beach. This being Wednesday, and early (she'd made summit at daybreak), she'd hoped not to encounter any tourists at all, at least not before she was off the mountain and on the beach again. She'd wanted sweeping, soul-cleansing views of granite and fog and trees and water. Wanted solitude. Birdsong. Sun catching the dew on pine needles, glinting off the sapphire water, lighting the shallows turquoise blue. But here came four clean-cut boys in their twenties, climbing the trail single file. She heard them before she saw them. Their easy laughter. Their shouts of good-natured insults of one another. Their observations of rocks. No, they definitely weren't from around these parts.

The leader spotted her and called, "Ahoy!"

He was medium in every measure: height, weight, general attractiveness, shade of brown hair. All four boys were brown-haired, clean-cut. All four were dressed in short-sleeved knit shirts and shorts and high socks and sneakers. The second and third wore dark-framed glasses. The third was half a head taller than the others. They looked like book-smart Jewish boys.

She raised a hand to her brow in salute, moving aside among some boulders to give the boys room to pass.

"Are you from here?" the leader said, stopping. The others stopped behind him. "We could use some guidance."

"*You* could use some guidance," said the second boy in line.

The one at the end said, "Max *is* in desperate need of guidance. Indisputably."

The third one said nothing. He just smiled in a manner that suggested he was there living his best life.

Marti's first lie occurred now, when on a self-protective impulse she said, "I'm just visiting. My aunt lives here."

"She's just visiting," said number four.

The lead boy, Max, said, "Are you here for the wedding?"

"Which wedding is that?" she asked.

"Ah, yes. It is June. There would be more than one, wouldn't there?"

"Idiot," the second boy said.

Boy number three spoke up. "The Bergman-Rabinowitz wedding," he said. "Bruce Rabinowitz is our friend. We all went to high school with him, in New York."

"Floral Park," said the fourth boy.

"On Long Island," boy three explained. "He's marrying Beth Bergman. By the way, I'm Leo Geller."

"Marti Newman," she said. They shook hands.

The other boys gave their names, but already Marti was paying them less attention. Something about this Leo Geller struck a chord somewhere inside her. This felt surprising and not wholly welcome. She hadn't been looking to pair up with anyone anytime soon. Maybe not ever again.

She said, "I don't know Bruce or Beth. I'm here to visit my aunt."

Max said, "But you do know—I'm certain you must know, given the direction of your travel—if it's worth it for us to continue our hike."

"*Is there really a great view?* is the question," said boy number four.

Leo Geller said, "You should come to the wedding."

"What, me?" said Marti, though of course he meant her.

"Yes, if you're free. It's Sunday evening in Bar Harbor, more or less. At the Bergmans' place. The wedding's going to be in their yard."

"Call that a yard?" said boy two. "A park is what it is. We had lunch there yesterday. They've got statues."

Max said, "Mr. Bergman is in finance with Mr. Rockefeller."

"Which Mr. Rockefeller?" Marti asked.

He shrugged. "Does it matter?"

"Anyway," said Leo, "you should come. If you want to, that is. As my guest."

Max said to him, "Would you look at you?" while Marti was doing just that, looking at Leo, who was looking at her and smiling that best-life smile. He beamed as if he'd eaten sunshine for breakfast.

His invitation was hard to resist. Not because she wanted to go to some rich girl's wedding, but because she felt warmed by Leo's smile and wanted to bask in it again and again. She was eighteen years old, and although she'd already been burned by false hopes, or maybe *because* she'd been burned by false hopes, this surprising warmth was ignition for romance, for longing, for things she could not quite articulate yet knew they'd be good for her.

She said, "It's a Jewish wedding, right?"

"It is very much that," said Max.

"Will any Rockefellers be there?"

"Low probability. I've heard their type are allergic to yarmulkes."

"What about Callaghans, the ones out of Boston?"

The boys' expressions were blank.

Marti said, "Never mind." Low probability there, too, she was sure. Mixing socially with Jews was still a thing most of those people wouldn't do.

She glanced again at Leo. What an open, genuine face. What an excellent smile! He was someone who could be counted on; she knew it just by looking at him. He wouldn't betray her, wouldn't crush her hopes or force her into terrible situations. He was a possible future, not an impossible past.

She told him, "Okay. Why not?"

"Should I pick you up?"

"Where are you staying? I'll meet you there. And yes—the view is wonderful."

In the intervening days, while Marti clocked her hours working at the farm that used to be her family's and now belonged to the smug McGilrays, who'd always acted superior to them, she replayed her encounter with the boys. With Leo. She knew almost nothing about him, but her impression of him was that he was exactly the kind of boy she ought to be with. Sunny. Respectful. Kind. Outgoing but not aggressive. As good as all of that: he was from elsewhere, and elsewhere was exactly where she wished she could be.

Two years ago, Marti wouldn't have paid a boy like him much attention. He wouldn't have seemed to offer enough of what she thought she needed. At sixteen, she'd been undone by her family's circumstances: they'd lost the farm the previous fall, forced out of the house she'd grown up in and into a mean little hut, almost, a bare-bones two-bedroom structure where their seasonal manager used to bunk, forced to be employees rather than employers. Her brother, Carl, after spending three nights there with their father raging drunk and their mother sullen, nasty, berating their father for her ongoing misery and his many failures, had enlisted in the Army and got sent to Vietnam. Marti had commandeered Carl's old Chevy and took a job waiting tables in Bar Harbor, to put herself in the way of a different path of escape: rich boys of summer. A dead-end path, as it turned out.

Now she mucked out the goat pen and thought about this latest boy, Leo. Was he rich? She didn't think so. In fact, she hoped he wasn't. That he hobnobbed with people who counted Rockefellers among their cohorts, if not their friends, was more than sufficient for what she now understood she wanted most.

"You should've seen how he looked at me," she told the goats, who bleated at her from the adjoining pen. "I could marry him."

Years later, when she recounted the story of how she'd known he was "the one" right from the start, she placed herself in her invalid aunt's dining room. "Aunt Rebecca and I—she was the loveliest old goat—were sitting down to dinner—potato soup with ham; she never bothered with keeping kosher—and I told her I'd met this wonderful young man, and that I believed I would marry him." There was, of course, no Aunt Rebecca. Marti had invented her that morning on the trail.

"What's this?" Marti's mother, Miriam, said on Sunday afternoon when Marti emerged from her bedroom wearing polished saddle shoes and a dress.

Marti would have worn heels if she'd owned any in good enough condition to wear. As it was, she was happy to have this dress, which had been fashionable when she got it two years earlier from a Bar Harbor boutique she'd set foot in only that one time.

Marti said, "My friend is getting married today."

"What friend?" Her mother sat at the kitchen table, smoking a cigarette and idly paging through a tabloid magazine. Her father was out. He was always out.

"Her name is Beth. You don't know her."

Miriam looked up from her magazine and pinned Marti with her gaze. "I don't know her because she's not real. You made this up to meet a boy—you think I don't know? Who is it this time?"

"She *is* real, and you can look her up in the newspaper when the announcement runs. Beth Bergman."

Miriam gave a dismissive wave and turned her gaze back to the tabloid. "You girls all believe marriage is going to save you. Didn't you learn anything?"

Miriam meant the rich boy from last summer, Chip. She meant the pregnancy. Marti's crushed hope that Chip would do right by her. Marti would never forget the day Chip's mother came here to say Marti was nothing to him but an amusement—an amusement!—and to give her two hundred dollars for an abortion. Marti, seven weeks into her disaster, took the money, and after less deliberation than she would have ever wanted to admit, she took the advice to put the whole sorry situation behind her.

Now Miriam was saying, "No one is going to save you."

Gathering her purse and keys, Marti said, "I know that, believe me." She left the house, silently adding, *I have to save myself.*

None of this meant that the love she would eventually profess for Leo was fabricated. So what if there was no Aunt Rebecca? You could wrap a truth around a lie and in that way change your fate.

"In case you're wondering: a smart girl likes to be practical," Marti said to Leo, meeting him in the lobby of his waterfront inn. The property was grand

and rambling, a onetime home to a Gilded Age scion who'd needed room to put up dozens of friends at a time. It smelled of sea and roses, scents carried in by a warm breeze through the rear doors, where a wide, manicured lawn ran down to a reedy stretch of coastline. Beyond it, so much blue and air so clear that the Porcupine Islands hopscotching across the Narrows looked near enough to touch.

Marti's remark was a preemptive one, in reference to her saddle shoes, which she showed off by extending one leg and pointing her toe. "Have you ever walked on a lawn wearing high heels?"

"Not yet," Leo said. "But then, it's only one-fifteen in the afternoon, and I haven't had any champagne."

"Precisely," said Marti. "A person has to be especially mindful of the champagne factor. I intend to consume every drop that's offered to me, and I don't like to topple over, or at least not in public."

"Tipple, but not topple. Got it," Leo said. "Besides, I happen to like saddle shoes. They have a sporty look to them."

As they walked outside, Marti said, "Are you a sporty guy?"

"I've been made to throw a baseball a time or two. I'm better at watching other guys do it. I hope you weren't looking for the Mets' next center fielder."

"I don't follow baseball," Marti said.

"Oh, well, that just means you're ripe for me to brainwash. Repeat after me: the Mets are the best team in baseball."

"I won't say anything I don't believe myself."

"Even better!" Leo said. "That gives me an excuse to make you come see them play and form your own assessment. Not," he added, "that I needed an excuse, if you should happen to find yourself visiting New York. I'd love to take you to a game regardless."

Marti laughed. "You don't even know me; how do you know you want to take me anywhere?"

"Are you familiar with Jung's idea of synchronicity?"

Marti shook her head. "What is it?"

"It has to do with there being a connection between every individual and the cosmos, the universe. It's about *meaningful coincidence*—like us meeting on the trail the other day, and now here we are, making plans to see the Mets play. It's about fate."

Marti liked the sound of this, the notion that their meeting was fate. She especially liked that he might think it was so. "I'd go to a game with you," she said.

"I'm going to hold you to that."

They'd reached Leo's car, a late-model Ford. "I borrowed it from my dad," he told her, holding the door while she got in. After he was in, too, he continued, "I live in Manhattan, and it just doesn't make sense to keep a car there. How about you? Where's home?"

This moment was her chance to come clean, to say that actually she'd grown up right here on MDI. She considered it. The weight, though, of that history. The risk that this sunny guy would be repelled by her darkness.

She said, "Are you familiar with Kentucky?"

"Well, I've heard of it. They race horses there, right?"

"They do," she said. "That's where I'm from. You've probably never heard of the town. Smithville," she said, since she couldn't name any actual Kentucky towns or cities with confidence. "It's so small it's not even on most maps."

"I'll bet it's *very* quiet, being so small."

"That depends on whether the neighbor's hounds are barking, or if anyone's running a tractor, or if the men get drunk and start arguing." Really, she was describing her life here on the island. She could've added, *and whether the TV is blasting a game show or soap,* since that's what her mother brought to the scene.

Leo said, "Make the dog a golden retriever and the tractor a lawn mower, and you've got life in the Long Island suburbs. God, I hate the suburbs— nothing against golden retrievers."

"I guess Manhattan is lots more exciting."

"It is! It's more of everything good: food, music, theater, sports. I'll never live anywhere else, if I can help it. You'll love it there."

Marti laughed again. "Okay, if you say so."

"I do say so." He reached for her hand and glanced over at her. "Will you come visit me there, for real? I know this feels fast. I don't want to scare you. I'm a nice, completely rational guy—hell, I'm an accountant! But I just have a good feeling about you. It's crazy, but I like it."

"I like it, too."

How easy it felt to sit there beside him on the car's wide bench seat. Thrilling, in one way, but also natural, like they were already old friends. Old friends who'd been apart for a while and had to fill each other in on what had occurred in the interim. She'd had one such good friend, Janey, who'd lived on the adjacent farm but then had moved down east when they were fifteen.

The drive was brief; the Bergman estate hugged the coastline just a few miles north of Bar Harbor, on Frenchman Bay. Parking for the wedding was being managed by a crew of skinny young men in matching black windbreakers, one of whom, when Leo pulled up to the porte cochere, directed Leo, "I'll take it from here," and handed him a plastic chip imprinted with the number 47.

Leo took his yarmulke from his jacket pocket and tucked the chip away in its place. Donning the yarmulke, he said to Marti, "Shall we?"

Marti sat frozen in her seat. Now that she was here, the whole scene was intimidating. The grand house, the parklike grounds, the kinds of people who were sure to be here . . . There was little danger that she would see anyone she knew. It was the atmosphere that paralyzed her, the scene of money and privilege and charmed lives and disregard for anyone who didn't have them.

Leo said, "What is it? Everything okay? I've scared you off, haven't I? You're trying to figure out how to get away from madman Leo."

"No, it's not that at all. It's . . . well, I just realized that I'm showing up without a gift."

"Oh, don't worry about *that*. They'll never know the difference."

She did not doubt that this was true.

Having relinquished the car, they were guided through the house and out to the rear of the property, onto a veranda that edged a tremendous treed park of a lawn, with the promised sculptures and paths and beds of flowers that certainly required a gardening staff. Under a stand of towering oaks, hundreds of white folding chairs encircled a chuppah erected on a dais. Each corner of the chuppah was beribboned, crowned with cascading bouquets of pink and white roses. Beyond this, three large white awnings covered tables set for dining. There was a wooden dance floor, currently empty. A chamber orchestra played some light and lovely tune.

Here on the veranda and out on the lawn, guests in summer finery milled and mingled. Waiters circulated with trays of champagne and canapés. "Fancy," Leo said, taking two proffered glasses. "Most times you don't get drinks until the reception."

Marti, on alert for any familiar faces, saw none, but noted a few women glancing at her shoes, some expressions registering amusement, others disdain. She held her chin a little higher. So what if she didn't have the money they did? She was here, wasn't she, same as they were? She was making a go of it. Living her life. In school, Marti had learned a Winston Churchill quote that stuck with her: "Success is not final, failure is not fatal: it is the courage to continue that counts."

She said to Leo, "Have you been to lots of weddings?"

Leo nodded. "It's like there's a marriage epidemic. I guess everyone wants to get it in before they hit thirty."

"You're not near thirty," Marti said. "Are you?"

"Twenty-five." He gave her a close look. "I know you're a little further from the big three-oh, but please tell me you're at least over eighteen."

"I am over eighteen," she said.

"Because, well—"

"You wouldn't want to date a girl who's got school in the morning."

"So to speak."

"Smart," Marti said.

"*There* you are, Geller." It was Max and the other boys, dressed, as Leo was, in simple dark suits, their hair slicked down, their shoes polished.

"You guys remember Marti," Leo said.

"Right," said Max. "Miss Newman, who is Not from Around Here. How are you enjoying your visit?"

"Better and better," she said, slipping her arm through Leo's. "How about you?"

"I count us lucky to have survived the bachelor's party."

"Oh?"

Leo said, "We should take our seats. That's not an evasion—the party wasn't *that* bad. They're signaling everyone, is all."

As they left the veranda and crossed the lawn, Marti watched the women pick and teeter their way to the chairs, some of them in heels too high or too spiky to be practical even on firm, level ground. Now the glances at her shoes were glances of grudging envy, of irritation that this nobody made them look foolish in comparison. Well, that was fine. She knew she didn't fit with this crowd, would never fit with this crowd. She'd tried once and failed. Move forward: that's what she told herself. Fate seemed to agree.

What a beautiful place for a wedding! What a beautiful day. Marti had never attended a wedding. She took it all in. Look at the groom standing there, somehow humble and prideful at once. Look at the bride, buxom and glowing in the satin gown bedecked in tiny pearlescent beads and yards of tulle and lace. How marvelous, this solemn yet joyous ceremony. How satisfied the family seemed.

An unmarried girl can't attend a wedding without imagining herself in the bride's role, in the bride's dress, thinking how the bride must (for good or ill) feel as if she's been made over as a princess or duchess, made the center of such pageantry as was happening here on the flower-shrouded, shade-dappled dais. Marti let herself pretend that she and Leo were the pair who stood under this chuppah and exchanged promises, that it could possibly be like this for her (even if not for them) one day.

The rabbi intoned the blessing, the groom stomped the glass, and voilà, a young woman became a wife, entitled and protected the way Marti hadn't ever been.

She couldn't help wanting some version of this. She was eighteen and damaged and eager, and so, so ready to make herself into something new. Something else. Someone else. Mrs. Some Good Guy, because that was what a young woman was supposed to desire and become, if she could. Marti hadn't yet been exposed to examples of feminine independence. Happily Ever After with Prince Charming, that was the thing to want.

If Marti was a fortune hunter, it was good fortune she was aiming for, nothing to do with money, everything to do with a second chance to be someone different from the Marti Newman who'd lain in bed with her pillow curled and pressed to her ears to muffle the insults and accusations her parents lobbed at each other in the next room. The Marti who'd gone hungry so often that her homeroom teacher began slipping her cheese sandwiches to help her get through the school day well enough to pay attention and make passing grades. The Marti who had dropped out anyway; cheese sandwiches could do only so much.

Twilight approached as the dinner ended, blessings were delivered, and the dancing began. The chamber orchestra now filled the air with romantic tunes. The wide wooden dance floor was rimmed with lanterns. Other lanterns were suspended from poles throughout the property, inviting guests to stroll the grounds as the fireflies appeared and the tree frogs took up their own music.

"Walk with me?" Leo said, rising from the seat where they'd had as fine a meal as Marti had ever eaten. A delicate poached salmon. Spring potatoes with some kind of herb she couldn't identify, cooking being one of the many things her mother never aspired to do. Asparagus with a delicious (and, to her, mysterious) sauce. More champagne. *What a life!* she thought, trying not to think any further along that line, the one that examined who gets to live this way versus who does not.

Marti finished her drink, dabbed her lips, and stood to join Leo. He held out his hand and she clasped it. He said, "I won't embarrass you with my poor dancing skills, but I'm great at walking. First rate."

"I don't mind. Not-dancing, I mean. I'm good at walking, too." She pointed at her shoes.

As they went, he said, "So, do you spend a lot of time visiting here? There's not much Kentucky in your voice."

Marti's face grew hot. She said, "Oh, yeah, well, I come here pretty often. Every summer since I was ten. My aunt, she's an invalid. Polio. I like to see her as much as I can."

"Generous of you to give up your summers."

"I never think of it like that. This is a beautiful place to be. Did you know that Bar Harbor was originally called Eden?"

"I did not! But your friends must miss you. And I'm sure there've been some boys who've wished you stuck around home."

"I met a boy here, though. His name is Leo Geller."

"Oh, *that* guy. I know him. He's swell. And lucky, if he gets to spend time with you. I'll bet he'd like to know what you'll be doing after your visit with your aunt is done. For example, would there be time for a stop in New York before returning home? And might you be going off—back?—to college in the fall?"

"Do you think I should tell him that I've got plans to move to New York later this summer?"

Leo stopped and turned to face her. "You do?"

"Yes," she said, and this part wasn't a lie; she'd been saving up to go. It was important, though, not to scare him off by being too forward or too eager. She invented the rest: "My friend Janey and I are planning to get an apartment. She's there right now to find a place."

"That's terrific! Leo will be delighted. He'll probably be so happy to hear this that he'll want to kiss you. What would you think of that?"

"I'd think he was moving pretty fast. But I think I'd like it just the same."

Then Leo did kiss her, and she did like it, and the die was cast. Or, she thought, had it been cast at time's beginning and they were merely living out the plan?

Whatever the case, by late July she would be in Manhattan with a room at the YWCA and a story about how Janey's plans had changed. Within a week of that, she'd have a job waiting tables and a spot in a secretarial program for the fall. She would invent and perfect a story for Leo that included Aunt Rebecca's sudden demise just before Marti left MDI, of being orphaned a few years earlier, of having no siblings, of being alone in the world. "But don't feel bad for me," she'd tell him, standing by Central Park's Angel of the Waters fountain while, around them, the city thrummed its particular New York rhythms, pushed those rhythms into her cells, into her heart such that she would come to feel she'd been born to the place.

She said, "I'm not the kind of person who stays sad too long or has lots of regrets. I feel so lucky to be here and to have you as a friend."

"More than just that, surely," Leo said.

More than just that: By the following February, she would have a husband along with her New York City life. But it had begun for them on Mount Desert Island, with a lie that would lead to something true.

12

Some Kind of Hero

n Bar Harbor the day after Marti's funeral, C.J. woke to a text from his
sister, Maya:

> Spoke with Avery but didn't say you were in Maine, like you asked.
> New job and fiancé keeping her busy. Gave her a nudge to connect
> with you. She was noncommittal.
>
> Will we ever get our family back the way it was, Cole?
>
> Nobody's perfect. Maybe you and Dad can call a truce, and then we
> can just be like every other dysfunctional family.

C.J. replied, Maybe we could. But why would we want to?

Now he, Deirdre, and Arlo were in the Callaghans' broad side yard, in
an open area that was sun-drenched today and would get plenty of light all
summer. C.J. forced a spade through frost-tipped grass into the thawing soil.
"This looks doable," he said.

Today there was no wind to speak of, making it easy to hear the ocean shushing against the craggy shore. Gulls cried out as they circled overhead in hopes of the handouts they'd been accustomed to in the warmer months. C.J. rendered the scene on a mental canvas: the stark contrasts of dun and evergreen and blue, with slashes of grayed white for shadowed patches of snow. A study of that craggy shoreline would require every shade of gray and brown for all the angles and depths of stone that climbed out of the ocean before yielding to the Callaghans' plateau.

Under Deirdre's direction, C.J. and Arlo had spent the past several days using stakes and string and neon spray paint to lay out the whole garden. Arlo had been earnest and cooperative, eager to learn and to help. Now the real work of the project could begin.

"You get that short shovel, there, and start here where we painted the line," C.J. told him. He moved a wheelbarrow to the spot. "Go shallow, like this." He demonstrated. "We want to take up the sod—that is, the layer of grass—and leave the dirt. Dump the sod into the wheelbarrow. Got it?"

"Got it," said Arlo. He pushed the shovel through the sod, as C.J. had done, and came up with about two square inches of turf, which he deposited in the wheelbarrow. He said, "I wonder if we'll find any arrowheads or bones."

"Only one way to know, right?"

The sound of a vehicle driving up to the house made them all turn to see a bright red compact car come to a stop. "Ah, that'll be the tutor," said Deirdre. "Did Arlo tell you she was coming? He said he would."

"I forgot," Arlo said. "Maybe it was a little bit on purpose."

"It's time he got back on track with his schoolwork. I've been helping him, but I'm not equipped to teach."

"Gram is smart, but she doesn't know *everything*."

C.J. watched a young woman get out of the car. She had big sunglasses and a thick brown ponytail, a gray wool coat. Deirdre left them to go greet her, moving with no more speed than C.J. had seen her use since she'd arrived there. Which is to say she was notably slow in every circumstance, it seemed. He hoped the house never caught fire.

He said to Arlo, "I'll guess that sometimes Gram has a hard time keeping up with you."

"I'm one of the slowest kids in my class and she's *still* way slower than me. It's because of something with three letters, my mom said."

"Which three letters?"

"C-something? I forget. It makes her heart need help, so she has a little box thing in her chest." Arlo tapped a spot near his sternum. "It's called a pacemaker? Gram says it only has one speed."

"Well, that would explain it. Let's you and me go over there to meet your tutor so that Gram doesn't have to walk back here."

"I already know her," Arlo said. "Miss Melissa. She helped me when I broke my leg."

"How'd you do that?"

"When Dad took me skiing, only the hill was a little too steep for me."

Stellar parenting, thought C.J. He said, "Still, let's go say hey. I'm sure she's gonna be happy to see you again."

They joined the two women. Up close the tutor looked mouselike, he thought. A pretty mouse, though: wide, dark eyes. Spray of freckles across her nose and cheeks. Slender nose, delicate chin. Under different circumstances, he might like to draw her, see if he could capture the delicacy of her features from various angles and in varying light. His serious drawing days were coming soon, once he secured himself a home. And now that Marti Geller had passed, he was going to get a look at her house on the lake. He hoped it would be a fit. Sure, the price would be higher than he'd intended to pay. He could afford it, though; even after the legal fees and his divorce, the money his grandmother had left him would cover the house and fifty or more years of living there simply, as he intended to do.

C.J. greeted the young woman. "Arlo tells me you're Miss Melissa. I'm C.J.—unofficial garden manager. Good to meet you."

She smiled shyly. "Hi, nice to meet you."

Deirdre told her, "C.J.'s a family friend who's here lending us a hand with a garden project."

"That's a nice thing to do," said Melissa. She leaned over to ruffle Arlo's hair. "I'm glad to see you again."

"What'd I tell you?" C.J. said.

Arlo turned to Deirdre. "I don't have to do school *today*, do I? Me and C.J.—"

"C.J. and I," Deirdre said.

"*C.J. and I* are supposed to be digging."

"And dig you shall, all day, if it suits you. School starts tomorrow."

Arlo said, "Miss Melissa, you can help us if you want to. I mean, if C.J. says you can."

"But it's not required," Deirdre told her.

"No, I'd like to." Again, the shy smile directed at C.J.

"As you wish," said Deirdre. "Let's get you settled, first."

C.J. nudged Arlo toward the car, saying, "We'll get Miss Melissa's things."

"We will?"

"It's what gentlemen do."

"I thought it's what workers do," said Arlo.

"It's both. And are we not working today?"

"I guess so."

"Then grab that backpack, there on the seat," C.J. told him, and took a suitcase from the trunk.

"She'll have the room at the end of the north hall," Deirdre said. "You go ahead; don't wait for me. Lunch at twelve-thirty. Dinner—"

"At six sharp," C.J. and Arlo said in concert.

"Correct. Don't be late."

Not twenty minutes had passed before Melissa joined Arlo and C.J. outside again. She wore suede boots and a green puffy vest and mittens. She did not ask for a shovel or offer to assist.

"It's nice out here," she said, squinting at them. "So sunny! Arlo, does the sun rise in the north, south, east, or west?"

"Gram said no school today."

C.J. laughed at this. "Too hard a question for you?"

"No. I know the answer. Why should I say it, though, when I don't have to?"

"Spirit of cooperation?" C.J. said. "Good manners?"

Melissa said, "It's my bad. Pop quizzes are never well received, even on school days. Here's a question you guys can help *me* with: is this island Mount *Dessert* or Mount *Desert*, and how did it get the name to begin with?"

Arlo said, "That's, like, three questions."

C.J. said, "Well, at least your brain still works for counting."

"Ha-ha."

C.J. told Melissa, "I had that very same question—the pronunciation thing, first time I came up here. I mean, look around: trees everywhere! Doesn't seem like any desert I ever heard of. But dessert makes even less sense."

Arlo said, "I like dessert to eat."

"Me, too," said Melissa. "Boston cream pie."

"Bananas Foster," Arlo said.

C.J. turned to look at him. "Bananas what?"

"Foster."

"What exactly is that?"

Arlo said, "You don't even know? It's bananas with ice cream and yummy sauce."

"What, that's all? Why's it need that fancy name? Double scoop of mint chocolate chip ice cream for me, waffle cone, thanks very much. Preferably eaten on a dock or a boardwalk in July."

Melissa said, "That sounds great. I'd go for that." She smiled at him in a way that seemed to suggest she'd go for more than just that.

He said, "Anyway, the whole 'how to pronounce it' thing is a debate that goes way back to the 1800s, maybe even earlier. Far as I can tell, you just have to make up your own mind on how to say it. Me, I'm team desert, because the name came from the French, and in French it means desert."

Arlo said, "Team dessert, because I want some." He gave C.J. and Melissa his most winning smile.

Melissa said, "Maybe we'll get lucky later tonight."

Did she wink at C.J. while saying this? He could've sworn she did. Then again, this young woman was probably no older than his daughter, and would she really see *him* as a prospect? And even if she did, it would be pretty damn forward of her to be flirting that way in a situation like this.

He was seeing things that weren't there. She was eager for some Boston cream pie, or whatever Deirdre might have on the menu tonight. Not for a middle-aged guy who could be her dad. He said, "Best thing right now is to keep our minds on our work. This garden isn't gonna build itself."

"All that fresh air is good for the boy," Deirdre said after Arlo, who'd nearly fallen asleep during dinner, was tucked into bed. She and C.J. were in the drawing room, where Deirdre had built a fire and was now sipping brandy. C.J. poured himself a scotch and sat down. Presumably Melissa categorized herself as "the help" and wasn't bold enough to behave differently around Deirdre.

C.J. said, "Fresh air's good for me, too. I'm sleeping like a baby."

"So is Arlo, which is what I hoped would happen if I brought him here. My Boston town house doesn't offer much in the way of activity for children, and frankly, we both needed a change of scenery. He really likes you, you know."

"I really like him. We can relate to each other. My upbringing wasn't all that different from his before he lost his folks."

"He doesn't really understand everything that happened—I protect him from that nonsense. He just knows his father wasn't such a great pilot after all. Did Joseph tell you the story?"

"He did. I'm real sorry."

Deirdre propped her feet on an ottoman and continued, "I told Anna way back that she had better never put Arlo on that airplane, unless she wanted me to report her for child endangerment. I told her she shouldn't fly with that fool of a husband, either. It's just a matter of time, I said."

"Why was that?"

"He had a drug addiction and the delusion that it had no effect besides the effects he liked."

"I've known guys like that," said C.J. "Can't tell 'em anything."

Deirdre nodded. "It's the money. It doesn't ruin all of them; my other children have done better. But Anna . . ." Deirdre shook her head. "She was a lot younger than the others—a surprise baby when I'd thought I was in the change of life, you know. When she first brought Forrest home to meet us—my husband Charlie and me; he died some years ago, now—when she brought Forrest home, Charlie tried to converse with him, but the boy was dull as a stone. His big accomplishment was that he could surf. We were sure Anna would get bored with him, but we kept our opinions to ourselves. You push children and they just defy you. Next thing we knew, the two of them came back from three months in Biarritz wearing wedding rings."

C.J. said, "It must've been awful hard to lose her, though. I really admire you taking charge of Arlo."

"There wasn't much choice in it, but thank you. My friends say I'm foolish to take him on full time. I'm eighty-six years old! I don't even have dogs anymore; they're too much effort."

"He'll keep you young," C.J. said, though he thought her friends were likely correct.

"Not young enough to be what he needs; I've decided to look into boarding schools," Deirdre said. "There are several very good ones in the region."

"What does Arlo think of that?"

"I haven't asked him, and I won't. I'll thank you not to say anything, either."

"Sure," C.J. said. It wasn't his business, after all.

Had she asked his opinion, though, he would've said he thought boarding school was exactly right for some kids, but for a wounded, introverted kid like Arlo? That was tougher to see. On the other hand, being parented full time by an old lady who, before losing her daughter, had been living a typical rich-old-lady life in Boston society, teas and museums and bridge games or whatnot, a woman who, for all her strength of personality, was not in the best health, was less than ideal, too. Lots of kids in the world had it far worse, though. That's what C.J. told himself, as a way to halt the other thoughts that tried to press in: thoughts like him taking on Arlo's care as, say, a foster parent. As a dad again, except better this time around.

Don't even think it, he told himself. *That is not on your agenda.*

Deirdre said, "Tell me, how goes the house hunt? I'm in no rush to lose you, but I know you've got a life to get on with."

"I suppose I do," said C.J. "Looks like I might have a chance at a place that caught my eye earlier but wasn't on the market. Owner passed away and the family might sell. Life's like a coin, isn't it? Bad fortune on one side, good on the other."

"A trite sentiment," she said. Then she smiled. "But true. And at least you didn't compare it to a box of chocolates."

Now Arlo was in the house with Melissa, the two of them seated at the kitchen table doing history and math while C.J. continued to dig out the turf along the stringed borders of the gardens-to-be. It was, he thought, akin to roughing out a subject in charcoal or pencil before rendering it with paint. Things had to be done in stages if you were going to get a result worth keeping. Stake and string the areas, dig out the turf, level the dirt, lay in landscape fabric to keep the weeds down, enclose the area with wooden panels, landscape timbers, or stacked stone, per plan, then fill it all with garden soil . . . If C.J. were to stick with this project the way Deirdre said she wanted him to, he could be here for a few more weeks, maybe longer. More time to get attached to the boy. More time to worry about his fate.

He looked back toward the house and saw Melissa watching him. She raised one hand in greeting. Smiled.

C.J. didn't return the wave. He was not the kind of man who'd shoot fish in a barrel.

Fact was, he wasn't the kind of man to shoot anything or anyone at all. But in the years before he'd fired the rifle and missed his father's head by maybe four inches, he had used to suit up in camouflage with his father and cousins and uncles for long weekends spent in duck blinds or deer stands, warming themselves with flasks of Macallan (Jim Beam was too lowbrow for these guys) and telling stories about past conquests of all kinds.

He'd been ten years old his first time out, and twelve when he bagged his first (and last) deer. The older guys had permitted (really: urged) sips of liquor in those years. Liquid courage, they joked, recalling their own nerves at that age. C.J. remembered training his rifle on the buck, seeing its breast in his scope, hearing the whispered exhortations to take the shot, the joy and then the horror when he'd felled the animal, that moment when he understood he had snuffed out its life for no reason other than something to do on a September Saturday.

He hadn't quit that day; he'd wanted to, but knew there would be questions, conclusions, judgment. Already they were razzing him about how he was better in art class than gym class. "Boy's a little soft," said his uncle Lindsey, poking his gut. "Watch that you don't get swishy, too." They all had a good laugh at that one. Not until he made the JV football squad could he extricate himself without consequence.

For a time after college, he'd been independent of his family, a young artist living in a creekside cabin outside Charleston, painting still lifes and creek views and working for a landscaper so that he could pay for rent and food. He thought of this time as Denise's "doctor years," when both of them were still trying to sort out who they wanted to be. In the meantime, he and Denise got on the phone regularly so that he could talk to his baby girl, which he was grateful to get to do.

Maya said Denise wouldn't call him so often if she didn't still want him. "Trust me," she said, "you'd never hear from her if there wasn't something going on, unless you had a court order saying she had to take your calls."

"Yeah?"

"Definitely."

C.J. thought Maya could be onto something, because Denise would drop suggestions like, might it be worthwhile for C.J. to at least *consider* the path of least resistance—that is, accept his father's standing offer for him to join the family business, become a Reynolds Fasteners executive? How difficult was his father, really? Surely Coleman Sr. was mellowing with age—and it wasn't as if C.J. and Senior would be working in the same room all day every day, right? He could still draw and paint to his heart's content in his time off. His mom and sister were saying it, too. His dad just said things like "When the hell are you going to grow up and face the music?"

He'd grown unsure of how he felt about Denise, but not about Avery: it was Avery saying "Daddy" that did him in. He worried that if he didn't make himself a daily part of her life, she'd start calling Denise's doctor husband by that name. She'd grow up thinking C.J. cared more about his art than he did about her.

He went to see his father and said, "Hey, so, I've been thinking we should talk about you putting me to work."

C.J., as VP of Operations, resigned himself to the suit-and-tie culture. He resigned himself to long, dull meetings with other suited white men. He tolerated the bland square office space he'd been given, with its square view of the bland courtyard. What he wouldn't do was put his feet directly into his father's tracks. Yes, he would learn all the ins and outs of running the multinational company the Coleman Sr. way. He also wanted to work on expanding their corporate philanthropy. Do more than make cursory nods toward funding new parks or donating to church charities. All kinds of arts programs were starving for financial support. C.J. was no bastion of virtue, but he did believe this was a better use of money than further fattening the board members' bulging wallets.

In his first week on the job, he'd gone to his father's office to give his pitch. He outlined a plan, then said, "These kinds of programs are as essential as the stuff we make out there in the factory."

Coleman Sr. leaned back in his chair and crossed his legs. "*Stuff*, you say. That *stuff* we make has paid for your whole life, including the years you spent screwing around in college finding your true identity or whatever horseshit that was. That *stuff* is allowing you to support a child, which Jesus knows you weren't doing too well from your shack on the creek. You ought to be thanking me.

"It's time you learn to do more than spend my money," his father continued. "I say this for your own good, son. Be the man Denise and Avery need you to be. And learn to play golf, for Christ's sake. No more of that artsy folderol."

"Sure, Dad," he'd said, and then he'd gone to Atlanta to persuade Denise to do what Maya was certain she'd be ready to do.

Two months later, C.J. bought Denise a diamond engagement ring she would be proud to wear in the company of all the other country club women who made up her social circle. Eight intense wedding-planning months after that, he put on his tux and watched Denise in the white gown of her (and her mama's) revised dreams, following little Avery up the aisle. He danced with her in front of four hundred guests. He sat on the rose-petal-strewn bed in their hotel suite, waiting for her to emerge from the bathroom clad in a figure-skimming white silk charmeuse nightie.

"It was worth the wait," he said to her, and to himself. He told himself he could withstand just about anything his father could dish out, because now he'd be raising his daughter in a pretty little low-country house, built new and decorated to perfection by Denise and her mama. Happy wife, happy life, that's what everybody said.

Somehow painting never seemed to fit into this happy life. He took up golf and rejoined the Reynolds hunting club so that Denise would still have a husband who kept himself busy with the right sorts of things. So that Avery would have a dad who fit in with her friends' dads. He did all the "guy" things while "his girls" did all the things they were supposed to do—day spas, weekend trips to cities with great shopping, getaways to various tropical eco-resorts for "wellness." These weren't bad activities, in and of themselves. It was the shallowness of the culture that troubled him. The idea that all of this was life's pinnacle. Denise, and then Avery, became everything a

certain kind of young woman was brought up to be. C.J. became their coun-
terpart. He tolerated this misfit life for twenty years because it was the price
for getting to be Avery's dad, for getting to see her grow up.

And now she wouldn't take his calls.

Those weekends in the duck and/or deer blinds, C.J. had nursed his
whisky, the shotgun or rifle resting in the crook of his arm. Whenever it
came time for him to take a shot at the duck or deer, he took careful aim
slightly above or beside or below his target. "Damn," he'd say when he
missed. "I ought to drink less before I shoot." Or "I think the sight's cal-
ibrated wrong." Or "A mosquito was biting my neck just as I was taking the
shot." He made himself into the Prince of Excuses. The others didn't care
that he always missed; his ineptitude made every one of them look better.
Years later, when C.J.'s uncle Lindsey testified at his trial, Lindsey said, "I
don't buy his excuse that he deliberately missed Coleman Senior's head;
no, sir, I don't. Why, I saw many a time when he leveled his rifle at a buck
in hopes of bagging it. Only reason he missed is because he's a terrible
shot."

Now C.J., out here on Deirdre Callaghan's lawn digging up sod, thought
of Arlo, imagined what kind of future was ahead for the boy, his careless
parents dead, his grandmother needing to shuttle him off to be raised by
an institutional staff for nine months or more every year. And in the other
months? During school breaks? Weekends? Who would put Arlo's needs
first? Deirdre wouldn't live forever, and the rest of the Callaghans, like
C.J.'s own family, were in large part a selfish bunch of hedonists. What
kind of influence was that for a child? He knew the answer all too well.

C.J. thought of how he'd seen Arlo that first day, digging in the flower
bed, talking about dinosaurs and precious gems.

He thought of all his failures. The excuses he'd made for the things he'd
done and the things he hadn't managed to do.

He thought about salvation—Arlo's, should he try to step in, if Deirdre
would even consider allowing such a thing; allowing him, the ex-con who'd

been charged with attempted murder, to raise her grandson. His own salvation, if that's what this scenario was offering.

A fantasy, he supposed. Him trying to be some kind of hero now, as if that would make up for everything.

13

Telling Stories

A t sunrise, Beck wore her orange coat and set off on her drive to Maine. She'd considered flying, but a road trip felt far less stressful than getting to and from airports—all the waiting, the reliance on airlines and schedules, and having to rent a car. *Simplify,* Beck told herself. Keep control of what little you can.

Though she was no less reluctant for the task ahead than she'd been on the night of Marti's funeral, she was (she told herself) resigned to the facts and had scheduled her time in Maine accordingly. She'd arrive this afternoon, take stock of the camp's condition, air the place out, and barring signs of anything dire, tomorrow morning have Carol Barksdale over for a preview meeting. "The worst thing I can do is waste my clients' time by showing a totally unsuitable property," Carol said when Beck spoke with her. "Not that I think yours will be that, but you know what they say: better safe!"

Beck stopped at the mini-mart to buy all her favorites for the occasion, treats she no longer allowed herself to keep in the house: Dove mini chocolates, seasoned rye chips, gummy worms, kettle corn. Comfort foods, so that maybe she would cry a little less than she'd been doing. So what if her mother had lied to her, to them, for decades? Have another chocolate.

At home she'd brewed mocha cherry coffee and filled two thermoses, waiting until Paul left the kitchen before also grabbing a slab of spice cake from the freezer, where they'd stashed the leftover shiva offerings. She'd be home again in three days and would eat clean for a week. She'd double up on vegetables.

Or maybe she wouldn't. Maybe she would eat chocolate for every meal and double the servings for dessert.

When Beck pulled up and parked at the camp, patchy fog hovered, shroud-like, in the trees and over the water. *Ghosts,* she thought. Her previously unknown-to-her uncle. Her newly revealed grandparents. Her mother, too, almost as mysterious as the others, and maddening because of that.

This green clapboard four-season house that most of the world would refer to as a cottage had almost nothing in common with the "cottages" that had been built for all those gilded families of the late 1800s and early 1900s, that era before income taxes made it so that the filthy rich had to scale back (for a while). No marble here. No iron gates. No golden decor. No music room, no conservatory, no library, no piazza. No servants to arrive ahead of Beck and prepare the place for occupation.

No, what Marti and Leo Geller had been able to afford was a one-story post-and-beam box comprising three nondescript bedrooms, one rudimentary bathroom, a kitchen that might have seemed modern in 1961, a high-ceilinged living room cluttered with comfortable but mismatched furniture, and a sunporch. The latter was, in Beck's opinion, one of its three graces—the first being its high ceiling, which lent the house a feeling of spaciousness, and the second being the stone-clad fireplace with its added blower. The sunporch had not only a full wall of windows but a heated slate floor, too. As a teen, she'd slept out there well into the fall on long-weekend trips, in part to get farther away from Claire and Sophie, whom Leo forbade from joining Beck. "Your sister needs her privacy," he'd told them.

"I need my privacy," she said now. "God damn it, Mom."

The only sounds Beck heard when she got out of her car were the ticking engine, water dripping from the trees onto last season's dead leaves, and a pair of loons—one near, one far—calling to each other across the distance of the partly thawed lake. Such peace! And the air smelled marvelous, so earthy, poised for spring's eruptions of green everything, everywhere.

The camp's setting was unchanged, yet from Beck's new perspective it seemed entirely different. Not foreign; rather it felt cell-level familiar: she was *of the island* in a deeper and truer way than she'd known. Her DNA had been formed in part from the soil and water and stone that made up this magical place. From potatoes, too, apparently. What did any of this mean, though? What difference, if any, did it make?

If only her mother hadn't directed them to sell the place. This tranquility, these scents, the promises of renewal and abundance, all would have been awaiting Beck every time she found time to come here to write. That, and solitude—which was different from the solitary time she had at home four days every week, while Paul was at work in the city.

To stay here would have meant not having to pay any attention to what Paul was doing at the moment or would be doing in the future or might want her to do later or sooner. It would've meant no obligations to socialize. It would have meant mental space in which to erect the scaffoldings upon which she would build her novel's plot and characters. At home in Irvington, she was Beck Geller the wife, the cook, the laundress, the neighbor, and whenever opportunity presented itself, the journalist. Here, she could've been Beck Geller the novelist—a taller, less aggressive Jo March. Not so brash as Jo, maybe, but fully as thoughtful and talented. She hoped.

Young Beck had thought Jo March a fool for rejecting Laurie. Young Beck had thought herself much wiser for marrying Paul. Older Beck was embarrassed by her young self, that earnest, naïve idealist who'd believed she had everything figured out. That nineteen-year-old girl who'd rushed into marrying sweet, unassuming Paul, a man she was sure could never break her heart the way his predecessor had.

Not counting her two kids and a freelance résumé of many well-placed, well-received long-form articles and about as many interviews, what did Beck have to show for her twenty-six years of adulthood? Some of those articles were important—or rather, the topics were. She was proud of her work. The trouble was, even with the internet, periodicals were ephemeral. But a novel could endure. It could become iconic. It could change people's lives. Most didn't, but still, even if all hers ever did was help someone pass the time in a way that was meaningful to them, it would be worth the effort.

If she ever made the effort.

She had wanted to make that effort *here*. But maybe her mother thought she'd just been making excuses.

Had she just been making excuses?

Beck unlocked the front door and stepped into the dim, stale space. It smelled of mothballs and the lingering molecules of meals long past. She opened the curtains on every window, turned up the heat, and went to the breaker box in the hallway to switch on the water heater—where she discovered and removed a mouse nest. That done, she assessed the overall condition of the house, trying to see it the way the Realtor or potential buyer would. Mostly the place needed some strategic subtraction and a few artful additions. For her current purposes, though, she'd focus on hiding the clutter and rearranging the furniture. If it turned out that this camp wasn't a good fit for Carol Barksdale's client, Beck would move ahead with further repairs and updates.

There was a knock on the door, and a woman called out, "Hello? It's Helen. Can I come in?"

"Helen!" Beck said, going to hug the elfin neighbor who'd lived up the road for as long as the Gellers had owned here. She was snowy-haired and had a slight hunch to her back, made more pronounced by her bulky down coat. Her black boots had a butterfly print.

Beck said, "Come in. You didn't have to trek over here! I told you I'd pop in for a visit."

"Gave me an excuse to move these old bones."

"Well, it's good to see you."

"You too, honey. I'll only stay a minute. I was so sorry to hear about Marti. Such a shame. You came alone?"

"Yes," Beck said. "Everybody else has to work. I'm between assignments."

"That reminds me, I read the interview you did, in last month's *AARP*. That funny actor. What's his name?"

"Steve Carell."

"That's right. I guess you know everybody famous by now."

"I've only done a few of those interviews. It's Sophie who knows all the celebrities."

"You New York City girls and your high-toned lives. Marti sure was proud of you, *and* your doctor-sister. My son manages a cardboard recycling plant in Iowa," Helen said. "Remind me, how long will you be here?"

"I'm not sure. It depends on what all I need to do to shape things up."

"What was your mother thinking, telling you to sell? You don't want to do that."

"You're right," Beck said. "I don't want to. I love it here so much! But it's not up to me."

"I forgot to tell you, the Barretts are selling, too. You remember them, the people from Pittsburgh? Dale's got the Alzheimer's and Mary had to put him in a home. She doesn't want to come here by herself."

"Oh, I hadn't heard about Dale," Beck said. "That's sad news."

"Entropy or disease," Helen said with a shrug. "One or the other is going to get us all. Are you hungry? I've got chowder on the stove."

"Thank you, but I couldn't eat a thing—I snacked the whole way here."

"All right, then. You'll come to dinner tomorrow. Don't say no. Are you the one who always loved my chocolate cream pie?"

"That's me."

"Then it's on the menu. Halibut, fresh from Hodgdon's, too. Come at five-thirty."

Beck said, "You're very thoughtful, but—"

"What I am is an ornery old lady who won't take no for an answer."

"I just don't want you to go to so much trouble on my account."

Helen waved off the remark. "Who ever thought of pie as trouble? You're doing me a favor by giving me an excuse to indulge. You wouldn't think that at my age I need an excuse, but it's hard to talk yourself out of eighty years of conditioning. You didn't ask for my advice, but I'll give it to you anyway: you want to change something about your life, don't wait till you're long in the tooth."

"Mom said she wished she had taken cabs more often."

"*That* was Marti's big regret?"

"One of them," Beck said, thinking of the video, her mother's hidden past. "Say, do you happen to know of a family that used to farm here on the island, their name was Newman?"

"Doesn't ring a bell. How far back?"

"In the sixties. Probably later, too."

"I came from Vermont in '77. Could be they were gone by then, or they moved in a different circle. Old flame of Marti's?" Helen asked. "I remember she said she used to come here summers to visit a sick aunt."

"Something like that."

"Here's another piece of advice: stop the regrets before they can start." Helen let herself out. "See you tomorrow."

Now sunset was approaching. The fog had dispersed enough to let the late-afternoon sun pour into the living room. Beck faced the window and closed her eyes, bathed in the light. Stop regrets before they can start? Easy to say, tough to do. Already Beck regretted agreeing to have the real estate agent come tomorrow morning, or at all. Though what else could she have done? Tried harder to persuade her sisters to keep the place, she supposed. Not that it would've helped. When they'd heard there was someone already interested in buying, their compasses pointed straight at him.

Beck put her coat back on and went outside. She walked down the stone path to the water's edge, then turned to look at the house, which glowed in the sunset's heavy orange light. With the Gramercy apartment gone forever, this property was her entire legacy—and maybe that wasn't much when compared with, say, the Rockefellers' holdings, but it meant something to her. She had connections here, deeper than she'd known, and ambitions that had nurtured her when it seemed that little was going right. A gay husband. A dying mother. A dead mother, now.

Here was where she was supposed to write her novel. Here was where she'd first fallen in love, as her parents had done. And although that romance had led to crushing heartbreak, that heartbreak had led to her marrying Paul. Which hadn't quite been what she'd thought it would be, but it had given her two great kids and a secure life, and who knows what she would have become if not for all of that? She might have ended up in Iowa, managing a cardboard recycling facility.

Beck wondered whether knowing about her mother's boy-of-summer heartbreak might have prevented her own, helped her avoid sweet-talking troublemakers in the first place and, in turn, led her into the path of a man who would've desired her passionately, out of bed and in. Though, in truth, Marti *had* warned her about summer romances (warnings Beck now realized had more behind them than she'd known) and she'd ignored them, same as any teen would do. Maybe some things really were fated to happen no matter what. Maybe God or the universe simply wanted it that way. She couldn't blame her mother for that.

What Beck did blame her for was this unexpected obstacle to her writing dream. Was it punishment for failing to have done more, sooner? Was it because, when it came to writing the novel (here, or anywhere), Beck had been all talk, no typing?

When it came down to it, Beck couldn't blame her mother for much of anything.

That said, Marti enacting punishment posthumously did seem out of character. She wouldn't have encouraged Beck all this time, only to then use her will to say, *Sorry, honey, you blew it*. Or maybe she would? Beck could no longer say with confidence what her mother would or wouldn't have done.

She sat on the dock and wrapped her arms around her knees, feeling displaced in every way. Was she a New Yorker, or did she belong in Maine instead? At the moment, influenced perhaps by the ghosts of her mother and her mother's family, she felt more inclined to a life here.

The more she thought of it, the righter it felt. Yes. Yes, that was the fix. She should *live* here, where she could get her cardio climbing the mountainside stone staircases laid in by MDI's first benefactors and then later by Civilian Conservation Corps workers during the Depression. Where she could exercise her soul by traversing Acadia's scenic carriage roads, same as Bar Harbor's founding millionaires used to do. If she lived here, she could write fiction every day. She could eat lunch with the harbor seals at Pretty Marsh, the way she'd done when she was a teen, she and her summertime girlfriends piling into a car to get away from the parents and the siblings so that they could sit around eating junk food and talking about— what else?—boys.

And speaking of boys: in marrying Paul when she was just nineteen, had she taken a wrong turn and simply kept going because she thought the path resembled her parents' path and would therefore result in the same kind of satisfaction they'd enjoyed?

As for her work, were articles and interviews her entire writing future, or could she resurrect the Jo March inside her and weave her own stories instead?

Not long ago, after a flower-arranging class in which Beck had created a stunning centerpiece on her first try, her friend Gina had said to her, "Is there anything you don't excel at?" and Beck had warmed herself in the compliment. "Thanks," she'd said, feeling proud of her work. She did excel at most things—because she almost never stepped outside the narrow lane of safe possibilities. She played only to her strengths, so of course she appeared to be one of those perfectly accomplished, perfectly together women who lived a perfectly happy life. She avoided the hardest things, the risks, the potential failures that would show the world how scared she was to feel vulnerable or be seen as *less than*.

Was that the person she wanted to be? No. *No*. She didn't respect that person or admire her. She didn't want her kids to go on thinking that was who she was. If her mother could see her, she didn't want her feeling justified in having directed the camp's sale because Beck couldn't follow through.

Beck said, "It's time to fish or cut bait. That's all there is to it."

After tidying up in advance of the Realtor's visit tomorrow morning, Beck went out onto the sunporch, turned on the lamp, and called Sophie. She paced as the line rang several times. When Sophie picked up, Beck said, "I want to talk to you about letting the Realtor come see the camp."

"Oh, right, that's tomorrow, isn't it? Sorry—I'm shopping for a friend's bridal shower and my brain is consumed by the banality of it all. Dildo-style lollipops, seriously? A tiara for the bride-to-be? Sashes—as if an impending marriage is the culmination of a beauty contest, with bride and bridesmaids parading in swimsuits and heels . . . It's fucking depressing. Why does everything that seemed so fun when we were all twenty-something seem so juvenile or sexist or pointless now?"

Beck said, "Is this a serious question?"

"No, I know the reason, and it starts with 'thirty-six.' As for your matter: you're doing the right thing. It makes total sense—it could lead to a fast, easy sale."

"But suppose selling it is the *wrong* thing to do."

"Wrong for *you* is what you're saying. I know you don't like it, but it was Mom's decision and I think we should follow her instructions."

"What if she was mistaken in thinking that's what we wanted. Befuddled about it."

"That's a word?" said Sophie. "Kidding!"

Beck ignored her. "Influenced by her meds—or the cancer might have spread to her brain."

"You don't really think that."

Beck said, "Okay, no, I don't."

"*I* think she wanted to cut the cord with MDI for good. She just couldn't face you to do it while she was alive."

This had not occurred to Beck. "I hope that's not true."

"Look, I don't know what's true, but I'm sure she had her reasons, whatever they were."

"Don't you wish you understood her better?"

"I do understand her," said Sophie. "As I said last week, none of this changes her for me—except maybe I like her even more, because she wasn't as squeaky clean as I thought. She hid things. I get it. If she'd told Dad about her past and it put him off, we wouldn't even exist."

"And we wouldn't have this camp, either. But we do exist, and we do have it, so we have to deal with what's real. Do you truly have no interest in keeping it? It's the only tangible piece of our history we've got."

Their father's parents had died when Beck was too young to remember them, so other than Leo's inheritance funding the purchase of this place, Beck had no connections to those Gellers. There was one other Geller, Leo's older brother, who'd never married; Beck had seen him only once before Leo's funeral, and not at all since then.

Their mother's family had been merely a sad story that Marti told with few details: the father dead in a workplace accident of some kind, the mother from an allergic response to a wasp sting. Both of them gone when Marti was in high school in Kentucky. Social Services had put her in foster care for the duration. No siblings. No extended family left. Little Beck, her head full of girl-child horse lust, envisioned young Marti as a lost filly, all long legs and flowing mane, wandering the Appalachian foothills, hungry and lonely as she made her way through wind and rain, eventually reaching the house of Beck's namesake, old, invalid Aunt Rebecca (the house torn down long ago, of course), where she magically transformed into a young woman—and then made a new family with Leo.

Yeah. Not quite.

"MDI is great," Sophie was saying. "Don't get me wrong. The history part is interesting, and I enjoy visiting. But camp is a bit, um, let's say *quaint* for my tastes."

"Well, sure, compared to how you live. But quaint is good! Quaint is comfortable and full of solid middle-class character. Like me—and you love me, right? Also, this quaint place is free! Nearly free—we just have to pay property tax and insurance. If we kept it, I'd be willing to shoulder that on my own—"

"I totally get it, but really, Beck, I just want to sell and be done with it. My love for you notwithstanding, money is way more appealing. I was browsing similar homes on Zillow, and we could be looking at something close to a million dollars in value."

Beck said, "I doubt that sincerely."

"And I assert it sincerely. Waterfront property, in one of the country's favorite summertime destinations—it's high-demand."

"It has one bathroom."

"But three bedrooms, and a sunporch, and acreage."

"Let's not debate it. Whatever the value, you don't *need* the money. Claire doesn't *need* the money."

"What you're ignoring is that neither Claire nor I are going to use the place, but I can assure you we both have every intention of using the money. You could use the money, too, you know. Buy your freedom, basically. Don't you want to do that? Why wait for Paul to make the first move?"

"No, sure, you're right," said Beck. "The thing is—well, I just realized that I want to live here."

"What, in Maine?"

"Yes—but don't say anything to Paul about it, okay? I haven't figured all of that out yet. Anyway, how about I pay you rent? Would that work?"

"Oh, honey. I'm sorry, but no, I need—see, I have this thing, remember? This start-up that I said I would invest in—"

"Okay," Beck said, thinking of other options, "then suppose I buy you out."

That would, of course, mean that everything she'd said the other night up in Tania's penthouse—about being ready for Paul to unburden himself and move forward on a separate path—had to be rethought; she couldn't get a loan if they were separating households and incomes. So then, okay, if it came down to it, Geoff, or whoever Paul might want to canoodle with, could move into the Irvington house. Why not? She'd hardly ever be there anyway; she'd be here, proving her mother wrong for thinking the camp could and should go.

Beck said, "I'd pay Claire, too, if that's what she wants. Would you go for that? Then there'd be no question about following the will or needing the court's consent."

"You're serious? Even if you take a conservative guess at value, we're talking about hundreds of thousands *each*. I didn't think you had that kind of cash on hand."

"I don't. I'd have to see if I could get a loan. Either a new mortgage or borrow against our house—mine and Paul's, depending on what kind of equity we've got. Obviously I haven't run any numbers yet—I mean, I'm still just spitballing here—but I might be able to swing it."

Sophie said, "It's your life. I guess if Claire's cool with you buying us out, I would be, too—but you'd have to pay us market price."

"I know," Beck said.

"And you should meet with the Realtor tomorrow, regardless. In case we have to go that route."

"No, right, I will."

"Okay, well, if you can work it out by the deadline for listing the place, I guess I'm good with it. Hey, I'm at checkout—gotta go. Keep me posted."

"Of course."

Beck ended the call and stood in her socks on the warmed stone floor while the moon rose, casting its glow over the firs and the naked hardwoods and the glassy black surface of the water. What if she could do this every night? She said, "There, Mom, what do you think of that?"

After calling Claire, repeating her plea, and getting the okay to attempt it, Beck poured a glass of wine and sat down with her journal to make notes and sort things out. If she got everything on paper, she'd be able to stop thinking about it so much and get some sleep. Then tomorrow she could put her plan in motion.

This morning's meeting with Carol Barksdale, the real estate agent, would not be a complete farce, though it felt like one to Beck, whose head was freshly full of details on how to get a loan. She'd been up at dawn researching home values and mortgage rates, looking at records of her income and assets. She'd need Paul as co-applicant on a loan, but he wouldn't have to pay for anything as long as he was willing to let her take out half of the money they'd set aside for the kids' college expenses and use it for monthly payments. That was fair. That was how they'd divvy things up anyway, eventually. She didn't let herself think too hard about *that* part of this—the divvying, or the emotional toll that upending their marriage would take, amicable as their split was sure to be. One thing at a time.

The meeting with Carol would allow Beck to gauge the accuracy of Sophie's and the internet's guesstimate of value—and possibly be a backstop, should Beck fail and have to sell after all. Which she wouldn't, unless she couldn't persuade Paul to cooperate. Hence this gathering of information before she even brought the matter up to him.

The Realtor arrived. "Hi! Thank you *so much* for agreeing to this!" The woman was as friendly and energetic as a golden retriever. "As I said when we spoke, I like to get a quick preview of new prospects, especially if they haven't been on the market for long, or at all."

"I'm sure your clients appreciate it."

"Realtors do *a lot* of homework. People don't realize this. They think we just show houses or stick a sign in a yard, and then collect a fat check. When, really, we're more like doctors."

"Doctors? How so?"

"Well, lots of ways. People come to see us with their problems, so that's one. And then we have to investigate and diagnose and treat the problems. Research things. Make referrals to specialists—say your house needs window repairs, or you've got radon to mitigate. Dr. Carol Barksdale, at your service."

Beck said, "Huh, I never thought of it that way. But sure, I can see it."

"Doctors and matchmakers: that's really the profession in a nutshell. Call me Dr. Yentl."

Beck said, "I think you mean *yenta*. Which is not actually the term for a Jewish matchmaker."

"Are you sure?" Carol said, skeptical. "I saw *Fiddler on the Roof* two times."

"The character is *named* Yente; she's not *a yenta*. You'd be Dr. Shadchan. That's Yiddish for *matchmaker*."

Carol wasn't convinced. "That sounds Chinese or something."

"I promise you it's not. A yenta's a gossipy busybody."

"Oh, well then, that's not me at all. I take my clients' privacy seriously. In that way I'm a priest. Or an attorney. Words are so interesting! My client— the one who may be in the market for this house—he and I had a similar discussion when we first met. And by the way," Carol added, gazing around, "I have to say, the house is surprising. I wouldn't have guessed it was post-and-beam. So much light and space for its size. It's got character."

"I was just saying as much to my sister."

"There are three of you, is that right? And you're all willing to sell?"

Beck said, "There are a lot of variables, but yes, we want to explore our options."

"Great. Now, obviously one big factor is going to be price. To get a good sense of that, I pulled the public records to check age, square footage, and so on—I told you, research! I've looked at comparable properties, recent sales, and so forth, and now that I see its condition, I'd say we're in the ballpark of eight-fifty, give or take."

"Really? Okay. Good to know."

"You sound disappointed. It's true that there are properties here that sell for much more, but those are larger, newer homes, or homes where everything has been updated to the latest trends."

"Of course," Beck said, pretending that she'd hoped for a higher rather than a lower value.

Carol said, "Even at that price, I do understand why your family might prefer not to list the property with an agency. The commission takes a big bite— not to say that we don't earn every dime! The problems that come up! You see why I have to use hair dye." Carol pointed at her presumably otherwise-gray hair. She said, "Anyway, the good news is that I can recommend the property to my client with enthusiasm, and if he's as interested as I predict he's going to be, you may have a quick and easy transaction to look forward to. Everything tidied up, everyone happy. That's what Dr.——what did you say the word was, the matchmaker word?"

"Shadchan."

"That's what Dr. Shadchan aims for. Then we'll all say *L'chaim!*" Carol pretended to raise a glass. Then she said, "If it's all right, I'll have a quick look at the rest of the house before I get out of your way. Do you mind if I take a few pictures? I'll make sure you aren't in them."

"No, sure, go ahead."

When Carol was finished, she returned to the living room. "Shall we set a time for me to come by with my client? I've got an opening late this afternoon, if that's convenient for you. Let's plan for four o'clock, and then if that's not good for him, I'll let you know ASAP, or you just call me if you need to change it."

"Four. Okay. Sure," Beck said, agreeing to this plan because the surest way to jinx *her* plan was to get overconfident.

As soon as Carol was gone, Beck prepared herself for her conversation with Paul. She told herself that what she was about to do was not lying so much as deferring the truth until a more convenient time. There was no real harm in doing it this way. It was a matter of expedience, that's all. He'd probably thank her for that, praise her forethought, consider it to have been considerate, Beck looking out for him the way she'd always done.

She placed the call. When he answered, she said, "Hi, do you have time to talk?"

"A few minutes. What's up? How was the meeting?"

"Everything went fine. But I have an idea and I need to run it by you."

"Let's hear it."

"It's about how to keep the camp and still abide by the will: we buy it from Soph and Claire. They've already said they're okay with it. I've worked out the numbers, and what we'd do is apply for a new mortgage—"

"Hold on. You asked them before even bringing it up to me?"

"There'd be no point in bringing it up to you if they weren't in agreement."

Paul said, "The reverse is also true, you know."

"Okay, yes," Beck admitted, hoping they weren't going to derail over this. "I apologize. I didn't look at it that way."

He said, "Do you really think the place is worth hanging on to? That is, I understand the sentimental attachment, but the expense would be significant."

"I—"

"Though if you're thinking of making it a vacation rental, I can see how it might pay for itself."

"Yes, exactly! You are a mind reader," Beck said. "So, that being the case, here's what I'm thinking: the structure is in good shape, but inside is rougher than I expected. Really beat up. Maybe some raccoons got in? So I think I should stay here and do the necessary work myself—make the fix-up fund go farther, you know? I can get the place ready to rent while I'm waiting for loan approval. And if for some reason we can't get the loan, the improvements will make it a lot more marketable. We'd get multiple bidders, no question." This part, at least, was the truth.

And she would take up the novel again. No time like the present, right? Make every day meaningful. Stop a possible regret before it could start.

Paul said, "Before you go too far, you should talk with some property managers and get hard numbers. Make sure the expenses won't outpace the income."

"Right, yes, I'm going to do that." (She was not going to do that.)

"And call Howard, see what the tax implications would be."

"Yes, good idea." (Just not one she planned to act on.)

"Will you still have your 'sisters weekend' as planned?"

"Absolutely. It'll be good for us to spend time together without all the commotion and stress of the funeral."

"What about clothing?" Paul said. "You didn't pack for an extended stay."

"True. I'll buy a few things—I think there's a thrift shop in Bar Harbor. It's not as if I'll be socializing much, anyway."

"Okay, well, if you're sure owning a rental is the route you want to go . . ."

"It is, definitely," she said. Another lie. "I should have thought of it sooner."

Once everything was done, signed, and sealed, she would tell him she'd changed her mind about renting. They could talk about other matters, too. What the future ought to look like for each of them. Beck living here full time, writing a novel—no matter what Paul thought about her chances of success. Paul doing whatever it was he wanted to do, with whomever he wanted to do it.

He said, "So I guess you'll be there a while."

"A few weeks, at least. It's going to take a lot of elbow grease. Fortunately, I don't have anything else on my plate right now, workwise; I wanted to take a little time, you know, to process everything."

"Yes, good," Paul said. "So all right then, I'll just fend for myself until you get back." He sounded almost cheerful about the prospect.

"Just don't eat out every night, okay? You need to keep an eye on your cholesterol."

"Don't worry, I will be moderate."

"But enjoy yourself. Go see a show with a friend. Take advantage of that city of marvels."

"I'll do my best not to mope around the house while you're away."

"Good," Beck said. "You deserve to have some fun."

She heard a voice in the background. Then Paul said, "Hang on, Geoff. Beck, I want to talk about this in more detail later, okay?"

"Yes—but you're all right with me proceeding with the loan application?"

"I guess so. It's not a commitment."

"Good. Okay. *Thank you.* Really. This means so much; I can't even tell you."

"I just want you to be happy."

"And I want *you* to be happy," Beck said. "Tell Geoff I said hello."

Thrilled by her success, Beck went outside to the dock, filling her lungs with crisp air. She wanted to cheer! This was really happening.

Beyond the lake's icy edge, the water's deep sapphire color contrasted richly with the gray-brown of the naked hardwoods and understory. Clouds were moving in, but for the moment, sunlight glinted on gentle ripples. Such stark beauty. And in the warmer months, a whole other kind of beauty. Long days and fireflies and visits from friends and the kids . . . She could have Leah here for a while every summer, give Zack and Binta time to travel by themselves. Beck imagined the profile of herself that might run in the *Times*, if she turned the entirety of her dream into reality: *Manhattan Native Beck Geller Pens Debut Novel After Reclaiming Family History on Mount Desert Island.*

"It will be a test," she said.

Part of that test now involved doing more home-improvement work than she had anticipated. Luckily, she was capable and experienced there. She'd watched HGTV at the gym so frequently and had applied what she learned so many times that she could host her own show if given the chance.

As soon as she'd filled out her credit union's loan application online, she would go into town to gather groceries and supplies, maybe find something pretty for the camp while she was at it, for inspiration. Yes, that was the thing. As for this afternoon's appointment with the Realtor and her client, what purpose would it serve? None, now that Beck had put off the possibility of selling for a few weeks at minimum, and maybe forever.

Before she left, she texted Carol:

> Beck Geller here. Apologies but I am canceling the house showing we arranged for later today. Change of plans. I'll let you know if and when we intend to sell. Thanks so much for your trouble.

The sky had darkened and was threatening rain. In Bar Harbor, Beck made a first stop at the hardware store, then found a parking spot on Firefly Lane beside the Village Green, which on this day was brown and barren. In summers long past, Beck had chased Sophie around and around the seventeenth-century Italian fountain donated to the town long ago by John Livingston, a soigné who'd built an imposing brick "cottage" over on Schooner Head Road. Beck didn't know much about the Livingstons, except that there were many of them and they had lots of money and numerous fancy homes in the area. They'd rubbed elbows with someone she did know, however: Edith Jones, who became Edith Wharton and chose to eschew Bar Harbor, where her brother lived, in favor of Newport, Rhode Island, as the Astors and Vanderbilts were also doing. Beck had always liked to imagine she was walking the same sidewalks young Edith had walked when she, too, was in her nascent writing years.

Edith's friend Henry James paid visits to Bar Harbor before he was her friend. Badass Alva Vanderbilt stayed here in her brother-in-law George's summer home in those days before he chose Asheville for Biltmore and compiled its library of 22,000 books. And a girl named Marti Newman met a boy here, a boy who would have ruined her if she had not been strong and determined enough to overcome her troubles. Then she met a better one. He, too, was now gone and yet not gone from Beck's recollections—especially now, when she was thinking so much about that seminal meeting between her parents on the Beehive trail. This island was filled with ghosts.

Beck provisioned herself in the thrift shop, then entered a shop whose display window showed it wasn't one of those tourist traps full of cheap, mass-produced generic prints of fir trees and sailboats and sandpipers. There were original paintings here—pretty good ones, she thought, scanning the woodsy, brightly lit space. The shop had only a few customers, including a tall elderly woman draped in an array of colorful scarves (*Me at eighty?* thought Beck), a cerebral-looking man who stroked his goatee as he peered at the offerings, and a sandy-haired middle-aged man who was crouched down beside a dark-haired boy pointing to and talking about one of the paintings.

Beck was struck by the warm intimacy of the scene, the obvious affection the man had for the boy—his son, she presumed, though there was no clear resemblance. The boy was pale, with vivid blue eyes. The man, whose style might be described as upscale grunge (expensive well-worn denim; T-shirt under plaid flannel; handsome wool overshirt; quality leather work boots) looked like the kind of guy who might've spent his winter someplace sunny—on a surfboard, maybe, or a sailboat. Yes, probably an expensive sailboat—no, a yacht, and it was anchored here in the harbor, and maybe the man was visiting his son who'd wintered here with the man's ex-wife, who was one of those leggy models from Eastern Europe, the kind Beck used to see on Fifth Avenue and in the Village. A Polish woman, maybe. Or Lithuanian. They'd married in haste, the woman attracted to his money and his golden-boy American good looks, the man attracted to the woman's remarkable body, her exoticism. They'd had some fun and had a child and then split amicably, each going their own way. The woman had come to Maine, or stayed in Maine, because its visual austerity reminded her of home.

I really should be writing, Beck thought.

Beck moved closer to the man and boy. A writer's job was to eavesdrop; it was part of the process. The man was saying, ". . . that's how you can tell the artist used a palette knife instead of a brush," and Beck heard the South in his voice. It surprised her; "South" didn't fit at all with the story she'd created; she'd been thinking Old Money New England.

The boy said, "You can paint with a knife?" and there was no South in his voice; his was the nasally Northeast. So that fit, at least.

The man said, "Sure you can! A knife, a stick, a feather, your fingers—there's no rules, see. Just possibilities."

No rules; just possibilities. Yes, Beck thought. *Yes, thank you.*

Or did she say it aloud? Something made him turn and look at her just then. He smiled at her and stood up.

"Giving the boy a little art lesson," he said.

His smile provoked her own. "A good one, from the sound of it. But I didn't mean to interrupt."

"No worries at all."

"It's such a gloomy day now, isn't it?"

"It could be better, sure," said the man.

"The end of winter is hard! Are you local?"

He said, "Just visiting."

The boy said to Beck, "Did you know you could paint with a knife?"

"I did, actually. Pretty neat, right?"

"It seems like it would be hard. But I know how to finger paint; I learned when I was a baby. I use brushes now."

Beck said, "I think artists should use whatever suits them."

"No rules, just possibilities," the man repeated, and smiled again, a half-grin that told her he didn't take himself too seriously. In that smile, something more—a spark is how she'd think of it later, when she was alone again and replaying the encounter, enjoying the sheer pleasure it elicited. A spark. And she was tinder. Married tinder, true, but flammable just the same.

She said, "Yes. Words to live by."

"More or less," the man said.

"Right. More or less." To prolong the encounter, Beck said, "I came up from New York to do a little work. I'm a writer. Working on a novel."

There, she'd declared it out loud in front of witnesses. That made it a pact with the universe, right? No matter what came of the camp's disposition, she was standing here right now, publicly declaring and committing to her goal.

Also, she sort of wanted to impress this guy. Test him, maybe.

He said, "We're not up to anything as cool as that," and Beck felt a ping of satisfaction. "Home improvement's our game right now."

Beck said, "This is the time to do it."

"We're building a garden," said the boy. "I'm going to grow pumpkins."

Beck nodded. "That'll be so useful when Halloween comes." She waited for the man to say what he would grow. When he didn't, she said, "Well, don't let me interrupt you further. You two enjoy your day."

"Hope you do, too," the man replied, his voice warm and rich like melted butter.

Beck moved along to the next aisle. Was he still smiling the way she was? Was he spending even a moment's thought on the tall, friendly, still-fairly-attractive writer in the bright orange coat? She hoped so. There was something about him, something compelling that snagged her, brought into sharp relief the fact that she had not had sex in a very long while. She browsed the shop with purpose, though she was also hyperaware of the man still meandering through with the boy. What a strange thing, this current of electricity flowing between the two of them. *He is*, Beck thought, *magnetic*.

After stealing a few more quick looks at him, she made herself attend to business, and left the shop a short while later with a small original oil painting of the harbor.

In her car, Beck checked her phone. Carol Barksdale had replied to her text:

> This is disappointing but of course you should do what's best for you.
>
> If I can be of service!

Beck tucked her phone back into her purse. Canceling on Carol hadn't solved everything. She still had a lot to put in order. There *were* rules and procedures, hoops to jump through, walls to scale. But, all right, there were possibilities, too.

14

Time Is a Harsh Mistress

Paul's phone chimed with a surprising text message. It was from The Resident: Hey, short notice but could you meet me for lunch? Need to discuss something with you.

Intrigued, he replied, What kind of something?

Tell you when I see you, she wrote. 1 pm at Ippudo?

Ramen did sound good. Paul wrote, Sure, see you then.

The Resident was there waiting outside the restaurant when Paul arrived. She looked good. Very good. Young and intelligent and dynamic. Sexy, too, though he was not going to think about that.

"It's been a while," she said. "How's the book world these days?"

"Good. Always something new and interesting. How are you?"

"Been busy. Let's go in. I'm famished."

Inside, en route from doorway to table, she greeted the host, then the waitstaff who had worked with her, then the cooks she could see through the window to the kitchen. "I miss this place."

Paul observed her, thinking how strange it was to see her in this context, even though this context was where he'd seen her first. At their last appointment, they had—well, it was best that he didn't think about that too specifically. Whatever the reason for this date, it was not *that*, he was pretty sure.

They placed their orders and then he said, "I was surprised to hear from you. Everything still on track with your residency?"

"Yeah, all good. You? Last time we met, you were still in half-denial mode. Like, 'I'm really not the kind of guy who does this . . .' It was cute. Thanks again, by the way, for that generous send-off tip. Funny, but the rich guys? They spent a *lot* more on services, but the tips were always paltry. Cheap sons of bitches, you know? Always wanting a bargain, an add-on freebie, 'good-customer discount'—like I'm Jeff Bezos with a vagina."

Paul ignored the visual her remark evoked. He said, "I think I'm still in that half-denial mode. I still don't really want to be the kind of guy who— but actually, never mind that. That's not your problem, it's mine."

"Not much of a problem, if you ask me. It's just recreational sex."

"Would you feel the same way if your partner was the one seeking it?"

"One: I'm pretty sure mine would never need to. Two: if mine *did* ever need to, then yeah, I'd be all for it. Why should anyone go without sexual satisfaction if they don't absolutely have to?"

"You make it sound so simple."

"It ought to be simple. Be the change you want to see."

"This is what I admire about your generation," Paul said. "Anyway, I know this isn't just a purely social call; don't keep me in suspense. What's up?"

"Okay, so, I wrote a book, and I need some professional guidance on what to do next."

"*You* wrote a book."

"What, is that so weird? It seems like I'm always running into someone who's writing a book, or who's with someone who is or someone who has. It's like an epidemic or something."

"I had no idea you counted writing among your other, um, talents and ambitions. Is it something you've done a lot of?"

"Not really, not before I decided to do this. Academic stuff, yes, but that's all. But last fall I read this great book and I thought, Hey, *I've* led a unique and pretty interesting life, and I bet there are people who'd be really interested to read about what I've been through."

"So it's a memoir?"

"Autobiography—is that the same thing?"

"More or less," he said. "You aren't . . . That is, I assume you're being as discreet on the page as you've been in conducting your business."

"Don't worry," she said. "All names and occupations have been changed to protect the guilty. Just kidding about the *guilty* part. A person's only guilty if they broke a legitimate rule or hid their actions."

"Are you trying to tell me that most of your clients don't?"

"I prefer to imagine that everyone is as on the up-and-up as I am. Realistically? I know most people are cowards. Which is fine. Reasons."

"That's right," Paul said. "Reasons. Anyway, about your book, I should tell you straight off: as a genre, unless you've got something pretty exceptional, a memoir is a hard sell. Also, publishing houses, including where I work, don't accept unsolicited manuscripts. You'll need to find a literary agent who'll be willing to represent you. Then they will advise you on all of the rest, send your book out, negotiate any offer you may get, and so on."

"I couldn't just give you a copy and see if you want to publish it?"

"I'm afraid not."

"Okay—but you could read it and tell me if it was any good, and help me fix it."

"Actually, no. That is, I'm capable of it, of course. But I only do that for books I'm publishing or might be publishing."

"Is this some kind of crazy catch-22?" she said. "You can't read it unless you're going to publish it, and you can't publish it because you won't read it, or at least not if it comes from me directly. And here I thought this business was all about who you know."

"Relationships *are* important, but—"

"Is it that you suspect my writing's not any good? Because I promise you, the feedback I've gotten from teachers and professors my whole life is that I'm a skilled writer. And it's a good story. Inspiring. A little salacious, too, but sex sells, right? I know *you* like sex," she said, and winked at him, then laughed, leaning back in her chair. "That was for old times' sake. I also happen to trust your judgment and taste. I read *Yankari Springs*—did I tell you that?"

"No, you didn't."

"A fucking masterpiece. I felt like I was *in* Nigeria."

"We're all very proud of that novel. But look, the thing is, I don't even acquire memoirs."

"Don't, but not can't, right?"

"I suppose that's right."

Taking a tablet from her bag, she said, "Indulge me for a minute or two, okay?" and then she read to him:

> *It's nearly two a.m. on a December night when the security guard makes his regular pass through the last rest stop on eastbound I-40 in North Carolina. This rest stop is in the middle of nowhere, in terms of surrounding civilization. A crossroads, almost, as the exit for I-95 is minutes from here. Between the two cross-country routes there are 4,479 miles of possibilities: hundreds of cities, thousands of roadside restaurants, gas stations, truck stops, motels, parks, hospitals. But for reasons unknown to the security guard and to everyone else from this moment onward, the infant girl who's crying weakly, lying on the chilly floor at the end stall in the men's room, was deposited here, in this washroom, this chilly, tile-floored stall, swaddled in a blue motor-oil-stained work shirt with the name patch torn off.*

Paul was pleasantly surprised. She'd said, ". . . the infant girl *who's*," not the usually encountered *that's*. She'd said *lying*, not the ubiquitous wrong-in-this-usage *laying*. For these two reasons alone, Paul would, if he had this manuscript, keep reading, memoir or not. But also: a mixed-race child starting life abandoned at a highway rest stop and then going on to be a sex-positive trick-turning premed student in Manhattan, and now a doctor somewhere—that was compelling. The way she framed it up—the elements of mystery and pathos—was compelling, too. She had talent.

He said, "I admit, I'm impressed."

"Thank you. So you'll read it?"

He laughed. "All right. Yes, but I make no promises as to whether or not it'll be right for me or my publisher—and I'm also going to send you a short list of literary agents I've worked with who handle memoir. Look them up, contact the ones who appeal to you—and any others you like. There are a lot of great resources out there on finding an agent. You need to have someone in your corner if I—or anyone—wants to publish your book."

"You're not in my corner?"

"I am, but I might not end up being your editor, and publishing is a business, and I'm trying to protect you. Let me, will you?"

She smiled. "Sure. And thank you. Listen, Paul: I may not know you very well, but I know you well enough to say with confidence that you're a pretty good guy. So let me offer you some advice: stop wasting time."

She took a bite of ramen.

Paul waited. When she didn't say anything more, he said, "That's it?"

She wiped her chin, then said, "You aren't letting that sink into your brain. When you do, you'll recognize that it's as profound as it is simple."

"All right. Thanks. It's nice of you to care."

She pointed at him with her chopsticks. "I'm pretty sure you're laughing at me. That's cool. I don't mind. But if you let yourself think about what I said and why I said it, you'll see the value."

Throughout the day, even as he traded emails with Beck, sending or signing documents needed for their loan application, Paul kept returning to this conversation. *Stop wasting time.* He let it sink into his brain. The concept of wasting time had, for most of his life, been synonymous with the concept of stealing moments for small pleasures. As a boy, he'd *wasted time* reading books about amphibians or rocks or volcanoes when he was supposed to be doing homework. In college, working as a teaching assistant, he'd *wasted time* listening to Elvis Costello CDs when he had student essays to grade. *Wasting time* during his fatherhood and professional years had often meant reading a novel solely for pleasure (that is, not in any way related to work). So to *stop* wasting time was, he thought, bad advice. He loved wasting time! The Resident—whose name, he'd finally learned, was Tabitha—didn't know what she was talking about.

A week or so after their lunch date, Paul stood at his bathroom sink with a towel wrapped around his waist, preparing to shave. With the days growing longer and the sun moving northward bit by bit, on this morning the sunlight edged through the bathroom window and caught Paul in its rays. Specifically, it caught his chest hair and lit up some gray hiding among the brown. He leaned closer to the mirror for a better look. Yes, gray. He dropped his towel and looked down at his pubic hair. A few gray strands there, too.

But, okay. Nothing to be alarmed about. Silver-haired Fred Rogers had looked distinguished. The graying had given him visual gravitas to go along with the wisdom he'd always possessed. Graying was natural, inevitable, if you lived long enough. The alternative did not feel especially desirable. Besides, Paul thought, he would like to be considered distinguished one day. Gray hairs were harbingers of good.

He stepped back from the counter in order to get a more comprehensive view of himself. There was little evidence of change; he looked much the way he'd looked at forty. This stasis, though, was an illusion. In the same way that he was physically not now the boy he'd once been, this current self would not last forever. As his father had done in recent years, Paul would likely grow thinner, develop stooped posture, saggy pecs, spotty skin. Unlike his father, though, Paul would not have spent the previous decades enjoying what anyone who'd seen his parents together could tell was an enduring passionate love affair.

Paul would have liked to have an enduring passionate love affair. But that hadn't turned out to be his lot in life, had it? He did have an enduring passion—it was just an unrequited one. Why was that? Well, in part it was because he'd been too fucking timid too many times. Too fearful of what might happen if he weren't.

The last time he'd fully rejected his fear, it was in the wake of Tabitha's telling him about her motto, about Bowie's remark that living in fear was the lowest depth of misery.

Fear fed misery, and misery could be a hungry bastard. Voracious. It could suck up all the remaining years of a person's life. Time, too, was a harsh mistress.

Stop wasting time, she'd told him.

Looking at his face in the mirror, Paul said, "Oh."

He was an editor. He helped fix stories. It was past time he fixed his own.

15

Fabulous Floating

Nothing against Manhattan, but Sophie would far rather have preferred to be in Los Angeles, where her boss, Benji, was eyeing a West Coast branch and where Sophie enjoyed unfettered access to her producer friend Jojo's Bel Air guest house. Benji did not need her in L.A. just now, though; he needed her here in New York for his first annual Spring Elemental, a gallery event specially mounted to bring in select clients and prospects to socialize with the artists, the gallery staff, and—as important—the other guests. Not a single piece of art would be on display tonight, all the works draped by white taffeta as if they were innocent brides-to-be awaiting introduction to future mates.

"But we'll unveil all of them at some point, right?" their new intern, Darren, had asked back in January when Benji announced his event vision to the staff. Darren was a twenty-one-year-old Korean American art history major at SVA, a logical, bookish young man who in his job interview said he hoped to one day work in valuation for an auction house or insurance company.

"We will not," Benji said.

"Some of them?"

"No."

"So . . . you mean no one will see any of it?"

Benji told him, "No one will see the work at any point during the event, that's correct."

"I don't get it," said Darren.

Sophie had watched him with sympathy, recalling how ignorant she, too, had been in the beginning of her career. She hadn't understood how different selling art was from selling ordinary commodities—even specialty items or luxury goods. How a good gallerist (and Benji was top-notch) was *so* much more than a salesperson of pictures and tchotchkes. How a gallerist had to cultivate a distinct identity in the same way a perfumer—a *nose*—created a distinctive scent. There might be five thousand gallerists exhibiting the art of some hundreds of thousands of artists, and so each had to be unique. Ochoa was its own brand, the way Clive Christian No. 1 was. Ochoa repped art especially for a particular type of discerning, informed collector (though Benji would not turn away a Wall Street bro who was ready to drop tens of thousands for a painting or photograph based merely on Benji's say-so). Ochoa's brand was *offbeat*. It was *mystery*. It was not sex so much as *passionate foreplay*. All of this, wrapped in high art's historical and philosophical breadth and depth, juxtaposed against the pop cultures of both now and soon.

Sophie told Darren, "Think of this event as a first date—"

"—in an era of so many one-night stands," Benji finished for her.

"Oh, okay," Darren had said, pretending to get it.

"Art's getting too democratized," Sophie told him, making it sound like a bad thing when in fact she was a secret advocate. She added, "The way it's being sold online now is like ordering a band's tour T-shirt when you didn't even go to the concert." This part she felt was true. The approach was all wrong. "With Spring Elemental, Benji is reinvigorating the personal and unique experience of art."

"Precisely," Benji said.

"The not seeing it," added Sophie, "is an enticement for getting to see it later, intimately."

Darren said, "Oh, yeah, okay. Smart."

Make no mistake about it, though: the event was also an effort toward lightening their inventory to make more room for new-to-Ochoa artists—Jordan Morgan, for example, the painter Sophie had romanced (platonically) in Dubai after her romance (sexual) with Hanif in that luxe villa. Hanif, who was a human rights attorney and had worked with Amal Clooney in the Hague (really, Sophie should call him). Amal Clooney, who was right now en route (Sophie presumed) to the Spring Elemental along with her husband, George, who was a friend of Benji's. Amal, who would tonight be meeting Marco Villanueva, the urban artist who, not long after Sophie's night with Hanif, had ghosted Sophie and who tonight was on his way (Sophie presumed) to the gallery with the woman who'd enticed Marco to leave her.

Benji gathered the gallery staff in the front room around an artful (of course) display of hors d'oeuvres that would be supplemented by a roving band of catering staff's trays of additional tasty bites, along with waters and wines. He'd dressed as he often did, in vividly colored pants (turquoise, tonight) with a crisp, collared white shirt unbuttoned to nipple level so that his hairless chest was evident. Benji was forty-one, and he was rich, and he was beautiful, and he was gay. He was also married (to Evan Arnold, an old-money Daddy Warbucks type, who'd underwritten the gallery in its early lean years). So for Sophie, Benji had been neither prospect nor threat—which made working for him much more relaxing.

"All right, people," he said to Sophie, Darren, Jamie, Denis, and Krystal, who he referred to as his "rainbow coalition," owing to their diversity. "You each know your roles. Everything looks marvelous—thank you to Krystal especially," he went on, indicating the artful food display curated by their new gallery assistant. "Talent will be arriving soon, doors open in thirty. Please eat now, not while guests are present. Drink at will, but remember, as ever: evidence of inebriation—"

"—is cause for termination," the group said in unison.

"Exactly, my darlings. Sophie, what's the final on your A-listers?"

"Happy to say I've got a pretty great lineup: the Clooneys for sure; Jia-Jia Fei—of course, and thank God; also Gaïa Matisse, Steve Cohen, Lenny Kravitz, A-Rod and J-Lo, a Kardashian, Liev Schreiber—"

"Stop," said Krystal, the newest hire, a young Black woman who'd come to New York from Miami, but who'd grown up in one of Florida's nondescript small interior towns after emigrating from St. John. Despite looking the part of hip young Manhattanite, with her keen eye for cheap, funky fashion, she hadn't yet fully grasped the beating heart of Manhattan's culture—that is, the heated intersection of celebrity and money.

Sophie said, "Stop what?"

"*How?*" said Krystal. "I mean, yes, I know this is the plan and it's part of what you do . . . but do you actually *know* all of those people?"

Sophie shook her head. "God, no. Only some of them."

"Oh, only some. Okay. She only knows *some* world-famous actors and sports stars and singers."

Jamie, the lithe androgynous beauty, said, "They all shit, same as you."

"Which Kardashian?" asked Denis. He was French—and therefore fabulous, in Sophie's view, before even doing anything. He was also an astute marketing and publicity manager; Sophie coordinated with him in running Ochoa's Instagram to subtle, maximum effect.

"All I could get was a promise that at least one would make an appearance."

Denis said, "Let it be Kendall, s'il vous plaît. *Not* Kim."

Darren said, "Um, Kendall's a Jenner."

"Please. Whatever," said Denis, waving Darren off. "Same pond, is it not?"

"Anyway, people," Benji said loudly, "the takeaway is always that where there are stars, there is press, and when there is press, we are not only cautious but on message, yes?"

"Yes," they said.

"Laissez les bon temps rouler!" Benji told them, clapping his hands.

Sophie helped herself to a stuffed fig. Krystal did the same, then said, "Okay, I knew we'd get some high-profile people here tonight. But I admit, I am kind of freaking out."

"I get it," Sophie told her. "It's a totally normal response. And here's the thing: you're going to say something stupid to one or more of them, I promise you, so just forgive yourself now, in advance. And remember that you'll do better the next time out."

"Oh my god," said Krystal. "I'm already regretting whatever stupid thing will fly from my mouth."

"Breathe," Sophie said. "And look at you, already a step closer to forgiveness."

Krystal asked, "Who's the most famous person you know?"

"Like, truly know?"

"Like, they'd take your call."

"That would have to be Tania Uccello."

Krystal was wide-eyed incredulous. "Come *on*."

"I'm serious. We've known each other forever. I'm housesitting for her right now—she has a place uptown, 432 Park Avenue. *Very* posh."

"Okay, but the rest of them—was it this job that got you connected, or . . . ?"

"Some. It's New York. I was born and raised here. You never know who you're going to see or what connections you might make, if you're open to the opportunities. I like to think I am."

Certainly, she talked a good game. *Played* a good game. She'd be nowhere, though, if not for that early connection to Tania, which had connected her to some key people in the music world, who had connections to people in the art world, and all of them had connections to people on Broadway, in television, in film, in finance . . . so many lines going in so many directions—much like the MTA, much like the airlines. And yet for all of her zipping from place to place, pollinating this flower and that one, she was herself as untethered as any hummingbird in flight.

She was tired.

Now Krystal was saying, "What stupid thing did *you* say, you know, back when you were a noob?"

"Oh—I don't know if I can tell you. It's so embarrassing."

"Yeah? Now you have to tell me."

Before she could answer, two of the artists—"the talent," as Benji had referred to them—arrived. One of those two was Marco, whom Sophie hadn't seen or spoken with since her return from Dubai. With him (the woman was managing to walk with both of her arms around his waist) was a socialite Sophie recognized from other high-profile events of the recent past: Linda Holbrook, the comely ex-wife of Jimmy Holbrook, billionaire financier, vintner, breeder of horses, etc. She was a fifty-something woman of no particular talent whom Marco had not that long ago remarked upon as being nicely well preserved—as if any woman who was past youth's blush was in need of augmentation.

This was a view he shared with too many young women, Sophie herself being on that group's fringe. She'd had strategic Botox and some careful minimalist plumping and sculpting. How to compete otherwise? And yet she'd still lost Marco. Which maybe was not nearly as dire an event as she'd felt it was when she came home to Tania's vacated apartment, exhausted and desperately missing her mother and expecting to be enfolded in the arms of a lover. Hanif had been akin to doing some cocaine (now unaffordable to her) as a quick pick-me-up-get-me-through. Marco was supposed to have been her comfort food. Well, whatever; like a pot of instant macaroni and cheese, he was bad for her anyway.

She went to greet the pair. Air kisses near his cheeks, then hers, *mwah, mwah*, and oh, Linda dear, so wonderful to see you again, can I get a selfie with you before the crowd arrives? Snapping the picture, Marco staring, smirking, enjoying this demonstration. Sophie smiling warmly right to his face, no *Fuck off and die* squint for him, nope, she wouldn't give him that satisfaction. He was never going to be a first-rate artist anyway; he'd already peaked, he just didn't know it yet. Benji knew it, though, and would soon be having *the talk* with Marco, about pricing and prospects.

Sophie left them to greet the other arriving talent. She felt strong, she felt ready for the night ahead. She'd dressed to impress, wearing a vibrant print satin dress from Proenza Schouler under a vintage black leather jacket she'd nabbed from Metropolis. Her yellow Gucci patent leather ankle boots were the killer finishing touch. She'd already posted a shot of them on her SimplySophie! account, posed artfully (of course) on Tania's ninety-first-floor windowsill, the twilit city behind them. Whatever J-Lo was flaunting tonight, whatever Amal had draped herself in, Sophie would be able to hold her own. That, in a nutshell, was the game.

Before long, the gallery was buzzing with beautiful and/or wealthy people eating delectable tidbits, drinking top-shelf liquor and the best Chilean wines, photographers circling and encouraging groupings they hoped would headline the social pages. Phone in hand (as ever), Sophie pollinated this pair and that trio and those five finance bros who were dying to get a selfie with A-Rod before it was too late (the celebs rarely stuck around for long). In a perfect world, she would also get to pollinate George Clooney; alas, she had to settle for a brief (but meaningful!) conversation and a posed photo that in that perfect world would have made her mother proud to buy extra copies of the *Post* when the picture appeared there. Behind or beneath the draped canvases, original works of art priced at USD $14,000 and $67,000 and $320,000 . . . Jordan Morgan's new mixed-media canvas, *A Correction for the Apostolic Wingman*, was being marketed at $585,000 but likely would sell higher due to demand. Benji was currently assembling a special collection of mid-century works that would almost certainly bring millions apiece. Even as Sophie had been striving all these years to be someone who bought such things for her own edification rather than someone who sold them for a salary, she couldn't help thinking that some people had too much money.

She would like to have too much money.

She didn't need to have that much money. Really, she didn't. Enough money, yes. Too much, though, and she risked becoming inured to the everyday problems of ordinary life and ordinary—which is to say, *not filthy rich*—people. On the other hand, they said success and wealth didn't alter one's character, it revealed it. Well, okay. She'd be willing to test that adage, under the right circumstances.

Spotting Krystal in conversation with JiaJia Fei, Sophie caught her eye and Krystal gave a tiny nod that might have meant *You were right* or—Sophie hoped—*I'm slaying it*. Either way, what Krystal was discovering was that you learned how to do this by doing it. With a few notable exceptions, every person in this room had *worked* their way up or in. The work wasn't in every case ethical, she was sure, but never mind that for now.

Sophie saw Liev Schreiber standing alone, his back to the bar. Clooney excepted, a better pollination opportunity could not be had. She made her beeline over to him and introduced herself afresh.

"Sophie Geller," she said, looking up at him. Even in her marvelous yellow stiletto boots, she was several inches too short for eye-to-eye engagement. They'd need to be in bed for that. "I'm the assistant curator and in charge of client services."

"Liev Schreiber, ace pretender," he replied, moving his drink to his left hand so that he could shake her proffered hand. "Benji speaks well of you."

"That's good to know. He speaks well of you, too. Question for you— and not an original one, I'm sure, but, do you just never shave?"

Her lack of originality was no detriment to them having an easy, warm conversation. They spoke about his recent voice work, including playing the role of Spots in *Isle of Dogs* and narrating the art history program *Civilisations* for BBC. Here was a man who had his priorities sorted. Just the same, as she stood there enjoying the chat, her marvelous yellow stiletto boots were taking their toll on her feet—something that had never used to happen when she was younger. In the old days, she could dance all night in heels this high—cheap ones, no less—and not think about her feet at all. She could be out with friends or with a guy and not have to have her phone glued to her palm, not fear that being out of constant contact meant she'd miss something crucial. Now her phone vibrated frequently, drawing her attention to its demanding little screen—and damn it all, here was a text from Tania: *Call me asap!!!!*

Sophie excused herself and went into her office. "Hey, it's me. What's going on? Are you okay?"

"Me? Totally."

"Where are you?"

"Umm, let me think a second, I just woke up . . . Melbourne! God. Melbourne, yes. Beautiful place. So great. Listen, you remember Jacqueline, my business manager?"

"Sure, of course."

"Yeah, well, get this: her father just kicked her mother out because, I don't know, her mother, Shari, was having a thing with some friend of theirs, I guess, and her father found out. It's ugly. Anyway, he's being a real dick and Shari needs a place to stay for a while and they're in Manhattan on the Upper East, so I said she could have my place until she gets something new of her own. This way you can get back to your own place, which I'm sure you won't mind doing."

"Oh! That's—wow, that is such a shitty thing for him to do to her."

"Right? It's so hard to find a great place in the city on short notice, which of course he knows. She's got a life there. Jacqueline said Shari has put so much of herself into decorating their place, and now, poof, she's locked out and she can't get into their bank accounts, either. She'll be fine, I'm sure. Eventually. Right now, though, this is the simplest solution. So if you can be out by tomorrow afternoon—"

"God, yeah, of course. No problem at all."

"I was sure you'd say that. Thank you. If you need more time, though—another day or two, just say so. She's in a hotel for the moment, but you know how lame that is—"

"Tomorrow's no problem, why would it be? Tell her she can get in at . . . two o'clock. I should be able to be packed up by then. Cool?"

"I love you. I can always count on you."

"I love you, too. Gotta go now, though—we've got a gallery thing under way and I just left Liev Schreiber hanging."

"Girl! He's single now, right? Go get him. I will only be getting coffee and whatever Melbourners—wait: Melbournians, that's it—do for break-fast."

"Too bad, you," Sophie said. "*Sad* life."

When Sophie returned to the gallery floor, Liev was re-engaged in the crowd, so Sophie re-engaged as well. She had to fight, though, to keep her attention on her work and not on the question of where she would stay to-morrow night, and the next, and the next.

Tried.

Failed.

Got herself a drink.

Liev was single, so, maybe, just maybe, if he had more than a friendly interest in her, she could engineer the date-leads-to-sleepover-leads-to-stay-a-while routine with him. Which might lead to more. To something genuine. It could. Who knew? He had kids, though, and a famous ex, and even sup-posing he really was into her, did she want to be a part of all of that? Usually she avoided dating actors; how could you ever trust that they were being real with you? And she always avoided children. This, though, was a special situation. Desperate times called for desperate measure, etc. Right?

She imagined approaching him now, making the date, snapping a sel-fie with him for her IG (*You only Liev once?* winking face emoji) and then meeting him tomorrow for dinner. Where would they go? What did it mat-ter? The only thing that mattered was where they ended up. A doorman building, surely. Which neighborhood was his vibe? What would they talk about? Did he really care about art, or was he here tonight because of A-Rod or George, or because his publicist said his brand would benefit from some elevation, lest he end up typecast in unshaven-Ray-Donovan-type roles for-ever? There was no telling unless she asked him straight out, and how weird would *that* be?

Sophie had cared so much about art—visual art, but music, too, and writ-ing and dance and fashion. Art was how people throughout human history had made sense of their worlds. Expression. Witness. Evocation. Calls to arms. She had needed to be a part of that, but she hadn't wanted the poverty-level hand-to-mouth life that usually went along with it. Dingy dark apartments with no space to even turn around in. Cockroaches. Rats. Or you shared a bigger place with your best girlfriends—she'd done that for a time—and got more space, maybe another two windows. No closet space, though, and no refrigerator space, and worse of all, no privacy. Plus, someone was always borrowing your best stuff. Or selling it, as had happened to Sophie.

Somewhere along the line, her ideals had gotten corrupted. She'd taken "fake it till you make it" way too much to heart. Working here for Benji, putting art into the homes and offices of people who never even looked at their credit card statements after shopping sprees, vacations, furnishing the Paris place . . . She'd pretended to be one of them—not only while on the job, though, which would be forgivable. No, she'd misled everyone, herself included, always assuring herself that the act was temporary, that soon she'd convert *faked* to *made* and life would find its equilibrium. Most likely this would occur via a path that led through some wealthy man's bedroom— where a $90,000 painting might hang, getting no notice after a while, just one more pretty collectible among so many other things.

Maybe Jacqueline's mother, Shari, had started to feel like just another collectible. Maybe that's why she had welcomed the fresh attention of another man. But was that the answer? The solution? There had to be a better way.

Later, when the guests and staff had gone and Sophie was in her office finishing the day's tasks, Benji called to her from his. "Sophie, darling. Would you come here for a minute?"

She went to his doorway, with the words *What's up?* on her lips. His grim expression stopped her. *Oh, shit,* she thought. First Tania and now . . . ? She had no clue what the problem could be, only that it looked like he was about to, in essence, add insult to the night's earlier injury.

He said, "Come, sit. Those boots, marvelous as they may be, are unkind to your poor feet. And you'll want to be sitting anyway, as I have a situation to discuss with you."

Sophie took a seat, saying, "I don't like that look on your face. What's going on? Did tonight not go even better than you'd hoped?"

Benji said, "The event was spectacular. You have the golden touch. I couldn't be more pleased."

They'd sold five paintings and two sculptures to a pair of competitive art-loving hedge funders who wanted not only valuable art but also a great story to tell about its acquisition. After all, who among their crowd could say they had acquired such expensive works—art that was in fact *hidden from view, can you believe the balls that takes?*—based solely on their trust in Benji Ochoa's guidance? Doing so bespoke a willingness to spend money incautiously. An *ability* to spend money incautiously. For these two buyers, owning art was a sport as well as an investment. The gallery grossed close to five million dollars on the sale. Sophie had just finished processing the men's payments and was now set to arrange for their deliveries.

"No," Benji continued, "the situation is unrelated. Something has come up, and I need to be out of town for a little while."

That was it? Sophie said, "Okay, well, I can manage everything while you're out. When are you leaving?"

"No, love—that's the thing. I'm closing up shop for the interim. I'm sorry. I have to furlough everyone for the time being."

"Furlough?" Sophie said, hoping it didn't mean what she thought it meant.

"For the time being."

"Everyone?"

"Yes."

"With or without pay?"

"Without."

"But not me," she said.

"I'm sorry," he said again. "I know it's sudden. I was hoping I'd be able to avoid it, but, well, it didn't work out that way."

"Furloughed for how long? Should I . . . You know, the staff, most of them are living on a pretty slim margin, here; they can't be out of work for long or they won't be able to pay their rent."

"I know, I know. It shouldn't be too long."

"Okay, but do they need to look for other work?" she said, her voice rising. "We can't ask them to just wait indefinitely. They've got lives—" She paused, collecting herself. "They're a top-rate staff, and they won't wait around, Benji. They'll get picked off by the other galleries. You do know that."

He held up his hand. "Don't get your panties in a twist, love. This is all going to be resolved quickly."

"Okay, good. So, then, I should consider this a vacation . . . week?"

"Yes," he said decisively. "A week or two of vacation, that's a good approach."

A good approach for him, perhaps. Not all that good for the staff, or for her. The death certificates still hadn't arrived, which meant the little bit of money coming to her from her mother's life insurance and whatnot was a month away, at a minimum. She'd maxed out one of her two remaining Visas and Amex had instituted a credit ceiling on her account. She'd risen to it.

She said, "All right. But, what's going on? Is it about the audit?"

"No, nothing like that. No, all of that's fine. This is something sudden. A bit of a surprise. Something I have to deal with right away. And anyway, tonight excepted, business is fairly slow at the moment, so the timing shouldn't really be a problem."

For you, thought Sophie.

She didn't like his equivocating. "Is it a cash-flow thing?" she said. "Because if that's the issue, we can run with a skeleton crew. Keep the doors open while you get it all sorted."

"Oh, it's nothing like that," he said breezily. "No, no. Everything is fine with our finances. No, this is something else. A personal matter."

"Then why not—"

"We needed to do some reorganizing anyway. So."

It was obvious she'd get nothing more. She said, "When are you leaving?"

"Tomorrow morning. Today was a long day, wasn't it? You, my love, appear to need to get those marvelous boots off of your marvelous feet. I'll see to tonight's delivery arrangements; you go home. Relax. Sleep in tomorrow.

You've been an angel, but you need some *you* time. My god, you just lost your mother! And yet you pushed on. Well, no more. I'll finish up for you here. And I'll keep you posted, don't worry about that. All will be well."

Sleep in, he'd said, not knowing what a terrible joke he'd made. Sophie felt sure she had no prospect of sleep at all.

Limping her way to the subway station, she passed a bedraggled woman seated on the sidewalk. The woman had a piece of cardboard underneath her, to ward off the concrete's chill. A half-full garbage bag of who-knew-what rested beside her, as did a small shaggy dog.

Sophie stopped for a moment, took off the yellow boots, and offered them to the woman. "They're legit Gucci," she said. "You can sell them for good money."

The woman looked them over. "What size?"

"Seven. Does it matter?"

The woman, who wore what appeared to be an overlarge pair of men's scuffed leather loafers, took off one shoe and peeled off one of at least two underlying socks.

Sophie said, "Are you shitting me? Do you want them or don't you?"

"Give me a second," said the woman. She took the left boot, pushed her foot into it, and got up onto her feet. The dog stood up, too. After trying a few steps, the woman said, "It pinches a little."

"Tell me about it."

"But, fine, I'll take 'em."

Sophie set the other boot on the sidewalk and continued on her way.

Nighttime in Manhattan had used to be Sophie's favorite. Work ended. Life began. Everywhere, there was a hot new band or singer, a new play, a dance club with strobing lights and pumping bass, a trendy bar, a party where she'd find equal chance to score some free blow or land a guy on whom to hone her guy-getting skills, or both. Everywhere, the steady trails of headlights and taillights moving people uptown, crosstown, down to the Bowery, the Battery, the bridges. The young people didn't drive, though.

They walked, they streamed into the city's steaming bowels to crowd into subway cars, laughing, jostling each other, ready for Brooklyn's scene next, for the Bronx, for Jersey City, for Harlem. Tentacles reaching outward from lower Manhattan, the city's heart. Lifeblood, these young people, pushing the city to become what it might be. She'd been poor and she'd been *electric*.

Like everything, though, it couldn't last. She'd had to grow up. Be responsible. Make a life out of the raw material of good looks and a pretty good brain and an interest in how the act of creating art not only defined a past but built a future. Her father had encouraged her to direct her energies toward Jewish art and history, maybe have a role in their synagogue's cultural outreach. Even then, though, Sophie hadn't wanted to define herself, delimit herself with the small existence her parents had been content to call a life. Where was the fun in that?

No, what she'd intended was to find herself a nice boy, Jewish or other, who could afford season tickets to the Metropolitan Opera, good seats for the best Broadway shows, tickets to hot concerts and Knicks games at the Garden. A nice boy whose family were benefactors to any or all of the city's art museums, so that she might have an in if she wanted to work in one of them. Because, come on, if she had to be a grown-up, she wanted the best New York version of adulthood she could get.

Good wasn't good enough; she wanted *better*. But when she'd thought about it, *better* didn't feel quite good enough, either; she wanted *best*. Even *best*, though, had a definition that kept shifting upward, maybe because of her proximity to Tania, whose trajectory, though not New York–specific, was like a rocket's. Sophie began to see what *best* might look like for a woman whose life was unbounded by conventional ideas of what was possible. And so she'd aimed high, too, elevating her tastes, trying to live the part (*fake it till you make it*), trying to rise fast—except the problem was that she couldn't make her own fuel the way Tania did. The problem was that she'd discovered she could only ever be a stowaway.

Upward.

Somehow.

If the doorman at Tania's building had any thoughts about Sophie's appearing at the entry barefooted, he gave no indication. "Good evening, Ms. Geller."

Sophie nodded her greeting and padded on, into the lobby and past the two similarly professional but certainly amused women who staffed the concierge desk. *Tough night,* their expressions seemed to say.

Upward from the original goal of pairing with a middle-class lawyer or doctor, say, to pairing up with a mid-level finance guy, to pairing up with someone at or near the top of the moneyed food chain. A Fortune 500 CEO or COO or CFO. A president. A starting forward, an A-list actor, a rapper-entrepreneur who was better described as a mogul. Yes. She had been in the market for a mogul of some type or other—but, no surprise, there weren't many such men outside of Hollywood who matched her progressive ideals, and whether in Hollywood or out, such catches weren't at all easy to spear.

Upward, to the ninety-first floor. To Tania Uccello's thirty-million-dollar halfway house for wayward women.

Inside the apartment, Sophie ordered up a bottle of chilled Veuve Clicquot, then tended to the plants while awaiting the delivery. Was Shari prepared to take on this responsibility until Tania's return next fall? Presumably—and if she wasn't, well, that was Tania's problem, because after this, Sophie was over it. Once she solved her immediate crisis, there'd be no more housesitting. She could not leave herself so vulnerable to upheaval at someone else's whim. She was getting too old for this shit.

The champagne arrived, and as soon as Sophie closed the door, she popped the cork, took a swig, and then, bottle in hand, went to stand on the window seat. There was the Chrysler Building and MetLife, the Empire State Building, the Freedom Tower. The bridges. Liberty. The bay. Countless buildings all around her, and not one of them to call home. Seeing her reflection, Sophie raised the bottle to herself. "Here's lookin' at you, kid. It's been a good run, but now the fat lady's about to sing."

But not until tomorrow afternoon. If she was going to get her money's worth (so to speak) from the rest of her stay, she had better get to it. She climbed down, went to the bedroom, slipped her feet into her UGGs, and headed for the elevator.

First stop: the residents' dining room, where she had the maître d' seat her at the room's edge so that she could take in the full view of the elegant space. At this late hour, she was one of only a few diners present. At any hour, most residents here who weren't eating out ordered for delivery to their own apartments. A waste, in Sophie's view, when you paid thousands *for this very privilege*. The fee did not even include food.

"Bring me a flute for this," she told the waitress, setting the bottle in front of her. "And I'll do whatever fancy salad Chef Hergatt's got going tonight. Plus the scallops, if they're still on the menu—yes? And . . . will you see if he'll do a quick haricots verts garlic-soy sauté? Like, just to the point where they get super bright green but they're still crisp. Oh—and let me have a glass of his best pinot noir. And some bread and butter? And let's put this"— she indicated the champagne—"in a bucket while I'm here, okay? Thanks. You're a doll."

When the meal was before her, Sophie arranged it to its photographic best and then leaned across the table, reaching to angle her phone slightly above, where she could get both food and face in frame. She needed four tries to get it just so. Her eventual IG post read, *Fine-y Dine-y Wine-y Mine-y*, with hashtags chosen somewhat haphazardly because who the fuck cared anymore? She was about to be homeless.

After consuming the delectables, Sophie dried the champagne bottle and left for the billiards room, hoping to encounter someone game for a game with a slightly soused Sophie. Alas, no dice. Or better to say, no cue? What-ever. No game.

Okay, fine. She'd rather have a swim, anyway. No matter that she wasn't properly attired. She'd get the concierge to send up a suit.

When that had been accomplished, she had a swim. "Long laps in lux-ury," she said to no one. "Fabulous floating." She did a few dolphin dives.

Some pampered paddling. Then out of the pool and into a warmed towel. Outside, Manhattan twinkled.

Fitness room next? Nah, to hell with that.

A turn in the steam room, then.

Soon after, an empty bottle. So be it. Time to pack what little she owned and get ready to vacate.

But when Sophie was back in the apartment, she once again pulled the alpaca comforter off the bed, wrapped it around herself, and curled up on the window seat. She could pack later, when the sun came up and a sense of urgency returned. Later, too, she'd line up a hotel room for tomorrow night, and start looking into possible housesit gigs to bridge this new sink-hole. She'd assess and calculate. She'd reclaim nimble. Right now, though, she wanted to be Small Sophie, snug and protected, painted by the city's nighttime glow.

For a while, she gazed out onto the city, calmed, numbed. Maybe she dozed a little. At some point later, she realized she needed to pee, and she was thirsty, and a headache was forming itself deep behind her eyes. Her brain's cogs started turning again:

What was going on with Benji?

When were she and her sisters going to, individually, get their shit to-gether?

Where should she stay?

Where *could* she stay? Her options were open, geographically. Maybe she could score a last-minute housesit someplace fabulous, travel costs included. She'd had a fantastic stay in Thessaloniki once, years earlier, before Benji brought her on board. She'd been between jobs then. She hoped she was not between jobs now.

After taking care of her urgent business, Sophie retrieved her phone and went housesit hunting. The hunt was brief, however; nothing aligned. She'd have to go the cheap hotel route once again and pray there were no bedbugs.

As she (once again) prepared to pack her things, she put in her earbuds and said, "Hey, Siri, call Mom," the way she would have done when in this situation before. Those times, she knew that she could go home to stay if she wanted to, if she was ready to admit defeat. She was not. Then, as now, she just wanted to hear her mother's voice.

16

The Pressure and the Rhythms

I n the pediatric intensive care unit, Claire finished her assessment of a sweet, groggy boy named River, who'd undergone valve replacement surgery that morning to correct his aortic stenosis. Then she stepped outside his room to speak with his mother, Heath.

"He looks good. You holding up okay?"

Heath said, "I guess, yeah." She kept one hand pressed to the room's window as she spoke. "It's hard to see him all wired up, though. He might be five, but he's still my baby."

Twenty-three-year-old Heath was hardly more than a baby herself. Or at least this was how it seemed to Claire, from age forty. Heath, like Beck, had jumped into motherhood without finishing childhood. Claire really ought to give Beck more credit for what she'd accomplished and less grief for not accomplishing more. After all, which of them had married Paul? Which of them was now still married to Paul? Which of them was right now using Paul as a measuring stick of accomplishment?

Claire ought not to look at Heath and see an ill-prepared victim of poor circumstances or poor judgment. This young woman with the extensive body decor (her neck was ringed with tiny birds; she had literary quotations on her forearms; her nasal septum and eyebrows and traguses were pierced) was clearly no pushover. As she'd told Claire, she was single by choice: River's father, an Ojibwe guy Heath had met while skiing at Spirit Mountain, had been her "totally spectacular one true love," despite her parents' refusal to even meet him, and the two of them had started building a house themselves on land he'd bought at auction. Then one spring night three years ago, he was riding his motorcycle home from work and he hit a moose. "People don't realize how big they are," she'd told Claire. "This one was maybe eight feet tall and a thousand pounds. Basically? It's like hitting a brick wall." He died at the scene. There'd been no one else in her life since then. She'd said she didn't *want* a man in her life, not unless he could be as spectacular as Eric had been, and no one could be as spectacular as Eric had been, and so that was that.

Heath had ditched high school at seventeen, and since Eric's death had continued to live there on his land just outside of town, where she and four other young women who were "done taking shit from society" built their homes and raised sheep for milk and wool. They had a compound of five small cabins, she'd told Claire, plus a community house with a big kitchen and several classrooms. It was rustic but had all the basics. River was the third child born to the group. Heath said, "Men can visit—and they do, right, because we are not trying to be celibates. But they're not allowed to live with us. Rules are rules."

Claire had listened to all of this with half an ear while doing River's initial exam. Then she had to ask Heath to either observe in silence or wait outside the room. "Right now I want to have a close listen to his heart."

Heath said, "He has such a big heart—which I know isn't what you're talking about; I just wanted you to know that about him. Right, buddy?" she said to the boy. "You love all the good people, just like Mommy does." And River said, "I'll still love you, Ms. Dr. Geller, even if you give me a shot."

Five young women living together cooperatively like an elephant herd, friendly toward the males of the species but not dependent on them. This seemed a much wiser approach to life than Claire's had been.

Now Heath wiped her eyes and said, "When he passed out that way . . . I just never imagined he wasn't in one hundred percent perfect health. Seeing him like this is hard. Even though I know he's all fixed up, now. He is, right?"

Claire nodded. "Everything looks and sounds *really* good, I promise. We'll keep him here in the ICU another couple of days just to be sure he's mending the way he needs to. Then he'll move onto the ward. I think you should expect to bring him home early next week."

"Yeah? Okay, that's great to know. Thank you so much." Heath paused to wipe her eyes. "I know this is routine for you guys, but to me it feels totally miraculous."

"It's never routine," Claire said, though in truth too many aspects of the work were exactly that. Other aspects were outright maddening. For example, the work-arounds Claire was required to use in order to get Medicaid to cover River's tests and treatment. She had not gone into medicine out of a desire to problem-solve bureaucratic bullshit.

"Dr. Geller? If you don't mind me saying, I can't help but notice that you carry *a lot* of tension in your upper body, neck, and head."

Claire glanced at the nurse's station, where her almost-friend Jennifer was tending charts. Jennifer looked up and gave a questioning look: *Do you need to be saved?* Claire's answering look: *Not yet.*

Heath went on, "It's not my business to ask what all makes you tense, but I will offer to help you relieve that tension. I mean, it's the least I can do, right? And don't worry, it's not drugs; that's not my jam. I think I told you that I teach yoga—"

Claire held a hand up to stop her. "Thanks, but I'm fine. Tension's a normal part of my day." Supplemented now with her anxiety about David's well-being whenever he was at Chad's. Then there was Beck's reluctance to sell the camp. And the fact that every conversation with Beck made her think about Paul, and damn it, she was tired of feeling guilty for a thing she hadn't really *done*; it had all been in her head.

Plus, she was suffering a low-grade malaise over Paul's suspected homosexuality. Seeing him at the funeral and at the house afterward, she'd wanted to punch him in the face, punish him for all the trouble he'd unwittingly caused. She knew he hadn't *actually* caused the demise of her marriage, but she was angry at the entire situation and somebody ought to pay. She had not punched him, and she also had not tested his sexuality when she had the chance, alone with him there in his office (where she hadn't expected him to catch her in the act of absorbing some Paul atoms). Why had she ever spent even two minutes on fantasies that involved his being so hugely impressed with her achievements that he'd throw Beck—her *sister*—over for her and they'd run off someplace tropical for hot sex and cold blender drinks? Why had she instead married a man whose way of showing love involved constant suggestions for correction or improvement? *You know, you could shed those baby pounds faster if you . . . You know, you'd look really good if you . . . You know, if you would relax more during sex, it would . . .* And now she was leaving David alone with him three nights a week and every other Sunday. Poor kid. She hadn't meant to do this to him.

So yes, tension, every day.

She said to Heath, "The stress is, unfortunately, unavoidable."

"You're proving my case. You need to do some yoga with me—I practice Anusara, heated—and my girl Tina is a trained masseuse. I'll get you loosened up, and then a deep tissue massage will unkink those muscles."

Claire said, "I'm familiar with the benefits of both. But—"

"But you never do either one, am I right? Basically?"

Claire kept her tone calm and friendly. "I appreciate your concern—"

"You don't," said Heath, her tone as friendly as Claire's. "You resent my concern. I totally get that; who am I to go inserting myself into your personal realm, right? But look, you helped me and River. Now I'm returning the good deed—offering to return it, that is—by inviting you to come out to the compound for yoga and a massage."

"That's very generous," said Claire, "but there's no need for favors. I'm paid nicely for my work."

Which didn't mean she was rolling in cash; her med school debt alone was still close to $200,000. Add to that two mortgages, alimony, child support, a car payment, malpractice insurance, a small retirement contribution, half of David's extra expenses, and what it was costing her for Goliath's doggy day care, there wasn't that much left at month's end.

Heath had a child in the PICU. Heath scraped by teaching yoga, and lived in a tiny cabin in the woods. Heath's upper body was loose, almost relaxed, even here, now. Her hands weren't clenched.

Heath said, "You *should* be paid nicely; what you do is hugely important. And I expect you to pay for the yoga class and the massage. It's not a freebie, Dr. Geller. The favor is the invitation. We're really particular about who we let in."

"Well then, I feel privileged to get the invite—but just now," Claire said, glancing at her watch, "I have to run. If I decide to take you up on it, I'll let you know."

Heath was not put off. She took a pen from the breast pocket of Claire's white coat, grabbed Claire's wrist, and on Claire's palm, wrote an address and a time. "This evening or Thursday: which do you prefer?"

"Listen, I—"

"Pick one," Heath said. "Seriously. Do it. You need this."

Claire was simultaneously annoyed and charmed by Heath's insistence. She said, "You are a very caring person, and I appreciate it. Honestly. But I'm not sure it's professional of me to interact with a patient's family in the way you're offering."

"Are you sure that it isn't?"

"Well—" Claire paused. "No, I'm not."

"Tonight or Thursday: choose."

"Okay, okay, you win," Claire said, to extricate herself. "Tonight."

"Excellent. See you then."

As Claire was on her way out of the ward a short time later, Jennifer caught up to her. "Hey, before you go, I wanted to ask you about kicking in twenty bucks for the floor's Lotto pool—are you still in? The jackpot's over a hundred mill."

"Oh, I forgot. Sure, I'll waste twenty dollars on the fantasy of becoming an instant multimillionaire." She took her wallet from her purse.

"That mom was really intense—albeit in a super-sweet way. So you're going to go?"

Claire said, "No. I just agreed to it so that she'd stop insisting. I'm really not in the mood."

"That's exactly why you should do it."

"Oh, now I have to debate you, too?"

"It's good for you," Jennifer said. "To go, I mean. Not to debate about going."

"I'd have to leave Goliath at day care."

"So leave him. The woman is right. Your shoulders are practically stuck to your ears. Try to get a sauna session, too, if they've got it."

Claire said, "Any other advice?"

"Wear a hat when you go outside."

"Aw, Mom."

"I know," Jennifer said, stern-faced, "but we don't want you catching your death out there, now do we?"

"If it means I can avoid having to go to Heath's nutty-crunchy compound . . ."

"You *can* avoid it," Jennifer said. "But you shouldn't. Besides, what else do you have to do tonight? David's at Chad's, right?"

Claire sighed. "Yes. Fine. I'll go. I'll go! Then you guys will get off my back, and that alone will ease my stress."

Jennifer said, "The good news is that we'll all be multimillionaires tomorrow. Then we can quit work and live like sloths. Very low-stress animals."

Claire took her toque from her coat pocket and headed for the doors, waving as she went. Endless free time to fill? No distractions from her failings? Now there was a stressful thought.

. . .

Fat snowflakes were falling, fast and heavy, as Claire left her house, having gone home to grab a quick bite to eat and change clothes. How could she have ever thought of snow as romantic? Ugh. It was going to be winter here forever. Perpetually cold. Ice and snow everywhere. Her cardio workouts would remain limited to shoveling the driveway and sidewalk forever and ever, amen. Why even let herself imagine anything different? She'd made her choices.

She navigated her Subaru up Duluth's rise from Lake Superior's basin and onto the plateau that stretched west of town. You didn't have to go far to feel like you were in the backwoods wilderness that characterized most of northern Minnesota—especially after dark and during this kind of wet, near-spring snowfall.

While snow coated the tree limbs and added to the piles along the roadside, the roads themselves were merely wet. For the twenty or so minutes it took for Claire to get from the outskirts of town to the address Heath had written on her palm, Claire drove in the Zen-like reverie created from the steady swipe of her windshield wipers and the constant barrage of snowflakes. Maybe all she needed was to keep driving. Just keep going west to Fargo, to Bismarck, to Billings, then Bozeman, Missoula, Spokane. Go all the way to Seattle and then get a flight to Maui. To Tokyo. To Seoul. Wait, no; stop at Maui. What was she even doing out here, anyway? Her existence felt inconsequential, even to her. Forget driving west; just steer, fast, into a ditch or a tree and be done with it all.

"Knock it off," she said aloud. "Get a grip."

The long roadway into the compound was icy gravel bordered by dense stands of vivid white birch. The snow fell more lightly here and danced in the headlights. At the road's end was a parking area bounded by a split rail fence. Behind the fence, a wide, rectangular planed-log structure with four evenly spaced windows on this side. Three pairs of cross-country skis rested against the building near one end, where a single bare-bulb fixture made a pool of light beside the door. A half-dozen hardy vehicles were already parked here. Who knew a place like this could be so popular?

Claire grabbed her yoga mat and water bottle, both little used, and followed the shoveled path to the building's door. Inside, she found a long hallway with fluorescent lighting and doors on both sides.

The first one on the left stood open to a small but surprisingly inviting yoga studio: the lighting here was low and warm, the walls painted soft mocha, the wood-plank floor glowing golden where it wasn't covered by mats.

Heath spotted Claire and came over to her. "Hey, you made it. I'm proud of you."

"Thanks," Claire said.

"We've got a few minutes before I start class; why don't you put your stuff down over there"—she pointed to a space near the left wall—"and let me give you the tour."

Along the left side of the hallway were a second, unheated yoga studio; two small, cozy rooms set up for massages; and a restroom. At the end, a wide, warm kitchen with a stone fireplace, beside which was a dining table flanked by two benches and a high chair. A young woman was at the stove making something that smelled amazing. *Probably packed with sodium,* thought Claire; as far as her taste buds were concerned, everything worth eating was off limits. She was still awaiting the promised shift away from craving salt, just as she was still awaiting acclimation to Duluth's extreme cold.

The young woman waved at Heath and Claire. "Welcome," she said.

Heath said, "Hannah, meet River's doctor, Claire Geller, the one I was telling you about." To Claire, she said, "When Hannah's not making fab meals for us, she does fiber arts. We'll see her domain next."

Hannah said, "Thanks for taking such good care of our boy. Stop back here before you leave; I have a care package for you."

Heath said, "Your famous spiced walnut bread, I'll bet."

Hannah nodded. "Yep. Among other things."

"Really, that's not necessary."

"It *is* necessary," Heath said, guiding Claire back into the hallway. "It is absolutely essential."

The first of the rooms on the right was outfitted with two industrial sinks and an array of drying racks and plastic tubs, some of them as large as a bathtub. The room had a faint odor of something like sour grass.

"Fleece-washing room," Heath said. "We shear the sheep, pack the fleece into these tubs, then bring it in here to wash and dry."

In the next room were wide tables surrounded by walls of shelves that held an array of spiky tools Claire couldn't identify, along with brushes of different sizes.

Heath said, "Picking, combing, carding all gets done in here. You have to process the fleece into a spinnable fiber. Oh—and in addition to cleaning the fleece in the other room, it gets dyed there, too. River loves that; he has a feel for color, you know? Hates the shearing, though. It's noisy, and he worries that the shorn sheep are cold."

In a third room was an assortment of spinning wheels and accessories, along with an entire wall of shelving that held skeins of dyed yarn in scores of colors.

"Stock for our online store. Not everyone wants to dye the yarn themselves."

"I want one of every color."

"Do you knit?" Heath asked.

"I don't know the first thing about it."

"It is incredibly satisfying. And the basics are simple. Even River knows the garter stitch. He made a scarf for his stuffed bear."

Claire said, "Come on."

"No lie. Ask him yourself. Here," she said, selecting a skein of vivid green. "Take this. I'll get you a pair of needles, and he can teach you. He'd love it."

Claire could not imagine finding time for that lesson, let alone time to actually knit things. Still, the idea appealed the way salt appealed. She said, "Okay, why not?"

"*That's* what I want to hear. *Why the hell not*: it's a life lesson for all of us.

We can be different. We don't have to all be sheep—no offense, sheep!" she called, in what was presumably the direction of their sheep.

Claire said, "To be fair: there are a lot of situations and occupations—mine, included—where you *have to* toe the line. Some kinds of conformity are necessary."

"Of course," said Heath. "Who said they're not? River has a bedtime. I pay my taxes. I'm not in favor of anarchy—well, maybe a little. Anyway, that's the tour! Time to get class under way."

In the yoga studio, new age music played at low volume. Eleven other women, old and young, every shape and size, were waiting there, talking to one another with familiarity and ease. Claire took her spot near the wall, seating herself on her mat beside an angular silver-haired white woman with crepey skin and a lotus tattoo on her calf. In front of her was a slightly younger (but not young) Native woman whose thick gray hair hung down her back. When the woman turned her head, Claire saw that her septum was pierced. These women were all what Claire was not: unconventional.

Here she sat, wearing designer yoga togs she hadn't used in a year or more, no ink anywhere on her body, nothing more than a single hole in each of her earlobes. She couldn't see everyone without turning around and being obvious, so it was possible that she wasn't the only uninked and unpierced and unpracticed person present. Others here might be anxious about looking wrong, about doing poorly and embarrassing themselves. The thought brought little comfort.

Heath seated herself on a mat facing the group. She said, "Good evening. Special welcome to Claire, who's joining us for the first but we hope not the last time."

"Welcome, Claire," the women said, turning to look at her. The white-haired old lady said, "Bienvenue." She had a gap-toothed smile.

Heath continued, "On a personal note: I ask for you to lend some good energy to the continued healing of River. And now let's begin with a re-minder of our primary intention, which is to be present and open so as to allow ourselves to step into the flow of grace. We open ourselves as vessels for Spirit, connection to all that is divine within and without, access to freedom, to ease, to love. Now let's each of us take a moment to set our personal intention for this specific practice."

To *keep a straight face*, Claire thought, then chastised herself. She should try harder to get with the program. Maybe there really was something to yoga practice; millions and millions of people thought so. Of course millions and millions of people also thought shrimp was food, and Claire was not among them. But all right, *breathe . . . reach . . . turn . . . hold . . .*

Claire and the other women spent the next hour in the dim warm room under the mesmerizing direction of Heath, who kept her voice just loud enough to be heard over the low music. Claire did her best to put her body into the correct positions (some of which were painful, some not remotely possible) while also trying to ignore how the old woman next to her was not struggling at all. Probably the woman didn't also work fifty hours a week doing her damnedest to treat sick children and raise a son and tend a dog and parry with an ex and pay her bills and grieve her mother's untimely if somewhat expected death. Probably the woman had been doing yoga daily for longer than Claire had been alive.

(*Focus, Claire. Remember your blood pressure.*)

On went Heath with her calm, affirming instruction. ". . . now inhale, lengthen the neck, and exhale into your third eye . . ."

Claire could not figure out how to exhale into either of the eyes she knew she had, let alone the one she knew she didn't. She settled for her nose.

Unlike Heath, with her pierced everything and decorated skin, Tina the masseuse was as plain as a glass of tepid water. She wore her ash-blond hair straight and long and parted in the middle. Her blue turtleneck and blue pants were a mere shade apart in color. Pale complexion, unremarkable features, and when she spoke to say, "I'll just give you a couple of minutes to undress and get settled, facedown, blanket over the top," her tone was gentle. She seemed entirely self-possessed, at one with the universe. Claire wanted to be Tina.

As in the yoga studio, the music here had a tuneless, soothing quality. Claire stripped off her damp clothes and folded them into a tidy pile on the wooden chair. Possibly because of the yoga practice she'd just done, possibly because of the snow falling outside the window, or the music inside, or the low lighting, or Tina's unthreatening mien, Claire was (for the moment) almost uncritical of her naked body. Yes, her breasts were a bit uneven in size and a bit lower and heavier than they'd been before David. Yes, she had some stretch marks on her belly and hips. She had cellulite and was heavier through her thighs and ass than either Beck or Sophie. (She resented Beck; childless Sophie she could forgive.) Just now, though, she felt grateful for having been capable of the (sometimes awkward) efforts her body had just made, grateful for the luck (it was so often only luck) that brought her continued good health, such that she could be there doing yoga in the first place. Maybe this gentler attitude was *being in the flow*?

When Tina returned, Claire lay, as directed, facedown under the blanket.

Tina said, "I've got warmed oil here, and I've warmed my hands, so we can get started. Are there any areas you'd like me to focus on or avoid?"

"I don't think so," Claire said. Her face was pressed against the padded donut. Her view of the floor below was of a mosaic panel made from smooth lakeshore stones, separated into a pattern of tonally similar colors and laid out in a Tree of Life design.

"Is the music volume all right?"

"Yes, fine."

"Good, then we'll get started. Let me know if I'm doing anything too hard, okay?"

"I will."

As Tina got under way, it occurred to Claire that no one had put hands on her unclothed body in more than three months—not since the night she'd seduced her neighbor from across the alley on Christmas Eve. From her kitchen window, Claire had seen Brendan standing on his back stoop looking out into the gloaming. He was cute-ish, and he looked so lonely; his two daughters were with their mom for the holiday. Claire went to her door and called to him, "Come have some grog."

The sex had been awkward and quick, but also satisfying, like scratching an itch. That itch, however, hadn't had much to do with Brendan. He was a good guy, pleasant enough but in no way a contender for future involvement. The itch was for guilt-free sex. Fun sex with not-Chad. Sex with a man who wasn't concerned with staging her just so for his own maximum enjoyment. *You know, if you'll just get on your knees and lean forward about forty-five degrees . . .*

Tina moved her hands from Claire's left leg to begin on her lower back. As she pressed, she elicited a sigh of pleasure.

"That's a good spot, eh?"

"Mm."

Sex with Brendan on Christmas Eve had also been a way to offset the trauma of the prior holiday—Thanksgiving, that trip to Chad's parents' home that had precipitated Chad and Claire's split. After the early afternoon feast, they'd spent the late afternoon watching the Bears beat the Lions. Chad's sister Michelle had persuaded Claire to join her for boilermakers. Everyone was having fun. The fun got interrupted by Chad's assistant, who called with some crisis, and Chad said they needed to head back to Duluth right away— documents in his office, only he could handle it, that's just how important he was, folks, sorry to cut the fun short.

While driving back, Claire decided to check in with her sisters. Beck and Paul hosted an annual feast with their kids and Marti and sometimes Sophie, plus the various "widows and orphans" from their network of colleagues and friends. This year Sophie was doing an un-Thanksgiving in London with her latest man-child, Marco. Usually Claire called Marti on the day after. Just now, though, here in the darkness of Chad's restored Saab, nothing to do or see, she was feeling buzzy and warm and congenial and wanted to extend the feeling, having had it abruptly ended by Chad.

So she'd tried Sophie first, got voice mail. Then she'd called Beck and

Paul's landline, telling Chad, "This way I'm sure to get her—she won't have her cell at hand." (This way, too, she might possibly get Paul.)

She'd gotten Cammie, who sounded like she was in a rush. "Hey, Aunt Claire! Happy day! I almost missed you—we're all out back, hanging around the firepit. I just came in to pee. If you'll hold on, I'll get Mom and Grandma to come in—"

"No," Claire said, deflated by the image Cammie's words brought, the fun being had without her there, no one even thinking of her absence. "Don't bother them. I'll call tomorrow."

"You're sure?"

"Yes. Go have fun."

"Okay, then. Give my man David a squeeze for me."

Claire said she would, and ended the call. "They're partying outside," she told Chad.

He said, "You have to hand it to Beck: she puts on a terrific Thanksgiving. It's a whole *event*."

"I guess."

"You guess? Every year it's a full formal dinner for at least a dozen people, and the house always looks like something from a magazine spread."

"Yeah, well, she's got time to do all of that."

Beck was known to start cooking three days ahead. She was known to create elaborate centerpieces using whatever materials were trending that year. There were always gourds and flowers and fabrics and candles and napkin rings and crystal, all of it coordinated expertly and laid out on their oversize walnut dining table and the mid-century sideboard that she'd restored herself, as well as placed in other high-visibility areas throughout the house.

"It isn't just about having time," said Chad, warming to his topic. "It's that she actively cultivates an entire holiday environment. The guest list, the menu, the decor—even her Facebook pics are first rate. Maybe it's the journalism training. She's got a real eye for what makes a good photograph."

"Yes, Beck is perfect. Perfect life, perfect kids—"

"Their *kids* aren't perfect. Cammie's got zero interest in college, and

Zack knocked up his girlfriend by accident. What kid from their class *does* that anymore?"

"It wasn't by accident. It was by arrangement. I told you that."

"It was stupid and naïve, is what it was. These kids think they can just upend all the norms and it'll work out like some fairy tale . . ."

"Also, she's got a perfect husband," Claire declared, only half hearing Chad.

"*Paul* is perfect? The guy's balding and he's not even fifty."

"So? Hair loss is not a character flaw."

"He makes his living editing books no one reads."

"I read them. Award committees read them."

"Have you ever noticed his biceps? You haven't, because I'll bet he's never even seen the inside of a gym. Beck could've done a lot better."

"Oh, because what Beck really deserves is a guy with six-pack abs? A guy like you, I guess. But you know what? Paul has a very attractive body. He doesn't need to be in the gym five mornings a week."

"Please. You think *he's* attractive."

"I do."

"Really."

"Really," Claire said. "I always have. If Beck hadn't already nabbed him . . ."

"What, then *you* would have?"

"Absolutely. Once I was old enough. I think he's an excellent person."

"Maybe you wish he was your husband."

"Maybe I do."

Chad laughed. "Sure. That nerd versus me."

"He'd win," Claire said.

"You're either out of your mind or you're drunk."

"Maybe I am a little drunk, but I'm also totally sane. I've loved the man since I first saw him when I was fourteen years old."

As all of these words had been emerging from her mouth, Claire felt simultaneously exultant and horrified that she was saying the unsayable. Saying all of it so *easily*, with such confidence in her declaration.

Chad said, "I cannot believe what I'm hearing."

"Believe it," Claire told him. "But, look, so what if I love him? It makes zero difference in anyone's life. He married Beck. I married you. *That's* all that matters."

Ah, but that was not all that mattered to Chad. Before the weekend was over, he'd labeled Claire as a deceptive, disloyal, disgusting human being. He could not—would not—abide being anyone's second choice. A consolation prize. He valued himself much too highly for that. He'd never be able to see her the same way again.

No amount of apologizing or explaining or denying could undo his suspicions that she'd fantasized about Paul while in bed with him (she had). By Sunday evening, he'd found a furnished apartment and that was it, the end. Her betrayal was unforgivable. He'd wasted too much of his life on her as it was.

This was not an unreasonable position to take. Just the same, she'd wanted him to be as pragmatic about it as she'd been all these years. To put aside the wound to his ego and focus on what was real. For years, she'd been able to live with the dissonance between what she wished were true and what actually was true; why couldn't he at least *try* to do the same? But no.

Now Tina worked on the muscles in Claire's upper shoulders and neck. "Hmm, you're still pretty knotted up here."

"I should do more yoga."

"You're sure this isn't too hard?"

"No, bring it on," said Claire. "I need it."

A little pain could be a good thing. The divorce had been painful, but now that she'd overcome Chad's total rejection of even her most contrite self, she couldn't fault him for his actions or his opinions. In his place, could she ever feel the same toward a man who'd always jonesed for someone else? No, she could not. She wanted the same thing Chad wanted: total devotion from one's partner. He deserved that. She deserved that. She'd had it—sort of; Chad had been totally devoted to the Claire he kept trying to create. Now she wanted the real deal or nothing at all. This was growth. This was empowerment.

Claire gave herself over to Tina's strong hands, to the pressure and the rhythms. Back done, front next. Scalp, ears, forehead, the base of her neck . . . It was sensual but not sexual, and so, so good. She felt sated, aglow with limp contentment.

When Tina had finished the last gentle strokes and was about to leave the room, Claire, eyes still closed, said, "This was exactly what I needed. Thank you. As I was lying here, I was thinking about how for way too long I've based a lot of my value on whether a man desired me. I'm done with that. I feel . . ." She paused, thinking of how best to describe her state of being. Then she said, "I feel whole. Reconstituted."

Tina patted her arm. "That is truly wonderful. I'm grateful to share in that with you."

Claire dressed in the change of clothes she'd brought. Really, she felt almost drunk; physiologically, this was an endorphin high. She knew it was so, yet just the same, she embraced the emotional shift she felt, tagged it as genuine. She was reconstituted for real. Free of Chad. Free of unrequited longing, of the resistance and anger she'd felt about Paul. Go with God, my friends, she thought, sending her message to each of them through her third eye into that purported psychic river of grace.

She felt so renewed that after paying for the class and massage, she signed up for a fiber arts one-day workshop for Sunday, when David was at Chad's. She had good hands; knitting shouldn't be too difficult to learn. She could start by making Goliath a scarf.

Outside, the snow had tapered off. Claire started her car, then checked her phone and was surprised to see a voice mail from Paul. Her heart, which had slowed to a mellow rhythm, got a fresh surge of adrenaline and forgot all about mellow. It forgot all about reconstituted, about states of grace. She might be a heart doctor, but here was further proof that her medical degree gave her no advantage over the most ignorant of the lovelorn.

What might her life look like today if he hadn't been at Eileen Greenburg's bat mitzvah, or if she hadn't? *Damn it, Paul,* she thought. *Why can't I quit you?*

Deep breath in, long slow exhale. Okay. There was just the one missed call and no text from him, so, not an emergency. She could ignore the voice mail for now. Avoid whatever business he had to transact; surely this call had to do with the will. Some document she needed to sign, some information she needed to provide.

Claire told herself to just leave it for now. Forget about Paul. Get back into the flow. *Deep breath in . . . Fill your lungs . . . Feel your heart expanding . . .*

She put her car in gear, backed out of the parking space, drove down the long birch-bounded driveway and out onto the road. One mile, two miles, three miles . . . Then, "You win," she said aloud—maybe to Paul, maybe to God, maybe to Satan (though she hadn't believed in Satan until right now). She pulled over, took her phone out again, and played the message.

Claire, hi, it's Paul. Listen, I've been . . . No, you know what? Just give me a call back when you get this, okay? There's . . . I have something I need to talk to you about. Okay. Hope you're doing well. Thanks. 'Bye.

Her car's headlights lit the roadside snowbank. Claire stared into the night, her pulse thumping in her ears. This was no business message, that was evident. What else it could be, though, was not evident at all. Why would he need to talk to her if it wasn't to do with the will?

Might he . . . be looking for a confessor?

He might.

Did she want to be that for him?

She might.

Or maybe not.

But at least then she'd know.

Call him back now, or call him from home? Have her (pathetic, improbable) dream ruined now, or later?

"Oh, screw it," she said, and placed the call.

He answered right away, and she said as casually as she could, "Hi, I just got your message. What's up?"

"Thank you for calling me back."

"Of course."

"Sorry if I sounded a little deranged," he said. "Maybe I should've thought better of it."

"No, you're fine. Is everything okay?"

"Well, yes and no. That is to say, everyone is okay. The kids, Leah. Beck, too, I assume."

"Assume?"

"She's in Maine. She didn't tell you she stayed?"

"No, she did," Claire said. "I just figured you must be talking regularly."

"Now and then. Anyway," Paul said, "everyone's fine. But . . . well, the truth is, *I'm* not fine."

Here it comes, Claire thought. He was going to puncture her fantasy, deflate it, leave it shrunken and withered along with her soul. All right. If that's the way it was, then that's the way it was. Nothing she could do, except continue to be his friend.

"Can I help?" she said. As she spoke the words, she noticed something dark and large edging into her headlights' beam. "A moose!" she blurted. "Oh my god, there's a moose right here in front of my car. Holy shit. It's huge!"

"What? Where are you?"

"On a back road, west of town." She watched the majestic bull as it meandered across the road. It had to be six feet tall and probably eight feet across. Its thick-furred body took up her entire view. "I've never seen one before. It's . . . wow. It's magnificent." Was it some kind of sign? Heath, moose, Paul—what was the connection? Was there any connection at all? Her father had liked to talk about Jung's "meaningful coincidences," and here she'd just spent two hours in the universe's flow . . .

Paul said, "Are you driving?"

"No, I'm parked."

"Okay, good, I was worried." He said, "You know, maybe this wasn't a smart idea. I shouldn't be bothering you with my—"

"No, no, you aren't. Please. Sorry to interrupt you that way. I just—"

"Right, of course. A moose sighting! I've never seen one, either."

Claire said, "He's going off into the woods now. You have my full attention."

No reply.

"Paul?"

"I'm here. Sorry." She heard him draw a breath. Then in a rush he said, "Okay: I'm thinking of asking Beck for a divorce. Never mind what the reasons are; that's complicated, and I . . . I'm not going to trouble you about that. My question for you is, how do you think she'd react?"

Claire was more surprised by this than she had been by the moose. She said, "We don't really confide in each other much, so . . ."

"Right, I know, but I thought that maybe lately . . ."

Claire thought of that night at 432 Park. The martinis. Beck's almost-casual attitude. "I . . . Wow, Paul, this is a real shock. To me. But maybe it won't be to Beck. I mean, if she knows what the reasons are, maybe she'll be on the same page."

"I'm not sure if she knows or not," Paul said. "My timing, though . . . it might be cruel. I'm concerned that I'm going to hurt her terribly."

Claire said, "Actually, I—that is, I can't speak for Beck with total authority here, but let's just say you might be surprised at how well she takes it."

"Yeah?" he said with clear relief. "That's good to hear. In a way. In another way, I should feel *terrible* about the idea that she'd be okay with it, because what does that say about how clueless I've been as to *her* feelings? On the other hand, it would be so much better for both her and me if, in fact, she really is okay with us calling it quits."

He added, "Saying all of this out loud is surreal."

Say more, Claire thought. Just say it, damn it. Get it all off your chest! *You'll* feel better, even if I won't.

She said, "Believe me, I understand."

"I thought you might—considering you've been through a breakup. It can't have been easy."

There it was again, his characteristic thoughtfulness, his caring tone. Why did all the best ones have to be gay? Presumably gay. Possibly gay.

Or not!

But then, as Sophie said, shouldn't Beck be able to gauge this possibility far better than she, Claire, could? Yes, Beck knew better.

She wanted to ask Paul to enumerate his reasons. Was it about Geoff, his assistant? Was he leading a double life? She could relate!

If she pried, though, she might upset him and spoil this moment, the crazy, stupid tenderness of it, her sitting here in the dark, light snow in her headlights, a moose in the woods, Paul's voice in her ear, in her head—maybe for the last time, if he and Beck were splitting up.

Claire said, "No, the breakup wasn't easy at all. But it was the right thing, in the end."

"Maybe one day we'll get together and compare notes."

"Maybe we will," she said. Was her tone wistful? She hoped it was not.

Paul said, "So, then, my other question for you, given your experience, is, how would you say is the best way to go about telling her? Not by phone, obviously."

"No," said Claire, "definitely do it in person. Be the same thoughtful guy you always are."

"I try to be thoughtful, Claire, but you know, I don't always get it right. I have flaws. Obviously."

"Everyone does. Just do your best. You guys are such great friends. That's not going to change."

"I'm not as convinced as you are. Well, it depends. But anyway, I don't want to keep you any longer. I'm sure you want to get home. Thank you for letting me lean on you this way. I really appreciate it."

"Glad to help."

"You take care, okay? Stay warm."

"I will," she said, and for the moment she actually did feel warm. That was the Paul effect.

"And, Paul?"

"Yeah?"

Claire was about to say, *Call me anytime,* and then thought better of it; she didn't want him to call her, ever, if it meant she was going to be tormented all over again.

That was the message of the moose's crossing: it was a warning, a reminder that the next encounter might be a catastrophe, and why take that chance? Why put yourself in the way of trouble when you could easily avoid it?

She said, "Never mind. Good luck. I'm sure it's all going to work out fine."

17

Hidden Truths

Because there was no Wi-Fi at the camp, if Beck wanted to scour the web for information about her mother's past (which of course she did), she would be best served to do so elsewhere—and where better than the nearby Somesville Library, where she'd passed so many summertime hours in the little white building beside the Mill Pond? It was hardly larger than the Geller camp, but for young Beck it had been as vast as her interests and imagination.

Seated now at the big wooden table facing the windows, Beck began her web search broadly. This was always her practice: casting a wide net first could yield richer and sometimes unexpected results. Once, when working on an article about so-called teacup dogs, she'd ended up reuniting twin sisters who'd been adopted by two different families and raised apart, only to both become teacup Yorkie breeders living on opposite sides of New Jersey.

Feeling optimistic, Beck googled her mother's and grandparents' names. And found nothing at all. Not a single hit that pertained to any of them. This wasn't that surprising, though; a lot of people had little or no online presence, especially if they'd lived most or all their lives before the internet's invention.

Next, she tried the local property records, marriage records, birth and death records, and found only slight evidence that the people her mother had named in the video existed at all and in the way she'd claimed. Stanley and Miriam Newman owned a farm, then lost it to foreclosure; Stanley died in 1973, Miriam in 1986—her grandmother had been alive for the first decade or so of her life, and Beck had never known! Carl Newman served with the U.S. Army in Vietnam and was killed in action. But Marti Newman didn't appear anywhere in these records.

"Where are you, Mom?" Beck murmured as she pulled up the MDI Historical Society's database. You never knew what ephemera you might find in these kinds of local collections.

There was nothing here about her grandparents, nothing about her uncle, nothing about anyone whose surname was Newman—with one exception: Martina "Marti" Newman, who was pictured in a photo of the Callaghan family "cottage" known as Cal Eyrie, where she and a squinting boy stood beside a red sixties-era Buick Wildcat parked in front of the grand house. The squinting boy was Roderick "Chip" Callaghan.

Was he Marti's ill-advised love? Almost certainly; the photo was dated '66 or '67, and the Callaghans seemed to Beck exactly the kind of people who'd have such heartless disregard for a poor farmer's teenage daughter. Beck had met a Callaghan kid one summer, gotten to know him a little bit. A little bit had been plenty for her; he'd been obnoxious and full of himself, just like Chip here had surely been.

But look at Marti, wearing bright green pedal pushers and a polka-dotted shirt knotted at her waist. White sneakers. A white ribbon in her wavy dark hair. She stood with the toe of her right shoe covering the left. Nervous, despite the wide smile. She'd known she was out of place, that she faced long odds of ever belonging to this scene. Yet there she had been, giving it a try.

"Poor Mom," Beck said.

What had Chip made of himself? That was Beck's next query. Google had more to say about him. Eldest of four, CEO (now retired), married (still) to Penelope Marie Whitlock Callaghan. Son of Roderick Sr. (deceased) and

Deirdre, of Boston. Father to seven—seven!—kids who, like Beck and her sisters, would not now exist if he had manned up and done right by Marti Newman in her green pedal pushers and polka-dotted shirt.

Roads not taken.

Enough about the Callaghans. What about the Newmans? Beck spent another hour at her task, trying every archive she had access to and coming up empty-handed. Stanley and Miriam Newman left no easy trail.

Beck snapped a picture of the photo and texted it to her sisters:

> Mostly a dead end on Newman history, but here is Mom with the guy who got her pregnant, I'm pretty sure.

> I might pursue Newman history further via print archives when I have more time. But maybe it's okay to leave it lay?

Sophie replied right away:

> Up to you but I think we know enough.

> Mom though!

> You looked just like that in high school. Except her clothes are cuter.

After a few minutes of browsing books, Beck selected a few, checked them out, then left the library and went to see if she could locate the house and land that had once belonged to her grandparents. The drive from the library was short and not especially interesting. Beck, though, imagined how it would have seemed to her mother as a troubled teen with few options. How she'd have dreaded coming home. How briefly hopeful she'd have been when she was welcomed at the Callaghans. How badly she'd wanted to leave MDI, once everything went to hell.

When Beck got to the part of Crooked Road where the farm was supposed to have been, there was nothing but trees and, way off in the distance, the weathered remnants of a barn. She pulled over to the roadside and got out of her car. No one was around to see her slip through the fence and walk a short way, then just stand there with the wind blowing through her hair and tugging at her coat.

"Homeland," she said, and scooped up a handful of dirt, though she felt foolish. This was hardly on par with a visit to Jerusalem. And being so sentimental about a place her mother had evidently not held dear felt foolish, too.

She tossed the dirt into the wind, saying, "Okay, whatever."

Claire's response to the photo came late that evening, after Beck had finished sanding the kitchen cabinet doors and was lying on the plaid couch icing her elbow and rereading *Little Women*.

> God that does look like Beck!
>
> I agree to let it lay. Ancient history. What else do you need to know?

Beck wrote:

> Maybe you're right. I just wish I knew why Mom thought we would want to let all of this go.
>
> Anyway, the loan seems to be on track, but IRS is being slow with tax return verifications. Appraisal is next Weds. I won't rest easy till I get final YES.

Sophie replied right away: LMK as soon as you hear.
Claire wrote:

> Goliath is puking something up and David needs help with his science project. I love my life! Got to go. Keep us posted.

Beck set her phone down and said, "Mom, if you're listening, I need you to help me understand. Show me a sign."

She waited.

Nothing but the sound of water dripping—the bathroom faucet needed to be fixed, but surely that was not a sign of anything except age and neglect.

"Maybe I should rephrase that: Mom, if you're listening, give me some kind of clue."

Beck scanned the living room, noticing the fire iron, a glass candy dish shaped like a crab, the Yahtzee game that was missing two dice. She saw ruffled curtains. A photo of herself with her sisters in a canoe, circa 1989. On the mantel, a row of five "snowmen"—a family project they'd done one summer, crafted from painted stones her father had glued together. Each was made to look like its artist. That was the summer Claire contracted chicken pox and spread it to Beck and Sophie. Claire was so fascinated by the whole experience that when they returned home to New York, she'd started reading medical encyclopedias.

When it seemed that Marti was not going to offer her anything, Beck returned her attention to *Little Women*, where, when she turned the page to begin the next chapter, a passage caught her eye:

Every few weeks she would shut herself up in her room, put on her scribbling suit, and "fall into a vortex," as she expressed it, writing away at her novel with all her heart and soul, for till that was finished she could find no peace.

"Fish or cut bait," Beck reminded herself. She set *Little Women* on the coffee table and opened her laptop.

Beck's Writing Room (as a note taped to the door now read) was the smallest of the three bedrooms, the room that had been Beck's, way back when. Her tiny, glorious room, even if only for brief bursts of time. She hadn't cared that it was small; she was used to having little space of her own. She cared that she could keep her sisters out. She could close the door and feel as if she were in a whole other universe.

She could open the window and let in the sea-scented air and be an orphan on a great maritime adventure where her bed was her boat and the gulls that called and cruised outside were her companions at sea, helping guide her to an island where she would rescue the cute boy who'd been kidnapped and was held prisoner there.

Or she could be the star of a Broadway musical, standing on the stage (her bed) belting out *Fame*'s title track or channeling the hopelessly devoted Sandy of *Grease*.

Or she could be Dickinson or Austen or Woolf or Plath or Didion, so earnest as she sat on the bed with a notebook on her lap transcribing her joys and woes into bad poems or short stories or essays that were more like diatribes. Every emotion had felt saturated then. Every emotion felt saturated now.

She made coffee and sat at the table she'd placed in front of the Writing Room window. On that table: her laptop computer with its blank page and its blinking cursor, waiting, waiting, waiting for les mots justes. Her writing plan was this: using the notes she'd compiled over the years, start fresh with the story and write 2,000 words every day. When she had 30,000 words done—a third of the story, give or take—polish it up and send it to her friend Gina, who was a literary agent and would tell her if the work was any good.

Every day since she'd been here, Beck had worked her plan. She wrote in the mornings starting at five A.M., getting words on the page quickly, uncritically; the important thing was to just throw the story down, to not let self-doubt paralyze her anymore. She would edit later. In the afternoons into the evening, she patched, she primed, she painted—walls, furniture, cabinets. She disassembled old plumbing fixtures and assembled new ones and scrubbed grout and evicted spiders. She hauled things off to the thrift shop and hauled other things back.

Only late at night, when Beck was lying in bed awaiting sleep, did she muse on how her mother had lived *every day* enduring the tension between truth and fear. Every summer visit to MDI, she must have been looking over her shoulder to ensure she wasn't recognized by anyone from her past. No wonder she had preferred to stick close to camp, and when she did go out, she chose Southwest Harbor over Bar.

Could all that suppressed anxiety have caused her cancer? Probably not directly—but what if it had made her more susceptible? The mind-body connection was a real thing.

"Mom, if you can hear me, I forgive you for the deception. Still not happy, though, about this sell-the-camp business."

But so far, Beck's solution (expensive though it was) was working: the credit union had given the loan preliminary approval, pending the necessary verifications—of Paul's and Beck's income and assets, of the camp's value—which, though they seemed to be taking *forever*, were merely formalities at this point. She'd texted her sisters to reassure them that their weekend together would be a celebration—and, Beck hoped, the first of an annual series of such gatherings spent here together, rebonding. As different as she and her sisters were, the faint silver lining in their mother's passing was that it had forced them to stay in close contact, and Beck, for one, really liked this.

In the meantime, she was showing her mother (and herself) what she could do.

Writing day one: "I am on fire!"

Writing day two: "I am living the dream—for the moment, anyway, and what else is there?"

Writing day three: "I can do this. I. Can. Do. This. I can do this!"

And so on, with varying degrees of confidence. Still, she showed up every day. She put words on the page. That was more than half the battle.

Again today she rose at five. She made the coffee. She sat down at the table and opened the file to the scene where she'd left off yesterday. Her protagonist, fourteen-year-old Caitlinn, was visiting her dying father in the hospital in Pottsville, Pennsylvania. He was sick with black lung disease, having worked in a coal mine since he was a teen. Caitlinn had been in the hospital room for nearly five thousand words already, and Beck had to get her out of there and on to the next scene, where she would visit the family's priest, distressed about her father's imminent death, and the priest, in a pretext of comforting her, would make sexual advances.

When Beck had discussed the story idea with Gina a few years earlier—casually, pretending it had just occurred to her that it could be a novel she might write if she were going to write a novel—which, she added, she wasn't saying she was going to do, Gina had cautioned her that the story might be too grim.

"Something upbeat and closer to your own experience might be the better bet," she said.

"Sure," Beck replied, knowing she would ignore the advice. Serious novelists wrote about serious subjects, especially if they were married to serious editors whose authors sometimes got nominated for major awards.

Now Beck watched the cursor while she tried to decide how to end the scene. Caitlinn and her father had a lot of unspoken business to deal with before he died. She *could* force Caitlinn to reckon with the unresolved stuff later. Have her father hang on a bit longer—maybe even have a brief rally? Except if Beck took that tack, she'd need to think of something different than the father's imminent death to upset Caitlinn and compel her to seek guidance from the priest. Hmm.

The cursor blinked.

Beck sipped her coffee and thought some more.

She typed some dialogue. More of a monologue, really, since the father could barely speak.

She changed her mind and deleted what she'd written.

Wrote something else.

Deleted it.

And tried to suppress the voice in her head that whispered, *Here we go again. We've been* here *before . . . Shut up,* she thought. *Just keep writing.*

When she looked up from the screen a while later, it was three o'clock and her word count showed a net loss of two thousand words. Which was not necessarily a problem! Except that Caitlinn was still in the hospital room.

"Fine," Beck said. "You can just stay there." She snapped the laptop closed, then went to make herself some lunch. Brain food; she had barely eaten anything today. No wonder she couldn't write.

Except that after lunch, she was still just as stuck. So much for the clear head. So much for the great energy.

"I will persist later," Beck said, and went to change into her painting clothes.

18

Sweet, Sharp

That morning, C.J. awakened to the sweet, sharp sound of a winter wren singing outside his window. He lay there listening, marveling at the purity of song, the energy the bird put into sending its message. He'd been trying to do the same thing with Avery—somehow convey the purity in his heart where she was concerned. But he'd been singing outside her window (so to speak) every few days since he left Broad River, and all he'd gotten was a thumbs-up to one text, basically acknowledging that she knew he was alive and free again, but didn't care enough to type a reply.

After breakfast, Carol Barksdale picked up C.J. for a second viewing of the house across from the Geller place. He still wasn't excited about it. He'd prefer to be seeing the Geller place. Carol had sent him some photos of the interior as well as the view; everything looked great. Typical lake-house decor, dated kitchen, and so on, but workable for sure. Unfortunately, there was still no telling the what or when of that one, so here he was, back at house five, the Barretts'.

Carol said, "You're smart to take another look at this, now that they've reduced the price."

"I was thinking that if I added a second story, I'd get at least a partial view of the water."

"There you go! Problem-solving—I should have thought of that. It's what I try to do, too. I'm sorry I haven't been able to get the Gellers to budge on a commitment to sell. I know you've been hoping. If I had to guess, I'd say they can't agree among themselves. Happens a lot."

C.J. stood facing the direction of the water. "If I could get up on that roof there, I'd have a better sense of the view, such as it may be. Think there's a ladder handy?" He was already heading around to the back as he spoke.

"Hold on," Carol called, following him.

"Here's one," C.J. said, spotting it lying on the ground alongside the narrow garage. He made to stand it up.

"Stop, no can do, I'm sorry," Carol said. "We'd need the sellers' consent, and there's a question of liability. Let me see if I can set up a time to get a builder out here to join us. He could get up and have a look for you, take some pictures."

C.J. looked at the ladder. It was *right there*. Just stand it against the house, climb up, have a look with his own eyes, climb down. Five minutes and he'd have what he needed in order to decide how or whether to proceed. He said, "S'pose I promise not to sue anybody? I can put it in writing, if you've got a sheet of paper."

"I'm sorry," Carol said again. "Better safe!"

He sighed. "Sure, of course, no problem."

"I'll try for tomorrow," Carol said. She began typing a text message.

It was a perfectly fine, relatively cheap house. Too small and too dark, and at best a partial distant view of the lake. But fixable. Available. Of course, who knew what kinds of problems he'd encounter once he started taking things apart? He wanted a place of his own, not a money pit or even a lengthy project.

He said, "You know what? Never mind. To be honest, I'm just not feeling it, even if I could improve the place."

"Are you sure? I might be able to get someone out here late today—I can make a few calls. It's no trouble."

"No, don't bother. I just need to be patient. The right thing'll come along."

"It will! You just keep the faith, like Billy Joel says. I expect there will be new places to see by week's end."

When C.J. returned to the Callaghan house, he found Melissa packed up and almost out the door.

"Did I miss the memo? Is this spring break?"

"Sort of. Mrs. Callaghan has decided to take Arlo back to Boston for some boarding school interviews. I guess she's looking at Hillside and Bement? I actually tried to get a job at Bement, but no luck so far. Anyway, Mrs. C. says I need to go home until next week so that I don't 'get in your way.' Maybe I'll see you when I'm back here?"

"Well, travel safe," he said.

In the kitchen, Arlo was bent over his bowl of Grape-Nuts, pushing the cereal around with his spoon.

"Hey, champ," C.J. greeted him. To Deirdre he said, "Off to Boston, then? I ran into Melissa on her way out."

"Yes. I was able to schedule interviews with two top-notch schools."

"Lucky," C.J. said for Arlo's benefit. "Man, I wish I could've had a chance with one of them. Boarding school? Dang. That was my dream." Deirdre gave him a look. Was he overselling it? Maybe. He said, "But you'll be back in a few days, right?"

Arlo nodded.

"I got some more house-hunting stuff to do anyway, so you won't be missing out on much here. If you want, I'll just push pause on our project until you get back. How's that?"

"Okay," Arlo said. He still hadn't raised his head.

Deirdre said to C.J., "He will be fine."

By whose definition? C.J. wondered. He said, "Better than fine. He'll be outstanding."

Arlo said, "You and Gram can stop acting like this is some great thing."

Deirdre took her coffee cup to the sink, saying, "C.J., I know you had to delay your run this morning. Maybe now you can get to that—you don't want to miss a day. Arlo, finish up, it's time to go."

"This is stupid," said Arlo.

C.J. put his hand on the boy's head for a moment. "Don't give Gram any trouble, all right? I'll see you again soon."

"Whatever," Arlo said.

That afternoon in the hardware store, carrying two gallons of the stain base he needed for the landscape timbers, C.J. stepped past the tall woman waiting at the counter so that he could set the cans there.

"I'm not cutting the line," he said to the woman, whose back was to him. "Just giving my hands a break while I wait my turn. Hope that's okay."

"No trouble," she replied, glancing over at him.

She looked familiar to him—and by her expression it appeared that she was making a connection, too. Then he placed her: the woman in that shop a week or so ago, when he was there with Arlo. She'd been wearing a hat, but yes, this was the same woman. Today she was hatless and paint-spattered— and she was smiling at him. She had a nice smile. Open. Faint lines at the corners of her eyes. He itched to sketch that precise expression, try to capture that enigmatic smile. She seemed genuine. Guileless. In other words: Melissa's opposite. He was glad the girl was gone. She was no temptation to him, just a mild nuisance, a bee you had to keep swatting at while it circled your head.

The woman said, "Oh, you're that 'no rules' fellow from the shop. How's it going? More home improvement under way?"

"The project's coming along," he said.

"Where's your little boy?"

"Arlo? Oh, he's not mine; he belongs to a friend I'm visiting." He pointed at her clothing. "Looks like you've been at it yourself. Home improvement, that is."

"What? Oh, yes. A little sprucing up is all. I ran out of paint with half a wall left!"

"Sounds like subconscious avoidance to me. I've known a few writers, and sometimes writing is the last thing they're ready to do."

"Well, there's some truth to that." Indicating her clothing, she said, "Funny how what improves the walls has the opposite effect on the person doing the improving."

"Oh, I don't know about that," he said.

"You're very kind." She smiled.

He smiled.

The clerk brought a can of paint to the counter. "All set," he said.

"Thanks." She picked it up, then turned again to C.J. "Guess I'd better get back to it."

She left, and C.J.'s. adamant wish to not complicate his life with feminine entanglement eroded further. Amended itself to more of a "not complicate his life with *difficult* women" rule. This one? She gave the impression of being easy. That is, not *easy*-easy. Low-maintenance easy. Easy like Sunday morning.

The thought provoked a longing for exactly that, if not exactly her. A partner who'd sit with him in a cozy kitchen somewhere, having her coffee while he fried their eggs and whipped up buttermilk pancakes. Or maybe she'd be a toast-and-jam kind of woman, eating while she read the newspaper's Arts section, and he'd come over to freshen her coffee, and he'd pick the crumbs off her pajama shirt (it'd be one of his old tees), and he'd kiss her and she'd smile and set the paper aside, and—

"Sir?" said the clerk. "What can I help you with?"

"Do you happen to know that woman, the one who just got that paint?"

"Sorry, I don't."

I'm sorry I *don't,* C.J. said to himself.

Returning to the house, he put the stain in the potting shed with the other materials. Much as he'd like to get right back to work on this, if only to have a mindless task to fill the rest of his day, he would keep his promise and wait for Arlo's return. Just as well; the wind had come up and clouds scudded the low sky. C.J.'s weather app said they'd get snow overnight. Not unusual for Maine in March.

Still, this, along with the lack of progress on housing and serious artwork, his anxieties for Arlo, even the encounter with the woman at the hardware store, made C.J. feel like he was backsliding. What was his deal? He was taking things one day at a time. He would find his house. He did not need any sort of relationship with any sort of woman. He did not need to be heartsick over an orphaned little rich boy.

Yet here he was, padding upstairs to that boy's bedroom because he was worried about him. He lay down on Arlo's canopied bed, imagined being an eight-year-old boy in this room, in the life that Arlo now inhabited. Arlo didn't talk about his parents. He didn't talk about his friends. He talked about rocks and fossils and how birds were the same as dinosaurs, just smaller. He talked about growing up to be "a chef at a taco stand" because, he said, people always got happy when they were eating yummy food, and the yummiest food was tacos.

C.J. had no business entertaining this romantic idea of him and Arlo pairing up any more than he ought to entertain that little fantasy he'd had in the hardware store about his Sunday kind of love.

He sat up, said to his phone, "Play Etta James," then went to his own room for his sketchpad and charcoal. That kind of love, at least, was suitable and at hand.

Preferring not to dine alone in the empty house, C.J. headed out to Leary's Landing, bringing along an old James Michener novel—paperback, about a foot thick, found among the hundreds of paperbacks that lined the Callaghans' sitting-room shelves. The book would keep him busy for many (many, many) such meals to come, if need be.

One of the great things about not being locked up anymore was that he got to choose when to be with people, or not. And if it had been a week or two or three since he'd done a push-up, that was okay, too. He could relax a little now. Ease up. Follow a schedule that he set for himself. He'd spent many (many, many) hours during his incarceration imagining what his life would look like once he'd done his time. Now he was three years older, three years wiser. Unwilling to be ruled by old impulses and desires. Proof? He'd resisted Melissa's overtures. He'd resisted presenting himself to Deirdre as an alternative to boarding school. He'd resisted pushing Avery to see or even talk with him. It was okay to want things but not pursue them, or not get them.

He parked at the restaurant. The lot was not even half full. Could be most people were at home appreciating the vivid sunset sliding in beneath the clouds, saturating the sky in deep oranges and pinks. C.J. stood beside his car appreciating the chilly, salty air on his face and in his lungs while he watched the sky's colors deepen to purples and sapphire and navy, stars now peeking from between the clouds, nighttime setting in.

"I'll just sit at the bar," he told the hostess when he got inside, then found his way to an empty seat at a mostly empty bar. Those who were seated here were paired up already; no other lonely old souls, or not yet, anyway.

The bartender wasn't in sight at the moment, so C.J. opened his book, reached for his reading glasses—and discovered he'd left them at the house. If he held the book at arm's length and squinted at it just right, in this dim light he could almost make out the opening sentence.

A voice at his shoulder: "Well, we meet again."

He turned and saw the woman from the hardware store. This time she was dressed in a chunky sweater, jeans, and tall leather boots with low heels. She carried an orange coat and made to drape it over the back of the bar chair next to his. "Okay if I join you?"

"Please," he said. "You know, if we're gonna keep meeting up like this, I think I should at least introduce myself. I'm C.J."

She took her time getting seated. "I'm Beverly," she said. "Pleased to make your actual acquaintance."

"That's a name you don't hear too often," C.J. said. Though the way she'd said it made him suspect that she was not named Beverly at all, and either was not a skillful liar or had not intended to lie until that very moment. No matter. If it was Beverly she wanted to be, then Beverly she was.

He signaled the bartender, who had reappeared from the kitchen. "The lady will have . . ."

"Gin and soda, lime twist."

C.J. said, "Laphroaig Lore; two cubes. And bring a couple of menus, if you would. Thanks."

His companion looked amused. "That's a very specific drink order," she said.

"And yours wasn't?"

"I take my liquor from the well."

"So you think maybe I'm one of those prissy types."

"But you're not that guy?"

"I'm the guy who's had enough bad whisky in my life to be willing to pay extra for the good stuff. Also the guy who's discovered he's too slow with his drink, so the ice melts and spoils the whisky. I learned I had better drink faster, or specify fewer cubes."

"Or drink it straight. Since it's top shelf and all."

"Or don't drink at all—and that's no solution," said C.J as the bartender set "Beverly's" drink in front of her.

"Cheers to that," she said, and raised her glass—with her left hand, where there was no wedding ring.

C.J.'s drink arrived. He lifted it and said, "Cheers."

She was very attractive. But this was not that kind of flirting, right? And he didn't need it to be, right? He put his glass to his lips and drank. The peaty, smooth whisky gave him something else to think about for a few moments. Liquid copper right out of a Scottish bog.

She gestured to his book. "Is that any good?"

"I thought so when I read it thirty years ago. Have you read any of his novels?"

"I confess I have not. But I'm glad to see that you read fiction."

"And if I didn't?" C.J. said.

"I might ask you to relocate to the other end of the bar. To quote Jane

Austen, 'He who has not pleasure in a good novel must be intolerably stupid.'"

"It's good I have this book with me, then, as evidence of my not-stupidity. A claim without evidence might be me lying just to avoid being tarred by Ms. Austen's brush, as it were."

"Saying 'as it were' would give you cred, though, irrespective of your claim. Here's a test, to prove conclusively that Michener's doorstop, there, isn't just a prop: name your favorite novel of all time. I warn you: if you say *Call of the Wild*, this conversation is over."

"One favorite? Of all time? I don't know; I think that's a fool's errand right there. I spread my love around."

"Is that so? I've heard of men like you. What's the saying—stay away from runaround C.J.?"

He liked her sense of humor, the bold smile, the assurance in her motions—she was tall, with a dancer's awareness of her body in space. His guess (his hope?) was that she'd been single for a while and liked it that way. She gave no sign of overeagerness, a woman on the hunt. He'd known plenty such women from his work travel over the years. Seen plenty of men, too, with that same smell of desperation. Like, *I have to find me a bedmate* now, *or else face another long and lonely night of alcohol and infomercials.* "Beverly" here was not going to glom onto him and have to be peeled off like a leech after a muddy-lake swim. Neither would he be that leech to her. Good. Settled.

He said, "When you aren't writing, what do you like to do? Are you otherwise employed, or are you a woman of independent means?"

"When I am not writing the novel that's under way, I write other things for pay. Freelance work. How about you? When you aren't reading Michener or doing home improvement projects, you . . . ?"

He thought about how best to frame his answer, then said, "I paint. Fine art, that is, not house painting—though as you saw earlier today, I'm not against picking up a bigger brush."

"What's your area? Landscapes or portraits or what? Or maybe abstract? What medium? I confess, I don't know that much about art."

"All kinds of subjects, in oil mainly."

"Do you have a particular style?"

He indicated his decorative shirt cuffs. Paisley, in contrast to the body's pinstripe. "I like to think I'm halfway stylish."

"Fancy," she said. "I'd give you three-quarters stylish. Don't sell yourself short."

"Used to be I was into the modernists and all their high-minded ideals. Now, though, I'm interested in the Baroque. The drama of it, the intensity of light and shadow. It gets at things differently, and that appeals to the older, wiser me." He shrugged, self-conscious.

"The Baroque—that was Rembrandt, Caravaggio, those guys—right?"

He nodded. "That's them."

"Huh. I guess I wouldn't have figured you as that kind of painter. They're so . . ."

"Incredibly talented?"

"Well, yes—but what I mean is, their work is so serious. And you . . ."

"I cut up in bars, and make fussy drink orders. It's true. And when did a southern boy like me ever make a serious go as an artist? Believe me, it's a question I have asked myself many times. What can I tell you? The muse chooses her victims, not the other way around."

"I think an artist can be anyone who wants to create art. You want to paint like Caravaggio and Rembrandt, you should go right ahead."

C.J. said, "Tell me about your book. The one you're writing now."

"You don't want to hear about that."

"Funny, I would swear I just asked to."

"You'll think it sounds stupid," she said.

"Did I not just bare my own artistic soul to you?"

"Oh, so we're doing 'I showed you mine, you show me yours'?"

He said, "That proposition is on the ballot, yes." And by his saying it, it was. He thought. He hoped.

"Okay—but if you think it sounds awful, don't tell me."

She described to him a story about an anorexic teenager from a coal town whose father has black lung disease and whose community is beset with drug addiction and abuse. "It's about loss and self-discovery and, you know, essential truths about being human."

"Sounds . . ."

"What?"

"I'm searching for the right word, here. Grim," he said with an apologetic laugh. "But that's not a criticism! Lots of great novels are grim."

"That's right. It has a plot, too," she added defensively. "Things do happen in it."

"Okay!"

"It's not some torrid romance or whatever else men think women write about. Shopping. Sex."

"Sex is fine with me," he said. "Romance, too. And I like shopping all right. My ex-wife did a lot of it for me when I was married, which I guess is pretty typical. Now I choose for myself."

"I think clothing is the outer expression of our inner selves."

"So who chose that coat?"

"I did! Isn't it excellent? My daughter's mad that I didn't get the same one for her. Do you have children?"

"I do," he said. "One daughter, and she's grown."

They talked, then, about daughters and parenthood and the relief you felt when the kid made it to adulthood without catastrophe. And they talked about how difficult parenting could be even when you were blessed with only normal issues to deal with. C.J.'s curiosity about her name aside, he felt like he was having a catch-up conversation with an old friend, a dear friend he'd missed and was delighted to see again. It was, he thought, a freakishly strange feeling; he felt like he knew her, somehow. What's more, he thought this dear old friend was hot; there was no other way to put it. This was not merely a judgment of her appearance (though it was in part that); it was a judgment of her spirit, her manner, the tone of her voice—low and earthy and tinged with humor and warmth.

Both he and "Beverly" had drained their glasses again. "Another?" C.J. said, ready to flag down the bartender.

"I had better not. Food would be a good idea, though."

They studied the menus in companionable silence. C.J. felt relaxed and happy. Yes, he was mildly sloshed. That, however, didn't explain the warmth in his soul. Though maybe it did explain how he could be thinking about *warmth* and *soul* together when he might otherwise find the concept of soul warmth kind of woo-woo. But this woman made him think soul warmth might be a real thing. "Beverly" the writer. Intrepid drinker of gin from the well, orderer of—

"Those pub fries look like a winner to me," she said.

C.J. nodded in appreciation. "S'pose we pair 'em with the mussels."

"Oh—and lobster bisque. That sounds good, too."

They ordered all of these and two glasses of house red—because, come on, all those calories would offset the alcohol and they were having a fine time and C.J., at least, was now very much in the mindset that more of everything was better. Especially more of this appealing woman who, it seemed clear, had zero desire to play games and was one hundred percent genuine, and how refreshing was that?

They ate and laughed and talked, and when they were done, they split the check. Then C.J. said, "A walk? Or is it too cold?"

"I'm a New Yorker; half of my life has been spent walking in the cold. But let me make a quick pit stop first."

"I'll do the same."

In the men's room, he took care of business, and then he also took out an insurance policy—which is to say, he put four quarters into a condom dispenser and bought himself some peace of mind.

He was leaving the men's room when he stopped in his tracks.

No wonder this beautiful woman felt so familiar to him: he did in fact know "Beverly." Damn, how could he have taken so long to place her?

Though of course it'd been decades since he'd seen her. It was that summer he'd stayed with Joseph. Wow. He *knew* she'd seemed familiar. Her name was Beckie. No—Beck. Beck . . . Something; he'd lost that detail to time, but, oh, shit, he hoped that she would not have a similar revelation, because if she did, she might get a whole lot less interested in wherever this night was headed. She might remember promises made and promises broken without explanation.

He hadn't thought about that episode in a very long time, ashamed as he'd been to have let himself pretend he was an ordinary college kid whose life wasn't a complicated quagmire of baby and family issues. He had desperately wanted to be the C.J. he'd shown her—a truer self in many ways, but an impossible one, too. Also, why torment himself with daydreams of a girl he might have loved best, given a real chance? He'd forced himself to let it all go, be the man he thought he was supposed to be.

Should he bring it up now? Apologize? Or hope that she wouldn't remember him and let it ride?

"Let it ride," he told himself. "Don't spoil the fun for her or you."

Beck was waiting by the door when he got there, her expression troubled. He was afraid to ask why.

She said, "It's snowing."

"Yeah? I saw that it might. Is that a problem?"

"Not for me, but I thought it might be for you, being from the South."

"I'm sweet, sure, but I won't melt."

"Then let's go."

Later, he wouldn't remember what they talked about in those first few minutes after leaving, but he would remember the exact spot where she'd taken his hand to pull him around to the side of a building, out of the streetlight, where she then backed him up to the wall and kissed him. He'd remember that her nose was cold. That the kiss was forceful but that she hadn't pressed her body against his—not then. Not yet. She'd steered him, kissed him, then stepped back and laughed and said, "Oh my god. Did I just do that? That felt so good!"

He and Beck may have known each other briefly a long time ago, but they barely knew each other now. Did that matter? Two consenting adults planning to have a little recreational sex—that seemed okay to him. C.J., seeing her half-sheepish, half-wicked smile, was all in.

They had to decide, then, whether to go somewhere else. Somewhere private, and warm.

C.J. said, "My place or yours?"

She said, "Mine's about fifteen minutes from here."

"Mine, then?"

"Yours it is."

"Do you want to ride with me, or—sorry, stupid question. You'll want to have your own wheels."

"I'll follow you."

When they arrived, she got out of her car and stood assessing the house, which was artfully lit by landscape lighting. Warm light from inside added to its appeal. As with so much of what he saw here, this moment would lend itself to being rendered—on linen, probably, or maybe he'd try it on panel as a miniature. His easy-Sunday scene came to him again, this time with him in his future studio, painting, while Beck was somewhere else in his future house, writing. The windows would be open. They'd have classical music playing on some public radio station. She'd take a break and wander in to see him, a mug of coffee in hand. She'd lean against the doorjamb and smile at him just the way she'd done a few minutes ago . . .

She said now, "This really is quite a house. Callaghans', right?"

"Correct," he said, feeling wary. Had they ever been here together? He didn't think so, but couldn't remember for sure.

"Who else is here?"

"Just us," he said.

"Okay, good. Shall we go in?"

After shedding shoes and coats, C.J. led her into the sitting room. She said, "I guess you must be a very good friend to be staying here on your own."

"We go back a ways."

"The little boy I saw you with—"

"Arlo."

"Arlo—he's your friend's son?"

"No, grandson of the lady whose house this is, Deirdre Callaghan. Poor kid was orphaned a few months back." C.J. outlined the situation, then said, "I really feel for him. And I think in some ways I identify with him. Not being orphaned, but being a family misfit."

"You? Really?"

"Let's just say I am not the man my father wanted for a son. Never mind all that, though," C.J. said, moving closer to her.

"If you say so."

"I do."

They kissed tentatively, as if each was retesting the other's commitment to what was (pretty certainly) about to happen. Testing whether what had seemed like a fine idea when they were flirting at a restaurant bar and then on a darkened side street was in fact what both of them wanted now, here, alone. Overcoming the strangeness of kissing someone new. Seeing whether the chemistry was likely to carry them past the awkwardness and, in his case at least, fear that he might not show her as good a time as they both wanted.

The chemistry was no problem: things heated up fast. C.J. led her up to his bedroom, but even as he did, he worried this was a wrong choice. Maybe quick, hot coupling right there in the sitting room, standing up with a wall for support, would've been the better option. Hadn't the guys in the pen discussed ad nauseam how determined women were to get TV- and movie-quality sex from their men? How *Hollywood* the expectations were nowadays? But he still wasn't sure about security cameras here. And, further, C.J. was not a young stud anymore (if he had ever been). He was an out-of-practice middle-aged guy. Best to set realistic expectations. Best to face this head on.

He drew her down to sit on the bed with him. "Just so you know, it's been a while since I entertained a lady this way."

She said, "It's been a while since I was entertained this way. We can pretend we're virgins."

"There's an idea," he said. "Eager, but nervous."

"Exactly."

They kissed again, long, deep—but then she broke away, saying, "You don't have any STDs, do you?"

He laughed. "STDs? No, happily, I do not. I suppose I ought to ask you the same question."

"Right, you should. No, no STDs. Also, I probably should have thought of this before I got here: I'm not supplied with protection. I wasn't anticipating anything like this, so . . ."

He took the condom from his pocket. "No worries on that front."

Now he would merely have to remember how to put the damn thing on with a modicum of grace and efficiency; he hadn't used a condom since way back when he and all the other kids had called them rubbers and kept one in their wallets starting at age fifteen "just in case." For three more years, while he grew taller and filled out, he'd tormented himself with the wallet reminder that he wasn't yet getting laid. He'd imagined that all the other guys were way ahead of him. What an idiot he'd been! Sex at fifteen, sixteen, seventeen—even if it happens, it's going to be awkward and bad and unwise.

He said, "I gotta tell you, there's a *lot* about this situation that's making me feel like a teenager," then regretted the words instantly. Any reminder of their history might trigger her memory. Though she'd been the teenager, not him, and they'd never had sex. Which would not matter in the least if she were to suddenly recall his bad behavior from back then. *Please, God*, he thought, *don't fail me now.*

He added, "But I hope I'm better at it than I was in those years. Should we find out?"

She pushed him backward and leaned over him. "Yeah, let's find out."

From there, the undressing went quickly, both of them eager to get closer to the state nature intended for this kind of thing. Whatever nerves they felt were forgotten in short order. C.J. had been without sex for so long that the smells and tastes and feel of Beck's skin beneath his hands and his mouth were nothing less than sublime. She offered her body to him like a feast to a ravenous man. He forgot his anxieties, lost himself in the primal mechanics and rhythms of the act. And maybe because it had been so long since he'd had sex, or maybe because this sex was with *this* woman, this one-time summer love to whom he owed an apology (and what better way to make up for his bad actions than to deliver a great performance tonight, even if only he knew the truth?), he was able to savor it, savor her, give her all the pleasure he was getting. When he came, he groaned and laughed at the same time, and she was laughing, too, and for those few seconds it was like a goddamned miracle of pleasure, like the first orgasms in the history of humankind, like they had invented sex, defined its terms, set the standard by which all future sex (theirs and everyone's) would be judged.

After a few dazed moments, they moved up onto the bed and stretched out there. They lay looking up at the ceiling. She said, "That was . . . Wow. I don't even . . . Yeah. Wow."

He laughed. "Me too."

"That felt crazy! My entire body is just . . ."

"Same."

"I mean . . . Thank you. Thank you! That was amazing."

She obviously wasn't accustomed to sex like this. C.J. felt kind of proud of himself. Also, he was delighted with *her*. It wouldn't have been so good if she hadn't been so *there*. So present, so connected, so generous.

He was lying there enjoying the endorphin buzz when she said, "All right," and clapped her hands once before getting up and retrieving her clothes. As she dressed, she said, "I had such a good time. Seriously. Thank you."

He sat up and reached for his shorts.

She said, "You don't need to get up. Stay there where it's warm. I can see myself out. I hope you have a good rest of your night. Maybe I'll see you around."

She left him there without another kiss or backward glance. He made to follow her, then held short. It was abundantly clear that she didn't want any further interaction. Better to let her go.

C.J. didn't know what to make of this abrupt ending. He'd been all about "no complications," and even now the rational side of his brain was congratulating him for accomplishing the objective of getting laid entirely for fun. Another part of him, though, was brooding, trying to decide if it felt hurt or used or disappointed or what.

She hadn't left him her phone number. He didn't know where she lived. All he knew was that she wanted him to think her name was Beverly (or maybe it was, and he was completely wrong in his recollection), and he'd just had some of the best sex he was likely to have in his life—because could sex be better than that? He wanted to do it again. With her, whoever she was. Soon.

Except . . . he kind of felt like he'd been used as mere entertainment. It seemed that his assessment of her as someone who didn't play games had missed the kind of game she was playing. Or was the quick getaway a game at all? Maybe it was simply a practice some women had finally taken up themselves, having so often been on the receiving end.

He pulled on his robe and went to the kitchen, which now felt emptier than ever. "Get over yourself, Reynolds," he said. He'd make some decaf coffee, eat a scone, do some sketching—remind himself what he had come here for. It wasn't for a woman, no matter how great the sex. It wasn't to build vegetable and flower gardens. It wasn't to befriend a lost boy. "Straighten your priorities, man," he said. He needed his own place. Yesterday.

Thinking of houses made him think *Geller*—and then it clicked: "Beck *Geller*."

Oh, shit. This was getting messier by the day.

Well, at least now he knew where to find her.

If he wanted to find her.

Did he want to find her?

No, damn it. He wanted to find a house. Period. Her mother's, if he could get it. Unfortunately, she seemed to be playing games there, too.

19

It Was All Beside the Point

Beck, with the same insouciance she'd exhibited when she left C.J. in his bed, climbed into her car and drove away. At the next corner, though, she turned and pulled over to the side of the road. Her hands were shaking. Laughter burbled out of her in little spurts of surprise and delight. What had she just done?

Exactly what she'd wanted to do.

Tonight she'd decided to be bold and vivid and sexy, the way she'd once imagined a vibrant, intelligent New York girl (or Anywhere girl) could be. *Should* be, in this era of self-actualization. She'd wanted to have hot, athletic sex with a hot, athletic guy. And so she had.

She was kind of proud of herself.

She was even prouder of how she'd extricated herself.

From the moment C.J. had told her his name, she knew that if they ended up in bed together (and she'd hoped they would), she was going to execute that unceremonious exit. *Use 'em and lose 'em*, wasn't that essentially the motto for the boys' club he and so many other guys were part of? It certainly fit what she knew about the Callaghan clan (including good old Chip), and clearly C.J. was still tight with Joseph, his college friend who'd been cute enough all those years back, but kind of obnoxious, too. Oblivious. Using C.J. the way she'd done just now was a sweet piece of long-delayed justice— not only for herself but also (in a very small way) for her mother—enacted fully on her terms.

The look on his face!

She had been *so* hung up on him that summer she was seventeen, when he'd been here with Joseph, cruising Sand Beach, chatting up the girls. Instant chemistry back then, same as the day she'd met him anew in the gift shop with the boy, Arlo. Young C.J. had been as taken with her as she was with him, or so it had seemed at the time. Ten glorious summer days of being basically attached to him at the hip. Lobster fishing. Ice cream. Lounging on the beach. Summits on Dorr and Penobscot and Acadia, Gorham and Parkman, South Bubble. And the Beehive, of course, since that's where her parents had met, and Beck had been nothing if not incurably romantic. No actual sex, but a lot of heavy petting and heavy breathing. A tearful goodbye. Promises to stay in touch so that there would be more of everything. Their romance had been a city girl's fantasy summer vacation come true, and who knew what might come of it over time? He had a year left of college. She had a year left of high school. Then, the future was all theirs.

Ah, but no. The city girl's fantasy come true was instead only a city girl's fantasy.

Oh god, all those sentimental lovestruck letters she sent to him before she realized that his lack of response wasn't due to his being busy or the mail being slow. He simply wasn't writing back. He hadn't really cared about her at all. He'd used her. She'd been as embarrassed as she was crushed. By the time she met Paul a year later, she was the sadder but wiser girl, ready to see in gentle Paul the answer to her prayer that God give her better material the next time around.

Tempting as it was to blame tonight's behavior on the dope she'd smoked before going out for dinner, it hadn't made her do any of this; she'd lit up hours before she had stripped C.J.'s clothing from his body and helped him do the same to hers. No, marijuana (and the drinks she'd had with dinner) had merely set the stage for her inhibitions to later drop their own drawers and embrace that good, excellent, bad behavior.

"Wow," she said, her mind spooling back to the sex. *This* was what she'd been missing all these years. Good God. The scope of the loss was barely short of tragic. People could have sex like *that*. She'd thought it only happened in movies and on TV. Now, though, she was enlightened. Filled to overflowing with light. Radiant.

Driving back to camp, she felt bad only about the fact that she didn't feel bad. She *should*. Some guilt, at least, for cheating on Paul. Some shame, maybe, for having this one-night stand. The slightest remorse for using C.J. for recreation. Nope. She felt euphoric. Youthful. Desirable. Alive. She felt as though she had discovered a portal to an alternate world that looked almost exactly the same as the one she'd been living in but in which she got to be the person she'd been suppressing all these years out of what she'd told herself was consideration for Paul's feelings, the kids' feelings, her mother's feelings . . . All of that was bullshit. Living in fear of the negative judgment of others was a bullshit way to live. Her mother had proven that.

"Not gonna do it anymore," Beck said to the darkened landscape, the sleeping eiders and loons and harlequin-like long-tailed ducks, the tiny buds that were just about to unfurl along tree limbs throughout the island and were right now waiting for the sun's return so that they could flourish as nature intended. Shouldn't she do the same?

If she had any regret about tonight, it was that she'd chickened out of telling him her real name right before she left—which would've made her conquest feel even sweeter. Oh, well.

Inside the house, she dumped her purse and coat and went to look at herself in the bathroom mirror. "Beck Geller," she said. "Lookin' pretty good, my friend. But what do you have to say for yourself, huh? Some people might call you a slut. Whore. Faithless conniving bitch." She frowned and wrinkled her nose. "Eh, that's pretty harsh."

She angled her face to the mirror, as if to present another Beck. A less critical, more accepting Beck. A Beck of Wisdom. *That* Beck was decisive. "I say, 'Don't look back.' I say, 'Damn the torpedoes; full speed ahead!'"

She studied her reflection a minute longer. "I say, would it be any more wrong to do it again? With him? No, not with *him*. That's over. Someone like him. Yeah?"

Or him.

No, not him.

She needed an informed opinion about extramarital relations, so although it was nearly one A.M., she called Claire.

Claire's voice, when she answered the phone, was slow and sleepy.

Beck said, "Did I wake you?"

"Sort of. I dozed off trying to catch up on my medical journals. It's Sisyphean. What's up? Everything okay?"

"Yes. That is, I think so. I'm going to tell you something, and I need your advice about it."

Beck related the night's events, stopping short of saying that the man was her long-ago summer love or describing in graphic detail the sex and euphoria parts. Because while she and Claire were sufficiently close for this surface-level confession, some things were still too personal, too private. Besides, not telling those details preserved them and made them feel all the more exceptional for being hers and hers alone. She'd had so little of *hers alone* in her life.

The whole time Beck spoke, Claire was silent—listening, Beck supposed, for her to get to the end of the tale before responding. Beck told her in conclusion, "So, you know, I figured that you of all people could appreciate why I did it, and maybe give me your two cents on where I go from here."

Claire made no response.

Beck glanced at her phone's screen to make sure she hadn't lost the connection. "Hey—you there?" she said.

"I'm here," said Claire. "I'm just . . . I thought this was going to be about something else. Never mind. Why me 'of all people'?"

"Because of your somewhat similar experience."

"What did Sophie tell you?"

Beck said, "Sophie? Nothing."

"Wait," Claire said. "What are you referring to, exactly?"

"Your affair? Sophie hasn't said a word, but I presumed you had an affair and that's why you and Chad split. Am I crazy? Didn't you allude to that, back when it happened? Was that not it at all?"

"I . . . Yes. That was it. I was indiscreet and Chad couldn't deal and that was that. But are you saying you plan to leave Paul for this guy?"

"No, not for him. For myself. Wait. Are you saying you *didn't* want to leave Chad?"

"It wasn't what I aimed for, no. My thing . . . it wasn't the same, okay. He's married, and we haven't had the sort of relationship that I'd say has any kind of real potential."

Beck said, "Maybe that's okay—because it's better if you aren't trying to marriage-hop. I have zero motive in that regard. God. I've been married my entire adult life! I'm not trying to find a new husband. One day, maybe. But that's not what this was. At all."

"No, right, that's good." Claire sounded more animated now. "You deserve to see what it's like to be independent, if that's what you want. Especially if what you said about Paul being gay is correct."

Beck said, "Change can be good, right? Though maybe I got it all wrong with you? Sorry, I don't mean to be insensitive. You're so tough that it's hard for me to imagine that you were hurt by Chad's reaction to your situation. But maybe you were?"

Claire said, "It's more about David than Chad. He doesn't understand why we can't patch things up."

"Why can't you?"

"Some people have a really hard time processing and forgiving betrayal. Understandably. When you trust a person and they abuse that trust so egregiously—"

"Makes sense. Chad's a proud person."

"He is," said Claire. "Frankly, though, if the situation were reversed, I'd probably have responded in the same way. Anyway, I don't want to get back with him. I just want him to stop punishing me and let us all get on with our lives with something like harmony, for David's sake. We don't have to be permanently acrimonious. I can't see Paul ever being like that with you."

"I hope not."

"So you'll tell him?"

"Yes. That is, I won't exactly confess; what he doesn't know won't hurt him, right? But we need to have a conversation about remaking our relationship. Unmaking our marriage. I'll talk to him about it after all this house stuff is resolved. God! I can't believe I'm actually going to do this!"

Claire said, "Life's too short to keep living unhappily. Who does that serve?"

"No, that's right," said Beck. "It's not as if I've really harmed anyone." Which she believed! Though she was now feeling the tiniest bit compunctious about her behavior. A tiny bit conflicted about her subterfuge—with C.J., primarily, maybe because that was the more immediate situation. She could feel bad about Paul later.

She said, "So, there's just one other thing . . ."

"What?"

"About the guy, tonight. I'm not looking to get into anything serious *at all*. I didn't even give him my real name or my number or anything that would make it easy for him to find me. But . . . I actually wouldn't mind a repeat," she said, despite every reason she should not see him again. The *sex*, though! What if she could keep him on a string, the way guys so often did to women? She wasn't sure she had it in her to be so Machiavellian, but it might be worth a try.

"Should I track him down?"

Claire said, "He didn't suggest a future date?"

"No. But I didn't really give him a chance."

"He could have, though, if he really wanted to."

"True. So don't try to force anything," said Beck.

"Exactly."

"Just leave it up to fate, or whatever."

"That's a good way to think of it."

Beck said, "Okay. Okay, yes, that sounds wise. Less fun, but wise. Thank you for helping me figure it out."

"I didn't really do much."

"You listened. You assessed objectively."

"What else are sisters for?" said Claire.

"I used to think they were mainly for annoying the shit out of me."

Claire laughed. "Same."

"Hey—and don't take this as an accusation, because it is definitely not that, but how come you told Soph about the affair but you didn't tell me?"

Claire said, "Have you already told her about your thing tonight—or if not, do you plan to tell her?"

"My thought was that you're the right person for this, given your experience. But I probably *would* tell her."

"*Would. Probably.* At the time, I felt she was the right person to talk to about it."

Beck said, "It's been months, though."

"Look, I say this without rancor: you can be pretty judgy sometimes. I didn't want to be judged."

"*I'm* judgy?"

"Put it this way: you have strong opinions about things, and you express them without reserve."

"You're right," said Beck. "Sometimes I do. I'm sorry about that. Will do better in the future." She sat on the warm rug. "I hope all my happy rah-rah talk about divorce isn't bad form, when you're still kind of struggling with yours."

"Not at all. I'm happy for you. It's kind of crazy, you playing Sophie's role here."

Beck said, "Oh, I hadn't thought of it like that. Guess she and I share some genes after all."

"Was there ever any doubt?"

"I did used to wonder if the hospital switched babies and sent Mom home with a little golden-haired goyish child."

"Wonder no more," said Claire. "And now I need to get some sleep. You're okay, right?"

Beck smiled. "Better than I've been in a long time."

What a lovely boost of energy and goodwill a bout of great sex can provide: after hanging up with Claire, knowing she wouldn't be able to get to sleep anytime soon, Beck went into her Writing Room and opened her laptop.

She reread the last few paragraphs she'd written earlier in the day. "Oh, these are bad," she said. She highlighted a block of text and hit the *delete* key. The preceding page was bad, too. She deleted it. "What was I thinking?" she said, reading what came before that. "This *is* grim. Too grim. He doesn't need to cough up so much black gunk here, does he?"

Beck leaned back in the chair. The whole scene now seemed suspect to her, and this was officially Not Good. This was What Always Happened.

"Let's do this instead." She opened Google, with its inviting little text box. In that box she typed "C.J. Reynolds."

It was not the first time she'd done this. Back when the internet had been a fresh and exciting and wondrous resource, she'd dialed up her AOL service and asked Jeeves to find information on this way-back love of hers, to see if she could learn anything about what he'd made of himself. There had been very little to go on—a mention of him in some Cornell publication in which he was referred to as "Coleman (C.J.) Reynolds" was all she found. Years later, when all the kids started abandoning Facebook and all the adults came on board, she had looked to see if C.J. had a profile. He did not. He was, however, listed among the corporate officers for Reynolds Fasteners, which suggested she hadn't missed out on anything special.

Tonight's initial result yielded a lot of nothing about her C.J. but a lot of information about a cool guy with the same name who taught literature in West Philadelphia. Beck watched a couple of his YouTube videos, making notes for a possible article to pitch, then went back to her primary task. "Coleman J. Reynolds," she typed, then hit *return*.

Mug shot?

Holy shit. A mug shot.

Arrest, charges.

She gaped as she read. *Attempted murder of his own father?*

"What the actual . . ."

Beck scrolled through article after article from news sources throughout the Southeast as well as some nationals, plus a few from other countries where Reynolds Fasteners had manufacturing facilities. Coleman Jenkins Reynolds Jr. had been arrested, tried, convicted, and sentenced. In the end, the conviction was for a lesser change—reckless endangerment—but so what? The man she'd sort of been carrying a torch for since she was seventeen years old, the charming, sweet, smart, handsome man she'd just bedded, who had not two hours earlier given her the best sex of her life, had a few years earlier taken a gun, aimed it at his father, and pulled the trigger.

"My god," Beck said.

Whatever bad blood existed between the two men, whatever C.J.'s motivation for what he'd done, he was obviously not a person she ought to be entangled with. She should have realized that even before she let her endorphins carry her into his Callaghan four-poster. Revenge no longer felt so sweet. It was all beside the point of why she was here, anyway.

What a poor judge of character she'd been! So what if he was charismatic and handsome? So what if twenty-seven years ago they'd had a thing? Clearly she was blind to his true nature and should be grateful she found this out before she did what she'd begun to imagine despite herself: seeing him again, telling him her real name, exacting an explanation for why he'd ghosted her way back when, forgiving him, and turning this new chance into something like what she'd thought the old chance was going to become.

No, what it had now become was exactly what it had been before: a goddamn disappointment.

Well, fine. Lesson learned. And relearned.

She'd been going to wait until morning to shower, but now she went into the bathroom and turned on the tap. She would scrub the evidence of him off her skin and be totally, completely, thoroughly, absolutely done with him forever.

After the shower, she dried off and dressed in a pair of Hello Kitty pajamas she'd found at the thrift store, then brewed some coffee and went back to her Writing Room, determined to finish the scene by sunup and have polished pages to Gina by Monday. Success would be her best revenge against the disappointments, past and present.

She said, "If you're listening, Mom, I have a message for you: I think I get your reasons for wanting to break up with MDI, but I'm doing this, here, now, and no one better try to stop me."

20

Once Developed, Extraordinary

Sophie, feeling creaky after a week of sleeping on a saggy mattress in a saggy Jersey City chain hotel, rang the brownstone's doorbell and waited. After a minute, a woman's voice came through the sleek speaker beside the door. "Who's this?"

Sophie looked up at the door camera. "Sophie Silverberg, at your service!"

"Oh, hey, you're early."

"Am I?" Sophie said, though she knew she was. The Uber driver had a heavy foot and traffic had been light, putting her here twenty minutes ahead of schedule. "Should I come back later?"

"Would you?"

"Sure! No problem! Can I leave my luggage, though?"

"Set it in the foy-yay," said the voice. Then came a buzz and a click.

Sophie deposited her suitcases just inside the door, not taking time to do more than glance at the surroundings where she would be dog sitting for a few days. Slate floor tile. Warm wood paneling. Industrial vibe. She loved the ways this part of the city was being revitalized. The Village vibrated with the energy of artists' souls. Not far from this brownstone, Gilded Age architects Richard Morris Hunt and Stanford White had kept homes and offices; sculptor and artists' patron Gertrude Vanderbilt Whitney had her private studio nearby. Throw a stone in any direction from here and you would hit a building that housed Berenice Abbott or Edward Hopper or Winslow Homer—not to mention the writers and musicians who'd called the Village home. And maybe it was becoming too gentrified in this era of excessive incomes, but if she had to choose, Sophie preferred industrial chic to artistic squalor. The vibe could still be felt here if you tuned into it. The brick and stone were permeated with history.

Dressed as she was for her low-key meeting as a housesit pro (hair pulled back, no makeup, J.Crew everything, sneakers), she thought a dash over to Ochoa would be a good use of her time. No one would be working, so there'd be no *Hey, I hardly recognized you!* remarks from the staff, who had only ever seen her in full sail. The subterfuge was of course deliberate; she couldn't risk the housesit clients recognizing her from Page Six and elsewhere. At most, she might get a *Huh, you look familiar*—which, in a city of millions, could always be dismissed with a shrug.

And now here she was at the gallery door. On the ride in from Jersey, she had messaged Paul to confirm that he had in fact mailed her checks to Ochoa's address, which she'd been using for more than a year—it made sense, given how peripatetic she had become. Oh, how marvelous it was going to be to be planted someplace where she'd have her very own mailbox. Her own bed. A shelf with her own books and little collectible whatevers. Maybe a cactus, too. Cacti, even. And agave. A spider plant. Basically, all the varieties of green things that Tania had cautioned her not to water much at all. It was going to be so, so, *so* great to stop worrying about money! Everything was coming together now. Slowly, yes, but it *was* happening.

As expected, the gallery was darkened, save for the small display window, which never had real art, only artful posters of art or posters about art. The exception being twice a year, when Benji held a contest for public high school students to craft some creative rendition of the Ochoa name using any medium. He then displayed the winners and runners-up in the window and paid a $500 top prize. The most recent winners were in the window now. *¡Ochoa!* shouted a colorful mixed-media sculpture that married design elements from Mardi Gras and the Day of the Dead.

Standing at the door, Sophie took out her gallery key ring and went to fit the door key into the lock. It wouldn't go. She turned the key over to try again, though she was sure it wasn't made to fit that way. Still no luck. Again she tried it right side up. No.

"What the fuck?" she said.

She tried every one of the six keys on the ring, feeling foolish (she *knew* which one was for the front door) but also disbelieving the obvious conclusion: the lock had been changed.

"No. No, no, no, no. God damn it, no!"

New York being New York, no one who passed by on the sidewalk paid any mind to the blond woman now standing at the gallery's door yelling into her phone, "God damn it, Benji, pick up!" Nor when, after she'd tried Benji's husband, Evan, with the same result, she kicked the door and cursed again. When she sat down with her back to the door and put her forehead to her knees so that she could think on what might be happening here, no one stopped to ask if there was a problem. But one woman, taking note of Sophie as she passed, stopped and offered her a five-dollar bill. Sophie took it.

The dying dog's name was Mathilda. "With an *h*," said the woman who was being dragged off to spend four days in Rio against her better judgment. Suppose Mathilda, an Irish setter, died while she was away? Sophie said, "She won't. I promise. Unless she's actually been waiting for you to leave her. I've seen it happen. She might want to spare you the grief of seeing her go."

"Oh my god," said the woman, who was an exceptionally well-preserved fifty-something textile designer. "I never thought of that. I might have been prolonging her suffering?"

The man said, "This trip will be a mercy. Now let's get moving before we miss our flight."

Mathilda was twelve years old. She had her own bedroom. Its decor was something like might be found in a hunting lodge: leather chairs, paintings of hunts, textured wallpaper that featured rabbits and pheasants, low lighting, and a wide lambswool dog bed set in front of a glowing gas-log fireplace, on which bed old Mathilda lay while the conversation took place nearby. In fact, she would lie there for all but about three hours of Sophie's four-day tenure in this four-story monument of wood and steel and glass and leather and lots and lots of gorgeous rugs and throws.

All weekend long, while Sophie lounged on this sofa and in that chair and on each of five different beds (but not Mathilda's) in a veritable *Architectural Digest* photo spread that, regrettably, she could not reveal much of on IG, she fretted about the gallery's changed locks and its missing owner and what these two facts might portend. She left Benji text and voice and email messages. She polled the other employees on whether they'd had any communications from the boss. None had.

Late Sunday evening, she got the idea to contact the two Wall Street bros whose purchases she'd been arranging to have delivered the night Benji had sent her home after telling her he'd tend to the last details himself.

Call number one, to voice mail: "Hi, Sophie Geller here, from Ochoa. I hope all is well. I'm just following up to be sure you are as delighted with your recent purchases as we at Ochoa hope you are. Let us know if there's anything at all we can do for you. Thank you again. We value your business tremendously."

Response to call number one, by text:

Hey, Sophie. Yeah, actually haven't received anything yet—my assistant was going to be checking in with you tomorrow.

Sophie stared at the text. "Fuck," she said, then replied, I will track it down. More soon!

Her second call, to the second client, also went to voice mail.

While she was leaving him a message, she heard the beep from an incoming call—Krystal, who, when Sophie called her back, said, "I know you're probably busy, but I'm at this house exhibition in Inwood, 204th and Vermilyea, and there's some pretty outstanding work here. Maybe you want to come up?"

Sophie hadn't been to a house exhibition—that is, an art exhibit put on in someone's personal residence, usually downscale, sometimes *way* downscale, sometimes even seedy—in ten years or longer. These were usually "starter exhibits," the kind that got staged because the artists were too green (or, often, not sufficiently talented) to have gotten much if any attention from people like Sophie who had become the gatekeepers. The tastemakers. Once in a while, the exhibition was some rich person's folly being indulged in a Upper East Side mansion, where money could buy fawning admiration— which was probably all the artist in question wanted anyway.

Sophie told Krystal, "Yeah, why not?" She needed something to offset the terrible, bad, no-good feeling that her life as she'd known it might be over. Of course, there might be a perfectly good reason for whatever the fuck was going on. Something she'd laugh about with Benji when he got back. Yes. Please. Some kind of innocent mix-up, a coincidence of some kind, and they'd laugh, and she'd tell Benji about whatever she'd seen tonight, and they'd go to get sushi at Tomoe, and everything would be fine, fine, fine. She told Krystal, "Text me the address."

The night was mild, so Sophie threw together a jeans-and-tank-top combo, going sockless in Valentino platform sneakers, and topped it all off with a Loro Piana baby cashmere cardigan that might have been Tania's, might have gotten somehow mixed up with Sophie's clothing, might have cost more than $2,000, who could say? Anyway, the kids she'd see tonight wouldn't know or care about its provenance or its cost. They'd care that she scouted for Ochoa. That is, if they found out. She texted Krystal to warn her not to give her away. The best way for her to see art was to be anonymous. Pure. Not that there was much of anything an artist could do or not do to influence her. She was not susceptible to bribes or to begging, not in this realm. The art was all.

Before leaving to meet Krystal, Sophie stopped in to check on Mathilda, who lay before the fire, eyes half lidded. Earlier, Mathilda had taken a brief walk in the courtyard, had peed halfheartedly in the patch of lawn designated for her, had accepted a few bites of the ground liver she loved, and now blinked and sighed when Sophie told her, "I'll be gone for maybe three hours. Four at the most. Don't wait up." Sophie kissed her warm nose, then went out into the April night.

"Oh, man, this takes me back," Sophie told Krystal when they met on the sidewalk in front of the apartment building. Around them, young people stood in small groups, some talking earnestly, others laughing on the steel switchback fire escape, cigarettes in one hand, red Solo cups in the other. "When I was in school at SVA, I went to open houses downtown, all these cramped little boxes of apartments tucked into the armpits of the East Village and the Lower East Side, where they'd cleared out all the furniture to make room."

"That's what we've got tonight," said Krystal. "That, and cheap beer." She raised her cup. "There's a keg."

"How could there not be? Lead me to it."

"*You're* going to drink this crap? Or—wait; it'll be a prop, right?"

"No," said Sophie. "I'm thirsty. It's beer. Let's do this."

They pushed through the crush of bodies in the hall and along the stairway, where the scents of incense and marijuana and cheap cologne and sweat mingled in the stale overheated air. There was so much noise and energy— but not the sort that you got in a bar or club or party whose purpose was merely social. This buzz had an earnestness to it. It was purposeful and real.

The keg and its tender were stationed outside the apartment door, which stood open for easy transiting. "Hey," said Sophie to the young man who leaned against the wall. Two of his friends stood nearby. "Set me up."

"Two bucks," he said, taking a red cup from a stack and pumping the keg. He filled the cup. Sophie gave him the five-dollar bill she'd taken from the woman outside the gallery. "Hit my friend again, too," she told him.

Krystal got a refill, then she and Sophie went inside. As expected, all the furniture had been cleared out. The walls were painted a soft white and were crowded with unframed canvases and photographs. A series of cheap floor lamps were set up to spotlight the works.

"It's five artists," Krystal said, to orient Sophie. "Three in here—one to a wall—and then two in the bedroom."

"Got it. Which artists are you excited about?"

"Me? I'm kind of nervous to say."

"No, come on, don't be afraid. Your taste, whatever it is, is legit. Later we can discuss the what and why parts."

"Okay. I like numbers two, three, and five. They all got *something*—just, those three got something special. I think. I'm curious to see what *you* think."

Sophie moved through the room slowly. She gave each of the numerous paintings, drawings, and photographs a close look, scanning for the telltale qualities that suggested a talent that might not have developed yet but that might, once developed, be extraordinary. So many people could execute well enough to, say, find employment creating homogenous, crowd-pleasing images for mass reproduction and sale in retail stores. Far fewer had the ineffable something special, the whatever-it-was that made gallerists like Sophie and Benji (wherever he was, god damn him) respond viscerally.

The real fascination for Sophie, though, was that this response was always subjective. How many times had she been to some hot new artist's show and felt nothing for the work? Or seen the winners of juried prizes and wondered how *that* could have won? At the same time, she'd learned to trust her own tastes and judgments, different though they might be, because she understood that there would always be others who shared her vision, and among those others, collectors who were eager to own those marvelous bits of captured lightning.

As Sophie viewed the artwork, she also spoke with the artists—casually, not giving away her knowledge or position. *My friend asked me to come,* she told each of them. *I like art. What's your background? What does it mean to you to create? Who's your audience?* She listened closely to their answers, but she also took in the conversation of the others in the room, their responses to what they were seeing. Their observations were more astute than she expected.

"They're all so enthusiastic," she said to Krystal afterward, when they were outside again. She felt buzzy from the beer and the stimulation. "The artists, but all these kids, too. It makes me happy."

"I know, right? I feel like they've got this pure thing going on. You forget, at the gallery."

"It's true," Sophie said. The gallery was a rarefied environment—intentionally so. They existed in a self-created and self-serving stratosphere that was also self-perpetuating by design. When Sophie was a student, she'd viewed the people who'd floated up there as "fucking snobs," and now she was one of them.

Krystal was saying, "No one here could buy even a tiny fraction of one thing we've got for sale. Might as well be a different planet."

"Seems wrong, doesn't it?" Sophie said.

"I guess they can buy from each other, though."

"They can. And I'm sure they do. But . . . I think they all want there to be something more to it. Something that elevates the values and experience to the height it belongs. Not how we're doing it at Ochoa; that's artifice—"

"Wow," said Krystal. "You're just coming right out and saying it. Props for that."

Sophie leaned toward her. "Feel my forehead; I'm probably coming down with something."

Krystal laughed. "Don't worry, I won't tell on you. I like to keep my job."

Yeah, thought Sophie. *Same.*

She said, "As to your numbers two, three, and five: from the Ochoa perspective, I'll give you five, and *maybe* two. And though Benji would disagree with me, four—that Haitian girl, with the charcoal and pastel portraits—there is definitely something happening there."

"I like her, too. But you don't think the subjects are too ordinary?"

"No, right, they are, definitely. It's what she's saying with her medium that's telling. To me, at least. I feel like there's a real energy flowing from her brain and eyes through her fingers. It's in the technique, not the subject. When she finds the right subject matter, she's going to be on *fire*."

"Huh," Krystal said. "I need to take another look."

"Go ahead. I'll wait for you."

It was nearly ten o'clock, yet people were still coming around. There was a feeling of promise to the night. Some of that was due simply to youth, but with that youth, a shimmering sense of optimism that surprised Sophie because it seemed unearned by the times they were living in. These kids weren't interested in playing by the old rules. They weren't letting the times bring them down, and maybe they wouldn't, ever. They were creating and seeking and pushing back. Sophie felt melancholy, thinking of all of this. How long had it been since she'd been real?

When Krystal joined her again, Sophie said, "You know what would make me *so* happy? Bacon and mayo on toast. Want to find a diner?"

"Let's do it," Krystal said. "Maybe I can get you to tell me your war stories."

"I warn you, that might ruin my famed SimplySophie! mystique."

"Nah," said Krystal. "I think maybe you're like number four, up there. What you show everybody isn't the best you've got. I think there's definitely more going on."

It wasn't until mid-morning Monday that Sophie had a response to her second follow-up query. This one came from the client himself, and she let it go to her voice mail because she had, by this time, attempted to log into the Ochoa business banking accounts and was denied access.

The second client also had not yet received his purchases. Nor would he, Sophie was now sure. She was also sure that if she had managed to find a way to get into the gallery, she would've discovered that it was a large denuded space. Had she been able to access the bank accounts, she'd find them bare as well. She suspected that the artworks that had hung on the now-empty walls would, bit by bit, show up on the international black market, and that not a dollar of whatever they sold for would make it back to the artists, ever. Nope.

She was increasingly certain that Benji and Evan would be using that money to pad their life in exile, wherever they'd escaped to, safe from the Feds.

"Those fuckers," she said to Mathilda as she lay next to the dog on the lambswool bed. "That lying son of a bitch." Mathilda blinked at her and sighed.

She texted Paul to tell him to cancel the checks he'd sent. Small crisis at gallery, she wrote. Mail ruined. Okay for me to pick up reissued $ directly from you tomorrow?

He replied that he'd leave an envelope for her at reception. Thank God. The money would get her through for a little while longer—but then what? The stink of whatever Benji had done was going to stick to her regardless of her honest claims of innocence. No reputable gallerist was going to hire her in the wake of this scandal-to-be. More than ever, she needed Beck to nail down that mortgage so she could figure out her next move, next self.

Just then, her phone pinged, reminding her that her Visa payment was due.

"Fuck. Off." Sophie dropped a pillow on top of the phone.

The thing was, Sophie could—if she chose to—count on Claire to give her some money to tide her over. She could do the same with Beck and Paul. Hell, she could ask Tania to front her significantly more money than either sister might have to offer, and Tania would give it, no questions asked. But to do any of this was to admit that she, Sophie, was nothing more than a failed pretender. All flash, no substance. This was an admission she just was not prepared to make, not if she could help it. If Beck's plan didn't pan out, the camp would go on the market right after that. Probably it would sell quickly. Hang on just a little longer, girlfriend, and in the meantime, think fast.

21

Altering the Ecosystem

After dithering for more than a week, Paul knew he had to take action. As hard as undoing his marriage would be, to leave it in its current state was unkind to Beck, and wrong. A deception. It had to be done now, in person. He would have to go to Maine, because who knew when Beck was going to return?

He was scared, though, that if he told her he was coming, he'd either have to lie and say he just wanted to see her, no agenda, or he'd have to explain his actual agenda, at which point they'd be having the conversation over the phone. And that would be all kinds of wrong.

So he didn't tell her. He just went.

Now Paul parked his car beside Beck's and got out. He stretched his arms above his head, bent to one side, then the other. Breathed in the cool, damp, piney scent of Maine in early spring. Down past the house, the lake was silvered by late-day light. A red kayak sat on the shoreline near the dock. The only sounds were of distant gulls and the wind in the trees. To say it was picturesque was to understate the impact of the setting. He could see afresh why Beck was reluctant to let it go.

Would she be as reluctant to let *him* go? He half hoped she would. But this was, he knew, the old, scared Paul talking, the Paul who wanted the universe to reorder itself so that he wouldn't have to do the reordering.

"You can do this," he told himself.

Beck must have heard the car. She came out onto the front steps, plainly surprised. She looked both familiar to him and foreign. Had she always been so tall? Her hair was longer. Softer, framing her face. She looked tired. Watchful. Wary? Yes.

She said, "Well, this is unexpected. Did I miss a message?"

"No. I . . . It's a surprise."

"If I'd known, I would've planned something. Lucky I stocked up for this sisters' weekend my mother insisted on. You do remember they'll be here tomorrow night, right? Do you intend to stay?"

"Just tonight."

"Oh. Okay."

Paul watched the questions play across Beck's face. But she asked none of them, saying only, "How was the drive?"

"Fine. No problems," he said, taking his overnight bag from the back seat. He pushed the car door shut and took a look around him. "I forgot how pretty it is up here, even at this time of year. Everything smells so good."

He came up the steps and they embraced. She felt foreign in his arms. Not just different but strange and new. Singular. Single. He had the immediate sense that a lot had changed in the few weeks she'd been gone, and not only with him.

She said, "Come inside. Are you hungry? I made a curry. It's vegetarian, but I think you'll like it."

"That sounds great," he said and followed her in.

The place was completely transformed. The dingy walls and dark wood trim were now fresh white. All the dated furniture was gone, replaced by simple, attractive pieces in complementary shades of blue. A few well-chosen pictures and some decorative accessories had been placed in well-chosen spots. Woven baskets, bright pillows and rugs, knitted throws, and patterned curtains softened the room and pulled everything together. It was definitely ready to rent or to sell to today's buyers, with their Pinterest-inspired ideas of what constituted charm. She'd built a fire, and its glow made the setting feel tragically romantic.

Seeing Beck, seeing this—the effort she'd undertaken for this place she loved—made Paul want to wrap her in his arms. She was a remarkable person. hardheaded but softhearted. He had always thought so, but he'd gotten used to her over the years and stopped noticing the ways she'd enriched his life. He'd let the sexual attraction factor (that is, lack of) supersede the domestic tranquility factor. Now, though, he wondered if he ought to rethink his conclusions.

"This place looks fantastic," Paul said, pushing away those thoughts for the time being. "I can't believe this is the same house. If you do end up putting it on the market, it's going to sell the first day."

"Yes, but fortunately, that's not going to be an issue. The credit union got the appraisal back, so now everything's ready for closing a week from tomorrow."

Paul set his overnight bag on the bench beside the door. Any other time, he would have taken it into the bedroom he'd be sharing with Beck. He couldn't imagine that they'd sleep in the same bed tonight. He might not be welcome anywhere in the house, once he'd said what he had to say. *If* he went through with saying it. Look at her, standing there with that quizzical expression. How could he hurt this woman, this lifelong friend? He knew her face so well. As well as his own, really. Had he just not seen her properly, all this time?

He said, "Are the bedrooms and bathroom redone, too?" She'd painted the kitchen cabinets and changed the backsplash and hardware. The table was painted and the chairs were new. A sign over the door to the sunporch said FIND YOUR BLISS. As though the doorway might be a portal. Maybe they could walk through it together and see what happened.

Beck said, "New paint, bedding, and curtains. No budget for new bedroom furniture, but I wouldn't have replaced it anyway; it's got character. Have a look if you want."

Paul did, then paid a quick visit to the bathroom. While he washed his hands, he looked at himself in the mirror and tried to replay that "Oh" moment he'd had, when he'd recognized that treading water and swimming were not one and the same. When he'd then gotten up the nerve to call Claire for advice. (Ostensibly. He'd wanted to hear her voice, feel the jolt he knew he'd get from the connection.)

What if he knew for certain that Claire could never, *never* consider him romantically, for whatever reason? He knew that she liked him fine. But he'd also let himself believe there was something more between them. Thought he could feel it like charged ions or electrons or what have you (he was a fiction editor, not a physicist). Now, though? Now he wondered if he had labored under a delusion for years, living as if in Plato's cave. Unchained, he couldn't quite tell what was real. Had he come here actually believing that Claire could be his future? Was he willing to undo what he and Beck had, no matter what followed?

"What would Fred Rogers do?" he asked his reflection.

"Old Fred would never have gotten into this mess."

Beck called to him, "I opened a new pinot noir that I like. Should I pour you some?"

"Please. I'll be right out."

Paul joined Beck, sitting in one of the two new armchairs that faced a loveseat. She poured wine for him. Her glass was already in progress.

She said, "I've been going out in the kayak in late afternoons. The thing is *ancient*. The paddle weighs a ton compared with new ones. I need to update all the gear. Still, it's been so great to get out on the water. A pair of eagles is making a nest in a tree on the southwest shore."

"Oh, nice." Paul pointed to a colorful carved wooden bird that sat on the mantel. It was whimsical in design. "Is that an eagle?"

"No; spirit owl. Made by a Wabanaki tribal artist. It spoke to me."

"Does it have a name?"

"I call him Ollie," she said. "Not exactly authentic, I know."

"Ollie the owl."

"Yes. Ollie the owl."

Paul watched the fire dance. It was soothing. The wine was, too. Even had she known he was coming, she could not be doing a better job of making this easy on him. But now he wasn't so sure what exactly he wanted to tell her.

Best to dive right in regardless. Be clear and honest, and let the matters sort themselves out—which he was confident they would, once he exposed them to light and air. He didn't have to know what the conclusion should be. He just needed to push the situation to its limits, push himself to his limits, and then he'd know for certain whether this was an opportunity for remaking their marriage or whether this was in fact the fork in their road.

She was waiting.

Just tell her everything, he thought.

Most of everything.

The necessary parts of everything.

Yes. Okay. Ready.

He said, "What else have you been up to?"

"Well . . . I've been writing. Fiction."

"No kidding? That's new."

Beck's gaze slid from his. "Actually it isn't. I've been messing around with a novel for years. I just didn't tell you about it."

"For *years*? Why not?"

"You know how you are. You have really high standards."

"And you didn't want me to discourage you," Paul said.

"Yeah."

"Well, damn. I hate that I made you feel that way. I'm sorry."

"Don't be. You didn't do anything."

"I inadvertently made you afraid to share your work with me."

"Then I guess you can be inadvertently sorry. But don't worry about it. Besides, it really could be shit and we'll both be glad I haven't foisted it on you. I've just sent thirty thousand words to Gina. She'll give me good, objective feedback."

"She will," Paul said. He swirled the wine in his glass. "But I wish . . . *years* is a long time to be working on a novel and never say anything about it."

"To you. I did tell Mom. I hope you aren't offended."

He was, a little.

He said, "No, not at all. I understand. I do, truly. Anyway, I'm sure Gina's feedback will be better than mine would've been." Paul raised his glass. "To your novel."

"Novel in progress," she said. "There's still a long way to go. But we can talk about that some other time. I'm going to guess you came here for a reason . . ."

Paul got up to stir the fire and gather his nerve. He knew he ought to face her while he spoke but couldn't make himself turn around. If he had to look at her, he might not be able to get this out.

He said, "You know, I don't deserve you," which was as good a beginning as any. "You've been my closest friend all these years, but I haven't always been straight with you. I've . . . well, I've kept things from you—not out of disrespect. The opposite, really. Out of respect, and kindness. That's what I always told myself, anyway."

Beck said, "Oh, hell. I was afraid that's what this was."

He pressed on. "For a long time, I've understood that I wasn't being wholly true to who I am and what I want and need. Which is not your fault at all—I made those choices. But, so, a few years ago, I . . . An opportunity presented itself, and I took it."

Beck said, "Was it Geoff?"

Paul turned to her in surprise.

She said, "That's my first guess. I noticed a difference in you, and I've been wondering if that's when you got together with Geoff."

"Oh—no, God, it wasn't Geoff. Did you—that is, you think that I'm—"

"Gay? Yeah. Or maybe bisexual. It would explain a lot. I've been waiting for you to feel like the time was right to tell me."

Paul was stunned. Beck thought he was gay? *Him?*

Straight-arrow Paul Balashov, executive editor, patron of XX-chromosome sex workers, unrequited lover of Claire Geller, whose face and body were longtime fixtures of his romantic and sexual longings. He could not be less gay than he was.

He stood there, speechless.

She said, "Because, I know we haven't ever addressed this—but we should have, and now if we're doing this, we may as well put it all out there—and maybe *I* should have addressed it rather than leave it up to you when you must have been feeling so vulnerable—but, anyway, we haven't had sex in a *really* long time. An abnormally long time, even for people who've been married for decades. And even when we did have sex . . . well, I just have to say it: It wasn't so great. Ever. Which was okay, but also kind of sad, too, once I realized that the problem was probably biological, not personal, and there might be great sex to be had elsewhere. For us both."

He said, "I—wow. A lot to unpack, there."

"Paul. This isn't literary analysis. This is our life. Come on. Just tell me. If it wasn't Geoff, then who?"

He rubbed his head. Where to start? He said, "God, this is hard . . ."

"Some other man? Someone who's not out? I swear I won't say a word. And we don't need to change anything at home, you know. I'd be fine with us just altering the ecosystem, so to speak, and leaving everything else in place."

"Beck. That's not what this is about," he said. "I'm not gay. At all. Not that I think there's anything wrong with being gay, if that's what I was. But I am entirely heterosexual." He slugged down all the wine in his glass, then said, "You don't even like sex. I thought I was doing you a favor."

Beck stared at him as if he'd spoken in tongues.

"What?" she said. "*What?* You thought you were doing me a favor when? How?"

"I didn't want to impose upon you—"

"Are you trying to tell me that you've been stepping out with another *woman?*"

"Yes. That is, sort of."

"Either you did or you didn't."

Paul covered his face with his hand. "I saw someone. For sex. It wasn't an affair."

He sang the whole sad song, then. (Almost all of it.) What he'd believed. The Resident. The Resident's replacement. His feelings of guilt and relief. Beck listened without interruption. When he finished, she got up and went to the kitchen.

"Do you want me to warm some bread to go with this?"

"I—sure, yes, that'd be nice," he said, following her.

She turned on the oven, readied the loaf, put it in. She did these things briskly and with obvious preoccupation. Which he could understand! He'd given her a lot to process.

"Can I help with anything?"

She turned toward him, the bread knife still in hand. "Tell me the rest. I know there's more. I *know* you. Well—maybe I don't! But I know this. What else? Whatever it is, you have to just say it."

"There's nothing else."

Her voice softened. "Come on, Paul. You're lying."

"All right. There is. But I can't . . ."

"Then why did you bother to come up here? This could have waited until I got home."

"I didn't know when you'd be coming home. *If* you'd be coming home."

She went about setting the table. "So . . . did you just never find me very attractive?"

"Beck. I think you're beautiful. That has nothing to do with anything."

"Was I difficult to live with?"

"Not at all."

"That's definitely a lie."

"We've had a pretty harmonious life together. You aren't a difficult person."

"What I'm getting at," Beck said, "is that I'm confused about the sex part. You sometimes seemed . . . not reluctant, exactly, but tentative. Like you weren't always sure you wanted to be doing what we were doing."

"I was concerned that you weren't really enjoying it."

"Why didn't you say something?"

"Why didn't *you* say something?"

"I didn't want you to feel judged!" she said. "It wasn't like we were terrible at it. When you were with the other women, were you tentative?"

"Not really. Not after I got over how weird it was."

"So you never got over that with me."

"What? No, it wasn't like that. I didn't figure out until later that—" Paul stopped. He'd been about to say that it was only after he discovered his feelings toward Claire that he recognized how different they were from his feelings toward Beck. "Never mind."

"No, tell me. Didn't figure out what?"

He said, "That sexual attraction is complex. And for us, it's less strong. For whatever reason."

"*When* did you figure that out?"

"A while back."

"Because of the sex workers?"

"No, that's a whole different thing. Like . . . enhanced masturbation. Sort of. Ugh," he said, rubbing his face. "This is really hard to talk about."

"I know. For me, too, but we need to get to the bottom of this. If not because of them, then . . . ?"

"Claire," he blurted. "Shit. I'm sorry, Beck."

Her brow furrowed. "What? Are you saying *Claire* is at the bottom of this? Claire, my sister?"

"Not the way you think. That is, she's not involved. I've never—this is all just me, Beck. Just me and my foolish, ill-advised . . . She has no idea I think of her as anything other than your kid sister."

"Oh my god. *Claire* is who does it for you. Claire."

Paul wished Beck would stop saying her name.

Beck said, "This is unbelievable. When did you—"

"Years ago. I tried to shut it down. I never, ever even *attempted* to act on it."

Beck sat down. "Well, shit."

"Yeah."

"She really doesn't know? The two of you haven't been—"

"No! As bad as I am, I'm not that much of a reprobate."

"So . . . you came here to say . . . ?"

"That I think it's past time for us to free each other."

"So that you can pursue my sister."

Paul shrugged miserably. "I don't see that as a likely option."

"Then why bother to do this at all?"

"It needed to be done regardless. I know you don't disagree."

She said, "This was a *lot* easier when I thought you were gay."

"I can see that."

"Because . . . well, I was using that to rationalize my own behavior," she said. "My own indiscretion. You may as well know."

"*You?* When? Who?"

"A week ago. Nobody you know. Just a guy I met here. Actually that's not true. I did just meet him, but I also met him a long time ago. Remember how I said I had my heart broken here when I was seventeen? Well, same guy. Only I didn't realize it was him right away—it was just a random coincidence. Though Dad would probably say no, it was a meaningful one—that is, fate.

"Anyhow, I had a one-night stand, if you want to call it that. And you know what? It was great. I'm just going to say it. It was really, really great sex. So I get it—there is a difference. But . . . Paul, come on: *Claire?* Why does it have to be my sister, for god's sake?"

"Fate?"

Beck put her forehead to the tabletop. She said, "You aren't even mad at me, are you?"

Paul tested his feelings about what she'd done, then said, "No, I guess I'm not."

"Proof," said Beck, "that we really are over." She sat up again.

He said, "*You* weren't upset, either, until we got to the part about Claire."

"And your point is what?"

"My point is . . . I'm sorry. Hurting you is the last thing I want to do."

She said, "So what now?"

What now? Paul thought. Now it was blindingly obvious that he had to move forward on his own, come what may.

Beck said, "Please tell me you aren't going to back out of getting the loan."

"I'm sorry—"

"No," she said. "No. You can't do that to me. We can . . . We can just live apart."

"That might seem simpler, but at some point it'd cause problems—for you, too. You need to be free to pursue whoever, whenever, however, without having to explain that you have a husband in name only. Besides, I can't have a new mortgage obligation now. I'm going to look for an apartment in the city, and you know how important it is to have robust financials."

She stared at him as if he'd just strangled their dog and was still holding it by the neck.

He said, "I know it's a disappointment, but—"

"I was going to live here," Beck said quietly.

"What do you mean, live here? You set it up to be a vacation rental."

She shook her head. "I only said that so you'd agree to take out the loan. I was going to tell you after it closed. Have 'the talk' after everything was set—but you beat me to it."

"You were going to leave me?" Paul said. "This whole time, you were lying about everything?"

"Not out of malice. I . . ." She let her words trail off.

Paul slumped into a kitchen chair. "I really blew it all up, didn't I?"

"It's not too late to take it back. Some of it, at least. You can keep the house—"

"I don't want to keep the house. We lived there for the kids' sake."

Beck said, "But I thought you loved not having to be in the city all the time."

"I love not having to *commute* five days a week. Hence my desire to live there now."

"Great, so I have to sacrifice the one thing that matters to me most so that you don't have to commute. That's fair."

"Oh, but it was fair for you to lie to me in order to keep this place? Besides, it's more than convenience, Beck. You know it is. I don't see why you can't be just as happy staying in Irvington. You've made that house as beautiful as this one, and you won't have any trouble affording the payments, once this one's sold."

"I belong *here*."

"And I belong in Manhattan."

Paul watched as Beck went to a cabinet and took out a bottle of gin. She said, "Alcohol won't solve this, I know, but right now I either toss back a couple of shots or I accidentally stab you to death."

Paul said, "I vote for the gin."

She found a tray and loaded it with a glass of ice, a lime, a knife, and the gin. She said, "I wish I could say that this is really fucking selfish of you—but I'm not a hypocrite." She took the tray from the counter and moved toward the hallway.

Paul said, "Are we not going to talk about this further?"

"We are not. And just to be clear: you'll stay in *Claire's* room, and then you're out of here at first light tomorrow."

22

Turbulence

I f Marti Geller was watching over her girls, she was now seeing Claire meet Sophie at a gate in Newark Airport after flying in from Duluth. Two of her girls coming together to meet up with the third, exactly as Marti had directed. What was unfolding for the Geller sisters, though—well, it wasn't quite what she had envisioned.

The day's weather was volatile. Flights were canceled or delayed. Travelers were anxious and frazzled—Claire among them. Her connecting flight from Minneapolis to Newark had been turbulent from the moment of liftoff. Claire's hands were stiff from clutching the armrests.

"I'm happy to see you again," she said, greeting Sophie with almost no time to spare for the connection to Bangor, "but remind me, *why* am I taking three flights on a day when the weather sucks and I don't even want to be in Maine this time of year?"

"Because Mom wanted you to," Sophie said. "Besides, what else would you have done this weekend?"

"Knitted something. I made a scarf in one day! Now I think I want to try making a sock."

The announcement came for their group to board. They moved toward the doorway. "You're serious?" said Sophie.

"I am," said Claire.

"Minnesota has really gotten to you! How did this quaint development occur?"

As they boarded the flight and found their seats, Claire told Sophie about River and Heath, then said, "I took a workshop. We carded raw wool, spun it, dyed it, and now I'm knitting things with yarn I made myself. In a few weeks, I'll get to shear a sheep, if my schedule works with theirs."

"Sounds like you're well prepared for your eventual pairing with Paul . . . Bunyan."

"Oh, ha-ha. Could you be any funnier?" said Claire.

"That was bad, I know. Sorry. Too hard to resist."

Claire said, "I suppose it is slightly funny. In a tragicomic way."

They passed the half hour before takeoff chatting with ease. When had they last had this kind of time alone together? Not since the summer before Claire left for med school, champing at the bit, her eye on the impending leap toward a medical career. Sophie's concerns had centered on suppressing acne and determining exactly how many more days remained until her sixteenth birthday, when she intended to lose her virginity as a gift to herself. Neither of them could recall any particular event or situation of enforced togetherness, but they agreed it had probably occurred at the camp.

Sophie said, "You do know that we'll still have to share a bedroom. Beck said she's got her old room set up as a little den."

"I did *not* know," Claire said. She and Beck hadn't spoken since that late-night phone call. "But I suppose I won't mind it *too* much. It's been a while since I had another human adult in my bedroom."

"Same," said Sophie. "But if you snore, then fuck this togetherness; you're *out*."

The flight attendant made the announcement about electronics as Sophie held her phone above her head and snapped some pictures of herself and of the plane's cabin. She said, "What are we supposed to do this weekend, anyway?"

"I guess we're just supposed to just *be*," said Claire. "As a tribute to Mom and Dad, or something."

"Hm," Sophie said, typing an Instagram post. "There," she said when she finished. "For whatever it's worth."

"How many followers do you have these days?"

"Three point two." At Claire's confused look, Sophie clarified: "Million."

"That's *insane*." Claire had started an IG account a couple of years ago. She'd posted three pictures and had twelve followers.

"I know it sounds big," said Sophie, "But it's nothing in comparison to the serious players."

"I don't even understand that world," Claire said. For that matter, she hardly understood her own world anymore. Nothing had turned out the way she'd thought it would.

The plane taxied to the runway, then lifted off into the low, heavy sky, where the air was so bumpy, the flight so turbulent, that the flight attendants had to remain buckled into their seats. Claire spent the flight fighting and then, with much embarrassment, succumbing to the urge to vomit.

She said to Sophie, "This weekend had better be worth it."

Wrapped in a long sweater, Beck waited on the front stoop as they drove up to the fog-enshrouded house. She smiled and waved, obviously glad to see them, but she looked as if she hadn't slept in days.

"I'm glad you got here all right," she said.

"Me, too," said Sophie. "The fog is *bad*. But Dr. Geller here is excellent behind the wheel."

"Do you need a hand with your things?"

Claire said, "No, we're traveling light."

"It's my Life Principle," said Sophie, stepping up to Beck for a hug. "Important for quick getaways."

Claire followed. A closer look at Beck showed that not only had she missed sleep, she'd missed showering, too. Her hair in front was in wild disarray. In back, it was matted, as if she'd been lying on a hard surface and staring upward. *Something* had happened, and Claire suspected it had to do with either Paul or the mortgage. Probably the mortgage, given that Beck hadn't yet returned home.

Beck's hug was quick. Then she was moving on, saying, "Well, this is it," and standing aside so they could enter.

"Wow," Sophie said, gazing at the remade space. "This place looks amazing!" She pointed toward the kitchen. "Are those cabinets new?"

"Repainted," Beck said. "The hardware is all new, though. Backsplash is, too."

"You did that?"

"I did. Painted everything. Got rid of all the curtains and roller shades, recaulked the tub . . . I did pretty much all the things I would've done if I knew for sure I could keep it."

"And now?" asked Sophie. "What's the status on your efforts?"

"I'll fill you in after you get settled."

Claire pointed to the Shabbat candlesticks, which held new tapers, lighted and glowing on a sideboard beside the old dining table, newly painted a smoky blue color. "That's really nice," she said. "Mom would like it."

"A small thing," Beck said without looking at Claire. "Mom said she kept these from the house she grew up in, but now I wonder if that's true. Here," she said, laying her hand on Sophie's shoulder, "put your things up; you've had a long day."

When they were in the bedroom, Beck called to them, "Dinner is leftovers; I haven't been in the mood to cook. Drinks first? Wine?"

"*Definitely* a drink," Claire said, trading her coat for a wool cardigan and adding heavy socks over the pair she wore. "Bourbon, if you've got it."

Sophie left the bedroom, explaining to Beck, "Claire had turbulence from

Minneapolis, and then we had *bad* turbulence coming from Newark to Bangor. The flight attendant called it 'shake and bake.' Claire threw up."

"Sophie was completely blasé about it," Claire said, joining them again.

Sophie said, "Turbulence alone has never downed a commercial airliner."

"Yet," said Claire.

"I thought you were a woman of science!"

"I am. What you have to remember is that science is always a work in progress."

They got their drinks and went into the living room. Claire said, "Okay if I get a fire going? I'm cold. I'm *always* cold."

"Oh, do!" Sophie said. "I love a fire."

Sophie and Beck sat down together on the loveseat. Sophie put her arm around Beck. "What a transformation, Beck. You really do have a knack for decorating."

Claire liked things better the way they had been. This was too bright and tidy, too . . . *decorated*. But she knew better than to say so.

"Thanks." Beck popped up again. "You know what? I'm going to heat some bread. Bread would be good, don't you think?"

As Beck went to the kitchen, Sophie whispered to Claire, "She looks wrecked. What do you think is going on?"

"Hard to say."

If Beck's condition wasn't related to the mortgage, thought Claire, it might be something to do with the guy she'd had her fling with. Possibly it was about both. Or neither; Claire actually had little idea of what else was going on in Beck's life, and she'd never been good at reading her anyway.

For young Claire, Beck had always been her big sister on the go, out in the world seeing and doing and then cataloguing it all in notebooks. She might share some of those thoughts with their father or mother, but never with Claire. In retrospect, Claire realized that some of Beck's ruminations and views and feelings must have emerged in the stories she sometimes made up for Sophie. Claire had paid them scant attention in those years, jealous that the stories were for Sophie and not for her. Or so it had seemed at the time. To Claire, Beck had been a cipher.

When Beck came back into the living room, she moved as if her personal gravity was twice that of Earth's. She sat, angled her body toward Sophie. Claire, seated now in an armchair to Beck's right, might as well not have been in the room.

Claire couldn't think of anything she'd done to put Beck off, yet as the three of them talked about what Beck had and hadn't discovered in her quest for Newman family information, Beck continued to keep her face and body angled toward Sophie.

"So then," Sophie was saying, "I guess you'll be carrying on the Geller family history here. I'm so glad it worked out."

"About that," Beck said heavily, and *now* she turned toward Claire. "You were right," she said. "About Paul. You didn't believe he was gay, and that's correct. He's not gay."

This jolted Claire. Paul wasn't gay! Her heart rose with unearned joy—

—except, wait: why, then, would not-gay Paul want to end his marriage? There had to be someone other than Geoff in the picture. Some woman. Claire's heart fell. Plummeted, really. Right into her gut, to churn amid the knowledge that she'd wasted herself on a fantasy that never had the slightest chance of coming true.

Sophie said, "So you finally got it out of him! When did this happen?"

"He was here—came up yesterday, left this morning. He *had* to talk to me. It couldn't wait, he said. We're going to split up. He wants to move to Manhattan, which means I can't—" Beck stopped midsentence. Sophie's gaze was practically burning into Claire. Beck said, "What?"

"*What* what?" said Sophie.

"Why are you staring at Claire? Did you know?"

"Know . . . ?"

"He told you, didn't he?"

Sophie looked perplexed. "Paul never told me anything. What are you talking about?"

"About Claire! How's he's been in love with Claire for years."

Sophie's eyes grew wide. Then she burst out laughing. "Oh my god! That's—oh, wow. That's just amazing."

Claire, though, couldn't react. She sat as if frozen in place, terrified to move or speak, as if any response from her would break the spell.

Paul.

In love.

With her.

Charmed, not cursed.

"I don't see how it's funny in the least," Beck said to Sophie.

"No—I'm shocked, that's all it is. It's shocking."

"It is that." Beck looked at Claire. Her expression wasn't hostile or cold, just sad. "How's *that* for irony?" she said. "I thought he was hot for his assistant, but no, all along it was you. I'm so sorry to spring it on you this way. I'd meant to be a bit more . . . delicate. Or not tell you at all. I hadn't decided."

All Claire could manage to say was "I'm glad you did."

Now Beck turned to Sophie. "You realize this means I can't get the mortgage, so we have to sell."

"Oh. Oh, *shit*." Sophie reached for Beck's hand. "Honey, I'm sorry. This really isn't going your way."

Sophie returned her gaze to Claire, her expression ablaze with knowledge and delight. Claire wondered if she should levy her own confession. No, god, what a thought! Right now Beck had sympathy for her, for Claire's being caught in the crosshairs unwittingly. Right now Claire was Beck's innocent little sister and Paul was the bad guy who had misled them both. There was no earthly reason to disabuse Beck of those beliefs.

She glanced at Sophie, who looked about to burst. Shit. They were never going to get through this weekend without Sophie's giving Claire away. Or so Claire told herself right before she said—

"It was—is—mutual."

Because it really did have to be said, and better her than Sophie.

Mutual. The fact of it rested there in her brain like radioactive debris, seeping into her body, altering her cells irrevocably.

She continued, "He doesn't know. I never told anyone except Chad, and then Sophie, when I explained why Chad and I broke up. That's why she was staring at me. I'm sorry. I hate myself."

Beck got up and went out the front door.

"Why did you *tell* her?" Sophie said.

"To beat you to it. Your whole body was buzzing with the urge. She knew *something* was up. I just—we're too old for keeping secrets. For pretending."

Sophie made no response.

"Now she hates me," Claire said. "I don't blame her."

"Fuck. What should we do?"

"Let her be."

Sophie nodded. "It's *a lot.*"

The two of them sat in silence for a time, and Beck still did not return.

Claire said, "We should just let her keep this place without having to pay us at all."

"Oh, no, no, we can't do that. Mom said—"

"Mom isn't here anymore. She won't know."

"Then what's a will even for," said Sophie, "if the family doesn't follow it?"

"When did you become so principled?"

"Since I—Hold on, okay?" Sophie got up and went outside. A minute later she was back with her arm around Beck's waist. She was saying, ". . . so as long as everyone is just dumping things on each other, I may as well join in."

Now Beck absolutely wouldn't look at Claire. She said, "I don't know if I'm ready for this, whatever it is." Still, she sat—at the kitchen table, as far from Claire as she could get while still being in essentially the same room.

Sophie remained standing. She squared her shoulders and clasped her hands in front of her as if beginning a recital. "So, here's the thing," she began. "I have eight credit cards, and I've maxed out every one of them—I owe tens of thousands of dollars. As much as ninety thousand, I'd say. I'm barely keeping up the minimum payments.

"Tania needed her apartment back and I haven't had my own in years—which is to say, I'm perpetually homeless. Everything I own is in my carry-on and one box that's now stashed in a locker. Benji has evidently run off to who knows where in order to evade the IRS, and the gallery is shuttered, probably for good. This means I'm jobless, and there's a good chance my health insurance is going to disappear along with my boss. I have a trickle of income from sponsors, but I've fallen down on the job of late—because, really, who truly fucking cares which lipstick *I* use or whose jewelry I wear or which club is my supposed favorite? I'm going to be thirty-seven years old soon, I have no partner, no parents, no children, no pets, no *plants*, even. I may as well not exist! And, so, although I would love for you to keep this place, Beck—as poor, guilty Claire here has suggested would put all your troubles to rights—I just can't sign on for that. I literally *have to* have the money."

"Well," said Claire, almost as shocked by this as by the news about Paul. "*That's* quite a speech."

Beck glared at Sophie. "What are we supposed to do here? Say, 'Oh, poor Sophie, *your* life is the worst; you win'? I'm sure your situation sucks. But those shoes on your feet right now? Those are *six-hundred-dollar* shoes. Your purse is a Fendi, which cost how much? Three or four grand, at least. I can't even guess what you spend to keep your hair looking like poured silk. *Your* troubles are largely of your own making."

"While yours are barely even real!" said Sophie. "I have to hustle every fucking day, while everything's been *given* to you. You've had it easy your entire life. Claire was just now ready to give you what you wanted because you'd gone outside to pout! Poor Beck, Mommy isn't around anymore to make her feel the most special."

Claire said, "Purses can cost that much?" She hadn't meant to pile on, it was just that the figure surprised her. "Why would you pay thousands of dollars for a *purse?*"

"Oh, thank you, Claire. So helpful," said Sophie. "Do I tell you how to spend your money?"

"No, but do I bury myself in debt and then ask for sympathy?"

Sophie said, "Do either of you at all appreciate how difficult it is to be relevant in the art world? No, of course you don't. You don't have a clue."

"And that bag and those shoes make you relevant?" said Beck.

"In a way, yes."

The three of them glared at one another. Then Sophie said, "I didn't think you'd be so heartless."

Beck said, "I didn't think you'd be so irresponsible."

"Why are you coming after me like this? *I* didn't betray you!"

Claire said, "It's not like I could help it. We don't *choose* who we fall in love with; it just happens to us. How is it a betrayal if I never acted on it? It made me miserable, but I kept it to myself and just suffered, okay? I just sucked it up because I had too much respect for you and too much love for you to do anything different. Doesn't that count for something?"

Beck had her hands in her hair and was clutching it as if to keep the top of her head from blowing off. She said, "No. Maybe. I don't know. I need to think about it."

She turned to Sophie. "I'm sorry I attacked you. I'm just upset. That wasn't what you need or deserve."

"Thank you," said Sophie. "Enough of this shit for right now, all right? We're sisters. I'm hungry. Dinner smells amazing. Shall we eat?"

It was mutual, Claire's brain kept reminding her, even as she knew she could lose Beck over this.

Mutual.

Her and Paul.

She had forgotten there was such a thing as food.

23

Better Angels

Beck told her sisters, "I don't have much of an appetite. You two go ahead. I'll see you in the morning."

In the bedroom, she closed the door, then dropped onto the bed. "You are a miserable wretch," she said.

And the ceiling knew the truth: she was a miserable wretch.

For a few minutes, she lay there wallowing in her misery, examining its shape and content. The things that had happened. Who was to blame.

This was Claire's fault.

This was Sophie's fault.

This was Paul's fault.

This was her mother's fault.

This was her own fault.

She got up off the bed and went back to the kitchen.

"The problem is, not one of you is who I thought you were, and how can that even be possible? I thought Mom was an orphaned Kentucky transplant, but no, she grew up on a farm three miles from here. I thought Paul was a closeted gay man, but no, he's a stupid goddamn saint who tried to do right by me even though he was in love with *you*"—she pointed at Claire—"who I thought had everything under complete control, doing all that amazing doctor shit, saving babies, earning three hundred grand a year—"

"Is that what you earn?" said Sophie.

"—being perfect Dr. Geller—I figured you and Chad split because you had found a guy who was actually *worthy* of you. Which I guess you did!" Beck's rueful laugh was half sob. "And you, Sophie: what the fuck? I mean, seriously, what the actual fuck?"

"I obviously can't count on anyone or anything and I don't understand what the hell happened to my life! All I wanted was to be able to live here and keep writing the fucking novel I finally started—again—after years of half-assed effort. That's it. That's all I wanted."

"What?" said Sophie. "A novel? That's *amazing*. I love it. When can I read it?"

"Obviously not before it's finished. And now I'm not sure it ever will be."

"No."

"What do you mean, *no?*"

"I'm sorry, but if it's what you really want, you can't just quit, not if it's your true heart's desire—and I don't actually give a shit if the cynics of the world would laugh at me for saying that. I'm so tired of those people."

Beck was caught short by this, and it softened her. Slowed her heart. Defused, somewhat, the anger, which was not real anger so much as anxiety and pain.

Sophie continued, "I'm sorry for my part in this. I never meant to get so caught up in all the artifice. I never thought the lifestyle would come to own me. It was a kind of addiction, I can totally see that now. But I'm determined to put everything to rights. No more debt. No more fake-it-till-you-make-it. No more fueling myself with the facade of adulation from strangers who think I'm more than I am."

Beck went to Sophie and hugged her. "I am so angry with you, but I'm also proud of you."

"Yeah?"

"Yeah."

Sophie was still working the problem. She said, "Claire, you don't *need* the money up front, right? So, maybe, Beck, you get a smaller mortgage. *Half* the amount. Would that work? I'm brainstorming here."

Claire said, "I'd rather have it up front—"

"A minute ago you were ready to take nothing!"

"Out of guilt," said Claire.

"And now you feel absolved? Come on, this could work."

Beck said, "I doubt I could borrow even that much on my own."

"Claire could cosign."

"No," said Claire. "I'm strapped as it is. No bank would lend that much to me."

"Well, I for one am not going to let a little matter like money stand in the way of Beck keeping this place."

Beck had to hand it to Sophie; it seemed money was no object with her, even when she didn't actually have any.

Sophie paced from living room to kitchen to bedrooms and back. "Think, people. What do we have to work with?"

"Eventually I'll have half of Paul's and my assets," Beck said. "But that's going to take months. I don't suppose you can wait a while longer?"

Sophie shook her head. "For all I know, thanks to Benji, I'll be adding fees for legal representation to my existing burden. I need all the cash I can get, as quickly as I can get it. But there's a solution to this. I know there is."

Claire said, "No offense, but this would be a lot easier if you hadn't spent like some drunken sailor on leave."

Beck said, "It would be easiest if Mom hadn't said to sell the place."

"For you," said Sophie. "For me, it's a lifeline."

Claire said, "Do you think she knew you needed one?"

"Maybe." Sophie stopped pacing. "She never said so to me, but it's possible. Mom could be weirdly intuitive."

The idea that Marti would use her intuition to shortchange Beck in order to save Sophie was irksome, but Beck kept her mouth shut. To complain about favoritism would serve no purpose at all.

Beck said, "Whenever and however you get the money, you might want to use some of it for counseling. So that you don't repeat the mistakes."

"Oh?" said Sophie. "Is that your professional opinion?"

"She's not wrong," said Claire.

"Well, Drs. Geller, thanks for your concern. I promise you I've learned my lesson. Not only that, but I've got ideas for how to move in directions that are more authentic to me. I'm down, but I'm not out."

Claire said, "Yeah? What's your plan?"

Beck watched her sisters as they discussed Sophie's ideas for building herself a new future as an art concierge. *We are all on the cusp,* Beck said to herself. The cusp of what, exactly, was hard to say. What was clear, though, was that this night was a fulcrum for all three of them, and that going forward, nothing would be the same. Would they fly, or would they fall?

Beck went to bed feeling exhausted. She slept for a couple of heavy, dreamless hours, then woke to soft, silvery light through her window and loon calls pealing across the foggy morning. She was warm and snug in her bed, with its fresh sheets and down comforter, having a perfect moment before reality's intrusion: yes, she still had to sell. There was no other way.

Which meant she had to decide how much longer she would stay here. She and Paul hadn't discussed any of the practical matters they were facing. Clearly, though, they needed to do that soon, and start the process of getting the Irvington house ready for market.

Beck didn't know where she wanted to live or what she wanted to do. She knew only that it all had to be different, because *she* was different. Yet she didn't know quite who she was, which made it hard to know who she should become. This was a conundrum.

"First, coffee," Beck said, climbing out of her cocoon and into the room's chill.

Sophie was in the kitchen, dressed for fitness in her designer everything. Beck said, "Going for a run?"

"Already went. Cadillac Mountain at sunrise, baby. I slayed it."

"Impressive. Looks like you slayed the coffee maker, too." Beck filled a mug and took it to the kitchen table. "Thanks for that."

"You're so welcome! As are you, Dr. Geller," Sophie said as Claire joined them, hair spilling over her shoulders. "You look like teenage Claire," she said.

"Don't look too closely."

"Now that you guys are up, I'm going to get a shower. Then I think I'll head into town for a while."

"You should," said Beck. She sat with her hands wrapped around her mug. "I expect to be rotten company while I wait for the Realtor to show up."

Claire said, "Soph, is it okay if I go into town with you? I promised David I'd bring him a souvenir."

"Yeah, of course," Sophie said. "Beck, what will you do?"

"Things. I should work up some ideas to pitch. I haven't done any paid writing since before Mom died."

"If you're still doing celebrity profiles, I could connect you to some people. Lots of publicists and managers in my contacts list."

"Why have you never made this offer before?"

"I couldn't; Benji said it'd be an ethical conflict. He was *so pure*. Ha. Evidently not."

"Then yes, please. I'm up for some new-directions puff pieces, reputation rehab, whatever they want to throw at me. They'll be good distractions."

"I'll see what I can do."

Sophie went to shower. Claire was rummaging in the refrigerator. She said, "I'm not much of a cook, but I'm capable of scrambling eggs. Want some?"

"Throw in some of those chopped vegetables, if you're willing—do you see the container, there, with the red lid?"

"Got it." Claire set to work. She said, "Listen, I just want to say again how . . . weird I feel about how this has turned out. I mean, I'm glad there are no more secrets, and I actually don't mind that Chad left me. We were never a great fit anyway. What he really wants is an adoring trophy wife whose greatest ambition is to keep herself and their house in perfect condition."

Beck said, "Well, you won't have that problem with Paul."

"As if," said Claire. "Just because he and I . . . I mean, it's hard to see how that can happen. Realistically."

Beck had half a mind to say *You know, he paid for sex.* To warn Claire? Or out of spite? She held that back, wanting to only display her nature's better angels. She said instead, "You know, when I thought he might be in love with Geoff, I was filled with concern over him being taken advantage of. The way I would be for any good friend. I didn't feel jealous or angry. I *genuinely* wanted Paul to be happy. To be true to who he really is. And you know what? I still want that. I mean, why should it be any different just because the object of his affection is named Claire? You're right that it's a challenge to imagine—but who's been better at facing down challenges than you?"

"How can you be so generous?"

"I'm not, always. I guess it's just that I love you, and I love Paul, and if I stay out of the way, the rest of it will sort itself out."

Claire said, "Dad used to say, 'I'm confident that the universe will take care of it.' Remember? He was never afraid of anything."

"Soph is just like him, isn't she?"

"More than I knew," said Claire. She filled their plates and brought them to the table. "I was thinking about how being here at camp with you and Soph is like being on an island removed from time."

"For me, too. I'm glad you came. Thanks."

"Thank Mom."

Beck looked heavenward. "Thanks, Mom."

But also, no thanks, she thought, her mind snagging on the thorns of *if only.*

A few weeks ago, Helen had advised her to stop regrets before they could start. Yet how could Beck avoid them when everything that mattered in that realm was completely outside of her control? She felt like she was made up entirely of regret, as if regret were an otherwise formless putty that took the shape of angry, guilt-ridden fools who hadn't been able to see the cliff before they leapt off it.

24

Bloom

Having been out for a run on Acadia's carriage roads, C.J. returned to the Callaghan estate to find that Deirdre and Arlo were back from Boston. Deirdre was standing in the dining room's bay window, looking out toward the potting shed. She saw C.J. and pointed through the window. "He's moved into the shed," she told him.

"Arlo has?"

"Yes. In protest. Though he says you might be permitted to visit him. I, however, am banned. We had a fine trip; Arlo was polite if not especially forthcoming, and the schools are quite eager to admit him. I've decided I'm going to go with Bement. It was founded by a dedicated suffragette. Arlo is not, of course, especially interested in that."

"No, I can see how it wouldn't excite him," C.J. said.

"Tell me, how goes it here? Any progress on your endeavors? You do know I'll gladly keep you here all summer; Arlo has made his preferences clear, and I don't mind admitting that you'd be doing me a favor. We'll have the usual suspects coming and going, of course, but if you can drink cocktails on a boat, you'll fit right in. I told Arlo he won't have to leave for his new school until August, though that is apparently no consolation. So he's found a place of his own to live."

"I'll go talk to him."

C.J. went back outside and made his way across the broad lawn. The grass had softened underfoot. Robins hopped about, pecking for bugs and worms. The hardwoods' branches were *so* close to unfurling those fattened buds; soon the trees would have a haze of reds and golds and greens, the promise of springtime's arrival in Maine in truth, not just a date on the calendar. *We are late bloomers*, thought C.J., *but bloom we will.*

His phone rang: it was Carol Barksdale. "Hey, Carol, what's up?"

"You aren't going to believe who I just met with."

"Martha Stewart?"

"The Geller sisters!" she said, making it sound as if they were a music group on par with, say, the Dixie Chicks. "Well, two of the three."

"Which two?"

"Sophie and Claire. Beck is the one I met that first day, when I took the photos."

He knew who Beck was. He didn't say this. "And?"

"They're giving you first dibs on their refurbished camp, if you want it. Otherwise, it goes on the market officially next week."

"Well, I'll be damned. Do you have a price?"

"It appraised at $864,000. I know that's a lot more than you intended to spend, but it's had significant updates since I took those photos, and of course the waterfront location means—"

"I'll buy it."

"Don't you think you should see it in person before you decide? Though sometimes my long-distance buyers do just rely on me to—"

"Yes. When? And then I'll buy it."

Carol laughed. "Let me find out the best time and call you back."

C.J. went to knock on the shed door, thinking words like *fortitude* and *patience* and *good fortune* and *fate*. As he knocked, he called, "Hey, buddy. I hear you've got a new address."

Looks like I might soon have one, too.

"Are you friend or foe?" Arlo shouted.

"Friend. Definitely. Is there any question about it?"

Arlo opened the door wide enough that C.J. could see he'd laid out a bedroll and had a space heater running. It was electric, and presumably had a thermostat and kill switch on it, but C.J. would make sure of that.

He said, "Looks pretty cozy in there."

"I'm not going to that school. If you came here to try to talk me into it, you can just go away."

"Heck no," said C.J. "I don't want to talk about that. I want to show you this rock I found today. I think it has a fossil in it, but I'm no expert." C.J. held the rock out for Arlo to see.

"Okay. You can come in," Arlo said. He took the rock, then moved to his bedroll and sat down.

C.J. sat, too. He watched Arlo examine the rock. "What do you think?"

"These marks *could* be part of a trilobite," Arlo said.

"Yeah? I was hoping."

"I forgot to bring my iPad in here, otherwise we could look it up."

"That's okay. Hey, so, Gram said she liked the Bement School. But I guess you don't?"

"Obviously."

"Is it the school, or just having to go there and not know anybody? 'Cause you'd make friends fast."

Arlo said, "I have my own money, you know. My mom and dad left it to me. So I don't see why I have to let anyone else be the boss of me."

"Sure. Well, you're a smart kid. Might be you could take care of yourself. I mean, you can't drive yet—but I guess you could hire a chauffeur. And you aren't much of a cook—but that's a skill you can learn. You could get a hot plate in here, sure. Microwave. Or just order in. Now, Gram will probably charge you for Wi-Fi—but you can afford that. Sounds perfect."

"You could stay with me. We could build bunks."

C.J. looked around. "Might be you've got space for that. But, I like a place with its own bathroom and shower. No offense."

"*I* like to rough it. Peeing outside is fun."

"To each his own," said C.J. He had a closer look at the space heater. No danger there.

Arlo said, "I thought you would want to rough it, too."

"Up to a point. Hot water, though . . ."

"We could make a solar shower like one I saw on Discovery Channel. That would be okay, right?" He looked at C.J. with those so-blue eyes, beseeching him. "Just stay here with me."

"You know, I would. But I just found out that a house I've had my eye on is for sale. Real pretty spot. So I think I'm gonna go that route, if I can. I hope you'll come visit me there."

"Will you have guest rooms?"

"Sure I will. Nothing like your gram's place here, but at least one or two."

Arlo turned the stone over and over in his hands. He said, "Okay, here's my offer: I come and live with you in your new house."

"How is that an offer?"

"You won't want to be all alone there. Being all alone is scary."

C.J. felt a lump form in his throat. He said, "It can be. You're right. I appreciate that offer."

"Do you accept?"

"Oh, buddy . . . Here's my problem: according to all the rules, it's Gram who's got the say in where you live. And she thinks the best place for you is at that school you visited. I can't just take you and go against that. If I did, I'd end up in jail."

Arlo started to cry. "It's not fair," he said.

True, it wasn't. So much of life was not fair, but did an eight-year-old really need to learn that lesson as acutely as this boy had? Yeah, other kids had it a lot worse, there was no question about that. This kid, though, was the one who sat before C.J. sobbing. Who wanted nothing more than to be something like a regular kid with something like a regular life. A life that fit him, not a life he would be made to fit into.

C.J. held Arlo until his little body stopped heaving and shuddering. Then he said, "Tell you what: I'm gonna go talk with Gram and see if there's any wiggle room, okay? I want to warn you, though—and you're old enough to understand this—I might not be able to change anything for you. Gram might just get mad at me for nosing into her business and kick me out, and you and me, we won't get to see each other anymore. It's a big risk. Are we prepared for that?"

Arlo looked up at C.J. and nodded. His eyelashes were clumped with tears.

"Okay, then," C.J. said, standing. "You stay put. I'll let you know how it goes. And remember: whatever she says, you and me, we're pals. Always."

"Do you swear it?" Arlo said.

"Cross my heart."

C.J. left the shed and returned to the house, wondering what he'd just done. Was this yet another impulsive act that was going to leave him and those around him sorry?

Deirdre had made herself some tea and was in the sitting room with her feet up. "How did it go?" she said.

"I believe we've come to an understanding."

"Oh?"

"I think so—but you're going to have to tell me for sure." He sat down beside her. "I just got a line on a house—real nice spot, a few miles from here. Quiet. Real pretty. Lots of room to roam. Arlo thinks that sounds like just the place for him, and I agree. We're not looking for any kind of special financial arrangement, nothing like that. We'd just be a couple of bachelors teaching each other about the important stuff in life."

"Well, *this* is not what I was anticipating." Deirdre set her teacup on its saucer. "It's irregular, to say the least."

"It is that. But you can't tell me he'd be better off at boarding school. Not this boy. Frankly, from what you told me about his folks—and this is not meant to disparage your daughter—but I don't think he's had too many days in his life where he got the attention and care he merits. And you want to do right by him, I see that. So maybe give this idea a chance."

Deirdre said, "I've already given the school a deposit."

"If they won't give it back, I'll reimburse you."

She studied him without speaking. Then she said, "Let's discuss that unpleasantness with your father."

Oh, shit, he thought. "Ah, yes," he said, hope sinking, dread rising. "Let me just say that I promise you, I never had any intention of putting a bullet in my dad; if I had, he wouldn't have lived to call the cops."

"So it was all a big mistake. A misunderstanding."

"No; he understood exactly what I was up to."

"You're saying you wanted to shoot at him, and miss."

"Yes, that's it in a nutshell," he said. "I'll tell you the whole story, and you can judge as you see fit." Maybe she wouldn't like it, being that she probably had more in common with his folks than she did with him. There was no choice, though. Let the trial begin:

It had been Thanksgiving weekend. C.J.'s whole family were gathered at his parents' home in Aiken. They'd done the big turkey dinner on Thursday, and on Saturday all the men and boys had gone out to hunt deer.

"I'd hated deer hunting my whole life," he told Deirdre. "When I was a kid, I wanted to stay at home and draw or paint. But art was a thing you bought, not a thing you did. Reynolds men were businessmen, and our hobbies were guns and dogs and horses and golf and maybe NASCAR, though that was a bit on the redneck side for us. Still, it was within the pale. Making a painting of sunrise over the marsh, say, was the kind of thing sissy girls did; that's what my cousins liked to say when we were all teens. When my uncles or my dad ribbed me, they put it in harsher terms.

'Painting's for faggots and queers,' they said. 'Can't think why you'd want to do it.'"

This particular Saturday, while they were out at the tree stand, C.J.'s father brought up the subject, though C.J. had been working for his father for twenty years and not painting at all.

"It was a thing he did from time to time," C.J. told Deirdre. "To razz me. Keep me in my place, I guess. Remind me that I'd never really been a man the way he and my uncle and cousins were men. My golf game was weak. I didn't like to smoke cigars. I hadn't bagged a deer since I was twelve."

And then there was Denise, who Coleman Sr. often joked had little use for C.J. beyond "getting smart about whose family her little girl ought to have," as if the doctor Denise had been married to was lesser because, being native to Michigan, he didn't have deep roots in the South. "Notice they've only managed to have the one child," Coleman Sr. told the group this Saturday, in the deer stand. "Big disappointment to me, as you all know. Who's going to carry on the Reynolds name? You had *one* job, son," he told C.J., shaking his head. The other men laughed.

C.J. said to Deirdre, "I'd been taking it from him for years, you understand. My entire life, basically, and keeping my mouth shut. Why this day was any different, I can't tell you. Might've been that Denise and me, we'd been having a rough patch, and I felt like nothing I did was right, and I wasn't doing anything that mattered to anyone. Least of all to myself."

When the men got back to the house, the others went about unloading the two bucks they'd killed. C.J. made to separate himself from that and the men as quickly as possible, but Coleman Sr. said, "Hold short there, son," and drew him inside the gun room, where he planted himself on a padded bench, telling C.J., "Lock up my rifle and then help me with these boots. Least then you'll be good for something today."

C.J. told Deirdre, "I was going to the gun safe, gritting my teeth as usual, and then I just thought, *God damn it, I have had enough. I'm going to put the old man in his place.*"

He turned and leveled his rifle, aimed it toward his father. *Toward* him, not at him.

"What fool thing are you doing?" his father said. Not scared yet, just irritated. "Put it away."

C.J. released the safety. "I am done putting up with your shit."

"Damn it, Junior," his father said.

"What are you worried about? I can't hit the broad side of a barn. That's what you always tell me."

"Even broken clocks get it right twice a day," said Coleman Sr., and now he sounded nervous. "Come on, son. Lower it. If I said something that made you mad, I was just kidding around. You know that." His voice quavered.

C.J. aimed carefully, the scope marking a spot several inches clear of Coleman Sr., then fired the gun, taking great satisfaction in seeing his father jerk and throw himself to the floor as the bullet went past his ear and into the wall.

"Damn. I missed."

His father looked up at him, fear turning to anger. "Keep talking," Sr. said. "Talk's all you've got anyway. It's all you ever had." But his eyes were still on the rifle.

C.J. returned it to the gun safe. "Hard to take you seriously when you're on your knees. Pretty funny—because, you know, I was just kidding around."

He recalled his father's cold expression. Those narrowed eyes in his jowly face. The grim, determined set of his thin lips. Coleman Sr. now knew that C.J. hadn't aimed to hit him, and knew, too, that he could plausibly claim that C.J. had.

Even before any of the alarmed family arrived in the room, Sr. was on the phone with the 911 operator reporting an active shooter in his home. "It's my deranged son," he said, staring at C.J. as he spoke. "He's trying to kill me—already shot once and missed, thank God. There's a house full of people here, and I don't know what else he might do. I'm holding him off, but y'all best get someone over here quick."

C.J. waited for his father to end the call. Then the room had filled with people. First the family, then the police. C.J.'s mother had greeted them at the door and assured them they could holster their weapons; no one was in danger. The cops came in, cleared the room, asked a few questions of both men, then cuffed C.J., who expected his father to allow the cops to haul him off to jail and hold him for a while. A point had to be made, after all. He had not expected to be charged with attempted murder.

It was Coleman Sr.'s panicked response that had done C.J. in. His father had been embarrassed, and he'd turned that embarrassment into anger and that anger into action. C.J. recognized this later, when he was sitting in the courtroom for his arraignment. He hadn't been wrong about the point he was trying to make, but he had misjudged the effect his making that point might have on such a man as his father.

"A serious miscalculation on my part," he told Deirdre. "He couldn't stand it that I'd seen him scared."

She said, "Your own father let you go to prison."

"He sure did. Coleman J. Reynolds Sr. wasn't gonna let anyone say he was soft." This wound still stung. His father had been determined to make him "learn his goddamned lesson," not only for the humiliation but also for the crime of ingratitude.

Deirdre asked, "Have you two spoken lately?"

"Not since my arrest."

"You might be surprised at what he's learned since then. I say this with my own history in mind; I have been . . . a force in my children's lives, let's call it. Not always to the good, it turns out. I think I understand why you felt the need to make such a dramatic gesture, after years of provocation. He might understand, too."

"He might," C.J. said, to be agreeable. If his father had changed course, he'd have heard about it by now. He said, "Look, I am nothing like a perfect man, but I'm pretty good. I try to be mindful of other folks, the environment, flora, fauna. All I want now is to start over again fresh. I'd say Arlo needs that, too."

Deirdre considered this, one hand idly stroking a spot on her chest just below her collarbone, the spot where, beneath skin and flesh, a small device regulated her failing heart. Finally she said, "You'd have to pass a drug screen."

C.J. laughed in relief. "*That's* what you've got?"

"Can you blame me, given what Arlo and I have been through?"

"No, ma'am, I cannot."

Deirdre said, "If I may be honest with you?"

"Please do."

"I've never witnessed Arlo happier than he's been with you these past weeks. *Irregular* just might be the right thing for all of us."

"I believe it will."

"Mind you, we're going to take this endeavor slowly and see what things look like at summer's end."

"Of course. I wouldn't expect anything different."

"I don't know *what* the family will think," she said.

"Seems to me they've had their say already. This is your call."

"I am an old woman, and I haven't always made the best decisions. I've forced my will on others—always trying to do the right thing, you know. But then I've come to think, right for whom? I believe you might be a godsend. Certainly Arlo thinks so. The others will just have to *deal with it*, as you young people say."

"Thank you."

"Then if we're settled for now, I believe I'll lie down for a bit. I trust you'll break the news to our boy."

C.J. smiled at this, the word *our*, the wonder of how right and easy this had been once he'd finally given himself over to it. Like maybe there really was such a thing as *meant to be*, and it had brought him here.

25

The Way to Beck's Heart

Returning to camp after meeting with Carol Barksdale, Sophie said to Claire, who was driving because Sophie had never learned to, "Will you miss this place?"

"I don't know. Maybe. But not like I'll miss the apartment."

"Yeah. Same. Everything's changing all at once. Mom dying that way was like a bomb being dropped into the middle of our lives. Boom! Fallout everywhere. I'm glad we could get this part of it settled, at least. Assuming that guy will actually want to buy the camp."

"I'm glad you had the presence of mind to think of contacting Carol. It's lucky he didn't already find something else."

"What did Carol call it?"

"Kismet."

"That's right. Kismet. I like that word."

Sophie put her feet up on the dashboard and resisted the impulse to photograph her Alaïa hiking boots. SimplySophie! was on hiatus for now, and possibly forever. Though she could see the advantage of morphing her social media practice rather than ending it. Turn those followers into patrons. Encourage them to *participate* in art rather than being passive scrollers whose attention to any image in their feed lasts mere seconds. People needed to slow down. To *engage*. Beck's notion to write a novel was one that Sophie embraced for exactly that reason (though also to support her big sister). Writing was art every bit as much as painting or sculpting or photography were. Filmmaking, too. Music. Dance. Theater. It was life, reflected in ways that actually mattered.

Claire said, "If Carol's buyer comes through, it will make things a lot easier on Beck. It takes all the drama out of the process. She needs less drama right now."

"No thanks to you!" Sophie poked her.

"No thanks to *you*!" Claire said.

"Well, I'm fixing it now."

"For yourself."

"And for you. And for Beck, too. In a small way—you just said that she needs less drama, and this should give her that. I wonder what she'll do next."

Claire said, "Settle up with Paul, I'll guess."

"I mean after that. Me, I'd hit the road for a while. Get out in the world."

"You should tell her that."

"She won't think of it herself?"

"She's mired in emotional mud right now. That makes it hard to see the horizon."

"True that," Sophie said, as they drove up to the camp and parked. "First things first, though. Let me do the talking, okay?"

"Please."

Inside, Beck was in the process of boxing up the stone "snowman" family. She said, "Do you guys want to keep the ones you made?"

"What, separate them?" Claire said. "Who'd keep the ones of Mom and Dad?"

Sophie said, "We can figure this out later. Beck, I didn't want to say anything before I was sure this could happen, but Carol Barksdale's client still hasn't found a house and is very eager to see this one. She's bringing him over in half an hour, so we need to clear out for a bit."

Beck said, "I guess I'm supposed to embrace this as good news."

"Well, yeah. If he buys it, we'll save more than twenty-five grand in commission. Every dollar counts! Also, having a cash buyer who's ready right now—that's our best possible scenario."

"Fine," Beck said. "I just want to get this over with. Should we go find some lunch? I could do Quietside in Southwest Harbor. I'd prefer to avoid Bar."

"Oh?"

"It's not a big deal, but I had a brief thing with a guy I met there, and I'd rather not chance running into him again."

"Oh!"

"I know," Beck said flatly. "Will wonders never cease?"

"Tell me more!" Sophie said.

"It was a mistake. I'm sorry I did it. The end."

"*I'd* call it a start. A step in a new direction."

"Did you not hear the part where I said I'm sorry I did it? Never mind. Let's just go, okay?"

At Quietside, Sophie ordered the Last Kiss: liverwurst with onions and sprouts on rye. "In Mom's honor," she said. "Did she ever eat anything different when we came here?"

"I'll have the same," Claire told the waitress.

"Same," said Beck.

Sophie said, "Plus three chowders, and blueberry pie all around." She wanted to cheer Beck, even if just in this small way, and food had always seemed to be a route to Beck's heart.

As the waitress left, Claire said, "I ate *so much* liverwurst when I was a teenager. It was the easiest thing to slap together after school when I had to go right to work."

"Did you eat it with grape jelly?" Beck said.

"God, no! I used mayo—which is horrible in its own way. Did you?"

"All the time," said Beck. "Disgusting, right? But I loved it. I'm surprised I didn't make you guys eat it that way."

Sophie said, "You tried to. Dad saw what was going on and made you stop."

"I don't remember that at all."

"I did put jelly on my gefilte fish at Grandma Geller's."

"That might be where I got the idea to put it on liverwurst," Beck said.

Sophie thought she looked a bit more relaxed, now. Or resigned. If that's what it was, that was okay. Better that than to tilt at windmills. Forward motion, that was the thing—though touching base selectively with the past could be good medicine, in the right dosage.

Sophie reached for Beck's hand, then took Claire's, too. "This is so good," she said. "Isn't it? This is just what we need."

They were getting into the car, Beck and Sophie in the front seats, when Sophie's phone rang. "Hold on—it's Carol," she told them, and took the call. "Hi, Carol. I've got you on speaker. What's the word?"

"The word is *hooray!* Mr. Reynolds loves the house and wants to offer appraised value plus five percent as an incentive for you to keep it off the market. Cash purchase, with closing set for as soon as can be arranged."

"That's a strong offer," Sophie said.

"Call me Dr. Shadchan!"

Beck took the phone from Sophie, saying, "Hold on: the buyer—what did you say his name was?"

"C. J. Reynolds. He's moving from South Carolina. He's *such* a nice man. This sale would be a dream come true for him."

Beck said, "Tell Mr. Reynolds we said thanks for his offer, but we prefer not to sell to anyone with a criminal background. We're going to see what the market will bear." Then she ended the call and shoved the phone into her back pocket.

Sophie said, "What the hell! Give me my phone."

"What, so you can call her back with a different answer? No. We aren't selling to him. Remember the guy I said I didn't want to see again? He's the one."

Claire said, "Wait, isn't C. J. Reynolds the college boy you were so wild about that one summer?"

"One and the same," said Beck.

"Did you know it when you——?"

"Yes, but I didn't let on, and he didn't recognize me. I lied about my name; he lied about his history. We made quite a pair."

As Beck started the car, Claire asked, "What did you mean by 'criminal background'?"

"He tried to shoot his father. He spent three years in prison!"

Sophie shrugged. "All right, so it isn't a match made in heaven for you two, but it is for the camp."

"*No.* I'm sorry, but we are not selling to him." Beck backed out of the parking space. "Someone else will come along soon enough."

"You don't know that."

"It's a safe bet."

"Yeah, well, I'm not interested in gambling on this," Sophie said.

Claire said, "Me, either. I can't see any good reason to take our chances on the market when we've got this sure thing."

"He *shot at* his father. Do you not care about that?"

"What does it have to do with us? Domestic situations can be messy and volatile," Claire said. "There were times I might have liked to shoot Chad."

"But you never did."

"I didn't have a gun."

Sophie was not about to let this sure thing get away. She said, "We don't know the circumstances behind what happened. It might not be what it seems. In any event, if he did his time and paid his debt to society, he deserves to be treated like anyone else. Didn't you ever see *Les Misérables*?"

Beck said, "It's not just the shooting. You guys don't understand. I know it was a hundred years ago, but he deliberately made me think he was in love with me when it was just an amusement for him—same as Mom and the Callaghan boy, only I didn't end up pregnant. At the time, it was the worst pain I'd ever felt. And then I meet him again and he comes on like Mr. Wonderful, but it's all a ruse."

They were back at the camp again. Beck parked and headed inside without returning Sophie's phone. Sophie followed her. She said, "I get that it's all fresh for you again. But what difference does any of what he did make, really? All of that is over and done with."

Beck said, "I don't want Helen worrying about whether her new neighbor is going to harm her."

"Do you *really* think he's dangerous?" said Claire, trailing in behind them. "Because, when you called me that night, you didn't seem to be scared of him."

Sophie said, "Maybe you just want to punish him for doing you wrong."

"Maybe I do," said Beck. "That doesn't mean the other reasons aren't valid."

"Honestly? It does. It seems selfish and irrational. Imagine how he must feel right now. We give him the green light to make an offer, and then we say, *Sorry, just kidding!* It's shitty, Beck, and it's beneath you."

"If I had known he was the guy, I wouldn't have given him the green light."

"Look," said Sophie, "having your heart broken when you were seventeen doesn't make you a victim, and it doesn't make you special—"

"Okay, but if he hadn't broken my heart, I wouldn't have married Paul and my life wouldn't now be a complete and total mess. I'm not saying it's his fault—"

"It sure sounds like you are."

"I'm saying . . ." Beck paused. "I'm saying he doesn't deserve to be the one, okay? I know it looks perfect to you two, but it just . . . it isn't the way this was supposed to go. None of it."

Sophie knew the only way through this was to harden herself to Beck's plight for now. She said, "Do you want to explain all that to Carol and him? Because *we* aren't going to do it."

Beck was silent.

"I guess we just have to put this to a vote." Sophie raised her hand and said, "All in favor of selling to C. J. Reynolds?"

Claire's hand went up. Beck crossed her arms. She had tears in her eyes.

"The vote carries. I'll tell Carol to write up the contract, and then we will just get on with our lives." Sophie looked at Beck. "You won't fight us on this, right?"

Beck wiped her eyes. "As if I have any real choice. For the record: I hate all of you."

Sophie put her hands on Beck's shoulders and looked into Beck's eyes. "It's going to be okay, you know."

"Easy for you to say," said Beck, shrugging her off.

"I know it seems like some things are breaking our way and not yours. You aren't the only person suffering, though. We all lost our mother, and none of this makes up for that."

"So, 'Get a grip, Beck,' is what you're saying."

"Pretty much."

"I'll work on it."

If Marti Geller was looking down on her girls that night, she saw them seated outside at the fire pit where the flames spit sparks into the cold night's star-spattered sky. The sisters were unequal in their contentment, but Marti would be pleased that they were here together, sorting things out in ways she could not have imagined would be necessary.

She would see Sophie pop open a bottle of Veuve Clicquot and defend the luxury purchase, saying, "Certain standards must be maintained."

She would see Claire wrapped in a down comforter, eased back in her Adirondack chair contemplating a plan she had a short while earlier dared to make.

She would see that the champagne, delicious though it might be, was doing little to soothe Beck's turmoil. That was all right; progress *had* been made: Beck was unstuck now, if also untethered.

Marti had been at Madison Square Garden in 1972, singing along with Mick Jagger when he reminded the crowd that although they couldn't always get what they wanted, they might—if they tried—still end up with what they needed. Beck's story wasn't over yet.

26

An Invitation

The Sunday-morning flight from Bangor to LaGuardia couldn't have been smoother. Calm, clear air from liftoff to landing. Yet Claire's heart pounded and raced the entire time. She didn't say so. Sophie seemed to intuit it, though; she held Claire's hand through most of the flight and talked the whole time. Her art concierge plan was going to be a real game changer, she said. She'd hire herself out to genuine collectors who weren't concerned with playing the game. People who bought art with no intention other than to own it, value it, respond to it. She had an idea for developing an app, too, as a method for democratizing things—not the art itself, she said, just the process of buying and selling it. She said, "I might call Liev Schreiber, too, because why not?" God bless Sophie for her enthusiasm, for her support, for getting them all through the fire.

When she and Claire were about to part at the security exit, Sophie said, "Hey, you got this, do you hear me? It's going to be fine. Better than fine. It's going to be fucking phenomenal."

Now Claire pulled her carry-on to the main terminal's food court. She switched the handle from her damp palm to her less damp one and wiped her free hand on her coat. Sophie's confidence was unearned: this was a bad idea. Really foolish. Claire should not have texted Paul late Friday night, asking, without context, if he'd be willing to meet her this morning.

An airport was no place to have this conversation. What if Beck had been mistaken, somehow? What if Paul had at one time been a bit too fond of Claire but wasn't anymore? Or maybe he'd merely used her as an example of how, having been emotionally disconnected in the marriage, he *could have* found himself attracted to other women, including her. Beck, in her surprise and dismay, might have misunderstood him.

Claire's phone buzzed, and she stopped to read the text: I'm here. Glad your flight was on time. See you soon.

She drew a deep breath, counted to five, held it for five, exhaled for five.

Entering the food court, she saw Paul seated, facing her way. He raised his hand in greeting.

Claire remembered the first time she'd seen him, standing with Beck at Eileen Greenburg's bat mitzvah, the two of them at the side of the dance floor watching the crowd. Behind them: flowered wallpaper, black with fuchsia blooms as large as their heads. *Wallflowers,* Claire remembered saying to herself, thinking how funny this was and how she might go to them and make some kind of joke about it. She'd chickened out: suppose the cute boy with Beck didn't think it was funny? Then she'd be embarrassed and want to die on the spot.

Claire remembered a day years later, at Duluth's Canal Park. A singular moment, when Paul had looked at her as if she hung the moon. A seminal moment, she'd thought as it was happening, but then it passed and nothing changed and she'd told herself, *No more.*

Ha.

Now she neared the table and Paul stood. They did not hug, as they would have done before.

She said, "Hi, thanks for coming. It's ungodly early, I know."

Paul pointed to his cup on the table. "Espresso, double shot. Can I get you one?"

"I'm off caffeine—my blood pressure's too high." It was probably very high right now.

"Oh, that's no good. But with your dad's history, I guess it's no surprise. You're taking care of it, I hope."

"Yes, working on it."

She sat.

He sat.

"So," she said, "Beck really surprised us with the news of you two splitting up. I know you said you were going to when we spoke that night, but I guess I didn't think . . . that is, I didn't realize—"

"Claire," Paul said, his gaze so soft and his voice so tender that her name was a poem. He reached across the table and held out his hand. An invitation.

27

Balance in the Universe?

Never had a morning felt so bitter to Beck, who had managed only a few hours of sleep before rising early to see her sisters off. Outside, though, the fog was lifting, revealing a washed blue sky and vivid green pines and abundant sunshine that streamed into her kitchen as if God himself directed the beam. She was cheered by this, despite herself.

Beck dressed for the outdoors, then went down to the shore and shoved the kayak's hull into the water, climbed in, and used the paddle to push herself afloat. Ice still rimmed the shore in places where the sunlight didn't reach. Soon those shaded banks would give way to the earth's tilt toward Maine's long warm days ahead, when Mount Desert Island would swell its population with those moneyed families returning to their summer retreats, the tourists flocking in like starlings to roost and feast before flying off again.

Now, though: long minutes of perfect silence, broken only by the rhythmic slice of Beck's paddle through the lake's glassy surface, by the wind whispering through the pines, by an osprey winging past and calling out—

—and by her phone's ringtone.

She took the phone from her life-vest pocket: it was Gina.

"Hi," Beck said. "I didn't expect to hear from you until next week some-time."

"Well, I know how anxious you are for feedback, so I wanted to get to it right away. Beck, I am—no surprise—*really* taken with the quality of your writing."

Beck thrilled to this. At last, some good news.

"Your prose is so skillful and clear. There's no question you've got the chops to write fiction."

Beck's eyes filled with grateful tears. "Thanks," she said. This was *just* what she needed today. Affirmation. Hope.

"You've created some really compelling imagery, and Caitlinn is a strong character. But here's the thing: The story . . . it's depressing as hell. I mean, right off the bat, you hit us with all this *misery*, and—"

Beck pulled the phone away from her ear. No. No. *No*, damn it. No. This wasn't how it was supposed to go. The fog was gone, the sun was shining—these things were supposed to portend a rise, renewal, even rebirth.

". . . you there? Beck?" said Gina's tinny voice.

It took all Beck's force of will to bring the phone to her ear again. "I'm here."

"Obviously this isn't what you wanted me to say, but I think there's a lot to take from this. You're a very good writer, no surprise there. It just seems as if—well, I don't think your heart was really in this. I'm certain that once you apply your talents to a story only you can tell, you'll have a winner on your hands."

Beck's chest was tight. She might split open at any moment. She said, "Right, well, thanks for your assessment. I owe you."

She didn't even say goodbye before she hurled the phone as hard and far as she could. It arced up over the water, then hit the surface and sank, and Beck did not even care.

She took up the paddle and lit out for the farthest shore. Never mind peace and silence and osprey; she went full-on, as if she were in a race for her life. As if each stroke of the paddle was a sword's slash at a demon. *There, there, there, there*, she went at the water, stroking hard, sweat beading on her face, trickling along her ears and onto her jaw and chin—or maybe that was tears. She didn't care, she would just keep slashing and sweating and crying until she ran out of water—

Beck lurched forward as the paddle split, half of it slipping from her grip and disappearing into the kayak's wake, where it sank almost as quickly as the phone had done.

She looked behind and yelled, "Fuuuuuck!" then slumped into the seat. The kayak continued on its heading toward a jutting bit of shoreline, the hull now grinding against the bottom and bringing Beck to a stop.

There was not another soul on the water, so no one to hear her scream or to witness her crying for real now, and after a minute or two, that felt like a small mercy.

Spent, Beck wiped her face with her shirt cuffs, then turned back for camp. The lake was easily eight thousand times larger on her broken-paddle return than it had been when she set out, and the return took what felt like ten years. By the time the dock came into sight, her shoulders and blistered palms were cursing her with every stroke.

At the shore, she threw the busted paddle onto the ground and got out, stepping into the icy cold water with the resignation of Job. What did it matter if she ended up with frostbite and hypothermia? So what if Helen came to say goodbye and discovered Popsicle Beck lying inert at the water's edge? Then her sisters would be able to split the sale proceeds two ways instead of three.

The fact was, whether she froze to death or not, she was beaten. After a lifetime of *being there* for her community, her husband, her children, and her parents—but especially for her mother, a lifetime of ever and always *doing the right thing*, she had finally stepped up onto the edge of the nest and launched herself, flapping *hard*. And still she'd crash-landed while all around her the others soared. Why?

Why did Paul and Claire get to have each other?

Why did Sophie get to have all the money she needed and then some?

Why did C. J. Reynolds get to have the camp?

As Beck stood there, an osprey passed overhead holding a wriggling fish in its beak. A moment later, the fish fell back into the water.

Lucky fish.

Unlucky bird.

Balance in the universe?

Beck didn't know, and it didn't matter, anyway.

She pulled the kayak out of the water and trudged back to the cabin, unwilling to indulge this pity party any further. It wasn't her style, it didn't feel good, and it didn't help anything.

Plus, now she was going to have to replace her phone.

She'd been bold, here on Mount Desert Island. She'd moved out of her comfort zone and taken chances and made choices and asserted herself. She'd worked hard.

Yes, she'd lied to Paul. Yes, she'd stepped out on him. Yes, she'd misled C.J. and used him for sex. But shouldn't all of that have been canceled out by the wrongs *they* had done to *her*? It was simple algebra.

Except life didn't really work that way. She knew this. Good things happened to bad people. Bad things happened to good people. You couldn't count on either kind of person getting what they deserved. Had she gotten what she deserved? Or had she been misused by fate, just another casualty of magical thinking?

For the first time since she'd completed her bat mitzvah and felt the letdown of no longer needing to fret over getting everything right for God and her parents, she wished she were a true believer. That the Gellers had been people not only of the culture but also of the faith. How much easier this day would be if she could lay her burden in God's lap.

"That'd have to be a really big lap," she said.

Inside, she got her journal and wrote,

Who am I?

Where do I belong?

Is all of this a curse, or a gift?

I want it to be a gift.

Please, let it be a gift.

28

It All Comes Down to This

Eight eventful months have passed since I left Mount Desert Island. And by *eventful*, I mean insanely stressful and packed full of hard lessons I wasn't ready to learn.

Until suddenly I was.

And now finally I have!

(I think.)

If you're flailing around in your life, as I was when Paul and I concluded what I now think of as The Great Undoing, and can engineer the freedom to go, I recommend Switzerland as a treatment, if not a cure (the cure has to come from within). Where better to ground oneself than in a land known for certainty and precision and, of particular appeal to me, neutrality?

—I needed so badly to feel I was not being judged.

There is little guesswork in Swiss life, and no chaos, and everything is very clean. Also: the clean trains traveling through clean stations are on schedule ninety-nine percent of the time, and when they aren't, travelers get an apology, a reason, and an ETA. Think of that! If I had a dollar for every time I've stood on a New York City platform in frustration, I wouldn't currently be renting a studio apartment in someone else's chalet. I wouldn't be conserving every penny that's come my way, hedging the money against a still-uncertain future.

Obviously, I'm not in Switzerland for the trains. They're merely a delightful side benefit of my impetuous decision to follow Cammie's example and decamp for someplace unknown. I made the reservation on a sweltering afternoon in mid-July, when the Irvington house was sold and I had to be out in four days. I was hauling a box of old DVDs to the thrift store and there was *Heidi* on top. The alpine scenery looked so cool and inviting that I put the box in the trunk, went back into the house, and after very short consideration, bought a one-way plane ticket to Zürich and a train ticket to Interlaken, having read that it was the most beautiful town in the Bernese Oberland. I reserved a hotel room for a week, which I figured would be long enough for me to get a feel for the area and decide what to do next.

From there, I lucked into a rental in nearby Grindelwald and, again following Cammie's example, got myself an unofficial part-time job. (Don't tell the Swiss government; I don't want to get anyone in trouble.) I've been here almost five months, but now it's time for me to move on.

To Paris.

Paris!

It's an indulgence I'm trying to believe I deserve. A short stay in comparison to my time here, and done on the cheap. Still, Paris. La Ville Lumière.

I hope to gather its energy and store it in my healing heart, as I've been doing here.

And then?

"It's really your last day?" asks Birgitta as I tie on my apron for my final shift waiting tables at this berggasthaus. We're more than two thousand meters up the slopes of the snow-clad Schwarzhorn, a minor mountain in these parts but one with an incredible panoramic view that includes the Eiger's legendary north face, that killer of deranged climbers since 1935. The view is what drew me up this mountain, and it's what has kept me coming back to work in this restaurant five evenings a week—after I've finished the day's writing, that is.

Before I leave for the restaurant each day, I print out my work and stack the pages atop my desk. The desk (a small table, really) is in a corner of the room that also holds my narrow bed, along with a low bookshelf that doubles as a dresser, a mini-fridge, a microwave, and a hot plate. The room has two windows, both with a view of the chalet next door. A pretty structure. Very Swiss. I can't see it when I'm writing, though—and that's okay, because my focus, after all, is meant to be on the page. The stack is substantial now. A novel, nearly done. It isn't Caitlinn's story, though. It's mine.

My career used to involve my interviewing someone and then writing about their experiences, their life. Always someone else's story, because mine used to be so ordinary. The public wants drama, action, suspense, a mystery, maybe some bloodshed and death, certainly some sex. I wanted all of that myself (except the bloodshed and death). So I sought it in others' lives, and I wrote about it in ways that let the reader live it vicariously. Always, I've tried to make you feel what my subjects felt, be it joy or anguish. It was as if I was in training for when my own time came, for when the spotlight swung around and directed its beam onto me.

I had things to say with those stories. I have things to say with this one.

Birgitta is a middle-aged Austrian-born woman with the sturdy build of someone who threw shot put in the Olympics (which she did). She's as tall as I am, and divorced. We've become good friends. For her, though, Switzerland is a forever home, not a way station. I always knew I wouldn't stay here; it's too far from my kids and my granddaughter (Leah will be two years old next June!). However, I still don't know where I *will* stay. I don't know how my story ends.

Birgitta and I set about refilling the salt and pepper shakers. Beyond us is a picture window that looks out onto snow-streaked mountain peaks, a massive line of jagged granite cut out against a pure blue sky.

Photos can't capture the grandeur, the depth of field, the scents of alpine forest and flora, the feeling of being incredibly fortunate to witness all of this in person while also knowing that I'm entirely inconsequential. It's an experience that's as humbling as it is awe-inspiring.

I needed to be humbled—I see that now. It's the antidote for self-pity, which I admit to indulging more than a few times during The Great Undoing, when I allowed myself to think about how well everything was going for everyone else. Stand on the trail that skirts Eiger and look up; or ride the train to its sister peak, to Jungfraujoch, and look down; then you'll know how small you are, how big the world is, how there are so many more important matters than whatever's happening in your own pinprick spot on the planet.

I say to Birgitta, "I'm sorry to be leaving this, and all of you."

"But why go now? You will miss all the holiday festivities."

"It's okay; I'm Jewish."

"But Jews also recognize the New Year, yes? Stephan's party is famous. Many attractive men will appear, not all of them gay."

There's been no shortage of attractive men in my world. Rugged types who arrive in the warm months to hike. Rugged types who come in the cold months to ski. Suave types who dress as if they're rugged types, only at a higher sartorial price point, and who ignore convention, tipping with an extreme generosity that's meant to impress their beautiful, fashionable friends as much as the waitstaff. *See how generous and kind I am? See how I appreciate good service?* Those types are not all bad guys. Some of them really do understand their privilege and want to spread some of it around.

The men who are old enough not to see me as a mother type chat me up with varying levels of interest and aggression, and I've responded favorably to a select few. I've snogged in a gondola car. I've been naked in some hotel spas (though that's not out of the ordinary here) and a couple of hotel beds. In the end, though, I always go back to my apartment, alone. I'm uninterested in complications. The companionship I like best is that of the cows that graze the high alpine meadows where I often hiked in the warm months. What sound is more pleasant than that of cowbells ringing out in lazy time with the animals' hillside roaming?

"I'm sure I'll regret missing the party," I say. "The thing is, I'm going to be spending New Year's Eve in Paris."

Birgitta stops her work. "You're meeting a man! Who is he? Why have you kept this secret from me?"

"I'm not meeting anyone—not everything is about finding a man, you know."

"Of course it isn't. The right men are fun, however, and I like fun. You do, too."

"I admit it *has* been a refreshing change."

"Rethink this Paris plan. If you want to be all alone on New Year's, you hike to one of the huts, you don't go to Paris. You are wasting your money. Stay here, come to Stephan's party with me. I'll lend you a dress."

I laugh at this ongoing joke between us. I never wear dresses, and she always does. "Thanks, but anyway, my lease is up and I didn't renew."

"I will lend you a bed."

"Don't think that I don't appreciate the offer," I say. "It's just . . . it's time for me to go."

"But then you will come back."

"Eventually."

"Soon. Bring your family."

"That's a lovely idea," I say, and I mean it. What that might look like in practice, though, is an open question.

Sophie is in Los Angeles for the time being, living in a guesthouse that doubles as her company's headquarters. She's got investors and a small team of techies, and her online gallery has membership that now counts in the tens of thousands. Her credit card bills are finally paid off. She texts Claire and me regularly, making sure we're okay, showing us that *she* is, occasionally alerting us to "unreal bargains!" on designer samples made by friends of hers. In March, we're all going to gather at Tania's place in Panama and light a yahrzeit candle in Mom's memory.

After wrangling with Chad over custody and visitation matters, Claire has taken a job in Manhattan at Mount Sinai's Kravis Children's Heart Center. They're lucky to get her (as is Paul). She and David (and Goliath) took an apartment on the Upper West Side. It's warm and messy, the way that Claire herself now gets to be. Paul is in SoHo. They're taking it slow—for the kids' sake, I gather, because all three are still a bit uneasy with this game of marital musical chairs.

Me? I've finally made my peace with all of that. Leben und leben lassen.

My Parisian way station is in Saint-Sulpice, spitting distance from the Luxembourg Gardens and Saint-Germaine, that Lost Generation literary haunt. In the week I've been here, I've been doing little more than writing and walking, putting my feet into the steps of Gertrude Stein, Djuna Barnes, Sylvia Beach, and Zelda Fitzgerald, among others.

What I love about Paris: the ongoing sensation of being wrapped in history and significance. So much of Europe must feel like this, not to mention the UK and Asia and the Middle East and Africa. Really, everywhere I haven't yet been. Americans can be so ignorant, with their smug and righteous superiority. We are the newcomers to world power, and sure, we've done a lot of things well (new *can* be good!), but we are getting a lot wrong, too.

Everywhere around me here, the buildings are *old*. The streets are old. They've inspired artists and armies. Parts of New York feel this way, too. I'm so at home in this city, as if Paris is New York's older, sexier sister and she's letting me come hang out with her for a while.

It doesn't hurt that Sophie arranged for me to stay in Tania's pied-à-terre. It's spacious and luxe and on the same street where Scarlett Johansson has a place. I suppose the two of them must know each other, though maybe not. It's no matter, because although I may be sleeping in a bed that belongs to a filthy rich pop star, I'm no more consequential (to her, or to anyone) than some duchess's poor relation. No one knows me here, which is fine by me. A comfort, even.

So far, my favorite places in Paris are the Luxembourg Gardens, Notre Dame, and the Pont des Arts—where, like Sabrina in the movie by that name, I go in the mornings with my coffee and my journal. I gaze at the Seine, its

boat traffic, the gulls that swoop and soar and bitch at each other over territory and scraps. I especially love that as I stand on the bridge, I'm flanked on
one side by the somber southern face of the Louvre, that repository of great
art, and on the other by the Institut de France, with its baroque cupola and its
five learned academies that have been extant since the 1600s. I'm as humbled
by all of this as I was by the towering Alps. Inspired, too.

Tonight, I'm treating myself to dinner out, in a bistro on Rue Guisarde.
It's an intimate and cheerful place—just the thing for this damp, cold night
when I'm a little weary, having written a scene where I'm in a kayak and
my friend Gina, the literary agent, calls me. My *emotional* memory of that
moment is that she says I'm hopelessly untalented. Perspective has brought
clarity: she didn't say that at all! Which doesn't mean that reliving it wasn't
rough! Less rough, however, than writing the preceding scenes—the one
with Paul at the camp, and with my sisters. And the one I haven't written yet,
possibly because I'm still sorting it out.

It was three days after Gina's call, and I was due to leave camp the next
day. That morning, I went off to hike while the home inspector C.J. hired
was doing his thing. Carol had advised me that the inspection would take
about two hours.

I waited an extra half hour before returning, then drove back feeling
pissy (truly le mot juste) about the whole situation. Whining to myself. Why
does *he* get *my* place? Why can't Paul just keep living in our house and help
me get my loan? Why am I somehow less deserving of happiness than everyone around me? When I came up the driveway, the inspector's truck was
still there, along with a car. I didn't know for sure whose it was, and I didn't
want to go inside and find out.

Before I could turn around to make my escape, though, out came C.J.,
and behind him, Arlo. They saw me. C.J. said something to Arlo and the boy
came skipping over to my window. He was smiling so wide. He said, "I really
like it here a lot. Thank you for selling C.J. your house."

What could I do? I said, "You know what? I forgot something at the
store. I better go back. You take care, okay?"

And I left. Cowardly of me, I know. I stayed away for another two hours, just driving and sulking. I thought, *Mom, if you're watching this, I hope you're happy now.*

That man and that orphaned boy, though . . . I keep thinking about the tenderness I witnessed between them when I saw them together that first day, and about the joy evident in Arlo's face—in his entire body—as he stood beside my car and thanked me. The C.J. I've built up out of self-pity and angst doesn't match the one Arlo clearly loves.

Arlo may know things I've refused to see or accept. What was it C.J. said that night, about being a family misfit? He'd sounded wounded. There's probably a story there, one that if I knew it would make me see him in a different light. His criminal past may not be so criminal as I thought.

Whatever the case, what I see now is that I need to let it go.

At the restaurant, I'm seated at a small table toward the back of the room. I ask (in very poor French) for tap water and a glass of vin rouge while I consider the daily menu's offerings.

Nearly every table is occupied. Conversation rises around me and swims about. French, Italian, something Eastern European that I can't identify. There's soft music playing, too. The clink of fork to plate. Laughter. A clatter from the kitchen. Along the ceiling is a string of colored lights—a festive touch for Christmastime, I assume. I wonder who among my fellow diners is wearing something gifted to them from their beloved on Christmas morning, now four days past? That vivid scarf. The handsome jacket. Cuff links made from ancient coins. Everyone seems jolly this evening. I'm feeling a bit jollier now, too.

With my wine, I have a simple meal of hearty cassoulet and crusty bread with a schmear of deep yellow butter. I'm about three bites away from finished when I hear the voice—I know it without having to look up, its southern warmth as attractive to my faithless ears as the sight of land to a sailor who has been too long at sea. A glance over my shoulder confirms that C. J. Reynolds is here.

Here.

C.J.

With him is Arlo, who walks ahead, following the waiter to a table near my own. Between Arlo and C.J. is a woman whose unbuttoned coat reveals that she's about six months pregnant. I notice, too, that she wears a wedding band.

"Fast work," I murmur, and turn away, angry; I am supposed to be done with him, damn it. Why should I care that he's found happiness with a woman who isn't me? I really, *really* don't want to care. I'm forty-five years old now; am I still not in charge of my emotions?

Evidently not.

Who the woman is and why Arlo is with C.J. and how they have come to be here in this restaurant on this night are all matters of intense curiosity that I refuse to pursue. I only want to leave without them seeing me.

It seems that they haven't so far. If I don't look their way, I might be able to pay my check and escape. I signal the waiter, give him cash. "Gardez la monnaie. Je vous prie," I add, slightly mangling one of the handful of phrases I tried to learn during my stay in Grindelwald. (A waitperson's favorite: Please keep the change.) Then I take my coat from where I draped it on a chair, slip it on, and take the widest possible path away from the trio, then toward the door—though *widest possible* is not especially wide in this room. Still, I am just one more body amid many, and my hair is long now and hides my face, and I am in the vestibule—

"Beck Geller!" he calls.

I don't *have to* stop. I don't *have to* turn around.

I stop. I turn.

"This is a surprise," he says, coming over to me. "I almost didn't recognize you! But, tall woman in a bright orange coat—who else could it be?"

My faithless heart has sped up, pushing blood into my neck and face. Even my ears feel hot.

"Almost anyone," I say.

C.J. says, "Nah. You're memorable."

He smiles, and I hate that the compliment warms me further. See, this is how he fools you! You think he's sweet and charming and you'd never, ever kick him out of bed. You think you can trust him to tell you the truth, to never keep things from you, to never take advantage.

There are people around us, and I don't have any desire to make a scene. I'll be polite, then I'll get the hell out.

"Are you enjoying Paris?" I say.

"One of the best places I know. I'm showing the boy my favorite art. What are you doing here? You with family, or . . . ?"

"Working. A writing assignment."

"Over the holidays? That doesn't seem fair—even if it is in Paris."

"Nonetheless. Speaking of which, I still have things to do, so . . ."

"Sure, sure. I just couldn't let you leave without saying hello. I feel like we ought to sit down and have a talk. Things got a little squirrely there on MDI and—"

"Water under the bridge," I say.

"It is, but I also owe you an explanation for way back. Should've led with that the night we . . ."

He doesn't have to say more. The recollection is vivid.

I say, "You knew who I was? That night—you knew?"

"I did. Did you?"

I want to lie so that I can feel indignant about *his* lie. But I say, "Actually, yes."

"Listen, if you've got some time tomorrow, can we go for a walk? Maybe it's nothing to you, but I'd be putting to rest some things that have troubled me for a long time."

I glance past him, to where his wife and Arlo sit watching us from afar. *Let it go,* I think. Let it all go.

I say, "I'm sorry. I'm tied up all day. After that, too. *Very* busy schedule."

I expect him to keep pushing me—to prioritize clearing his conscience over my desire to be left alone. But instead he says, "No, right. Totally understand that."

"None of that stuff from the past matters to me anymore, I promise you."

"Okay," he says. "Okay, sure. Well, nice to see you. Have a happy New Year."

I'm already turning away.

The wet streets reflect light spilling from windows along Rue Guisarde. It's so beautiful and romantic and wasted on me. I feel ready to combust. I need the sting of sleety snow on my face. I need motion. So I stride up Rue Princesse, Rue du Four, Rue de Buci, Rue de Seine—an almost-beeline to the Quai, it turns out, to the river, to my bridge.

Only when I'm halfway across do I stop. I rest my hands on the railing and begin to calm down. Amber lights reflect on the water and along the streets. People pass me, umbrellas unfurled. Around the river's bend, the Eiffel Tower sweeps its beacon over the city. It's here. I'm here. All these other people are here. It's okay that C.J. and company are here, too. What difference?

If what I said to him about none of our history mattering to me isn't wholly true, I *want* it to be true. I can make it true. My life is about so much more than any man.

And now it comes to me: *That's* why I'm here in Paris at the same time C.J. is here! Because the universe knows I'm truly, finally ready for this last growth spurt.

And I'm ready to write the end of my novel.

Then I can go back to New York and see what more I might make of myself.

Yes?

Yes.

But as I turn to walk back toward the Quai, there's C.J., twenty feet away, waiting for me.

I stop in my tracks. "You followed me?"

"I did," he says. He walks toward me. "Seems I can't help myself."

"What about your wife?" I say. A challenge—thinking, *Don't do this to her. Don't do this to* me.

"My—oh!" He laughs. "No, that's Avery. My daughter. Her husband's joining us tomorrow. You thought . . . ?"

"How could I know? It's been plenty long enough."

"No, right. That's my trouble with you: I keep giving you opportunities to get me all wrong." He comes closer. "Will you let me fix that, Beck? I hope you will."

Now he's so close that I can see the raindrops on his hair and face. We are foolish to be here without umbrellas. His scarf has come loose. I reach for it, wrap it around his neck.

"You'll catch cold," I say.

"Worth it."

He smiles. I smile.

All of this has been worth it.

A few pages ago, I told you that I didn't know how my story would end. Now I can tell you:

It ends with C.J. and me together in the middle of the Pont des Arts.

It ends with explanations and apologies.

It ends the way so many favorite stories do: with a promise, and a kiss.

(And This Coda)

L ife is too often short and messy, full of complications, difficulties, be-
trayals, mistakes. Full of unfairness and loss. And questions. So many
questions! Mine often begin with "Why?"

Sometimes the answers come. Sometimes they don't.

I've been thinking about Mom a lot. What she went through, how it
shaped her. What I've been through and how it's shaped me. The costs and
benefits of lies and truth.

I don't believe Mom wanted us to sell the camp so that MDI was no longer part of our lives. I don't think she knew that Sophie was desperate for
money. I think she knew that if she didn't push me in just the way she did—
covertly, making me guess at and argue with her intentions—I might have
played things safe forever. Mom knew all about playing it safe. There *are*
benefits, but there is a price, too. In making me choose whether to fight for
my dream, she gave me a chance at true satisfaction, and I am grateful.

I like to think she was looking over my shoulder as I wrote our story.
That she guided my recollections, nudged my conclusions—mothered me,
the way she always did in life. I imagine her like Marmee March, telling Jo,

who, following rejection, had written a story for her family and seen it well received,

> There is truth in it, Jo, that's the secret. Humor and pathos make it alive, and you have found your style at last. You wrote with no thoughts of fame and money, and put your heart into it, my daughter. You have had the bitter, now comes the sweet. Do your best, and grow as happy as we are in your success.

Am I right about any of this? I don't know for sure. It *feels* right, though, and I'm trusting that.

In life, there are so many different lessons to be learned. So much wisdom to be gained if we are willing to humble ourselves, to make mistakes, to be messy and vulnerable sometimes.

Figuring things out and getting them right is a lifelong odyssey, and no one ever really completes it. But maybe it all comes down to realizing we should accept the hand fate deals us and make as much of it as we can.

Break the rules when necessary.

Embrace the possibilities.

And then there is the matter of love—in all its forms. Who among us prefers to do without it?

Love. Yes. You may see it differently, but for me, it all comes down to this.

Acknowledgments

I'd like to express my gratitude to all the usual suspects for the ways in which you have supported my writing efforts these many years and especially in the past two (as of this writing), when the pandemic wreaked its havoc on the launch of my previous book, *A Good Neighborhood*. In comparison to the greater trauma experienced by too many, the book and I came through fine. But there were some dark times just the same, and it was out of that darkness as well as the darkness of the world around me that the idea for this new novel arose.

Having just published my modern take on classic tragedy, my publishing team at St. Martin's Press might easily have balked when I came to them with the premise for a messy-families dramedy, with its wry humor and joyful resolution. I have written so-called women's fiction, historical-biographical fiction, and literary tragedy; never this kind of bighearted, upbeat tale. But instead, as they've done before, they embraced my new idea with enthusiasm, and for that I am grateful. Thank you Jen, Lisa, Dori, George, Jess, Marissa, Sallie, Kejana—and of course Olga Grlic, for this truly delicious cover design, which convinced everyone that we had the right title.

Throughout the process of getting this book written, Sarah Cantin, who was my editor for *A Good Neighborhood*, proved that she, too, is no one-trick pony. Not only that: when I was in the thick of trying to shape this story's plotline while also dealing with some mysterious and troubling health matters, Sarah's astute editorial assessments of each draft and her cheerleading for this book and me have a lot to do with it being in your hands now.

No book of mine has ever gone to press without my dear friend Sharon Kurtzman's name in the acknowledgments. The same is true for Wendy Sherman, my agent, advocate, and friend, and Jenny Meyer (if you're reading this in anything besides English, it's because Jenny made that happen). Thanks, ladies, for all the different ways you keep me on track.

I have three great kids (two born to me, one acquired by marriage) who completely take for granted that I've got another book done and am able to write fiction for my living—which is actually a supreme compliment, when you think about it! I'm so lucky to have them (and their partners) in my life.

And speaking of luck: what good fortune it has been to spend the COVID-19 pandemic with my own partner, fellow author John Kessel, whose belief in my writing talents came before anyone else's did and whose nightly pillow talk with me is one of the reasons I still believe in love. Let's keep being saps together.